# VALUING ONLY US

CORY DESMOND WOLFE

Manufactured in the United States of America

This book is a work of fiction. Any references to historical events, real people, or real places are used fictitiously. Other names, characters, places, and events are products of the author's imagination, and any resemblances to actual events or places or persons, living or dead, is entirely coincidental.



Cover Design by Richard Ljoenes
Executive Editor: Rachel Eve Moulton
Co-Editors: Carlee Fountaine M.D., Julia Winje D.O., Taylor Wolfe D.O.
Marketing: Heather Wallace, Courtney Corlew

The Library of Congress has cataloged the edition as follows:

Name: Cory Desmond Wolfe
Title: Valuing Only Us
Registration Number: TXu 2-422-050

Hardcover ISBN: 979-8-9913018-0-0

Paperback ISBN: 979-8-9913018-2-4

EBook ISBN: 979-8-9913018-1-7

*For my love, Taylor*

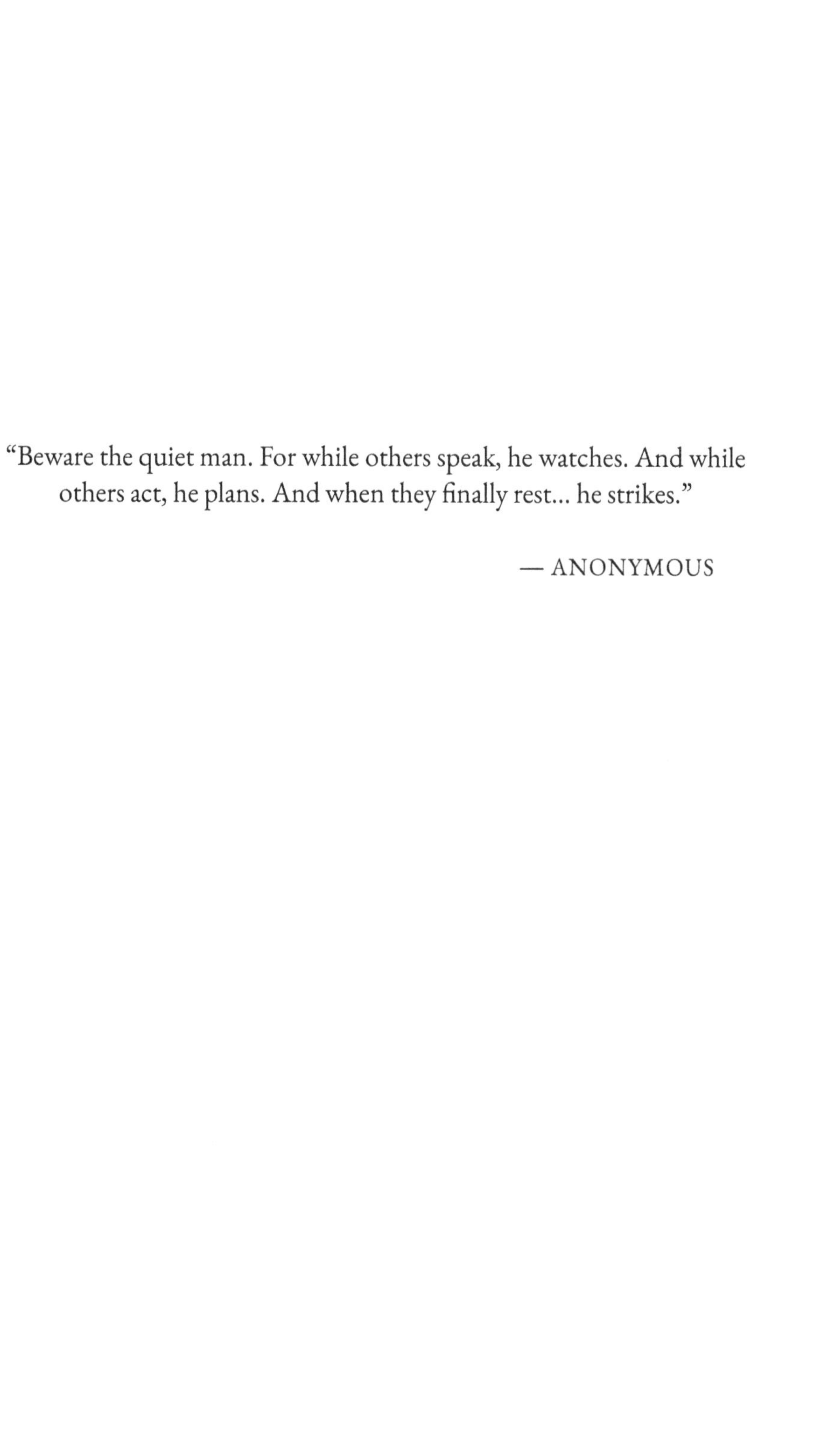

“Beware the quiet man. For while others speak, he watches. And while others act, he plans. And when they finally rest… he strikes.”

— ANONYMOUS

# Q1

# 1

## Ted Sullivan

I am a gentle liar and a ruthless charmer: a flawed human with a nutritious personality of sugar and salt, leaving everyone's bellies satisfied. The salty acid is in my blood, bouncing around the walls of my veins. It's paired with a sweet, vibrating toxin, not even dialysis can filter. But don't sweat; I would never lie to you, for I feel we both crave change; we share similar convictions—taking a carnivorous bite of cured corporate revolution. They pretend that the future will sustain us in the same way it had sustained us so far.

Looking out the window, I could still smell the manure and wet soil from circle and square farmlands below, fitted and stacked along highways, nestled at the base of mountains, trailing rivers like an organic game of Tetris played by the Gods of Capitalism. Even the burial remains of dried-up crops were visible, sprouting life replaced by tumbleweeds and metal legs.

My hands rested on my tray table as I ran my finger over the face of my cufflinks, tracing letters S and Y circled in a timeless gold trim, snuggled tight in their velvet-coated box. They seemed to shine a tad brighter as our moment had come. After years of planning, late-night think tanks fueled by cold brew and lead-dense aspirations took their place on stage, sucking in air one last time before the rise of the curtains -- Showtime! The cufflinks were a gift, a gentle reminder of our plan. Alec had gotten them for us us when we began our MBA programs as a reminder we were our company, even though it hadn't come to fruition yet.

After landing in LaGuardia, I fought the crowd at baggage claim and hailed a cab to the St. Eleanor's in downtown Manhattan, watching as the iconic city, once only accessible through movies or dreams, grew and circled around me. The awe-inspiring visuals popped my pulse as I zipped deeper into the concrete jungle, nudging closer to ground zero while feeling the VIX volatility of wall street stridulated. The slaughterhouse of high finance.

As I squinted from the Holland Tunnel, all the matured stone buildings and glass skyscrapers were familiar. The way they hugged each other over century antique streetlamps, exposing its cables and frail pole —truck-sized advertisements towered the edges of every intersection. Exit 4 - Downtown - Third Right, the stunning Freedom Tower stood the most recognizable as we passed under the green sign. The circular pad sprawling above her radiant collar and the clouds' glimmering reflection boosted my purpose. She held an amazing capacity to mesmerize and motivate. Those desires intimate—a sense of power.

This was my first winter season meeting the city; Murray's Pizza still insisted it was the finest pizza joint downtown, with a green, fluorescent bulb that read so. Preoccupied professionals in ink and beige trench coats hustled across the streets with their cell phones sewed to their ears. A line of toddlers shuffled like penguins while strapped to a safety rod as steam barreled out of metro air vents on both borders of the street.

The town car braked in front of St. Eleanor's as the bellman rolled his cart and waited for instructions, to his luck I only packed one suitcase. I entered my room and slid off my boots to sweaty socks, my feet appreciating fresh air; I noticed a letter resting at the foot of my bed.

*Welcome to the Kauffman Schwartz Innovator Awards Ceremony.*

Alec and I were both nominated for the award within our respective divisions. It was all part of the *plan*. I worked in the Private Wealth Investments division or PWI, focusing on our high-net-worth clients, allocating, and implementing financial goals for them. The fat, greedy, 1% piggies. Whereas Alec worked in the Investment Banking division, working with corporations, governments, and institutions on merger and acquisition (M&A) deals. We were both in our *reputation era*, making our names echo across the market before we set sail to start our own company, so winning the KS Innovator award was imperative. Vital.

Reality shot through my body, where it warmed my chest, and fish-hooked my lips. The time had come. I sat down on the king bed and re-read the letter. Modern elegant furniture surrounded me, dizzying views of the city jetting out toward Freedom Tower, all proof I had accomplished my goals. Tangible outcomes of keeping your eyes on the prize, nose in a book, your brain taking a beating, pushing your mental stamina to its limits: crunch, crunch, crunch. Then, you pick your head up, and you're visiting Manhattan while working for the top investment bank in the world.

ALEC MET ME IN THE BUSTLING LOBBY AT ST. ELEANOR'S. Our hug felt like an eternity of bliss. My ear pressed against his chest. The smell of his cologne and the sound of his heartbeat, churned a tidal wave of emotional memories.

"Are you ready for our lives to change?" Alec asked.

"Ready as I'll ever be," I said as I pushed him away to admire his suit. I tightened his tie and rubbed my palm down his cheek, grazing his stubble like organic acupuncture. "This is new."

"Thought I'd grow it out. See how it looks."

"I like it. You look sharp," I said, rubbing my finger across his Kauffman Schwartz pin nestled on his suit jacket. "You suck up."

"Hey, we have to where we can. We're not all as smart as you," Alec said, exposing his bone-white smile, turning those resting puppy dog eyes to me again. Like being back atop your favorite mountain, his view swallowed me whole. There's a youthful eagerness to his eyes, like a credulous lamb. Those features were the cherry on top of his existing

Gold Standard aura. His full lips, light blue eyes that sometimes brimmed near silver with full eyelashes of a newborn. Alec Young was complex, a multidimensional being whose edges shine and reflect like a mirror ball, who positions those facets to cater to those he's interacting with. Who Alec was to his colleagues was not the same person he was to his family or the same person he was to Emma. To me, he's all of them; he was his full self. The most fluid, intellectually complex Greek god I had ever met. As if Zeus and Hades birthed a mythical son, heir to the entire kingdom above and far below.

"I figured we could grab a table at the restaurant here before exploring the city. The ceremony is at Whisk. I researched it; it's your standard burgers and soups, but you know, artist anal," I said with a wink as Alec, and I settled into our seats. An attentive server followed behind us, scribbling down our orders, and disappeared behind swinging doors only to re-appear shortly after with overpriced yet exceptional avocado toast. The combination of olive oil, salt and pepper, and dried seeds were out of this world. My mouth flooded with saliva. Another discovery this high-class lifestyle had exposed.

The New York streets still felt surreal, despite having been here dozens of times throughout my three-year career with Kauffman Schwartz. Growing up a farm boy from Oklahoma, I think they will always feel that way. Warm and alive, even during the dead of winter. Alec toyed with his gloves as we stood by, waiting for the pedestrian light to change. His beard stubble looked good, enhancing another layer of handsomeness I hadn't imagined was possible.

I strived to be in the moment at Brookfield Place as we window-shopped various department shops, bookstores, and cooking floors, but they all seemed like chores. Anxiety robbed me of enjoying anything relaxing as I trailed Alec through an aisle of Williams Sonoma barware.

*You will not win the Innovator Award, Mason said.* His voice played a continuous loop. A slithering noise.

*You. Are. Not. Going. To. Win.* The sad part was I believed him. What if he's right? What If I'm not good enough?

I lifted and twirled a crystal martini glass and choked on the price ($229). "How's *Operation Rolodex?*" I asked, to distract my mind. To gain a sense of control.

"Showing bullish projections," Alec said as he gripped and compared the weight of two meat cleavers. "We're going with her parents to this charity event. UNICEF, I think?"

"Another charity event? The last time you scored zero business cards."

"This time will be different," Alec said as he handed me both cleavers. "Which feels heavier?"

"And why will this time be different?" I held both; the wooden handles softer than satin, but I fixated on Emma.

"Because she will have her parents to distract her as I work the room."

Alec met Emma Peterson during his MBA program at The Finance School three years ago. She was the daughter of consulting titan Roger Peterson, founder of the intimate yet prestigious Peterson Consulting Group. He'd been an *angel investor* for a few startups that took off. It wasn't until eight months ago when Alec attended an alumni event at The Finance School in Pennsylvania that they 'reconnected'. In reality, we had had our eyes on her for some time. We thought Emma would be the easiest to manipulate. It was then we brainstormed our next plot: *Operation Rolodex*. A black ops mission. My charming spy. A quick return of exploiting Emma's connections. Worming in close enough to snag her Rolodex. The plan involved social engineering until we exchanged the right business cards. Then it was time to cash out, *ruthless entrepreneurialism* kindling our plan. *Valuing only us*. In the world of business, reputation, connections, and appearances, we saved gray areas for the ethics committee. Nothing would stop us from creating our company. From building an entity that is half me and half Alec. A merger of equals.

I handed Alec the meat cleaver in my left hand. "This one's heavier."

We made our way out into the bone-crushing air with our noses running pink. On our way back to the hotel before the ceremony, a neon green sign caught Alec's attention. He drifted off to the side, peering through a stage window of animal skulls, crystals, and other tarot witch shit. *Fortune* read the sign. I let out a slow sigh while digging my hands deeper into my jacket pockets.

Before I could usher him away, he said, "We should go in."

"Are you serious? We're going to be late."

"I think it'll be fun. Get our fortune told before the ceremony."

Alec turned and opened the door as I rolled my eyes and followed. We swam through a wave of incense and half-melted candles. The room was dimly lit except for the small gift shop in the corner. Alec talked with the lady at the front desk and bought the most expensive package on their pyramid of options, a consultation with Lady Oculist. I rolled my eyes again and chuckled at the MLM vibes and prices of silly, made-in-China junk. We were taken to a room with a small round table and pillows on the floor. When we entered the room, we saw Lady Oculist already seated, waiting for us, her gray frizzled hair a cloud around her head barely restrained by a silk headband. I tried not to laugh. I looked over, and Alec seemed stoked.

She asked us to split the tarot deck while considering what questions we wanted to be answered. I wasn't sure how long this went on. Five minutes? Maybe Ten? Long enough for me to whisper to Alec, "We're going to be late."

Lady Oculist waved her hand, and Alec stopped shuffling. From the top of the deck, she drew three cards. I wasn't interested in the slightest degree as my eyes wandered the small room. She mentioned something about three of swords, reversed five of cups, and the death card. My attention snapped. The death card? Lady Oculist remained quiet.

"What does the death card mean?" Alec asked.

"Change is coming," Lady Oculist said as she moved her hand to each card. Her voice was all incense smoke and vinegar. "Physical and emotional pain. Past grief is threading its way into your present. And change. Big change."

"What kind of change?"

She leaned down and pulled out a golden bowl that was charred on the inside. "Place a single strand of hair inside the bowl," she said. "Both of you."

Bubbles made their way into my stomach as we each plucked a single strand and placed it. The witch then poured some juices into the bowl while mumbling in Latin. Again, I tried not to laugh, but my intrigue was growing. She pulled out a small box of matches and struck. Combustion lit up the room as she dropped the match into the bowl, followed by a flash of green fire that quickly died out. Lady Oculist held her face over the bowl and inhaled deeply. I looked at Alec with confusion. Her eyes were closed, crystal necklaces swayed.

Suddenly, her eyelids flapped open. "You will *both* sit upon your throne," she said as she sat back in her chair. A half grin stretched across her lips as she looked at Alec. "Cold tone. Alone. Craving the unknown. Nestled upon your throne." Then her eyes started on me. She looked right through me—eyes like laser beams. "And you. A part of you will be dead." A light chuckle slipped off her lips.

I cranked my head at Alec, then back to her. "I'm sorry, what?"

"*But you will both sit upon your throne.*"

OVER FIFTY KAUFFMAN SCHWARTZ COLLEAGUES MINGLED AT Whisk—a trending new spot meters away from the stock exchange, large enough to host convention-style gatherings. Sleek crafted wood lined the ceiling and support beams with beautiful accents of ivory and silver splashed on the walls, giving a soft feel next to beige silk curtains on every window. A few asymmetrical canvases gave the room some vibrance: bright reds lining warm yellows, mixed with fresh whites and lush greens.

The coordinators gave us personalized name tags. Alec helped me pin my name badge on as I scanned the room. A sea of crisp suits hummed around the room; each group of people echoed a different topic. Only a handful of people looked familiar, with senior management being the bulk of the attendees.

"You'll find your name tent on the table for seating. It's divisionally grouped," said Kelsey Burns, Talent Management Coordinator sans serif on her name tag. Alec jetted off to network with the other investment bankers, and like a lion in the grass, I watched as Alec engaged with strangers and hypnotized them with his charisma. Watching him work was one of my favorite pastimes.

A cold draft brushed my neck. *A part of you will be dead.* The witch's words came back.

"What about you, Ted?" a stranger said.

My attention snapped back to the group of colleagues around me. The people in my department were from all over the world as we discussed our background, current hobby, favorite food, and which KS office we were stationed in. The surrounding women were beautiful with iron-like confidence, custom suit jackets, and designer handbags that dangled from their shoulders. All their Cartier watches were synced. Hypnotizing me. I battled back self-consciousness, everyone at this firm had money. Maybe not Emma Peterson kind of cash or Alec Young's family money, but enough to blend in. Enough to give a first impression statement that stated you were one of them, enough to be deserving of the KS Innovator award. I tried not to let my insecurity get the best of me.

TINK. TINK. TINK. Everyone in the room looked around.

"Hello, everyone, please take a seat, and we will begin shortly," Kelsey Burns said, fidgeting with the microphone.

"Hello, hello!" A sleek older gentleman walked into the center of the room. It took me a minute to recognize him, our CEO. "For those of you who don't know who I am, my name is Frank Bernstein, chief executive officer," The crowd laughed. "I wanted first to begin by saying how extremely excited we all are to have you here today. Every one of you showed exceptional expertise and a fiery passion for serving our clients. You all thought outside the box in tremendous ways. Stepping up your game in order to become nominated for our annual Innovator Award." Frank clapped, the rest of the room joining with him, as our food arrived, followed by champagne's pour. "As much as we want to give all of you the surprisingly heavy glass trophy, only one of you from each division will win. So please enjoy the food and drinks; we'll begin here shortly!" The room erupted into cheers and clapping as a ringing crept into my ears.

*A part of you will be dead.*

The food was bland with a dried outer edge, as if it was prepared hours ago. The bubbles in my stomach returned as the show began with speeches, clapping, more speeches, award one, clapping, award two, clapping, award three, clapping, until we reached the Investment Banking division's turn to shine. I looked at Alec from across the room while squeezing my hands together under the table. It was as if my lungs went flat and airless at the sound of Alec's name echoing from the speaker, barely audible over a wave of clapping.

He won! Alec won!

I adjusted my glasses as I admired his walk up to the center of the room to accept his award and pose for a picture with our CEO and other senior members within the investment banking division. I was so proud of him. His face and smile illuminated the room and everyone around him. Our dreams were one step closer to reality. Our reputation as legitimate financiers was taking shape. Our names, Sullivan Young, would be respected.

As Alec walked back to his table, he looked my way. It was difficult to see the fine details, but the wink he threw me was crystal clear. Air made its way back into my lungs, filling and inflating as my heart began to pulse rapidly. I reached for my champagne flute, but it was empty. I was next.

"The Kauffman Schwartz Innovator Award for the Private Wealth Investments," Kelsey said, drawing out the words as my jugular enlarged with each passing second.

Tunnel vision swirled and narrowed as I focused on her hands, her wrists, the diamond ring on her left finger.

"Goes to..." she fumbled, opening the shiny blue envelope... "Chaz Perez!"

# 2

Alec Young

Alec paced back and forth, willing Ted to come, to make the climb, to room 2209. He placed a Dom Pérignon bottle into the ice bucket and positioned two flutes. After the ceremony, he hadn't been able to locate Ted. Ted didn't reply to texts or phone calls. Alec realized Ted required alone time. Ted hadn't won, what was in Alec's mind, a meaningless award. But the echo of Chaz's name rang, like a fresh wound, vibrant and hostile. *The news would've been less painful had it been anyone but Chaz. Anyone, anyone, anyone, but Chaz,* Alec thought. A knock jerked his attention as he scurried to the door in his dress socks, still in his navy suit. His mind scrambled like eggs on a hot sidewalk thinking of what state of mind Ted would be in, a concerned partner who never wanted to hear his love in pain.

Alec answered the door to reveal Ted.

"This is bullshit. This is fucking bullshit. Out of all the wealth advisors they chose Chaz? Chaz fucking Perez?" Ted said as he raced in while correcting his glasses. Alec followed behind Ted, silent. He recognized his best course of action right now was to let Ted vent, then they would brainstorm a path forward to strengthening Ted's reputation across the market. "He was sitting at the table next to mine, and I swear he sneered when I looked his way." Ted paced along the window with the skyline in the background. "He doesn't deserve the award! He's a hack! He goes out of his way to prove me wrong during management meetings. Tries to prohibit me from engaging in the LGBT Network meetings. God. Ever since we were both up for a promotion last year, and I landed the Grant account he's been this little cun—"

"Come here," Alec said as he reached his hand forward. Ted stopped pacing and drifted toward Alec. "You're an innovator." Alec held Ted's hands. "Corporate politics got Chaz the award. Not because he's better at his job than you, or because he works harder. It's because of corporate politics. Nothing more."

"It doesn't change the fact that he won. Now our entire timeline is all fucked up."

"You don't need a pointless award for investors to realize your value."

"How will it look to the market though? *Alec Young, winner of the prestigious Kaufman Schwartz Innovator Award and Ted Sullivan, a no one from Oklahoma, start their own firm*," Ted said as he freed himself from Alec's grasp and rested on the bed.

"Who cares what people think?"

"I know what they'll think. I want to stand next to you, not below you."

"They will only see Sullivan Young. One unit who holds the innovator award. Since I won, you also won."

"I want to carve out space on my own terms. Achieve something for myself by myself. I don't want to be under your shadow."

"What do you mean under my shadow?" Alec's eyebrows furrowed together. "Sullivan Young is both of us."

"I know, Alec. But that's not how the market will see it. You will make the headlines, the interviews, the investors, the notoriety. I will only be an *asterisk*. A footnote in the story of your success." Ted slumped his head and removed his glasses.

"What do you propose we do? Apply for contests? A Financial Times interview?"

"It's not about the clout," Ted said, thrusting his knuckle deep into his eye for an itch he couldn't scratch. "It's about achieving something on my own. So, when we announce Sullivan Young the market will state, 'That's a good duo. That's a smart partnership. I want to go where they're going. I want to be a part of their future."

"Do you have a plan?"

"I do," Ted said. He rose and made his way toward the window. "Every year, *Forbes* presents a list of the top wealth advisors. I'm going to make the list." Ted peered out the window then turned to face Alec. "We're going to make the list. I researched it and the deadline to be nominated is toward the end of Q1."

"Since it's Forbes, does Kauffman Schwartz have to submit the nomination?"

"They do. When we're back in Scottsdale, I'm going to have a meeting with Reid about the nomination."

Alec poured the citrusy bubbles into the two flutes. "I knew you'd find a solution. You always do." The hair on Alec's neck stood to attention as he picked up his glass. He sampled his champagne. The almond, cream notes, and carbonation tickled his belly. Ted took a sip as Alec ambled toward him. They were resting by the window overlooking Manhattan, and Alec placed his arm around Ted, kissed the side of his head, and turned the lights out with the remote, the city lighting up.

Sapphire and emerald signs illuminated newspaper-ridden, pedestrian-heavy sidewalks. The great New York City, the city of dreams. The place where everyone strives with and against each other in cramped subways, nauseating ferries, crowded bars, and trash bins—connecting everyone through shared experiences. Alec's eyes took a moment to adjust to the darkness inside, the bright lights outside. Its presence—an eerie beauty haunting all who have come and gone—reminded all that it is possible for those who refused to give up. Refused to settle for mediocrity. Refused to accept defeat. As they gazed out over the city, the longing ambition of what was yet to come combined with the anticipation of what they could become.

*You will sit upon your throne*, Alec thought.

The boys will succeed in buying Young Industrials and secure their first stepping stone by converting the oil-dependent into a green unicorn. Alec and Ted had no interest in trying to save the world by fighting climate change, nor do they plan to buy Alec's family company out of spite, well not entirely at least, but there was money to be made in alternative energy. *Green energy*. There was market share to devour and a chance for them to make a mark on this world. Alec would *seize* this opportunity.

"This city is so beautiful," Ted said.

"It has a beautiful mind, like yours." Their breathing synced. "We made it, Theodore. We made it. Still doesn't feel real. Our plan will transform humanity; it will save lives. I'm confident about that." Alec clinked his glass against Ted's. "Cheers. To our plan. To our empire. To *valuing only us*."

ALEC ROLLED OVER, BURIED IN FEATHER PILLOWS, AND barricaded his arms around Ted under a fluffy duvet as the blackout curtains recoiled, light reflected off the surrounding buildings piercing through, warming their eyelids mixed with a roar of honking and police sirens. Alec pressed his ear against Ted and sunk under the covers. As much as he wanted to be, Alec was not an early riser. His body and mind begged for the snooze button every morning; it took effort, courage even, to silence his alarm and creep out, dizzy, and slow. Adding Ted to the mix, their legs twisted together following rhythmic breathing, contributed to his desire to stay in bed.

Ted sludged out of the king, planting his feet on the carpet while digging rocks from his eyes. He stood like his bones were growing and assembling back into place as he shuffled to the bathroom.

"You said your flight was at noon? Two?" Ted's voice echoed off the tiled walls and floor, an orchestra following the flush of the toilet and crank of the shower.

"Noon," Alec said, crawling across the bed in search of his phone. "I have the UNICEF event tonight. I tried to get on your flight, but it was full."

"What?" Ted interjected, poking his head out of the shower.

"My flight is at noon! I have a layover in Charlotte."

"Lame. You should have booked my flight."

Alec rolled his eyes as he skimmed emails while multitasking with a round of Sudoku. Rainbow confetti fell from the top of his screen as he won his daily challenge, juicing him up with a surge of dopamine.

The summer Alec's Sudoku addiction kicked into overdrive was the year Alec and Ted met as Kauffman Schwartz interns. A fraction over six years ago. The day had inched toward being the second hottest in the valley of Scottsdale, beating down on one of the fastest-growing cities, and Alec was tucked under an umbrella perched on a rooftop bar. The sleeves of his white button-up rolled tight around his tan forearm as he sucked in the dry air, appreciating silence after a group of his female colleagues had soaked in his striking eyes and intoxicating aura with flirtatious pats and intellectual teasing. It happened right after the app downloaded. Alec picked his head up and saw cowboy boots and blue Wranglers stroll in. A heart-throbbing moment. The first time Alec set eyes on Ted. Admiring quick details, he drooled over minor mannerisms, from how he adjusted his glasses to how he held and took drags of his beer. Alec strolled over.

"Cody James?" he'd asked.

"Close. El Dorado." Ted took a sip of his beer while adjusting his glasses. "The one place I expected no one to know the brand of my boots. But here you are. I feel there is a story behind knowing boot brands."

"Lucky guess. El Dorado was my second thought."

"Was it now?" Ted smiled as his pinecone brown eyes squinted behind round glasses. Alec told Ted about his life and the story behind knowing boot brands. His father was Bradley Young, the cutthroat cowboy who built Young Industrials, an agricultural machinery manufacturer selling massive hundred thousand dollar combines, harvesters, and grain extractors. Fifty-ton industrial machinery with enough potential to compete with John Deer, AGCO, or CNH Industrial. They headquartered their main factory on flat terrain a few miles west of Des Moines and their multiacre Young Estate laid just south of the city. Ted pretended to not have heard of the name, teasing in between digs that his family only used John Deere equipment. A few smiles later Ted caved, admitting the tractor his family owned was from Young Industrials, which spider-webbed into flirty remarks Ted gave on how he was like most farmers, and Alec was the 1%. Uncalloused hands, never-gave-a-pig-a-shot-in-the-ass-cowboy type.

A girl tapped Alec on the shoulder, his ride to the event, and said they were all going to an intern's house to continue celebrating. An invitation rooted somewhere. The boys didn't want to be painted by the rest of their intern class as boring or anti-social. Alec and Ted went to the party. Optics. But instead of toasting, shooting, dancing, smoking, or snorting, the two explored and found themselves on the roof. They watched the sunset over a flow of conversation, and with every passing minute, their fingers crawled closer together. The collision of two equal atoms rippled through the universe like a brush fire catching an upward draft.

"By the way, my boots are Justin's, not El Dorado. So, it looks like you were wrong twice."

"You know, Justin's was my third thought."

More animated confetti fell from atop Alec's phone as Ted strolled out of the shower and sat on an end couch to put on his shoes. He soon turned into the human equivalent of a ping-pong ball, bouncing off the walls as he collected papers, his phone charger, mathematical-themed Stance socks Alec got him, and his used paperback copy of Animal Farm. In between, Alec grabbed Ted by the arm and pulled him back toward the bed.

"Alec, I have to pack," Ted said as Alec snuggled his head in his lap. "You should have booked my flight, and we could have left together."

"Oh, yeah?" Alec said, showing no sign of easing up, no sign he wanted to let Ted go. "I'm trying to savor this moment. Let me savor this moment." Ted ran his fingers through Alec's hair, scratching the sides of his scalp and making his way toward the top and back to the front.

"Now back to reality. I hate pretending we're only colleagues. It's so hard staying away from you when we live in the same city. Work in the same building. But I know it'll be worth it."

"I don't want to think about it."

"We should establish a spot. A place we can go for check-ins and alone time."

"Your apartment?" Alec grinned.

"I was thinking somewhere more mysterious, but that works. Have you heard from Emma?"

"No." Alec dug for his phone, checked his screen, and double-confirmed. "No."

"I'll call you when I land. I'm going to spend the weekend getting ready for Monday, so I won't see you for a few days."

"Stop reminding me."

"I'll stop reminding you when you let me finish getting my stuff." Ted ran his fingers along Alec's eyebrows. Alec sank his head into Ted's lap, exhaled, and released him. Alec kissed Ted goodbye and stepped into the bathroom to start the day, where he discovered a note Ted wrote on St. Eleanor's stationery written in black ink next to his cologne.

*V.O.U.*

~

THE ARIZONA UNICEF GALA WAS A FIVE-HUNDRED-DOLLAR per plate admission, with the proceeds going to support the work of UNICEF USA. A husky server holding a round tray of champagne floated up to Alec. He nodded his thanks, lifting a glass from the tray, and continued scanning the crowd. He wanted to make the most of tonight, which meant collecting a few business cards; only then could he toast himself for his accomplishment.

Everyone who had already finished dinner grouped up in small pockets of conversation, a game of communal musical chairs, where Alec was the odd man out. The Arizona Governor had the largest orbiting social circle. Alec peered in Emma's direction. She was still at their table, cracking the top of her second crème brûlée and washing it down with her fourth glass of champagne. Her strawberry hair was curled and pinned back, showcasing her diamond earrings and Cartier necklace. She was skimming through an article on her phone titled *Scottsdale's Most Expensive Game Nights*. It featured Emma and detailed her love for social settings; her lavish inventory of board games, first editions and custom boards; and shameless name-dropping, the social media influencers and kids of business executives who'd attended. Alec's competitive edge was nuanced and specific. The bottom line, *who* was he competing against? He and Ted were similar in the sense that they wouldn't waste their energy on frivolous competitors, whereas Emma competed with *everyone*.

"It's all about the quality of your clients, not the quantity," Roger told Alec as he took a sip of Moet. "Perception is critical. Especially when you're starting out. Let your client list do all the talking. Would you rather have ten mid-sized nobody companies or one fortune five-hundred titan? I've built a career catering to those titans. Waving at my competitors every time we onboard a new one." And it's those titans, those well-connected entities Alec's eyes were on. In the game of *six degrees of separation*, Alec was now within two degrees of their reach.

Alec did a lap, waiting for the opportunity to meet more influential pawns. He wanted it to look casual, not forced, so he kept waiting.

"I notice you found the quiet side of the room," a voice said with a beautiful intonational flow. Alec turned to find a tall woman with cocoa silk skin and short hair standing close to him. "Hi, I'm Yemi. Yemi Bankole."

"This is the best spot in the room," Alec joked. "Nice to meet you, Yemi, I'm Alec. Alec Young."

Yemi gave him a bright smile as they shook hands. "So, what does Alec Young do in the world?"

"I'm an investment banker for Kauffman Schwartz. I'm here with my girlfriend and her parents."

"Wonderful. I'm glad you both could make it. How long have you been with Kauffman?"

"Almost three years," Alec said. "It's been a steep learning curve, but it's the people who make Kauffman what it is. I'm fortunate for the opportunity."

"Yes. Kauffman Schwartz is a big player on Wall Street. Although they could focus more on giving back to communities."

"And what does Yemi Bankole do in the world?"

"I started a non-profit two years ago. Well, almost two years," Yemi smiled. "The Helios Foundation. We offer solar technology to developing countries with no access to power." Yemi pulled out her phone and showed Alec pictures of her foundation's recent success story. "This here is a small village in Nigeria, and before we stepped in, they relied on fire and candles to see at night." Yemi displayed before and after pictures. "And now you can see several small solar panels installed all around the village. Here is the current result." Alec's eyes widened. The village housed pockets of lightbulbs with children kicking a soccer ball, smiling toward the camera under the midnight sky. The next photo showed inside a hut, illuminated by the solar bulbs and a mother of two, sitting on the dirt floor weaving together strands of bark with both her newborns clenched to her breasts. And another photo showed a group of young girls cooling themselves off with small rechargeable fans.

"And what about this one?" Alec pointed to another picture.

"This is one of my favorites. It's a video," Yemi said.

The ten-second video started with three Nigerian children standing close to a glass bulb, shocked when they saw, for the first time, the light flare to life within. Like watching a magic trick, their mouths and eyes opened wide in disbelief, as they looked at one another with pure innocence and wonder.

"These are fascinating," Alec said.

"We provide them with basic rechargeable necessities to make life a little easier. A little more bearable. And about once a quarter, we do check-ins to make sure the solar panels are still functioning correctly."

"Which manufacturer makes the panels?"

"We went with SolarX. A startup in Silicon Valley," Yemi said. Alec took a mental note. *SolarX. SolarX. SolarX.*

"Do you ever experience pushback? Prideful tribe members who don't want outside help?"

"Every community we've helped has welcomed the technology."

"I mean, statistically, some are bound to discourage change," Alec said, nudging again.

"There was this one man who did not want our help," Yemi said, caving. "He was prideful, one of the senior members who lived in a small tribe in Namibia. He knocked down the solar panels and smashed the light bulbs." Yemi sounded like a schoolteacher having to admit one of her students misbehaved. "Things escalated fast."

"I bet."

"It got very confrontational."

"What happened? Was he excommunicated or something?"

"The tribe killed him," Yemi said, her voice staying strong. Alec went silent, regretting poking for more details on this rogue member. "They tend to take a utilitarian approach."

"Sacrifice one for the many," Alec said.

"Let me show you another fun video," Yemi said.

Emma walked over with glossy champagne eyes and tapped Alec on the shoulder. "Are you ready?"

"You must be the girlfriend," Yemi said.

"Yes. Emma, this is Yemi. She founded this amazing non-profit. Yemi was showing me photos of the great work they are doing."

Emma gave her a friendly smile. "It's great to meet you. Are you ready to go?" she asked, looking up at Alec.

"I was planning on staying a little longer. Network a bit."

"I thought we were only staying for the free dinner with the tickets my dad bought?" The way Emma said, *my dad* with a superior tone, reminding Alec of their peculiar power dynamic.

Yemi thanked them for coming and walked away, sensing a small argument brewing.

"Let me call you a Lyft," Alec said, pulling out his phone.

"Wait, so you're not coming?"

"I want to stay and mingle. Look around. So many fascinating people are here. I haven't introduced myself to the Governor yet."

Emma rolled her eyes and picked up her fifth champagne flute from a passing tray. "Fine. Tell me when my Lyft is outside."

Alec arrived late with his phone pressed to his ear. It felt automatic, a four-year-long marriage routine. Mimicking yesterday's actions, the day before yesterday, and the day before that. Alec threw

Emma a wave of acknowledgment, continuing to talk business while peckishly searching the fridge for a quick snack.

"Yep, yep. Okay, sounds great," Alec said. "Thanks, Roger." He set his phone down and wrapped a cheese wheel from its wax casing, savoring the mild tang while making contented hums.

Emma remained on the couch with dampened hair from the shower, her body dried by a beige wool robe. Alec continued humming to himself, oblivious to Emma's annoyed demeanor. She looked at him from the couch, and her head didn't move, only her eyes: quiet, analyzing.

"You're home early." Emma rolled her eyes, peering at the clock on the wall.

"I couldn't leave without meeting the Governor and the founder of Oasis Wave." Alec tossed the last nibble of the cheese wheel into his mouth and began wandering to the bedroom. His oblivion to the fact Emma had yet to look at him face-to-face was causing the temperature in the condo to swell, only feeding her paranoia.

"Are you going somewhere?"

"Shower then crash."

"I know your secret," Emma said, the words spewing out like acidic word vomit, warm and sour. Her belly tightened as she struggled to hold down another purge.

"My what?" Alec paused and swung to see the flame in her eyes and the throb in her lower lip.

"You heard me. Are you using me?"

# 3

Ted Sullivan

My team was in the office no later than 6:30, which gave us thirty minutes before the opening bell at the Stock Market, 9 AM eastern. I wore my navy-blue suit with a nostalgic, light brown belt and dress shoes I purchased at Marshall's for $19.99. I sat at my piano with fifteen minutes to spare, Nocturne No. 2 in E-Flat Major by Frederic Chopin. My fingers hovered over the keys; the pressure of my suit constricted my arms as I moved my hands across the keyboard..

A perk of being some of the first in the office, one you wouldn't think would become a pleasure, was empty elevators. Zero pressure to engage in small talk or listen to a phone conversation. A fifteen-second pondering chamber to reflect. Our work floor was a buzzing sea of computers. Tall state-of-the-art printers, whiteboards on wheels, a high-tech professional computer lab with high energy and a sense of purpose. Every KS floor hummed the same vibe. Massive flat-screen TVs lined the walls next to the floor-to-ceiling windows. Each set to the same MSNBC Stock Market channel. Bright green and red numbers ran across the screens. At all hours of the day, the TVs showed exclusive interviews with industry professionals, virtual Zoom clips from the Chief Financial Officers from various companies, and anchors debating the economic outlook while providing insight into the new public offering of a hot startup.

The line of desks didn't support high walls separating us, not like your traditional cubicle style office. Instead, our desks and computers were two feet apart, seven per row. After three years I still got an air of nostalgia with it all: the lighting, smell, Cisco phone sounds, clacking of keyboards, and everyone speaking fervently into their headsets. Before I took a seat, I saw the hack Chaz Perez a few rows down, showing off his stolen award to a group of new hires. Chaz and I started around the same time, but whereas I was fresh out of grad school from Oklahoma, he was a lateral hire from Goldman. Chaz was a member of the firms LGBT network. I recalled the question on the application of sexual orientation. Convex or concave? Left or right? Top or bottom? It didn't take long for me to realize being overtly gay was Chaz's brand. He was aggressively gay.

"Ted, come here," Chaz said as the group of new hires turned their heads toward me. "Do you want to *hold* my award?" He was taunting me in front of them.

"No, Chaz. I don't want to hold your chode." They all busted into laughter as Chaz rolled his eyes and returned to conversation.

Footsteps slowly grew louder behind me, not clunky or boxy, but smooth, like they were floating. Expensive dress shoes make a unique sound, noticeable to an outsider. I turned around to find Reid, taking in his tired eyes and greasy hair. He was clutching folders in his hand, wearing his usual perfect attire like he had installed a dry-cleaning service in the basement of his house for his custom wardrobe. Keeping the suit pressing gears rotating. A disposable wealth he embraced from his purple pocket square, Gucci loafers, and a single diamond wedding ring, which seemed to have some wear to it.

"Ted, are you free to meet?" His voice dripped with an English accent.

"Yep. Finishing up an email."

Reid Wallace was the top dog, the head honcho, whose main goal was to oversee our team's client relationships. He had the final say when we presented the client with various portfolio options for managing their ungodly amount of wealth. Is the client more open to risk, or do they prefer a more moderate approach? We would put together the pitch books, and with Reid, present them to the client over dinner. We do the bitch work, dig the holes, get our hands callused—the tedious, mundane, soul-sucking coordination and processing. We present the client with an assortment of livestock and advice on which is the best. Our job is to cut, hang, and drain the carcass. Process, package, and deliver the meat. In a roundabout way, our goal is to make the rich richer. Manage, preserve, grow.

Reid dropped off the papers at his desk and wandered away as I prepared myself for the worst. I sucked in air as I gripped the chilly metal knob of his office door. Reid was sitting, elbows on marble, typing an email on his phone. The steam from his flowery tea danced above the surface. He wasted no time jumping in, informing me Mr. Grant was satisfied with the investment opportunities I had supplied him: various call options on pharmaceuticals, and how I was doing a phenomenal job. I was catching the attention of clients and management.

"How was the ceremony? I heard our office won the most awards this year," Reid said as he took a sip of his tea. "Across all divisions. My youngest is still sick.Otherwise, I would have attended."

"It was okay. The food was bland."

"Sorry you didn't win."

"I've moved past it. Did you see my email?" I asked as I fiddled with my cufflinks, rotating them side-to-side.

"Yes, I got your email about the Forbes top advisor nomination."

"And?"

"And I let John Barret know. Your name came up in our management meeting as a potential candidate for the nomination. There are a few things I wanted to outline to help you maintain the course."

"I appreciate it." I was on track, but was I in first place? Did he also have this conversation with Chaz?

"You want to make sure you don't become a yes man. The double-edged sword of being labeled a yes man is you open yourself up to becoming overwhelmed and thus having things fall through the cracks. Make sure you maintain the right balance."

"Thank you, Reid, for the feedback. I can see how taking on too many projects, responsibilities, and tasks can set one up for failure. Going forward, I will establish a balance."

"Management is pushing investment interest in several companies. If clients discuss opportunities, you're authorized to advise on." Reid paused, fumbling through his notes like the words dangled from the tip of his tongue. "Pebble Arrow and Blue Horizon. Energy warthogs Kauffman probably has some investment in."

"I'm up to date on the market with several profitable green opportunities, but I'll add those two to my toolbox." Reid seemed unfazed as he rested his head against his palm, pinky resting at the base of his chin. "Are you saying I can only use those two?"

"Ted, I'm saying your name is being tossed around for the nomination and management's top-of-mind investments are Pebble Arrow and Blue Horizon. The committee will decide in a few weeks."

It was hard trying to remain present during our LGBT meeting, and not wander down the mental trail of angst from Reid's quid pro quo. This was the first time I'd become nervous about my nomination prospects, the first realization that I could be overlooked because I didn't prioritize management's top-of-mind investments. I could not dwell. I would make up the slack in other areas, somehow. I couldn't indulge; these investments went against the reputation we were building; they poisoned the story we were crafting.

The firm's LGBT network was one of many spices in the cabinet, including, but not limited to women, veterans, and black and Asian networks. Inspire. Engage. Educate. Not only did I have to be perfect at my job, but being involved in networks could help my career take off. Using the *network stage* to broadcast my name through the firm and make it my own.

A large flat-screen television displayed LGBT Network with a small Kauffman Schwartz logo on the top left corner. A bowl of rainbow suckers sat in the center of the table, a similar complimentary gift to what you would see in a dentist's office or Urgent Care waiting room.

I sat in the middle of the table and traced my palm down my blue and yellow striped tie as each person congregated around the large wooden oval table, accompanied by KS leather notebooks and KS Bic's, with their phones sunbathing under fluorescent bulbs. Chaz Perez entered last, juggling his phone and water bottle.

"John, you are going to absolutely love my idea," Chaz said. "It's so good."

I gave Chaz a side-eye as he continued to kiss ass. His pink bowtie and red velvet loafers were begging for attention. The attention a middle child in a family of eight strives to get from his parents but can never receive. Trying again and again, with more deliberation and outlandish acts going unnoticed. A small piece of me felt sorry for Chaz Perez's over-the-top flamboyancy, all in the name of attention. Scrambling from spotlight to spotlight. As if every day he lived in his own reality television show.

"Nice bowtie," John said.

John Barrett was a managing director of the Scottsdale office in the private wealth division. He was tall, just over six feet, wearing a well-fitted suit that didn't quite manage to hide his belly. As he folded himself into his chair and stretched his legs out, signature red soles peeked out from under his shoes. He was Reid's boss and had been with the firm for twenty-two years, a few of those spread out between New York, Chicago, and London.

"I propose we host a mixer at The Masters," Chaz said. "We could cascade it to everyone at the firm, so members and allies can attend. I've already talked to the manager, and she said they could close off the bar for a specific timeframe and have a private event. Hence, it's only for KS employees."

"Sounds like fun, Chaz. I'm assuming this wouldn't be a KS sponsored event?" Alan Takahashi asked, a Vice President in the technology division. Earlier in the morning, the firm suffered a significant technology issue, preventing clients from accessing their accounts, unable to check their investment summaries, place trades, or view our derivative pricing. Alan was the driving force in fixing it and still looked a tad stressed, checking his phone like a junkie waiting to hear from their dealer. I peered across the table. What was John thinking? I held myself back, waiting to chime in.

"I was going to ask; I wasn't sure of our budget."

"I would prefer we use the Network's budget accordingly and with a career-driven outcome or community engagement," John said.

"If we could comp the first rounds, it would be a killer turnout," Chaz said. "Since this would be our first event, it would send a powerful message having an amazing turnout. All eyes would be on us."

I cleared my throat and raised my pen. "I have a suggestion. Now the networking event is a solid idea. I think it would attract many people and attention to our network, but what if we could align with what John mentioned, a career-driven aim?"

"I'm listening," Alan said.

Chaz took a quick sip of his water.

"I propose we also incorporate a top-down networking event. We invite senior leaders from various teams and divisions, allowing the junior population to network with those leaders and give management the chance to know the names of the people at the bottom, in a more relaxed setting."

John arched his eyebrows and looked at Alan.

"Ted, I think it's a wonderful idea! How do you propose we go about organizing this?" Alan asked.

"I think we should email senior management first, from the Networks email distro, informing them of the event and how their attendance would be imperative to the success of their teams. John, we can CC you on the email since you are the head of the network. Maybe you can come back on the email saying how great the idea is. You look forward to seeing everyone there." I looked down at my notes. "Then, we send the official invite to the entire building."

"Sounds like a plan," John said. "Alan, can you help draft the email going to management? Chaz, when did the manager say she could host?"

"Well, I didn't give her a set date, but I'm sure she is open."

"Great, work with Ted on finalizing the date."

Chaz crossed his arms, grabbed his phone, then recrossed his arms with a fuming eye roll. A tea kettle spewing steam as it reached its boiling point. Our eyes made quick contact, and he looked away. It wasn't Chaz's fault he was placed in my way as I climbed the corporate ladder, and he didn't ask to be humiliated and look unorganized in front of the entire network and our Managing Director. When I thought more about it, I pitied Chaz. Once I delivered my actual idea, everyone would know I have substance, whereas Chaz is only surface.

"I can't wait to see the response to this," Alan said, rubbing his hands together as if he had won the lottery. "Does anyone else have any ideas?"

I raised my pen again. "I have an idea. I've been doing some research, and I think we could partner with the Big Brothers and Big Sisters LGBT here in town. Offer volunteer opportunities to people in the network and the firm to hang out with, mentor, and befriend the program's kids. A lot of the kids come from low-income households, with the majority experiencing domestic abuse." The attention of everyone around the table was on me. "You guys don't know this about me, but I'm adopted, raised on a farm in Oklahoma and I know those kids could benefit from everyone in this room."

"A farm? Like with chickens and pigs?" Alan asked.

"Yes, but no small stock. My family raised lambs, swine, and goats, then sold them. It was when I was younger. My dad sold the business."

The room drew silence, a bleak-hearted, almost somber silence.

When I said I was raised on a farm I meant it literally—acres of grassy land with dozens of cattle, goats, and lambs. All surrounding our vintage two-story farmhouse. The sun-beat blue paint chipping off almost every corner—continuous wood-creaks in the house from wind, steps, cats, dogs, and ambition. I was an only child who became friends with the farm animals. I named each one and gave them reasons for acting the way they did. Helped bottle feed the baby lambs, heard their excitement every morning to see me, blasted country music as I gave them baths outside in the grass by the barn.

Our family's asset-producing business was in selling animal carcasses. Slaughter. Blood. Death. My grandfather started the company, and my father took over, providing enough cash flow to bring me on and have my mother be a full-time housewife. Two of my deplorable uncles and *my evil cousin* worked with my father. There was a plan for me to take over, so I was met with snarky commentary when I decided to pursue finance. I knew how to drive a tractor before I learned how to drive a car, a monster green multi-contractible ground plower, Mongoose XR200 by Young Industrials LLC.

"Ted, this is a terrific idea and thank you for coming so prepared," Alan said. "Let's meet later during the week to draft the networking email and contact the organization on volunteering."

I smiled in affirmation and scanned the table. John's lips pressed in a straight line; he seemed impressed.

I CONTINUED MY TRIUMPHANT MARCH AS QUICKLY AS I could, a slight gallop in my step, as much as my dress shoes allowed. I was buzzing from today's wins. I determined that a vital puzzle piece of my success hovered around becoming more available to our clients, answering all their questions, complaints, inquiries, suggestions, conversations, insights, and ideas before Chaz. My strategy was two-fold and simple. Prioritize and hustle. First, I created a spreadsheet for all our clients, ranking them on net worth, location, and personal relationship with Reid. Had they been his client for ten years or ten days? The hustle aspect of pushing my mornings up by an hour would catch attention from Reid and our top-tier clients.

One client had already sent him a one-liner email on my performance with me CC'd, a corporate gold star.

The dry Arizona winter clipped my nose as I turned the corner a block away from our office; I heard a familiar call. Dry and hoarse from the ground said, "Always on the go, always on the go."

I ignored the homeless man lying on a crushed cardboard box. A stench of feces and molding musk invaded my nostrils.

"You're nothing," said the man as he adjusted his smeared written sign begging for help. "You work for them. Money owns you. You don't know who you are or what you believe in. You are nothing."

"I'm sorry?" I replied, standing dead in my tracks. I blinked, knowing damn well I did not have the time to converse with him.

*He scares me, the little adopted boy said.* His voice was scratchy and distant as he woke up from his nap buried in blue sheets scattered with glow-in-the-dark dinosaur prints. *Leave.*

No. I see him every morning, and every morning he always had some cynical comment. Some vulgar phrases about what makes him better, overextended remarks as I walk by.

"Always on the go, always on the go!" The man shouted, revealing black and missing teeth. "Money owns you; you think you're free? I am free! Slave! Cock sucker!" His beat-up coffee can sat empty of change from passers-by. His left foot became exposed as he threw a sock. Missing a shoe, month-old facial hair dirty and crusted.

I pictured Mason's crooked teeth covered in a yellow film, protruding high canines you want to flick off like a bug. His face wouldn't leave.

*Young 6600 Series* was a high-powered wheeled tractor. Used for hauling trailers, cultivating the soil for fields by dragging a combine harvester, it was helpful for harvesting corn or other grains. Pulling sharp blades, rotating metal wheels, the scorching sun, and those exact scissors caused the gory event one summer day. Mason finished harvesting a field for one of our neighbors when he lost his balance on the tractor. Got swept into the machine's gears. They found the tractor running in circles on cruise control in the middle of the field. No driver. Only the soft humming of the engine and the scratching of rotating metal. And a few feet away, they found shreds of Mason. His pureed organs were scattered around with an unrecognizable face as the tractor sliced over him several times. His fluids stained and rotted the crop soil. His cruel laughter spewed out of the man in front of me and rang in my ears as a rich metallic aftertaste burned the roof of my mouth, like sucking on a penny, warm iron, blood, making its way under my tongue.

I sensed my ears growing hot with anger, the blood steaming my face. I strolled toward him and removed my glasses, using the silk cloth to clean them. I refrained from showing my rage in a hostile manner.

"Slave!" he yelled again as his right eye twitched twice.

I leaned down, and we were at eye level as I put my glasses back on.

"You always fail and sink to the ground. No one can hear a little boy, yet to be found."

The man remained quiet as I looked him in the eyes, glossy yellow opticals that kept looking away. The last sentence lingering, I reached into my pocket and tossed a single penny into his coffee can.

# 4

Alec Young

"Am I what?" Alec paused and swung to see the flame in her eyes and the throb in her lower lip.

"You heard me. Are you using me?"

"Using you how?"

"Don't fucking play dumb with me, Alec."

"I would love to answer your question if I knew what you were talking about." Alec took a few steps forward. The brown in his eyes was a Rorschach test.

"Using me to get business connections with my dad. You're always on the phone with him. You know it's a girl's dream to have her boyfriend become close to her parents, talk on the phone as much as you two do, but all you ever talk about is business." Emma got up from the couch and used her hands to accentuate every word. "When is the next event? Where is the next event? We never fuck. Every time we go to an event, you vanish, collecting business cards like a junky. We don't go on dates anymore. You sleep on the couch more than in our bed. Oh and we never fuck."

Alec remained frozen. He felt exposed, like the scar on the back of his skull. The skin around his temples and eyes tightened. The electricity in his brain lit up like a plasma ball he used to play with as a boy. He had to say the right thing. He knew he couldn't take the straightforward way out of agreeing with her and packing his bags. Emma drove the karma bus, and in the world of reputation and appearances, there was nothing more dangerous than an angry, powerful woman. Alec walked over with his head down.

"I didn't want to bring this up to you until I found a solid path forward, a strategic game plan." Alec took another step, and Emma crossed her arms in a ball of fury. "What is the one thing that sets us apart from everyone else? I'm not talking the shit you find on a resume; I'm talking deeper. What is the one thing both of our fathers did?"

"Built a company?" Emma said, her eyebrows pinched together.

"Exactly, and what is the one thing your father thought you would eventually do?"

"We talked briefly about me taking over. Down the road. Years from now. Where are you going with this?"

"*Succession* sounds like the obvious choice. Now, compared to what your father thought you would never do? Think of all your undergrad professors, old friends and exes and the image of you they have. What they expect you to do, and what no one in a million years would think."

"Start a company?"

Alec's lip drew up in a half-smirk. His puppy dog eyes were sharp, courageous, and believable.

"This will be your chance to prove everyone wrong. Show the world you are your own person with entrepreneurial blood." Alec grabbed Emma's hand. "I'm sorry for making you think I'm only using you. I didn't want to get your hopes up if things didn't work out. You know the facts. If you say your plans out loud, it lowers the chances of you following through with them. I kept this idea under wraps until I felt we could succeed. And I'm not talking about filling out some incorporation paperwork and passing around business cards. I mean hit the ground fucking running with clients already lined up before we even begin."

"I don't understand why you didn't tell me. We are a team. Aren't we?" Emma pulled her phone from her robe and held it in the air. "Or should I call my dad and tell him what you've been doing. How you've been using me and him."

The room went silent.

"Exactly," Emma said as her fingers tapped her phone, Roger's name plastered across the screen.

"You're right. I fucked up." Alec threw his hands over his face, then ran his fingers through his hair.

"Hi, Daddy," Emma said with an optic high as Alec sank on the couch. His eyes turned glossy. Emma paused while twirling a strand of her hair, her jaw pressed to the left, right then centered. "I wanted to say thanks for tonight. Alec and I had a great time." Alec exhaled warm air, then sucked in through his nose. "Alrighty, love you too."

The room grew silent as Emma burned Alec with her eyes. A half grin came and went as though she was enjoying toying with him. She towered over him.

"I'm sorry," Alec said. His eyes fixed on her feet then up at her. "I should have informed you sooner. And hell, maybe I read it wrong and maybe you want to continue working for your dad." He stood up and caressed the surface of her blushed cheek with his pointer finger. A feather coasting her skin. "I wanted us to create something together. I'm sorry if I don't show you love in the way in which you're used to. I know I'm a bit different, but..."

Emma interrupted, "You...you love me?"

Alec sent a malevolent smile. Emma's eyes watered until tears ran down. Slow moving, happy tears hit her lip. Alec used both hands to dry her face then kissed her. "You're right, no one would expect that, at least not from me."

"See, now let's prove them wrong."

"How far have you gotten? You mentioned having clients before we even start?"

Alec sat on his thoughts, pensive.

"That is where Ted Sullivan comes into play."

"Your friend at KS?"

"He's on the private wealth side and he can draw in clients. So, we will have to bring him on board. From there, you can do whatever you'd like. Advisory, consulting, you name it."

Emma smiled and folded her arms around Alec. "I'm sorry for snapping at you, and I'm...."

"No more apologies," Alec said. "I'm glad we could have this conversation. We have to keep everything under wraps until we are ready."

"Have you talked to Ted?"

"No, not yet. But he's a crucial piece."

Emma zipped her fingers across her mouth and tossed an imaginary key. Electricity in his mind was sparking more than ever. He did not prepare for impulsive reactions. He had no choice now but to loop Emma in or risk her going rampant. Alec needed to break the news to Ted that Emma was now involved.

Alec recalled The Finance School alumni event. Regret rumbled his belly. They went into the early evening salivating over plump scallops marinated in lemon and butter topped with crisp parsley. They shared a bottle of wine, which they sipped, not drank. Emma wrapped her red hair in a high bun, highlighting her fair-skinned neck and narrow circular gold earrings. A fresh clear glaze on her nails with a gold Cartier bracelet: her darling. Alec remained cordial and neutral, letting Emma do all the heavy lifting, directing the conversations. Alec didn't feel put off. Instead, he knew the less he gave, the more she compensated.

After dinner they wandered the chilly Philly streets close to campus, trying to not let the proximity influence conversations about which professors they admired or loathed, spicy gossip about colleagues' families or market prospects. Instead, they embellished their childhoods with bedazzled lies, speaking only of the good parts in perfect little packages: creating their best selves. Describing these filtered, polished versions of themselves left a sweet but sour aftertaste: the kind that causes the jaw to clench and shrivels up the tongue like a raisin.

They walked until they came to a park, or at least it was advertised as one, with park hours and grass punctuated by pebble and asphalt tracks. It was a cemetery with perfectly paralleled headstones in all builds and sizes.

Visiting a graveyard on an initial date would be, an interesting first.

Emma intended to show Alec she was wife material with an edge and the steel stomach required to run a corporation or offer up skulls to shrink the bottom line. She found it insulting that her past boyfriends didn't see her potential and what she brought to the table, but Alec did.

His intentions were to make Emma keep doing what she was doing. She grabbed his hand and in they went.

~

ALEC SAT BACK AT HIS DESK AND RAN HIS FINGERS THROUGH his hair. Took a deep inhale and logged back into his computer. Alec's team faced the city's west side on the Investment banking floor, the perfect spot to witness the grand desert sunsets. Pink and purple light flashed across the dry sky, followed by the slow awakening of the city lights.

6:15pm.

Alec sipped his coffee and squinted around the floor. Only a few souls left, all junior bankers pulling eighty-hour workweeks fine-tuning the pitch books, re-valuing the target companies, and crunching the numbers in excel one last time. Once the junior bankers finished the PowerPoint arts and crafts, the associates would come back with notes regarding the book: what to exclude, what to include, and where the *fuck* did this number come from?

The work of an investment banker was not glorious work. It was more about the gates it opened in the realm of high finance: *the exit opportunity*. It was not the work itself that lured young aspirational grads but the prospects of what could come by being a part of something exceptional: to be a part of history, corporate history.

The work wasn't rocket science with complex mathematical equations; it was a tedious occupation mixed with administrative tasks that involved stamina and keeping Andre and their managing director updated on every market move their deal was interested in. Humans created the obstacles and answers investment bankers were looking for–taking simple questions and making them complex from the perspective of the layman. It wasn't like space or medicine where the questions lingered long before people could understand them, or at least attempt to understand them.

Alec's team sat on the buy-side of M&A activity within the industrials space. And what comes to mind when you think of *industrials*?

Machinery and environmental products? Construction and engineering? Electrical equipment? Road and rail? Ford? General Electric? John Deere?

The answer was yes, yes, and yes.

Whenever those grease-filled conglomerates wanted to gain or unite with a competitor, they would hire Kauffman Schwartz to lead the way. Alec's team was a lighthouse to guide the ship.

"Has Andre sent over the markups yet?" Chris asked, tossing a jellybean in the air and catching it in his mouth.

"Negative," Alec said, taking a sip of his coffee. "If you want to head out, I can hold down the fort. It's not a problem. I'm sure the changes will be manageable. I've learned my lesson from the last time we fucking included the wrong price points on the operations improvements."

"That was my bad. I spaced and already provided Andre with those price points. Again, I totally spaced."

"Andre is such a gentleman though; any other VP would have chewed our asses out." Alec laughed. "But really. You're good to head out. I know a few guys were heading to Masters for drinks. If I run into any issues, I'll call you."

"And that is why you're the man, Mr. Young," Chris said as he gathered his belongings. He possessed a vulnerability for social surroundings, notably ones involving tequila and promising young women. Chris stood on the heavier side of life, demolishing In-N-Out triple burgers, fries, and a milkshake with ease. He never let his weight weigh on his self-esteem. He saw it as a positive. Justified it. Kings and the opulent were heavier back in the day, a sign of wealth and boundless resources. Splash on some Ferragamo shoes and order bottle service in today's race, and the ladies will flock.

A total king.

After work, Chris leaned hard into the pop culture persona of an investment banker bachelor. The cracking shock and awe! The flashing lights of a lavish nightlife during a quick weekend in Tulum or running on zero hours of sleep following a few bars from Vegas to Miami. Living life to the richest, one coke bump at a time. Chris was a good banker. Not great, but good. And he was okay with only good, for good allowed him to continue doing what he was doing with a bare margin of responsibility. One day, Chris would stay home on weekends, take up a peculiar hobby, maybe settle down and have some kids, share family photos on Facebook, and build a solid dad friend group. But until then, Alec would not view Chris as competition.

Since joining the firm, Alec had worked on a few dozen deals, putting in countless hours, only to have a small majority of them drop off at the last minute. There were factors out of his control as the financial landscape kept shifting. Alec tried not to let it sour his spirits or play the internal *could it have been him that did something wrong?*

A few hours passed and Alec had yet to hear from Andre regarding the markups. He refilled his coffee and did a few laps around the floor, thinking about work and life, life, and work.

Ted's charming smile, the way his cheeks wrinkled inward and his eyes charismatically squinted and folded, flooded Alec's mind.

*The plan*, simple in theory, like reading microwave heating instructions, soon took on a life of its own. Revealed unforeseen mental obstacles. Crawled through mud under rusty barbed wire with no guidance or pleasant reassurance that their decisions would keep them on course.

Alec Young (positive) and Ted Sullivan (negative) were two atoms of equal purpose and disposition until they met the summer of their junior year of college as KS interns. Colliding into each other with unimaginable force, their undulating energy swelled and swelled.

The two had been gearing up for this moment, this exact situation, with the hope that it wouldn't feel as lonely as it sounds. They had to cleave this formed molecule. A homolytic bond cleavage. Become two clever radical atoms to divide and rule. Again, simple in theory.

Alec sat back down at his desk and to his surprise, Andre had finally sent over instructions for the next step. Alec pulled up the KS internal directory before diving in, with his other half still on his mind, and noticed Ted's status *online*. Alec smiled, pulled out his phone to send Ted a text.

Valuing only us.

~

Apricot jam and soft burrata stuck to the tips of Alec's fingers as he attempted to craft an Emma-approved charcuterie board. She sent him aerial photos of studio-level boards garnished with fresh thyme, sage, and rosemary. How to pinch and fold prosciutto. The right balance of fruit, cheese, and meats. "Make it perfect," Emma said before disappearing into the bedroom. *Perfect, sure*, Alec thought. *The world of zero flaws like a colorless diamond had coddled Emma her entire life.* Alec rolled his eyes at Roger and Grace for enabling this behavior and to a slight degree, encouraging it.

Alec wondered if it began the year Santa brought twelve-year-old Emma her most treasured board game: Monopoly. Precision-wrapped in shiny paper with snowmen and Rudolph patterns bound by a bright red ribbon. Grace hired a company to wrap all the presents: everything had to be perfect, staged, like a display window at a shopping mall. For, in her mind, she was building memories. Lasting picture-perfect memories. Roger fed the fireplace with chopped wood and a few unique pinecones that turned the flames blue and green, adding another layer of tradition. The wood cracked and popped as Emma ripped open gift after gift. She took a few seconds in between to appreciate her new Nike running shoes; a thin, customized iPad with her initials engraved on the metal; an aurora night light that turned her bedroom ceiling into a rotating nebula with sporadic shooting stars. Until she reached the rectangular box: small pieces shifting and sliding inside. She knew what awaited, but still acted surprised.

"And what could this be?" Emma teased as she peeled back the tape; their little girl was about to scream with excitement. But the climax fell flat. The only reaction they got from Emma was a few blinks, her white eyelashes fluttering. An unsatisfied daughter.

"It's the game you wanted, sweetie," Grace said. "Your dad is excited to teach you how to play."

"I already know how to play," Emma said, crossing her arms.

"What's the matter, sweetheart?" Roger asked, taking a sip of his coffee, and scratching the top of Emma's head.

"Emma?" Grace folded a strand of Emma's strawberry hair behind her ears.

"This is the poor people's version," Emma pouted. "This is the same one everyone else has. I don't want the same one as everyone else."

Roger and Grace glanced at each other. They were unfazed by their daughter's unappreciative demeanor and only cared about giving her what she wanted.

"What kind of version did you want?" Grace said with a slight panic that this year's Christmas wouldn't be perfect: memorable.

"The rich people's version. Jake in my class has one with a wooden frame and glass pieces."

"Oh... Okay," Grace said. "Let me and your father get you the version you deserve."

"It's going to be okay, sweetie," Roger said, as he sat at his computer and began searching the web.

Alec dried his hands, following a few knocks, and opened the door to the condo. Emma's ditsy friend Chrissy, who she nicknamed Starfish, walked in holding a bottle of rosé with Ron, her new boyfriend of four months, and Emma's junior colleague at Peterson Consulting. In undergrad, Emma would set her friends up with guys in her business classes, sit back, and watch things unfold. Later, probe them for questions like, "So how big is his dick?", "Is he good in bed?", "Do you have pictures? Show me pictures, you must."

Chrissy and Sean got comfortable in the living room, picking at grapes and cheeses as Alec walked over with an empty wine glass and a few beers.

"I haven't done game night in so long," Chrissy said, twisting the rosé open and helping herself to a generous pour.

"We are excited to have you both," Alec said, handing Sean a chilled pilsner when a knock at the door caught his attention. Emma ran to answer and returned clutching the hand of an edgy woman with thin black tattoos of seemingly random symbols on both her arms: a compass facing north, cat eyes, a triangle, a narrow circle inside a square, a pencil line around her wrist, the shape of a grey daisy above a quote, *Be the Hero of Your Own Story*. They complimented her long black hair parted down the middle and G.I. Jane's lace-up boots.

"Everyone, this is my best friend, Sloane Marshall," Emma said as everyone threw a gentle wave. Sloane was a *journalist* for the *Arizona Tribute*, the largest daily in the state and had known Emma since they were teenagers, as her mom worked at Peterson Consulting. She resonated confidence with a sprinkle of assertiveness.

"So, what game are we playing?" Sean asked.

"My favorite game of all time. Monopoly," Emma said, setting down the box. She removed the lid and pulled out the board: quality color dyed leather stitched to a thick wooden board. Small drawers with tiny silver knobs housed the colorful currency, deal decks, and classic tokens.

"Are they gold plated?" Leon asked as he picked up the top hat and analyzed the shininess.

"They are pure 24K," Emma said.

During the game, Emma detailed her upcoming birthday party and showcased her idea for party favors.

"This is from one of our new clients." Emma handed Alec and everyone a rectangular box with the words *Double Helix* in pop purple inked across the center. The first line in the 'x' was a colorful DNA sequence that grew larger and larger, like a squid tentacle. "They do direct-to-consumer genetic testing. These are sample kits. I was thinking about handing them out. The idea struck when the client asked to sample the product."

Sloane applauded the idea and ended up with the most cash at the end, only attributing it to her confidence. She meshed well with everyone. She laughed at unfunny jokes, and sipped frequently even when the drinks were terrible. It was as though she got along with all except for Alec, their dynamic forced. Alec wondered if Emma flooded Sloane's perception of him in a negative light after the UNICEF event. *Why doesn't she like me?* Alec thought. *She's only said two words to me the entire time. The game is like three hours long. What is her fucking problem?*

Alec walked down the hall of the condo to the restroom and Sloane stepped out as the two did an awkward dance around each other. It must've been the booze as Sloane turned toward Alec.

"Emma is my best friend. I just know, I'm watching you," she said.

Alec froze. *Did she say what I think she said?* Alec thought then smiled and rested his hands on her shoulders and said, "It's not polite to watch people use the restroom. Excuse me."

"You know what I'm talking about. *Opportunist*," Sloane said as she rolled her eyes and continued down the hallway.

# 5

Ted Sullivan

The market dropped 600 points, and every line had been ringing nonstop. The market volatility injected personality disorders into our clients. They all called to test our vigor and white-glove service. How deep would we bow before we broke? Today had been shit. A fucking dumpster fire of a scene. Eric Zimmerman was Reid's second most crucial client. They had a lengthy history, and Eric always appreciated Reid's British, no-bullshit advisor style. He was on the board of various old-school Fortune 500 companies. General Motors, U.S. Steel, and Mobil. The man was short-tempered when jabbed with issues that hit days ago, issues that cut his wealth. I observed firsthand when he brought our colleague, Mel, to tears one afternoon, over a thousand dollars (a lot to me, but pocket change to him). I heard him howling through her headset: "How could this fucking happen? You better fix this! Fucking unbelievable, Melanie! Conference Reid into this call now!" A few days ago, Eric traded a modest chunk of his stake in Globecast, Inc, a ripened telecommunications company in Los Angeles. Their profits had been steady, so I'm certain the move was to free up cash. Whatever the reason, I booked the sale trade, and when I verified the status, our internal systems reported, *incomplete.*

What. The. Fuck.

I phoned the manager of our operations team, who removed legends on restricted securities, which sounded simple, a straightforward process unless documents were missing or misplaced in their giant library of pre-signed client stock powers and legal opinions. Both are required documents to remove a restriction and while Gabbie and I debated on the chances of those documents being in the library, Eric kept calling and hailing and calling for an update.

Everyone knew the phrase 'in chaos lies opportunity' if studying it through a specific lens. Even financial hacks like Chaz knew the phrase, knitted in with his ambition for blind power and hollow leadership of title only. Shoving Pebble Arrow and Blue Horizon down his clients' throats, stroking their heads as he did it. "*Seize this opportunity,*" was his second most trending phrase today, and the past few weeks. His number one trending whisper, "*Pebble Arrow and Blue Horizon,*" milked softly as it rolled off his tongue. Mel pitched them a few times to her clients, but nothing like Chaz. The ignorant car salesman who assured you the diesel wagon tested below emission standards. A real-world example of narcissism for money and grand ideas of self was multiplying, taking shape in the desk next to me.

Gabbie shot an IM that they found the documents. All was right in the world. She worked her magic and delivered all the documents to remove the restriction. I closed my eyes, took a deep breath, put my headset back on, and called Eric back. The moment of peace was short-lived as two more clients called.

Days like today made my work so thrilling, the ludicrous issues yearned to end your career and influence, until you crushed the task. The dopamine onslaught of triumph and the euphoric high of confidence made it all worth it. Those extreme situations preceded the onslaught of success and the pure, electrifying high that came with it. It catapulted you to a peak high, where you remained, until the next disaster, and again, catapulted you even stronger once you killed it. And again, and farther. I ground my fingers against the sides of my temples; they were pounding. I fought back a dizzy sensation. I drew a sharp inhale and snooped around the floor. Things were tamping down with the market closed and critical inquiries completed. It wasn't so much my body, but my mind felt empty.

Reid walked past my desk, carrying his slick briefcase. He held his phone up to his ear. Mel mentioned how behind she was on non-urgent tasks that flooded her inbox as she pressed her lips to her custom mug, chugging her coffee. Chaz sat at his desk reading emails with his Air Pods blasting unrecognizable pop tunes while typing with a surge of anxiety.

~

THE BIG, GAY DAY ARRIVED. WE EXPECTED A SUBSTANTIAL turnout of our thirsty colleagues eager to network, chat, and drink with senior management across the firm and each other. The excited chatter of anticipation saturated the floors for hours leading up to the event on what time they should head over and lunch bets on who could get the most drinks bought for them by their bosses. Every time I heard such talk, a disguised sensation of pride manifested: the man behind the curtain—the invisible influencer.

Alan purchased a bulk order of rainbow pride pins to pass out during the event. They would display a symbol of solidarity and acceptance across the entire bar.

"Ted, right on time. Here are your pins. I asked Gabbie to greet people at the door. If you see someone without a pin, please give them one," Alan said as he handed me a Ziplock. "This is going to be fun."

"I'm excited to see everyone enjoy themselves. The other networks will be jealous of what we put together."

I felt the weight of pins in my hand as I scanned the room. There were so many colleagues I had never met. Within half an hour, the bar filled with local kings and queens mixed with the worker bees, generating a soft murmur. Diversity pools of Compliance, Operations, Investment Banking, Risk, Private Wealth Investments, Global Equity Research, and Legal socialized with draft beers, dirty martinis, neat whiskey, and old fashioneds. A small group of suit bros was standing on the patio trailing cigarettes and taking rips from their vape pens, fast-talking as smoke lingered out and carried with the breeze.

Alec walked up.

"You made it."

"I can't stay too late. I have to help with Emma's birthday party."

"I forgot it was tomorrow." My eyes kept darting at John like a sonar mechanism monitoring his whereabouts.

"So, he is John Barrett," Alec said as I handed him my drink and wiggled the pride flag pin needle through his suit slit. "He looks like an asshole."

"Most managing directors do," I replied. "Once the surrounding mob dies down, I think I'll head over and chat with him. I don't think we'll get another chance to network with senior members. I'm saying since you mentioned you couldn't stay long."

Alec remained 'okay, you're right' silent.

"We should divide and conquer," I said. "Are you not getting a drink?"

"I'm going to have my boss order me one." Alec winked.

"You get double points if someone not from your team orders you one. Now go work the room, boy." I could feel the booze loosening my demeanor. Alec laughed at my forwardness and disappeared into the crowd.

*You're nothing, Mason said.*

*You're nothing.*

I emerged from the bathroom to find the crowd around John kept growing and growing. He appeared to be telling a story as the circulating, insignificant planets nodded and laughed, laughed and nodded. Entranced by his gravitational pull and the intoxicating proximity to power. I drew my phone out, feigning to read emails when Mel and another girl walked by in shoulder-padded jackets over black skirts that bound their thighs as they forced quick shuffles, heels clacking.

"Can you believe Chaz organized this entire event?" Mel said.

I wrinkled my forehead. Is Chaz telling people he single-handedly organized this event? I made a B-Line for an open spot at the bar. The two bartenders were multitasking to their fullest extent. Pouring draft beers, squeezing the citrus from an orange peel, and cashing out bar tabs. I pulled out my sack of rainbow pins, controlling them as my icebreaker.

"Here you go," I said, sliding the metal rainbow to the woman next to me as the bartender slid her a glass of white wine. She towered over me, sporting a short haircut. "I noticed you didn't have one. Hi, my name is Ted."

"Ted? Is it short for Theodore?"

*She doesn't care about you.*

"Yes, it is. I am a member of the network, and I hope you are enjoying yourself, and again, I notice you didn't have a pin." The lady grabbed the pin and dropped it inside her light brown purse, a sleek and simple bag. She took a sip of her wine.

"How long have you been with the firm, Theodore?"

"You can call me, Ted."

"Catherine, it's great to see you," John said, emerging from behind as they shook hands. "How are the boys?"

"They're off at their father's cabin. He has them this weekend. But they're well." Catherine took another sip of her wine. "Are your kids still trying to learn piano?"

"They are, they are. It's not going well." I felt a sinking sensation as they pushed me aside. "Oh, I'm sorry. Was I interrupting something? It's good to see you, Ted."

"You're fine," Catherine said.

"I told my comrades I would buy them a drink for listening to my snowshoeing story. May I?"

"Yes, of course," Catherine said as her purse vibrated. She pulled out her phone and wandered off. I continued to stand there, holding my bag, blinking fast, trying to process what the fuck had happened.

"Ted, would you like a drink?" John tapped the concrete bar slab with his silver AMEX.

"Yes, please, I'll take a shot of rye."

"Whiskey man."

"John, I hope you are enjoying yourself. This is an amazing turnout. I am so pleased with what we put together."

"Me too."

"I was wondering if I could put some time on your calendar. Share some investment ideas and better understand other top-of-mind investments that management might have. Oh, and I also teach piano lessons."

"Reach out to my assistant about scheduling some time." The bartender slid me my shot and John his five drinks. He stepped back, and the flock of worker bees grabbed their liquid poison. Why did it feel like I was struggling at this event?

*It's because you are, faggot.*

Reid, Alan, and Chaz clustered around each other in the corner. I took my shot and crinkled my lips. What were they talking about? Why was Chaz wearing that hideous pink bowtie, again?

I filled my water cup and cherished the hydrating coldness running down my throat, feeling a little overwhelmed. I hoped Alec was having better luck. Never give up. I sucked in air and walked up to a circle of people, plastering a friendly arrival smile and focused on the king we were around, listening to his story about his first year as an analyst in the Risk division, followed by high-level advice that could apply to any job.

I found myself back in the restroom. Substituting water for every drink was becoming a burden. Dark whispers were coming from the end stall, the faint sound of more than one person, followed by quick successions of snorting, whispers, and more snorting. Some of these suit bros could not go one weekend without amping up. The stall opened, and out came three suits. They hustled out, their heads looking forward, one pinching his nose.

"Sup," the last guy said. After I gave a nod through the mirror, I rolled my eyes.

I came out of the bathroom and went to the silent crowd, a little concerned. Alan and John began clapping in the center of the room, which transcended into the entire bar clapping, including the bartenders.

"Thank you to everyone who came out to support the LGBT network. Both members and allies, it's people like you this world needs. We need to continue to push the envelope and fight for equality and acceptance, not only in Corporate America but in America itself," Alan said as he raised his champagne flute. "And a huge thank you to

Masters for allowing us to host this first of many events, and to Chaz Perez, our *innovator* of the LGBT Network, for organizing this successful mixer."

I nearly vomited.

"Yes, thank you, Chaz, and thank you to everyone who came out to show your support." John echoed as he, too, raised his glass and everyone in the room followed suit. I half-assed raised my imaginary glass and watched as Chaz waved at everyone, blew kisses, and took a snag of his cosmopolitan. I couldn't determine if, deep down, I wanted this dynamic.

Alec explained one rule of power to me. Get others to do the work for you, but always take credit for it. His words resonated: *"Never do yourself what others can do for you."*

But that's not what was happening. Surface-level Chaz kept getting all the credit and notoriety from senior leaders, our boss, and our boss' boss. He pitched the idea for this event, but I elevated it to fruition.

"Theodore Sullivan, thank you for organizing this successful, spectacular event, one might even call it extremely intoxicating. Many, many thanks for all that you have done and continue to do." Alec smiled as he handed me a glass of champagne. My saving grace.

"I want to go home. Reset my brain. This event didn't work for me as I'd hoped."

"Don't forget about Emma's birthday party tomorrow. We'll have another shot."

"Do I have to go?"

"Yes. Alice is flying in tonight and my buddy Raj is in town and said he would stop by. A few of Emma's coworkers and friends are coming."

"Is Roger going to be there?"

"No," Alec said as I exhaled louder than normal. "Also, I don't want you to worry or feel uncomfortable, but one of Emma's clients gave her a box of sample DNA testing kits she plans on passing around."

"Random. Weird fucking party favor. *Does she know I'm adopted?*"

"No, I haven't told her."

I downed my champagne and cashed out my high bar tab. I guess I didn't have as many senior management buy me drinks as I thought I would.

. . .

I ARRIVED HOME AND SAT AT MY PIANO, YEARNING FOR ITS ability to make me feel better, to take me away from reality. I pressed one key when my vibrating phone brought me back to earth.

"Hi, Mom, how are you?"

"Hello, Ted. I'm doing good. I was out picking the veggies from the garden all morning. You wouldn't believe the size of the tomatoes this year. Enormous. How are you doing? Sorry for not calling yesterday. The Martins came over to help expand the garden and after Barb and I drank iced tea out on the back patio."

"Glad they could help you. I've been busy building my reputation. But I'm good." My guts winced as they twisted around each other following the words, "I'm good." *I am good, aren't I?*

"Are you getting enough sleep?"

"Of course." I lied. "You should send me some pics of the garden."

"I'm setting up a booth at the farmers' market this Sunday. I'll send a pic of my stand."

"How fun. Pretty soon you're going to have an empire. So, what else is new around town?"

"We felt the aftershock of another earthquake."

"Again?"

"It wasn't as bad as the one we felt in March, but it was surprising. Your cousin Dana was dropping some bags of soil off and came inside to chat. We were in the kitchen when we felt it."

"How is Dana doing?"

"Poor dear, she is getting a divorce. Jim is not good for her. When was the last time you two spoke?"

"Gosh, it's been a while. I should call her."

Out of all my cousins and relatives, I was the closest to Dana. She was a few years older than me, but the age difference never stopped us from having a great time. One summer, we used farm pallets to build a fort under a Bur Oak Tree with the make-believe craftsmanship to live in it, forever. We spent all day hammering nails and tying the corners of the pallets with twine. Shelly questioned where the extra blankets went, ones that found a new home as our fine carpeting. We roofed our fortress with cardboard and hung battery-powered lanterns. We spent most summers out on Litchfield Lake, choosing the water over chores. Running after the hens to only be chased by the roosters, screaming all the way back inside the house, or jumping on the trampoline scattered with soccer and tennis balls; you were dead if one of them touched you.

I should call. Dana deserved someone better than Jim. A wormy-faced hick who spent all his free time hunting and fishing. I had never liked him since they dated in high school, a place where he peaked, and she was only beginning to blossom. They got married after graduation, hoping to live the American dream. Stable jobs and growing 401Ks. The white picket fence with kids running through the sprinklers all summer behind landscaped hedges type of American dream. Family, ever after. But their authentic story involved tropes of four miscarriages and three different jobs a year, which brought stress to that dream.

"I'll call her."

*No, you won't.*

"Albert wants to do Mason's anniversary dinner at the park." My mom continued, but a ringing overpowered her voice. Scratching metal gears. A repugnant ring in my ear as my lip curled and my arm tied to my phone twitched. A muscle spasm in my biceps.

*I'm a true Sullivan, the little adopted boy said. I belong. I belong. I belong. I'm strong.*

"He lost his job at the pipeline and is applying to Rex Mining. They might have to move to Wyoming."

"Mom, I'm sorry, but my other line is ringing."

*No, it's not.*

"You're good. Go ahead. I wanted to call and chat. Have a great day, love you."

I stared at the black and white keys, the room silent. I didn't have someone else calling, and to be honest, I wasn't sure why I reacted so fast. I always pushed through the cold sludge of memories, but this time I sank.

This time Mason grabbed my ankles, dry and loveless, and pulled me into the rotating gears with him.

# 6

Alec Young

Alec topped off everyone's glasses and rushed down the hall to the elevator and down to the lobby, where Ted waited. He was dressed in a black V-neck tee under a grey suit jacket. A scrumptious combination. Ted was gripping the champagne bottle Alec had brought him.

"Nice bottle."

"I figured it could become a back-and-forth trophy. Our version of the Stanley Cup."

Alec grinned and wrapped his arms around Ted. "Well, in that case, I am honored. We have a full house up there. I know you don't want to stay long."

"I drank way too much at the mixer. Advil is holding my headache at bay."

"You don't have to stay long. So, once you grab a plate and meet Alice and Raj, you're free to go."

"Thanks for being so thorough and thoughtful with my schedule. I knew you'd make a brilliant assistant," Ted said as they stepped into a vacant elevator.

"Ha! I'd make an outstanding assistant. Only for you though."

"You better keep up the good work."

Gravity pulled at their bones as they were lifted from one story to another.

"While I have you alone," Alec said, moving his hand to Ted's arm, then stretching his neck, kissing Ted once, twice, then an energetic third. The elevator stopped and opened, and the boys were in their original spots, a middle urinal distance between them.

The scent of toasted bread and roasted garlic permeated the entrance. A meter-long charcuterie board, warm pies, prime rib, and pounds of veggies covered the massive island. Soft music from portable speakers mixed with pockets of conversation, college football-loving men shouting at the TV, forced laughter, and throat gulps of white wine.

"Theo, so glad you could make it!" Emma said as she reached her hand out. "Theo" was a new one. She was well put together in an olive jumpsuit like a curvy paratrooper, with her poppy hair slicked back and coiled in a bun. "Here, I can take those. Thanks for bringing a bottle. This is nice champagne. I like the look."

"Thanks. You look spectacular.."

"Here you go, help yourself. We have everything you could ever want." Emma handed Ted a weighted plate with a gold swirling pattern on the outer rim. He loaded it with an arrangement of fresh veggies and garlic mashed potatoes, found a calm spot at the table, and picked at pineapples and grapes.

"Theodore, this is my little sister, Alice."

"Alice, wonderful to meet you! Alec has told me so much about you." Ted dried his hands and stood up, looking at a younger female form of Alec with sun-kissed freckles across her nose.

"Likewise. I'm glad I could make this trip work. It's been so long since I've seen this turd. He never calls or comes to visit," Alice said as she poked Alec. A six-year gap stretched between Alec and Alice, the Lexington exquisite equestrian. Alice was a champion at driving the thoroughbred through numerous obstacles showcasing to judges its perfect form, bascule, and her elegant showmanship as she's hurdled through the air on a thousand-pound mammal. Alice picked up the hobby at four, an attempt to be like mamma, and a need to make her daddy proud. It didn't take long for her to display a natural ability in the sport, winning local and state competitions, and getting her a scholarship to the University of Kentucky.

"Hey now, I'm busy."

"So, Alec tells me you ride horses for UK?"

"I do. It's so fun. We made it to the championships last year and hope to repeat this year. The practice has been relentless, another reason I'm thankful this weekend worked out."

"Oh, I can only imagine," Ted said, "forgive me, but is it like the Kentucky Derby? Where you race? Or...?"

"No, my team doesn't race. It's a similar setup to track and field events. But they are hunter seat and western. In those two categories, you have sub-events you compete in."

"And which do you do?"

"I do hunter seat events, so driving the horse through the various fences and flat obstacles."

"Wow, sounds challenging, but also fun. I'm assuming you started when you were little?"

"I rode my first horse when I was four at our family's ranch," Alice said, looking at Alec. "But this guy wasn't into horses."

Alec rolled his eyes. The family resemblance was uncanny, as they stood side by side. The kind puppy dog eyes, scarlet lips, and competitive attitudes—the prolonged baby blue-eyed contact they gave when talking or their hands running through their hair when listening. Alice's glossy brown hair sprawled over her shoulders with a silver Tiffany & Co. heart-carved pendant snuggled at the base of her neck.

Emma walked over clutching Sloane's hand. "Alice, this is my long-time friend, Sloane Marshall," Emma said as Alec jetted to the restroom, and Ted went on picking at his fruit, hearing pieces of their conversation. Her recent story had gained some traction within the market, a shadowy exposé piece detailing the DUIs of the kids of business executives and how money and influence let them off the hook.

"Touchdown!" Two guys yelled from the living room while doing a victory dance as their girlfriends filmed. Ted rinsed his plate and headed onto the patio to admire the eccentric clouds and lavish vines dangling from the penthouse terrace above. The newly potted mini palms gave the warmth of a five-star resort off Mexico's coastline or a remote villa in Hawaii.

Paradise.

Then a stranger bearing a sapphire blue turban with a shiny handlebar mustache walked onto the balcony and lit a cigarette, leaning on the railing next to Ted.

"Would you care for one, man?" he asked.

"No, thank you. Do you know Emma?"

He pulled the cigarette out from under his well-groomed mustache. "I met her today; I'm a friend of Alec's," he said. "I'm Raj. Raj Bhatt." His voice mixed smoothly with the cigarette smoke, triggering a tingling sensation in Ted's brain.

"You're Raj! Nice to meet you. I'm Ted. Ted Sullivan."

"And you're Ted!" He said as they shook hands. "I've heard a lot about you, man. Great to meet you. Alec and I go way back. We met in undergrad."

“Did you attend the finance school as well? What do they call it? A Whartonite?”

“Nah, I got my MSE in data science.”

"Smart stuff. It's always good to meet an old friend of Alec's."

"Man, Alec is awesome. Did he ever tell you the story about how he saved my life once?"

"No, he didn't!" Ted's head inclined with intrigue.

"We were out sailing, one of our buddies was taking us out, and a sudden wind gust came and swung the mast, and the metal pole smacked me and our other friend in the head. We both fell into the ocean. Fucking crazy. I can't swim. I'm from India, man, so I never learned." He laughed jumbled with cues of sadness, "but Alec jumped in and rescued me.”

“And what about the other guy?”

“He drowned,” Raj said in a low tone. “Sad fucking day, man.” Raj flicked his cigarette as ashes fell from the terrace.

"He never told me the story. Wow. I'm glad you made it out."

"I said I would never go into the ocean again. No fucking way, man."

"I don't blame you. So, Alec tells me you work at Bridgestone Analytica?"

"Palo Alto all the way."

"It's good to meet a non-finance guy. How do you like it?"

"Man, I love it. The pennies are nice, and the fucking girls in California, my god. You guys should come out and visit. I'll take you to all the hottest places."

"I would like that. I've never been to California."

"Dude, you are missing out."

Alec emerged onto the patio, enjoying a neat whiskey.

"There you are. Ah, I see you two have met," Alec said.

"Man, I was telling Ted you both need to come to Palo Alto."

"I'm always down for a vacation, and Ted has never been."

"Exactly," Raj said, drawing another pull of his cigarette.

"So, Arizona State won, and everyone inside is demanding we take victory shots," Alec said.

"Let's go," Raj said as he doused his cigarette in water and tossed it in the trash.

"Assistant, I think I'm going to head out," Ted said as they all stepped inside. "I've checked off the two items on my to-do list."

"Another item appeared on your agenda, last minute. Keep Alec Young company."

"I think Alec Young is in great company."

"But not the company he wants. Mr. Sullivan Young."

Alice and Sloane passed around chilled vodka. Alec took one, and Ted gave a passing nod as the room went silent in a domino effect. All eyes were on Emma as everyone sang happy birthday. A wave of unsynced melodies and hums somehow morphed into a harmonized collection.

"Thank you." Emma blushed. "So, I have this new client, who is in the beta stages of analysis and development and asked if myself and my dearest, closest friends would sample their product." She sat her shot glass on the island and pulled out the DNA test kits. "They do direct-to-consumer genetic testing. Saliva, not blood. And what sets them apart from their competitors is ethnicity accuracy, and not some vagueness.

Oh, someplace over there or here. Random party favor, I know, but it would be awesome if you all would try it." Emma picked up her venom and lifted it in the air. "Here's to you and here's to me, may we never disagree. But if we do, fuck you, here's to me." And everyone shot the liquid down their throats.

"What a lovely toast," Ted whispered. "Okay, give me a hug. I also want to squeeze in a nap."

"I'll walk you out," Alec said.

Ted said his goodbyes to Alice, thanking her for making the trip with plans to meet again in the future. The same with Raj, pats on the back following, promises to visit Palo Alto. As they headed toward the door, Emma perked up, handing Ted a Double Helix box.

"Don't forget this. I'm sure I'll be seeing you soon."

"Thanks... Emma," Ted said.

The two sat in the spacious lobby next to a gas-lit fireplace waiting for Ted's Lyft. A chandelier dangled above with a hodgepodge of oddly shaped mirrors, paintings, and wall-mounted gardens.

"My headache is coming back," Ted rubbed his forehead. "You and your sister are so much alike, and Raj is cool. Glad I could meet them both."

"I'm happy she made it down. It's been a while since I saw her last," Alec said. "Yeah, Raj is a great dude."

"Why didn't you tell me you were in a boating incident? I didn't know you saved his life."

"Hopefully, his is the last life I have to save. Raj and I were good friends before the incident, and after, we became best friends."

"And another guy drowned? Jesus, Alec. I'm sorry you had to go through that."

"It was definitely a turning point in my life."

Alec wanted to kiss Ted goodbye but couldn't find the spot in time as clusters of people kept filling the lobby. A discreet squeeze of Ted's hand sufficed, his palm was warm and soft. He watched as Ted walked through the doors and into the night, then made his way back to the condo and one by one, the room emptied like birds chasing the sun: pecking at trays one last time, bellies full of nuts and wine.

They packaged and sealed leftover food while letting the dishes soak:

a cleaning task for the morning. Emma and Alice brushed their teeth, sipped cold glasses of water, although something prompted Emma to finish her martini and throw on pajamas. They flipped through the various streaming services until the perfect movie appeared. Surrounded by throw blankets and down pillows, the cozy environment induced a taming of breathing and heavy eyelids, and Alice drifted off within the first ten minutes.

Alec and Raj were lounging on the patio, the sky dimly lit by the city lights, shying aside the stars from sight while dancing the catch-up on life game, weaving with occasional banter over icy beers. Brief snippet flashbacks of amusing and awkward encounters during undergrad life in Pennsylvania. A forward-moving timeline until they reached the present. In the years following the sailing incident, Raj became highly loyal to Alec. A staunch indebtedness. A dedicated confidant. Alec didn't have to tell Raj about the plan. He didn't need to pile him in a mountain of minutiae, for he knew Alec would shape his own path. Conversation soon turned to work as both shared stories and career achievements. Raj giddily told Alec about a new client Bridgestone Analytica onboarded and how he was their direct contractor. A startup specializing in sensor technology. *Vision AI, Vision, AI, Vision AI*, Alec thought.

Raj held his cigarette between two fingers and tilted his head upward to exhale smoke. Took his time to admire the clouds grow and shift.

"So what you're saying is you're concerned Ted won't get nominated for Forbes top advisors?"

"I could be paranoid. But yes. Ted is one of the most hard-working people I know, and he shouldn't be overlooked because of corporate fuckery. Ted is light years ahead of the guy they might pick."

"You always did look after your friends," Raj said, scratching his skin under the lip of his turban. "Is there some sort of vouch letter you can write? Or have people in the org sign a petition?"

"No, I can't have my name on this. There must be a way to organically make his management reconsider nominating this Chaz something guy. Fucking hack."

Suddenly, Emma stepped onto the patio, securely wrapped in a silky robe. Her dirty martini glass was topped off with a plump olive and she munched on a baby carrot.

"What are you guys talking about?"

"Work stuff," Alec said.

"Thank you again, Emma, for hosting this. It was great," Raj said.

"You don't have to thank me, Raj," Emma said, pulling up a chair. "Is everything okay with work? What's going on?"

"Everything's fine. I was telling Raj I'm concerned Ted won't get nominated for Forbes top advisors."

"But he's been working so hard."

"I know. He's been working very hard. I can't think of a way to nudge his management in the right direction."

"You can nudge them into knowing what a wrong decision would be," Emma said, sipping her martini while letting her vagueness linger. Alec's eyebrows knitted together with confusion. Raj sat back, invested in where the conversation was going.

"What do you mean?"

"We all know reputational risk is everything. Especially with a firm like Kauffman."

"Yes."

"Leverage reputational risk to have them make a different choice, or at least entertain the thought. When I was at Alpha Kappa Alpha and we wanted to kick out a *sister*," Emma said, using air quotes, "we would leak photos or stories, or have the frats spread things around that she supposedly did, and using code of conduct and reputational risk, disgracing our image, we had grounds to remove *her*... I mean, them."

"The deception," Raj said. "Love it."

"So, leak embarrassing or unprofessional things Chaz has done?"

"If that's the guy's name, then yes."

"Kauffman vets their employees thoroughly. A complete heat-press-dry-clean of our past and records. If there was anything out there, Kauffman would have already found it."

"Find private information. Hack his computer," Emma said casually, her cheeks glowing lush.

"Okay, Mr. Robot, let's focus on achievable steps."

"Actually, it is pretty achievable," Raj said while fidgeting with his mustache.

"Hold on, this is all hypothetical. For all we know, Ted will be nominated."

"But it's better to be ready if he isn't," Emma teased. "Raj, you can hack someone's computer, right? Snoop around and pull anything incriminating."

Alec noticed the more Emma drank, notably when her lips kissed the rim of a dirty martini, the further her devious traits manifested. Her true self was brought forth thanks to *liquid cuntness.*

"To be blunt, yes. But it would take time and creative workarounds if his computer is protected."

"Well, there you go, Alec. The solution to your dilemma."

*I don't know if I'd call that a solution,* Alec thought. *I still needed to tell Ted how Emma was involved with Sullivan Young. Fuck.*

Alec parked his silver pickup truck outside Ted's apartment and sat with his own thoughts, debating left brain, right brain on why Ted hadn't answered his phone. His eyes darted from the dashboard to the cup holders, then up to the assortment of buttons on the steering wheel.

*I need to tell Theodore about Emma,* Alec thought. *Why isn't he answering me? Could he have found out about Emma knowing our plan and his way of punishing me is the silent treatment?*

The lamp post he parked under flickered. The last remaining bugs before winter were swirling around, diving headfirst into the glass bulb as if trying to break its barrier. Alec headed up the stairs. He could hear plaintive piano keys seeping through Ted's walls: low muffled C sharp minor melodies, a nocturne trance. Alec gave the door two knocks. The piano stopped and the door slowly unlocked and opened. Ted's nose and cheeks were red, and his eyes bloodshot.

"Have you been crying?" Alec asked as Ted grabbed his glass of wine and slumped on the couch.

# 7

## Ted Sullivan

A tingling sensitivity near the base of my belly bubbled and fizzed. Everybody spoke in rosy whispers with hints of nervousness—quarterly review and *nomination* day. I got an IM from Reid as a spray of adrenaline coursed through me, kindling in my heart then sailing to my feet and back up my spine. Last room on the north side, his ping said. Time to check my top-tier item.

*A part of you will be dead.*

I sucked in the clammy air as I walked in, ingesting the wandering fumes of dread from those who came before me. Reid gave me a warm smile, surrounded by folders and confidential papers flipped face down as I took a seat, sensing the past bodies who'd warmed the leather chair before me, like a luxury car feature, a wet feeling.

"Over the past," Reid skimmed his notes, "three years, myself, along with our clients, have been incredibly lucky to have you be a part of the team. We've noticed you've done a phenomenal job. You scored an *outstanding* in regard to your risk management. Your ability to protect the firm and our clients' assets is unparalleled. Good job."

"Thanks."

"You scored an *outstanding* on your market sensitivity while escalating and providing guidance on issues. Wonderful job."

"Thanks."

"You scored an *outstanding* on your support of company culture. I've received notes on all the great work you're doing in the LGBT network, so again, really great job."

"Thanks."

"There is no question that you are a brilliant young man. And on behalf of myself and our clients, I want to say thank you, and as a result of your hard work and outstanding Q1 work performance, your salary will increase by ten percent with a lump sum bonus of thirty-five grand, leaving your overall take home pay increased by twenty percent. Congratulations."

Music to my ears. Pomp and circumstances melody blasting from all directions. My brain was humming, warm with flashes of electricity. The nomination news was next. I could feel it.

"Thank you so much. I'm happy all my hard work didn't go unnoticed," I said, smiling from ear to ear. "Mr. Grant called today and insisted I call him Robert."

"Did he now? That is a great sign. Good ol' Robert. We've received a lot of positive feedback on your performance."

"What's the update on the Forbes Top Wealth Advisor nomination?"

A slight pause lingered.

"I'm going to stop you right there, Ted. We've received a lot of positive feedback on your performance, but senior management decided to nominate someone else for the Forbes list," Reid said as he fiddled with a stack of papers. I didn't know what to say as the vinyl record in my ears scratched and paused. I kept staring at Reid. My genuine smile stretched into a fake grin. This was not possible. "You will have plenty of time in the next few years to make the list," Reid said as if those words would improve things. "Besides, we had heard through the grapevine that you weren't really interested in the Forbes list, that all you wanted was an outstanding on your quarterly review, which you got with a sizable bonus. Congratulations again. So, did you have any other questions?"

"Who did they nominate?"

"We're going to announce it next week in our quarterly client call. Best to keep the suspense alive."

I was furious—a stinging red inferno brewing inside me as I tried not to look ungrateful.

"Who doesn't love suspense? Thank you, Reid, for everything. I'm very grateful."

"Not a problem, mate."

I felt the eyes analyzing me as I walked back to my desk. Hungry for details on what transpired inside that room, but I gave them nothing. I kept the best fake smile radiating, not hinting I was in a corporate car accident. How the fuck can they decide based on hearsay on what I truly wanted? More eyes flicked my way as I sat back at my desk.

Finance 460: Financial cases and modeling were a required group-based lecture course at my business school. Our professor was a retired veteran turned chief financial officer for an old soda company in the '80s. He always wore corduroy overalls and smelled of caramel candy and butterscotch that had been sitting in a hot car. Our groups were chosen by the random excel generator formula. As a result, I got paired with two of the unluckiest kids in the class. They were unlucky the same way people say so and so was unlucky because their car was always broken, or their chain-smoking aunt's lung cancer came back. I lost count of how many times their Wi-Fi went down, so they couldn't upload their portion of the financial cases.

I did everything.

But the one thing these unlucky kids were lucky at doing was convincing Professor Leech of their sob stories. Their victimized narrative. No amount of fervent prayer will save Auntie Flow this time.

At the end of the semester, I learned that I was the unlucky one. Me. I never complained to Leech about their lack of contribution. I thought they would get what they deserved in the end. And yet somehow, they both got higher grades at the end of the semester than me.

I refused to allow myself to be unlucky for an opportunity I deserved. My aspirations went beyond sitting at the same desk in a Kauffman Schwartz office grunting through the bitch work.

My goal, *our plan*, was more significant than my desk, or Chaz's, or Reid's. My thinking was always three steps ahead of where I currently was, focused on the stone path; but what if I got lost by not peeking my head up, not taking accurate temperature checks, and by keeping my head down for too long? I could feel my phone buzz twice inside my pocket, but I paid no attention. My inbox notified me that I had three new unread emails, but my eyes were glossed over. Since I didn't get the nomination, my top-tier item was still live, begging to be fed while delaying our launch.

*You're not one of them, Mason said. You don't belong. Homeless boy.*

"Ted, everyone is thinking of going to O'Conners down the street for drinks. Do you want to come?" Mel said as she spun around in her chair and slid across to my desk. "Also, don't say anything because they haven't announced it, but *Chaz got nominated for this year's Top Advisors.* I'm not sure if you've heard of it, but Forbes does a list every year. So exciting!"

I fucking knew it.

I controlled my breathing and focused on my chest: inhale, exhale. "That's exciting, and thanks for the offer, but I have plans tonight with a friend," I lied.

"Uh, like a boyfriend?"

"Maybe?"

"Oh my, Ted has a boyfriend?"

*Jesus H. Christ.* "Like I said, it's a friend who, yes, is a boy. I wouldn't get too excited. But again, thank you for the offer, and you'll have a great time. Have a drink for me."

"Okay, be boring, Ted," Mel said as she rolled back to her desk and immediately pulled her phone out. She was probably texting Chaz, that fucking spectacle. A useless spectacle whose only purpose was being on all fours, pit-roasted between subprime mortgages and junk bonds. He didn't deserve the Forbes nomination. He didn't understand sacrifice and would only use this opportunity to update his LinkedIn profile to project egomania, elevating himself to a more prominent figure than he actually was. *Tulipmania* was more like it. I could feel my anger taking over. I needed to go for a walk around the block, decompress in the fresh air and figure out what to do next.

A few dog barks and car horns echoed as I completed two laps around the park, around two and a half miles. The light towers were lit up, and the lake's flawless ducks were floating in a pack. l My hands pulsed, my chest tightened, and my legs wobbled. Letting my body catch up, I took a sip of water at a fountain on the south end, with my office and other buildings in sight. Before heading home, I would jog to the office, maybe go up to my floor to use the restroom or admire our beautiful lobby and people watch. Receive an injection of inspiration from the people who are still working. Tame this power imbalance I was feeling.

I stood waiting for the pedestrian light to change when I could see several gleaming police lights ahead. Near our office, but a little off to the side. What schmuck got pulled over or arrested? As I got closer and closer, a moderate group of people began forming. The blue and red lights were extensive and robust. An accident? I got as close as possible when I saw an inky black tarp on the ground and in the center under it, a large object—a sizable skeletal object.

"Hi, miss. Do you know what happened?" I asked a stranger next to me—an older curly-haired lady with a pink fanny pack around her waist.

"A homeless man overdosed," she said, eyelashes fluttering, putting her phone back into her fanny pack.

"A homeless man?"

"Apparently, he was having a seizure, and people kept walking around him until someone called the cops." She shook her head. "I don't understand how people can be so cruel to other people."

My mind raced. My head drowning in paranoia. Could it be him? Drugs cost money, and his coffee can was empty.

"The man who called 911 said while he was seizing on the ground, he was clutching a cardboard sign that said, *Lost Boy.*"

Goosebumps crawled up my spine. The body under the tarp kept growing larger and larger. The words I said to him repeated in my mind.

I unlocked the door to my apartment and poured myself a glass of wine and sat on my piano chair, staring at the white and black keys, trying to not let my grim guilt overpower me. I didn't know what to play or what to think. What I did know was that I had yet to tell Alec about the nomination. My phone buzzed again with another check-in from him, four in total of unanswered explanations. I didn't want to tell Alec the news because telling him would make it real, and I knew he would ask me what my plan was, and I didn't have one yet. I didn't know what to do. I felt like he already got a hint that the update would not be acceptable by the fact that I hadn't responded. Our one rule was complete communication above anything else.

I closed my eyes. I desperately tried to keep the weight of everything, from not landing the nomination to missing Alec, from collapsing my spirits.

*Look what you've done, the little adopted boy said. Look what you've done.*

The string's vibrations were low and melancholy as I held my foot on the pedal. Releasing and pressing again to flood my mind with doleful notes.

A knock at the door jolted me back to reality. Who could be here at this hour? I unlocked and opened the door to Alec.

"Have you been crying?" he asked, as I turned around with red and itchy eyes. I took a second to answer. Paused.

"No."

"What's wrong?" Alec shut the door behind him. He could always read my mood better than I could. I grabbed my wine glass and sat on my couch.

"Nothing," I said, a humorless smile crossing my face, an exhausted, detached from reality smile.

*Why did you lie to him? The little adopted boy asked. Why did you lie to Alec?*

"Ted, what is wrong?" Alec probed again. "Did you hear back about the nomination? What did they say?"

"I should find out tomorrow." The lie came easily, even though it shouldn't, especially to Alec. "Just having one of those days. I feel so small. Like an imposter. Like I'm nothing. Powerless."

Alec squeezed the back of my neck. His palm was warm as he

massaged out the calcified stress knots. He could always control my inner demons. Tame them with a crack of a whip and force them into submission, and in this case, my guilt. I looked up at Alec's rosy, red cheeks and doll lips. I leaned in and kissed him, my purple-stained lips pressed firmly against his. He tasted like fresh honey as he kissed me harder; we both inhaled deeply. The scratch of stubble on his chin tickled my cheeks. My nostrils hummed from the woody citrus cologne he sprays behind his ears. Light-headed and shaky from the rush of serotonin coursing through my body.

"Yummy grapes," Alec said flirtatiously as he licked his lower lip, removing his ball cap and tossing it aside. I laughed, kissing him again, moving my hand under his shirt, and rubbing his smooth chest. Then moving my hand lower, grazing his bushy happy trail and squeezing his crotch. His throbbing erection through his jeans grew harder and harder. The warmth of his groin could melt ice. He kissed my neck as I squeezed another handful, released, and pressed again.

"Let's make you feel powerful again," Alec said as he picked me up and carried me to the bedroom. My bedside lamp gave a faint glimpse of my room. He flung off my sheets and laid me down gently, helping me take off my shirt. He kissed my neck, reaching my collarbone and my chest, then trailed his tongue down my belly. My erection found its way through the bottom of my jogging shorts, then into Alec's warm mouth. My breath went deep with every stroke and lap of his tongue. Alec slid off my shorts and unbuttoned his pants. I stood up on my knees, and Alec plopped down on my bed as I slid his pants and briefs off from around his ankles. The right side of Alec's naked body, muscular butt, and hairy thighs was glowing. I drizzled lube down his crack and crawled up, pressing my chest against Alec's back. He grabbed my hands as I wrapped them around him. My fingers were cold as my blood rushed to my groin. I kissed his beard and then his cheekbone as I slid inside him. Tight and warm.

"Are you okay?" I asked.

"I love you," Alec said as his moans grew louder and longer. I stuck my tongue in his ear and felt his goosebumps run up his spine. He clenched as I continued to thrust harder and harder. Pleasure was building until the peak climax bursted out and I tried to catch my breath. I love being inside Alec, and conversely, I love him being inside me. After I finished, I rolled over onto my back with my legs spread apart, and Alec slowly slid inside me.

# 8

Alec Young

Alec searched for his phone, struggling not to wake Ted. He had drifted asleep, promising to stay for warm cuddles: feeling security in each other and nourishment after a drought. It had been too long, Alec thought as he lay awake. The room was silent and somber with the ceiling fan making a click sound every few seconds. Alec drew his arm from under Ted's pillow and found his shoes, using the faint light from his phone screen. He hadn't predicted he'd find Ted drunk on wine, sulking at his piano: a sight he never wished to see again.

Alec had grown very protective of Ted, his well-being placed front and center. As time moved forward, he regretted more and more the way he handled Emma's outburst. Alec beat himself up for not lying better, for not crafting a creative explanation, guiding Emma away from their plan. A secret Alec must now keep. Since he got them into this mess, he must find their way out: continue scanning her father's Rolodex, then drop off the hitchhiker. He looked down at Ted wrapped in blankets, his head poking out with darting eyelids, his little dreamer. Ted's dry lips were purple from wine, even after a shower they'd taken together. Alec tucked his phone into his pocket and gave Ted a kiss on his forehead, brushing his hand through his hair with tender strokes, and plucked a pen and wrote in an elegant hand

*V.O.U.*

on a sticky note, leaving it on Ted's nightstand, and off he went into the night.

WHEN ALEC ARRIVED AT THE CONDO, A CORNER LIVING room light was on. The vintage bulb with twisting copper coils produced a golden-esque light. Hazy visibility for him to sense where things stood. *Did she leave the lamp on for me?* Alec thought, tiptoeing across the room and gravitating toward the couch, when he stopped himself. The cat was out of the bag. Time to play the part, so he flipped the light and headed to the bedroom.

The sun rose fast. Alec turned off his alarm, then groggily laid his body back down, despising the silent hurricane of a ceiling fan above him, missing the unbalanced clicks of Ted's. He looked over and Emma was already in the bathroom getting ready. The sound of small taps and clinks from her makeup bag came from the bathroom as she applied her war paint, followed by a loud whoosh of the blow dryer. Alec waited five minutes before getting out of bed, reading pre-market trading numbers, and scanning emails when a jolt of adrenaline shot through his body. He bolted out of bed in his maroon briefs and ran to the closet.

"Good morn... someone's in a hurry," Emma said, testing the temperature of her curling iron: one tap, two taps.

"The deal I've been working on is moving forward and the client wants a call."

"When?"

"In one hour," Alec said, in a sort of, *fuck me*, way, thrusting his hairy thighs through his narrow gray slacks. Palatable sausage casing.

"Well, that's exciting." Emma whirled around, cooking a wrapped chunk of hair. "So, I was thinking we should go visit my parents in Boston."

"When?"

"I don't know. Soon."

"Sounds great," Alec said distractedly while adjusting his suit.

I'm glad you came into bed with me last night. You were talking in your sleep."

"Was I? That's weird."

"I couldn't make out what you were saying. All I could make out was Theodore. You said his name like three times. Have they posted Theo about the Forbes nomination yet?"

"It might be today," Alec said, walking out of the closet transformed.

"Your ass looks so good in those slacks," Emma said, looking Alec up and down.

"I should get some new ones. These are getting tight," Alec said before giving Emma a goodbye kiss. "I'll probably be home late, so no need to wait for me."

ALEC LEFT WORK EARLY TO MEET TED AT HIS FAVORITE PARK, his hands gripping the steering wheel the entire drive over. The reality freight train was barreling toward them at unimaginable speed, rumbles rattling the tracks as the train roared its steam whistle warning. But Alec was prepping to flip the railroad switch, forcing reality to take a different, unknown path. The shifting weather was transforming the trees. The pond of social brown feathered ducks seemed unphased by the disappearing Arizona winter.

Alec stopped walking and faced Ted.

"Theodore, you need to tell me what happened."

Ted stood in silence.

"I'm sorry I didn't respond sooner. I didn't want to believe it."

"You didn't get the Forbes nomination."

"I didn't," Ted said as he pressed his ear to Alec's warm chest.

Hearing the calm thump, thump of his heart. "It might have something to do with Pebble Arrow and Blue Horizon. But before you go on about how I should have tried harder or how I should have solidified my position at all costs, I want you to know—"

Alec interrupted.

"Theodore, it's okay...." Alec kissed the top of Ted's head. "I can only imagine how stressful that was. I'm not upset."

"You're not? But this will set us back by a year, probably."

"No, I'm not upset. There is still *time*."

"Time? Reid told me point-blank I'm not nominated. They're going to announce it next week."

"I factored in the possibility of you not landing the nomination, and, being the risk fluent that I am, derived countermeasures, just in case."

"What countermeasures?"

"I can't tell you. All I can say is that the wheels are in motion."

Ted pulled his head up.

"What do you mean you can't tell me?" Ted said, annoyed. "Wheels in motion? You know I hate when you do things without telling me. Especially when it involves our future."

"Let's keep walking," Alec said as he grabbed Ted's hand. "Plausible deniability. I am shielding you from knowing too much."

"Jesus, Alec. I'm a good *liar*, just tell me."

"Once this is over, I will explain everything, I promise. But, for right now, I think it's best if we keep you in the shadows."

"You know I don't like it when you go rogue and do things without my input. When are you going to stop doing that?"

"You're right and I'm sorry. How's this, do I have your sign-off to move forward?"

"I don't even know what you're moving forward to."

"I want to keep you in the dark, but let's say I can hypothetically reveal some minor details that might make your management reconsider Chaz." Ted pondered his thoughts "Hypothetically of course. So, do I have your sign off?"

The wheels in Ted's mind kept moving.

"Yes, you can move forward. But I don't want whatever you're doing to get back to us."

"It won't, I promise. And just to confirm. It was Chaz Perez who got the nomination, right?"

Ted rolled his eyes. "Yes, it was him. God, I still can't believe it." Ted slumped his shoulders. A defeated stance.

"Hey, things will work out. We still have time."

Alec's phone sang ching-ding-ding, ching-ding-ding. Alec snugged his phone from his pocket. Raj was Face Timing. His intestines twisted around each other. Ching-ding-ding.

"Is that Raj?"

"Yeah." Alec declined. "I'll call him back."

"You can take it. I don't mind."

"It's okay. I'll call him back. I'm spending time with my Theodore. Let me walk you home."

Alec looked at his phone and saw a text from Raj. The spaces between the words swelled with diesel smoke from the reality train. The text timestamp: a vulgar ding of a grandfather clock striking midnight. Truths were unshackled, forced to surface, bursting through water, swallowing lung-popping air.

Found.

> Hey man, this dude should be in jail. I found
> some fucked up shit. Call me back.

*What Raj found must be dealt with,* Alec thought, then looked over at Ted watching strangers from a distance. Ted's hand recoiled slightly as strangers inched closer, and Alec gripped harder. He would make sure Ted's dreams ran true and ruthlessly manage these undiscovered truths, whatever they may be.

*What did Raj find?* Alec thought. The surprise enlarged with every passing second. The itch to unbox the mystery grew and grew until Alec couldn't help himself. When they returned to Ted's apartment, Ted badgered Alec about what he was planning, sensing something was happening. As much as Alec didn't want to, he caved and told Ted about the plan for Raj to hack Chaz's computer. He emphasized their discretion and carefulness, assuring Ted that it wouldn't be traced back to them. Ted sat on his couch, curious about the mechanics of such a scheme and hungry for what Raj found. Alec sat next to Ted and called Raj.

"Hey man," Raj said as his groomed mustache and blue turban appeared on the screen. "This Chaz guy is fucked up!"

"Raj, what did you find?" Ted said, leaning forward.

Raj shook his head in disbelief as he, too, got comfortable with Palo Alto illuminated in the background from his condo.

"You actually got in?" Alec asked.

"Yeah, man. I spammed his email for a few days. Several emails a day about 50% sale on Gucci belts, Chanel sunglasses, etc."

"I don't think Chaz is dumb enough to fall for lying spring sale emails," Ted said.

"He didn't fall for them." Raj took a sip of beer. "It wasn't until he clicked *unsubscribe* on the email that he granted me access. And I found a lot of fucked up shit on his computer."

"Like?" Ted said.

"Per the time stamps, he's been doing this for a few years. I can't identify any of the men in the videos, but your boy Chaz likes to secretly record himself abusing unconscious guys. Straight, gay, I don't know." Alec and Ted's eyes widened with shock. "In a few videos, you can see Chaz slip something into their drinks." Ted's hand made its way across his mouth. "And fifteen minutes later, they were out, and Chaz took their pants off, then took pictures with a polaroid while groping, you know..." Raj took another sip. "Shit's fucked up."

"Please tell me you're joking," Ted said.

"Man, I wish I was. I can't unsee that shit." Raj shook his head.

"We have to go public," Alec said. "If he's nominated and the story breaks, it would destroy Kauffman's reputation."

"I hoped to find something slightly embarrassing, but nothing like this."

"Let's not go public quite yet. Raj, how can we get access to the evidence?" Ted asked. Raj dictated a long web address as Ted wrote it down. A sequence of uppercase, special characters, and lowercase nonsense. The code rerouted them to the dark side of the internet. Dozens of video and photo thumbnails soon appeared. The camera's angle was tucked behind laundry, atop a bookshelf, and mixed with random objects. Hidden.

*What the fuck*, Alec thought.

Ted gasped. "Wait a minute." He leaned forward and pointed to a video. "Open that one." Alec's finger graced the touchpad, and seconds later, the video started. "No. Fucking. Way!"

The mystery man wasn't unconscious like the others as he bent Chaz over a beige sofa and sodomized him. He slapped Chaz's ass as his blue checkered necktie bounced off his belly with every thrust.

"Are you my naughty boy?" The man asked out of breath.

"Yes Daddy. This ass is all yours," Chaz squealed as the big man moved his hands from Chaz's hips up to his shoulders, then back down to his hips, thrusting harder and harder. "Come for me, Daddy! This ass is yours!"

"What? Who is that?"

"Our smoking gun. That's our managing director, John Barrett!"

THE AIR GOT BONE DRY AND UNEXPECTEDLY COLD HOURS after the sunset clashed with the warmth of manufactured air. Alec and Emma got comfortable in a corner booth, browsing the drink menu and admiring the unique lighting. Overly attentive servers swiftly bustled around, pouring wine with one hand and lighting scentless candles as couples sat at their tables, effortlessly delivering fresh gourmet rolls and toro sashimi. Steep and sophisticated, it was the perfect place to host evenings of celebration and recognition of all kinds.

"So, did you do it?" Emma asked while browsing the scrapbook-looking menu with her Burberry coat snuggled around her hips.

"Yeah," Alec said.

"Life is exciting, should we try fugu?"

"Maybe."

"Did you mail the package with attention to Sloane Marshall?"

"Yeah."

"And you dropped it off at a blue street bin?"

"I went to the one next to the mall when I was on my way home from work the other day."

"Perfect. Now we wait. Does Theo know?"

"No."

# 9

## Ted Sullivan

I lingered outside until someone wandered out of the building, and I slipped through the closing door, my phone pressed to my ear as though I was in a deep conversation, too diverted to converse with the crowds leaving. Pretending I, too, lived in the building.

"Third floor please," I said. Faint words trickled from my phone; unbeknownst to the strangers, it was Anderson Cooper summarizing today's news. Last year I had to collect a work laptop from a 'sick' Chaz to complete the Bachelier summary, so I recalled his apartment number.

I gave the door two knocks. The volume of the TV quickly sank, following a stomp and pause. I could sense him peering at me through the peephole. The fucking creep. The door opened.

"Ted? What are you doing here? Like, how did you get in?" Chaz said in a black Britney Spears the Circus Tour tee over teal satin pajama shorts.

I barged in, quick to make myself at home. "I was going to text, but some people were coming up so I walked with them." The disgusting beige sofa gawked at me as the video of John fucking Chaz replayed in my mind. From the ridiculous look on his face to how Chaz bent and arched his spine. "Interesting sofa."

"What can I help you with? I'm watching Real Housewives," Chaz said.

"Would you ever want to be a housewife?"

"What? What do you mean?"

"A housewife. If you had the option to be a stay-at-home-fuck wife, would you?"

"Ted, what the hell is your problem?" Chaz opened the door. "Leave. I don't know what you're doing here."

"I think I'll stay."

"Leave. Now!"

"Chaz, we need to talk." I walked around Chaz's living room, scoping for a hidden camera.

"What are you doing? Stop going through my stuff."

I glanced up. "Nice ceiling fan. Is it a break away model?" I reached his bookshelf, removing objects and tilting book spines.

"I said stop going through my stuff! Don't make me call security."

"Oh, I'm just making sure there isn't a hidden camera. Don't want to be filmed without my consent." Chaz ran pale as he slowly sealed the door. "Like, what are you talking about?"

"You know exactly what I'm talking about." I studied Chaz's pathetic worried expression. He was not doing a good job of suppressing his emotions. Amateur. "You greasy, little, slime ball." I chuckled. "I knew you were fucked up, but I didn't know it was to this degree. Really Chaz? Exploiting unconscious men?"

"I still don't know what you're talking about."

"Sure you do." I walked from his living area to his kitchen, hating the entire nude and beige palette, faux fur, and overly Target decor. I point to a basic white vase with salmon plumes tucked inside. "Is this from Scully and Scully?"

"I don't know what that means." Chaz whimpered.

"Of course you don't. And that is because you don't belong in our world. You're a fraud. A slithering snake who fucked his way to the top." Chaz stood silent. "So, here's how things are about to go. You're going to send John, your daddy, with the entire management committee CC'd that you're no longer interested in the Forbes nomination."

Chaz's eyes widened. "Don't you think that looks suspicious? Like, why would I no longer be interested?"

"I don't care how it looks. Make up some story. All I care about is you withdrawing your application," I said as I twisted around to appraise the city lights. "How much do you pay for this apartment? You have a terrible view."

I spun back around, and Chaz was crying. Silent tears ran down his round cheeks as he struggled to dry them with his palms.

"Why are you doing this? I know you and I have gone back and forth, but it was innocent banter. Why are you doing this, Ted?"

"My reasons are none of your concern. You're simply an obstacle in a larger path. All you need to worry about is sending that email." Chaz used the bottom of his concert tee to wipe his eyes, but the more he tried, the more the tears gushed. "You look like you might need my help. Hand me your work phone." I reached my hand out.

"No. Nuh-uh," Chaz said, swaying his head. "I'm not doing this."

"Chaz. You either don't and everyone finds out, forcing Forbes to blacklist you and the firm to fire you. Or you comply and no one finds out and you get to keep your spotless reputation."

Chaz read the floor, tears dripping onto the laminate wood, purposefully not making eye contact.

"You and I have to be up early tomorrow for the Q1 town hall," I said. "Tick-Tock, Chaz. What will it be?"

He stood frozen and sniffling, a petrified posture of uncertainty.

I was about to give up when he moved. Chaz tiptoed toward his desk and handed me his unlocked work phone, still not making eye contact. I smirked, and as I arranged the email to John and the committee.

Chaz poured himself a hefty drink. The sour sting of tequila permeated the apartment.

"You've made the right decision," I said, hearing the guzzling. I drafted the email short and quick, harnessing the voice of Chaz. Keeping the tone irrational yet highly self aware.

*Dear John,*

*I formally withdraw my candidacy for The* Forbes *Top Wealth Advisors. As much as I appreciate the nomination, I still have tremendous room to grow, and thus need time to focus on myself and the industry. Please accept my apology for the last-minute decision, and I hope to be a viable candidate next year, when I'm ready.*

*Sincerely,*
*Chaz*

Sent.

"I know John is going to ask you about this email tomorrow," I said, watching an already intoxicated Chaz hoover the glass to his lips. "What are you going to say?"

"What do you want me to say?" Chaz drew a greedy sip, then poured another batch. The frozen tequila bottle condensing in the stuffy apartment air.

"Good answer. Nothing too wordy. Keep it short. You simply aren't ready. Nothing more. He'll probably get insecure and ask if it was him. You're obliged to say no."

~

Our overtly religious new hire, Thomas, and I sat in the massive lecture halls on the top floor at KS, drinking coffee and water at five-thirty as we waited for the seminar to begin. At the end of every quarter, our division hosted a *nod to our past, a glimpse of our future* Town Hall event. Various managing directors took center stage to highlight and recognize all the hard work we've done. Using data to tell their story plastered on PowerPoint slides, they took us through the numbers from that quarter in our division and compared us to our competitors.

*Q1 did not show promising signs. Client activity went down with a low new client onboarding number.*

Reid must have received those numbers early when he stressed increasing engagement. I had offered a solution: nominate me, and I would bring in all the clients as a Forbes *Top Advisor*. Showcasing the trophy like a grand champion market steer at the county fair. Pick me! If those numbers hadn't improved, I couldn't feel bad. They had it coming with their poor decisions.

Chaz and Mel were sitting in the front row beside another girl, speaking of poor decisions. His hair seemed more robust with the top combed back. His wardrobe also seemed enhanced, mimicking the persona of Reid and the other managers. Rose gold cufflinks and a thick parsley tie knot. Resonating as if last night didn't happen. I wonder if John already spoke with him? I needed to chat with Reid as soon as possible to solidify my position. What if I wasn't next in line? What if last night was all for nothing?

*You will sit upon your throne.*

"We did terribly this quarter," Thomas said.

"Yes, we did, and I have a feeling it's only going to continue."

"I wonder what the cause is. Our competitors made bank."

"I don't know. Incompetent managerial decisions, maybe?"

John Barrett's remarks seemed to be all fluff. Ensuring everyone we had a stable and bright future ahead. Our office was expanding because of our success and looking to increase headcount by 5%.

"We simply need to move the goalpost. Don't dwell on last quarter's numbers, the firm is currently content, and content is king," John said. "We want to empower all of you to do right by our clients. A few of us have to bite the bullet, head back to the drawing board, and re-run the numbers. Management has strategies in place, several thought-out plans. Once we've ironed it out, we will hit the ground running. Going forward, we ask each of you to be daring. Let your creative minds wander and bring ideas to your managers."

The hall clapped as John stepped off the stage and Audrey Stone walked on. Global Head of Private Wealth Investments. People's attention rose, putting away their phones, and opening up their notepads—her power to control a room just by walking on stage was impressive. That's the level of prowess I strived for.

"Everyone, I ask you to look at the person to your left, then to your right. We've filled this room with the best and the brightest in the industry. You were all selected to work at KS for a reason. Don't lose sight of that reason," Audrey said, pacing about the stage while using her hands and fingers to emphasize her words. Accentuating that what our firm was going through was temporary, and we would bounce back.

"How bad do you think the firm is doing? Enough to fly Audrey Stone out to talk to us." Thomas asked.

"Well, she is doing a good job of convincing us otherwise."

"If the firm continues down this road, I might jump ship."

"Have faith Thomas, you're good at that, right?"

"And with that, we will announce to our clients later this week our nominated list for Forbes Top Wealth Advisors!" Audrey said, followed by clapping. "Congratulations to all who made the list. You are the gold-standard that sets Kauffman Schwartz apart. I leave you with a quote by Michael Jordan: talent wins games, but teamwork and intelligence wins championships."

"Ted," Thomas said under his breath, tapping me with his elbow. "Look." I grabbed his phone to see a notification from The *Arizona Tribute*.

*KAUFFMAN SCHWARTZ NOMINATES SEXUAL PREDATOR TO* FORBES.

My eyes darted up to Thomas.

"What the fuck?" I pulled out my phone. "I didn't get a notification."

"Download the *AZ Tribute* app. What does the article say?"

"I'm reading." I held his phone between us as we shared the experience.

"Chaz! The article is about Chaz," Thomas said as we both looked up at Chaz, then the room to determine if the word was spreading. The article noted that video footage of Chaz Perez, a private wealth associate for Kauffman Schwartz, drugging and raping men had shocked the valley. I elbowed Thomas and pointed to the line, then following it said, *they recently nominated Chaz Perez to represent Kauffman Schwartz of the Scottsdale office for the yearly Forbes Top Wealth Advisors, exposing the background process conducted by wall street.*

This cannot be real; the article was fake, and this was not real.

Alec, what did you do?

I took out my phone and sent him a text. It didn't take long for more and more heads to twist as whispers emanated a humming vibration. I fixed my eyes on Chaz, who remained still. If only I could see his face, his expression would reveal everything.

The town hall soon became a collision of bodies and shuffling as everyone poured into the elevators and back to their desks. In the stampede of worker bees, Chaz vanished. I stood on my tiptoes, peered down the hall, and combed the elevator as it filled to near capacity, but he was nowhere in sight.

Not even when I arrived in our row, the desks, except for mine and Thomas', sat empty.

Fuck, now what?

Q2

# 10

Ted Sullivan

I demanded Alec come to my apartment to explain everything, pacing back and forth in my living room. Re-reading the article. This was fucking insane. What would the firm do? My coffee maker beeped just as Alec arrived at my apartment. He pushed the door open after I unlocked it. I poured myself a cup and stared out my kitchen window, letting the silence of my mood known. Leaking the news seemed sketchy, dripping blobs of risk.

"Theodore, can you take a seat?"

"I'm fine right where I am." Alec walked into the kitchen, unlacing his dress shoes. "What the fuck is wrong with you? Why would you leak the evidence? I had everything under control! Chaz caved and withdrew his application. We won, then you go and do this? I hate not knowing what will happen next."

"Did they talk to you today?"

"No, not yet. Chaz was nowhere to be seen after the story broke."

"I bet."

"Everyone was whispering, and Reid wasn't at his desk all day.

Alec, they will probably place him on leave while they investigate. They're not fucking around," I said, slamming the mug on the table. "They will find out who sent in the evidence, and then what? What if they trace the information back to you? Or worse, fill in the blank areas with me and how I was the only one set to gain from it? We'll lose everything!"

"Theodore, no, you won't. Please calm down," Alec said as he took a loud inhale. "Do you have a beer in the fridge? May I?"

"Fine." He rummaged through my drawer until he found a bottle opener, throwing the cap in the trash and taking a big gulp. "What if the firm investigates and finds out it was you, or Raj, who sent the evidence to the *Arizona Tribute*?"

"They won't. We wrote a profile of Chaz, mentioned his Forbes nomination and what we found on the tapes. We put all the video files on a USB drive and taped it to the letter, and mailed it to them, with attention: *Sloane Marshall.*"

"Emma's friend."

"Yep. I dropped it off at a blue USPS bin and never looked back. Theodore, I know you're upset about the news, and yes, he is your rival and your colleague, but he preyed upon those guys. Chaz is fucked up. He deserves whatever comes his way next."

"What about the video with John?"

"We didn't include that one. Only the ones where he drugged the men."

THE NEXT DAY AT WORK A STICKY FRAGRANCE PERMEATED the floor, its pissed-stained aroma infused the cloth of our suits, the threads in our buttons, and even the oil glands in our hair, becoming an uncomfortable itch we couldn't scratch. Everyone could feel it. Our team was in the spotlight, and not for a good reason. I could sense eyes on me every time I got up to use the restroom or refill my water bottle in the kitchen. People wanted answers, and I tried not to let it distract me. Focus on your clients. If anyone asks, defend Chaz. He was your colleague, and it's all based on rumors.

*You know it's true. He reminds me of Mason, the little adopted boy said.*

"This is so outrageous," Mel said, arriving late.. I wondered if she spent the night with Chaz? And if so, if Reid agreed to let her come in late?

"Have you talked to Chaz?" I asked.

"Yes, I spent the night with him. He's not doing good. I don't believe the article, not for a second." Mel flunks a loose strand of hair over her shoulders. Fuck. Did Chaz tell her I blackmailed him? Did Chaz detail how I showed up to his apartment and taunted him with what I knew?

"Is he coming in today?"

"He's staying at home, where he should be until this all dies down." Mel placed her hand on her forehead. "I feel so bad for him."

Reid's desk sat empty, but his teacup and briefcase proved his existence today, somewhere. The lights to John's office were off with the door wide open. My phone lighting up re-centered my attention. I threw my headset on and the hairs on my neck stood surprised when Reid answered, asking me to come into the conference room. A million scenarios entered my mind about what he wanted to talk about. The conversation with Alec echoed in my mind. He had wanted me to have plausible deniability. I wished now I had listened. Time to flex my superpower. I took one last inhale as I opened the door.

Sitting at the table were Reid, John, and Catherine, the abrasive woman I met at the LGBT mixer. I tried not to glare at John or make any indication I knew he was fucking Chaz. It was a hard pill to swallow, made even more difficult as John wore the blue checkered tie. I bit my tongue.

"Hello, Theodore. Thank you for meeting with us," Catherine said.

"You can call me Ted. What is this about?" I took a seat, opening my notebook.

"I am head of compliance for the Private Wealth division. We're not sure if you are aware, but an *Arizona Tribute* article recently came to light about Chaz Perez."

"Yes, I saw that. But it's hearsay. Unsubstantiated rumors."

"The firm has to investigate when such accusations are made about one of its employees," Catherine said, clearing her throat, looking at John and Reid. "The firm needs to distance itself from this until we find a resolution. Chaz was placed on leave for the duration of our investigation."

"Okay, and what is it you need from me?"

"We will need you to cover all of Chaz's clients," Reid said.

I paused. Are the gates opening? "I can make it work," I replied.

"We understand it's a lot, as you are probably at capacity with your clients," John said, leaning against the table. Once you see your boss's orgasm face, you can't unsee it. The way his eyelid squeezed together, and his lower lip looked like it was caught by a hook, then folding to reveal his teeth. His was peculiar, emphasis on the liar. "And given the great feedback we have received, not only from Reid but from various clients, we are going to nominate you for the Forbes list. The client call is tomorrow, and we want a name to give them. So, if you could, please keep it under wraps until then." Did he say what I think he said? The golden light was drawing me in. "You'll be traveling to New York for a few days. Forbes is hosting a ceremony, and you'll get to meet the other wealth advisors. A quick press junket."

"Along with everything we discussed in this meeting, this should remain between us. We don't want rumors flying around," Catherine said. "This needs to be contained."

"Yes, I won't mention anything," I said, still processing, both dumbfounded and excited simultaneously. "Thank you for the nomination. I promise I won't let you or our clients down. You can count on me."

"That's what we like to hear. Thanks, Ted," Reid said.

I plopped down at my desk, staring at my black screen. Did that really happen? I made the Forbes list. *I made the list!*

Mel spun around as her eyes lingered, thirsty for an update on what my meeting was about. I paused. Forcing my reaction into a pleasant, firm line of my lips, causing Mel's eagerness to swell.

"What did they say? Was it about Chaz?"

"They want me to cover his clients."

"For how long?"

"They didn't say."

"So now what?"

"Now we wait. Serve our clients. Nothing much more we can do."

"He was so excited when he made the list."

"I bet. I would have killed for the nomination."

THE CITY WHISTLED A NEW TUNE AS I ADMIRED MY PHOTO and bio on the Forbes website, trying not show how fucking excited everything felt. Surreal. I would forever remember that day: the way the buildings towered above, the flash of the camera and font style of my name tent at the celebratory dinner. Every step, every second was noteworthy. Our reputation was booming.

My phone vibrated on my lap as I shuffled into the hall.

"Have things calmed down?" I asked.

"Sloane was over yesterday. She and Emma were gossiping about the article. I guess she's been getting a lot of press because of it. Sloane, along with her boss, sat with the authorities."

"Do you think anyone might suspect?"

"No, they don't know who sent in the leak. We're covered. Raj has been doing a great job of pushing the article on almost every social media site. It's circulating pretty fast."

"Well, make sure they can't hear you. And do you think it's necessary? We already got the firm's attention. I made the list. My face and name are on *Forbes'* website. I'm afraid this might get too big and, I don't know, backfire. Promise me no more until I return."

"I promise... Are you still flying to Oklahoma for the weekend?"

"Yeah. It's been long enough. My mom misses me."

"Alice called me this morning to tell me my dad hasn't been feeling too great," Alec said. "They are taking him in for testing."

"I'm sorry. When was the last time you chatted with your dad?"

"It's been a while, probably close to a year."

"You might call him? Optics. I won't blame you if you don't, though."

Alec rarely talked about his dad. The few times he did, he wrapped it with disdain and resentment. His cowboy boot-wearing dad was

Bradley Young, the cutthroat businessman who turned Young Industrials into today's heavy hitter. He was your typical strict parent who was impossible to impress. Emotionally traumatizing with his snarky comments and blunt reactions.

A malignant presence.

Alec took the front-line assaults being the firstborn, freethinker, and overall different. As a result, it deepened the divide between them. When Alec was seven or eight, I can't recall the exact age, but when he was in second grade, Bradley got word that Alec tried kissing a boy on the playground. He turned his mafia-sized gold ring around and clocked Alec, inflicting a six-stitch wound. Bradley and his mother, Ruth, told the doctors Alec was playing in the warehouse and it resulted from farm equipment.

"Last time I did, he asked if I was still fucking around with banking and proceeded to list off all the wonderful things Alice was doing," Alec said. "I was never into the whole farming, agriculture, horses, country club shit, and it pissed him off. Our relationship was never good. I'm not pouncing on the phone. He won't ask if I called."

"I'm sorry, Alec. When you were younger, I wish I could have been there. I would have protected you."

"Likewise."

"I did reach out to my Aunt Dawn about Young Industrials," Alec said. "Told her I've been reading things about the company. Is it as bad as people are saying? If anyone has inside knowledge about the health of the company, it's her."

"Is Dawn trustworthy?"

"Yeah. She and my uncle Spencer oversee operations. She's over playing corporate family politics."

"Good. Keep me in the loop on what she says."

I walked back to my table in the lecture hall feeling top-notch, in control when chaos happened. The slimy sensation sidetracked the repetition of success and smiles—a tumultuous earthquake of whispered gossip and darting eyes from every direction at me. I squeezed my hands together under the table and tried to make my appearance calm, undistracted, and unaware. My stomach tightened and turned. I tried to guzzle water to quell the nerves, but it only made things worse.

I quickly got up and hustled to the bathroom stall right before a warm vomit of water, orange juice, and creamy oatmeal poured out. Sour saliva. My hand was across my chest to hold back my tie as I dry heaved anxiety. A caustic odor burned the inside of my nose.

I was no longer in control, choking on imposter syndrome. No longer in possession of a situation that had now grown into a monster.

MSNBC, The Journal, NPR, Politico, ABC, CNBC, Fox, Huffpost, and CNN published their own articles about Chaz, and it was the number one trending topic.

Clickbait headline:

*Kauffman Nominates Predator.*

Now famous for each piece, Sloane was referenced as the lead investigative journalist. My phone buzzed every five minutes from inside my suit.

I sat back down in the lecture hall—my eyes still watery from throwing up. I heard a whisper off to the side.

"Ted... Ted, did you know Chaz?" A stranger asked. I made eye contact with him and gave a nod. He leaned over to the person next to him. "Yeah, he knew him. Fucking crazy. Dude, the company stock is down, and Frank Bernstein sent a company-wide email about it. What the fuck? This is nuts."

The email from our CEO was brief and to the point. The firm does not represent or condone its former employee's actions and to not divulge gossip or communicate with the press. The firm took care of the situation, and our stock will stabilize. He used the word former. They must have already let Chaz go. Everyone now will associate my name with Chaz since we were on the same team. I can hear them now.

You know the sexual predator, Chaz? He was on Ted's team back in Arizona.

Ted and Chaz hung out.

Ted and Chaz were friends.

Did Ted know what he was doing? Is Ted a sexual predator? Don't accept a drink from Ted, because it's drugged.

It was hard to determine how long after every news outlet cursed the name Kauffman Schwartz that my work phone seized uncontrollably. It was Reid.

"Fuck. Fuck. Fuck," Reid hammered.

"What's going on?"

"Fuck, fuck, this is not good. Okay, we're going to loop in Mel, Thomas, John, and the firm's resource specialist."

"Resource specialist?"

"Yes. They will outline all the resources the firm offers. Etc, etc."

A chime rang.

"John, hey, thanks for jumping on. This is a fucking nightmare."

Another chime rang. Then another, another, and another.

"Thanks, everyone, for hopping on this call. We have some difficult things to talk about," John said. His voice sounded remorseful yet flat. "On the line, we have Rachel Jones, a VP in Employee Relationship, and she will go over the resources the firm offers. Also on the line is Catherine McCay, head of Compliance."

"Thank you, John," Rachel said. "The firm has 24/7 counseling on and off-site. It is entirely confidential, and they will not charge you for the first five sessions. We strongly recommend you take advantage."

"Reid, what is going on? Can someone please tell us what is going on?" Mel asked.

"John, do you want to take over?" Reid said.

"Mel, we got news not too long ago. Chaz was involved in an accident in his apartment. I know this news is a bit of a shock, which is why we wanted everyone on the line. We want you all to know we support you, and you have the full backing of the firm for your mental health."

"Oh my god, what are you talking about? What kind of accident? Is he okay?"

"We understand this is tough news. We strongly recommend you use the firm's resources that Rachel has outlined."

"That is right. Please take full advantage." Rachel echoed.

"Did he die?" Thomas asked in a low tone. A pause lingered. The vein in my neck enlarged as the silence continued. One Mississippi, two Mississippi, three Mississippi.

"Unfortunately, *yes*," John said.

"What? No, no, no. This is not happening. Oh, my god. No." Mel sobbed.

My throat became dry. I leaned to grab my water cup, but it was empty.

"Mel, I know you two were close, and we have coverage in place for you to take the rest of the day off," Reid said. I couldn't talk or breathe. This was not happening.

"How... Did it happen?" Mel gasped, searching for her words. "Oh, my god. No."

"Once we learn more from the family, we will inform the entire floor about funeral service dates and times," John said. "You all will be the first to know."

"Reid, may I say a prayer?" Thomas asked.

"That *isn't* necessary," Catherine said.

"What *is* fucking necessary?" Mel cried.

"Mel, let's chat offline," Reid said. A ringing in my ear drowned out the voices. I could feel Mel's pain crack in her voice.

This wasn't the red-hot anger of fury, rather the bile toned anger of guilt and grief. The kind that dumped you in the middle of an empty desert with no intention of bringing you back to see the ones you love. Without a care for what you're going through or what you're feeling.

It dissolved all the luminous-colored emotions like acid.

# 11

## Alec Young

Alec held the highlighter by his teeth, a soft clamp as he flipped to page twenty-two. He propped his feet up, facing through the office windows. Undistracted. Highlighting here and there data and insights that captured his attention. His colorful pink and blue striped socks were eye-catching against Venezia's black leather Berluti.

On Alec's desk sat five different confidential information memorandums (CIMs), six hundred and eight pages in total. Alec had matured into a voracious reader of non-fiction: facts, stats, and figures. Although some read like fiction, a sprinkle of imaginary projections with comical vagueness about how their companies achieved *magnitudo.* He would catch himself saying, "yeah, okay," proceeding with a "ha!"

Every few pages, Alec would wake his computer from slumber to multitask. His brain fired between the two. CIMs to archive research, CIMs to more archive research. He was familiar with Kauffman's financing of oil, fracking, and rich carbon-producing projects.

Chris Bell tossed a paper ball toward Alec. "Yo, the boys are off to get Mexican. You want to join?"

Alec's first instinct was to decline, but his belly must have been eavesdropping. It growled before he could.

The ceiling in the restaurant was a tapestry of unmasked air-conditioned pipes and vents, electrical wires zip-tied in bundles and painted over water damage. Hanging in various spots were green ceramic parrots with red foreheads and large sombreros tacked to the walls around plastic vines.

"Man, you know the food is authentic when the menu is on a peg board next to a giant Coca-Cola ad," Chris said. One of the other guys agreed.

"I want that," one guy said, pointing as a server walked past, holding a tray of sizzling enchiladas and cheesy refried beans. Mouthwatering. The aroma of spice, lime, and cilantro circled. Alec's stomach agreed.

The four assembled at a red tabletop and talked about the only thing people at KS talk about: work. It was the sole factor they shared. The only experience around which they could relate. The only noise their bodies could shove out of their mouths.

Alec stuck out in his black suit and blue tie while the other three wore the same iconic light grey Patagonia vest sporting the KS logo, like a group of sorority girls. The simplest way to spot an investment banker in the spring during hunting season.

"Bro!" one guy said, glued to his phone, but received no response from the table as Chris continued venting about, you predicted it, work. "Dude," he said again.

"What?" Chris said.

"That Chaz guy died." He peered up, then back at his phone. Alec's head shot toward him.

"How do you know?" Chris asked.

"This girl I've been fucking, Mel. She's on the private wealth side. She said he got into an accident in his apartment. I guess they were on the same team and management told them."

"Who?" the fourth guy said.

"He's been in the news. Go back to sleep," Chris said. "What kinda accident? That can't be a coincidence. First, he's called a predator by almost every major news outlet. Suddenly he dies?"

"Do you think the firm put a hit on him?" The third guy laughed.

"Are you certain it was Chaz?" Alec asked.

"That's what Mel told me."

"I'll be back, gotta make a phone call. One of my buddies knew him." Alec got up, walked into the brisk air, and stood in anxious silence with clammy skin. A wave of goosebumps crawled up his spine like a dozen brown recluse spiders. Alec paced down the outlet passing strangers outside: Happy Nails, Bad Apple iPhone repair, Jared Jewelers, Bangkok Thai, Subway, and called Ted.

"Alec!"

"Is it true?"

"Hold on, I'm walking toward the pantry," Ted said with conversational chatter in the background. "They told us about half an hour ago. I still don't believe it. Where did you hear it?"

"Your teammate Mel is telling the entire world. Spreading it like a virus."

"She is good at that."

"Do you know how it happened? How did he do it?"

"They didn't say, but knowing how these things play out, it won't stay secret for long."

"How are you holding up?"

"I'm okay. I'm still shocked."

"Don't beat yourself up."

"I'm not. Chaz did what he did. This whole thing had me feeling exposed, with all the media attention, and now.... They're going to have a field day. You're certain nothing is tying us back to this, right?"

"I'm certain. Fuck, this is a mess."

"How are you doing?"

"Scatterbrained, but I'll be fine," Alec said. "I know you're busy with your Forbes press junket, so I'll let you get back to it. And if you need to talk or something comes up, call me. Remember, *valuing only us*."

A white pickup truck pulled into the spot in front of Alec, with cracked paint around dents and scratches. The side displayed, City of

Scottsdale. Two men hopped out, pulled industrial-sized tubs, and started taking down city-sponsored holiday decorations. Alec watched as they removed silvery lights circling around bushes and trees, wrapped from the trunk up to the highest branch, plastic wreaths hanging from small poles and support beams with red and green bows sprayed in a glitter coating. The clean-up of a scene people once admired and cherished, designs to boost hearts and invoke smiles. All removed.

Chris whistled toward Alec while pointing at an empty to-go box. The two other men shuffled out, exploring the next trending topic. Alec sent a thumbs up and skimmed his contacts.

"Hey man, how's it going?" Raj said, following the drop in volume from ambient TV voices.

"Are you alone? I need to fill you in on something."

"I'm working from home today. What's up?"

"What I'm about to tell you, I want you to know we did the right thing. Sometimes doing the right thing has consequences for those who don't. After this call, what I'm about to tell you, we will never speak of it again. Eyes forward."

"Okay."

"Chaz Perez died by suicide in his apartment. Things are still being flushed out. The media has gotten ahold of it, but I wanted to tell you. Hear it from me and not from a random source."

"Fuck. Well, that's a shame. I one hundred percent agree with you, man. He made the conscious decision to take advantage of those men, and he made a conscious decision to end his own life."

"Like I predicted, Ted made the Forbes list."

"Beautiful."

"I'll let you get back to work, and thanks again, Raj. You did great, forcing a monster to confront his demons."

"Before you go," Raj said, clearing his throat. "Whatever you end up achieving in the future, fuck, it can be filing people's taxes out of your garage or racketeering the grass mowing market. Whatever, I want to be a part of it. I'm not saying you have something in the works. All I'm suggesting is that I want in if you create something. Whenever you feel it's right."

"I appreciate you saying that. When something cooks, you'll be the first person I'll call."

~

The investment banking floor roared its business-as-usual turning of the money-making gears, a distraction Alec welcomed. His mind demanded productive use. He resumed where he left off, only now a cold enchilada accompanied him. Alec popped an antacid tablet to settle the burning sensation when he spotted Andre in the corner of his eye. He motioned his hand and angled his head, a silent meeting invitation. These catchups were twice a month and always danced around deal updates and pulse checks. But this talk, the silent invitation felt, ominous. Alec knew he shouldn't fret until he knew what hand they dealt him, flexing his energy of calm self-talk, talking himself through barbed wire and electric fencing. Andre wasted no time cutting to the chase. The big reveal. The intellectual opportunity Alec craved.

Travel.

Alec couldn't hold this excitement to himself, it trickled out as feet jitters and knuckle pops like an antsy boy on a drive with his parents to a water park in the heart of summer. Shifting and fidgeting around in the back seat. Palm trees engulfed the various slides, growing taller and taller, with red doughnut tubes and colorful swimsuits lining the stairs, families indulging in the spontaneous summer soak day. Families from all backgrounds traveled close and far to see the smiles on their kids' faces: common families. And Alec's family, his parents, his upbringing on the Young Ranch Estate were anything but common.

Alec never told his parents about winning the Innovator Award. He knew what Bradley would say, "still fucking around with banking I see." And Ruth, passive-aggressively interested in one thing, "Oh, is that right? So that means I can expect a grandson soon? You know I don't want to pressure your sister, with her riding career, and you were the firstborn. The first grandson must come from the firstborn. All my friends at church ask me, and I feel so embarrassed because I don't know." They never attempted to get to know their son. Once signs emerged, he may differ from their expectations. Challenging their views and beliefs of the world. This was how it was and how it should be. Stop being different, boys don't do that. Do what you're told. Stop crying, boys don't cry. And instead of learning who he was, Bradley and Ruth tried again. Determined to get it right the second time with Alice. Alec's uncles had a nickname for him when he was younger, one used in front of Bradley, one he never opposed, but instead agreed with.

The dud.

Alec sent Ted the update. Blushed cheeks plump from a grin of success. Stretching his wrists and thumbs in a circular motion. He was making progress, long strides fueling the plan.

Success adrenaline was a thing. Unleashing the potential to crank out work projects, tidy up administrative tasks or purge your inbox. Creating new rules in Outlook catering to your newfound success: if an email contains this in the subject, send it to this new folder, and if an email relates to travel or XYZ client, send it to this other folder.

THE PRESENCE OF EMMA AND SLOANE THREW ALEC BACK when he arrived at the condo. The reality train arrived again after a lengthy layover. The tip of Sloane's nose hummed pink as she wadded used tissue into a ball to dry her eyes. Both her feet under couch cushions snuggled knee to chin while juggling wine, tissues, and her phone. Emma would rest her hand on Sloane's knee to lend a few consoling rubs.

"Hi, Sloane," Alec said, unbuttoning his wool peacoat. "Is everything okay?"

Sloane rested her fingers against her forehead and stared down.

"No, things are a shit show," Emma said. "Did you hear the news?"

"What news?"

"Chaz Perez, the guy who Sloane exposed in her article."

"I remember the article. What happened?"

"People are saying he apparently died by suicide?"

"No. Not apparently. He did. He *hung* himself, and my story was a direct result," Sloane said as her cheeks flushed with disappointment.

"I know, I know. I'm sorry." Emma leaned over and splashed more deep red into Sloane's stemless glass. Alec's senses heightened, like an animal cornered. The thick pour was slow but loud, like they were consuming the blood spilled in a ritualistic sacrifice. A black and white Nickleodoen of Chaz binding a cord around his throat constricted Alec's mind. *What type of cable or rope did he use?* Alec thought. *Where in his apartment did he do it? Who discovered him?* Morbid questions everyone speculates, but no one seeks.

"I don't understand it," Sloane said. "I don't understand any of it. This all came out of nowhere." Her phone vibrated and whistled. "God, everyone is trying to get a hold of me now. But, do you know what I mean? All this came out of nowhere. Someone addressed the package to me. Why?"

"Babe, you can't keep doing this to yourself," Emma said.

"I feel used. I want to report the truth, be a vehicle for justice, but I don't want death to be the outcome every time I reveal the truth."

"It won't be."

"Now I have to live with that guilt. It was my article. I thought, when I got the package, it was too good to be true, that I was going to make a real impact uncovering the truth, and I never thought twice about where the package came from or why they chose me."

"It's your reputation of being an outstanding journalist that had you targeted, I'm guessing." Emma glanced over at Alec.

"I'm not saying what was on the thumb drive wasn't fucked up and creepy. It was. Trust me. Having to watch that sick fucking shit." Sloane brushed her hair behind her ears, revealing an industrial bar on her left and a gold helix and daith ring on her right. Her wet eyelashes clumped together. Unlike Emma, Sloane never wore heavy makeup. Her natural beauty, strong Armenian features, didn't require thick layers of clay, mud, and mascara. It required a hands-off approach.

"Is your boss being supportive?" Emma asked.

"Very supportive. They told me articles like mine, career altering investigative stories are common, but the outcome, more uncommon. This was my breakout piece, and they want to make sure it doesn't dampen my spirits or place into question the journalist industry. They told me during their careers they have received tips from unknown sources. Leaks from inside, which are done from some type of motive. I just don't know what the motive of mine was."

"I'm sorry this is happening to you Sloane," Alec said, taking a seat at one of the high-top chairs around the island. "Not the success, but the outcome. How it's making you feel. Everyone is always trying to knock Kauffman down a peg. Look at it from that point of view. A competitor trying to smear Kauffman's name. Have their stock price take a hit."

"True," Sloane said, taking a sip of her wine.

"Because if you think about it, the driving factor that caused your article to go viral was the fact that Chaz Perez worked at Kauffman. The headline was total click bait. Not to say what you wrote was fluff for click bait, but if Chaz worked at Nordstrom or cleaned cars, you wouldn't have seen the traffic you did."

"I get what you're saying. Thanks, Alec. And that's the reason I feel like someone's puppet, and I hate that feeling."

"Puppet or not, you helped expose a sick man. See some good in that," Alec said, bending down to untie his shoes. "It's been a long day. I'll let you two get back to it."

"Have a goodnight," Sloane said, readjusting her feet and throwing a blanket over herself.

"How is Theo doing?" Emma asked. "Have you heard from him?"

"He is still in New York. I'll call him tomorrow."

"Call him now. I don't think he's heard," Emma said, sipping her wine. Her eyes squinted.

"Who is Theo?" Sloane asked.

"His name is Theodore. Not sure if you met him, but he was at my birthday party. He's a friend of Alec's and works at Kauffman."

Alec knew what Emma was doing. Dancing and playing around the situation like a game, thanks again to liquid cuntness.

"It's late in New York. I'll call him tomorrow," Alec said, walking toward the bedroom as his shoelaces whipped the hardwood. "Have a goodnight you two."

"Dream of me." Emma smirked, and Alec responded with a thumbs-up.

Alec's dreams and dread ran rampant as he flipped through his phone in bed. He struggled to read his non-fiction paperback, but the market hailed his name. The thirst to be plugged-in pulled him in. Quicksand. The Chaz story was morphing into Frankenstein's monster, a grotesque chain of conspiracy theories around his suicide was forming.

# 12

## Ted Sullivan

I could never sleep on a plane, even at night. Rest, sure, but I never fully drift off. This time, Chaz was a driving factor, his purple face preventing me from dreaming.

After I touched down in Oklahoma City, I picked up a sizable cold brew and the keys to a black F-150 rental and embarked two hours east on I-40 to Litchfield. It was nostalgic driving a truck while back home: the dirt and gravel roads next to Bermuda grass under star-soaked nights.

When I reached home, several lights in the living room were on as I maneuvered in between my mom's Explorer and my dad's '96 blue Ford whose tires had melted into the dirt from years of resting in place. Everything felt the same.

"You made it!" my mom said. "Let me get one of those."

"It's so great to see you," I said, as she gave me a bear hug and kissed the surface of my cheek. She smells the same, all vanilla and wet soil. Her salt and spice hair was down and natural, with her cooking apron still strapped on. "It feels good to be home. I haven't seen the stars in so long."

"I'm glad you're back, even if it's just for the weekend." My mom rolled one of my suitcases into the house.

"You still have my graduation tassel hanging up?"

"Of course! I'll never take it down. Fried chicken and corn are on a plate in the fridge. I washed your bed sheets and dusted your room and brought out extra sheets in case you get cold. I'm so excited you're here." My mom threw me one last hug, sang how past her bedtime it was, and headed upstairs.

I settled in.

Aside from slight upgrades, the living room felt the same—the television standing in the corner as the coffee table cuddled the blue velvet couch. I took two steps to the left, crossed the entryway into the air current's path and received the tender remembrance of home from the cold draft brushing my neck. I strolled into the next room. An array of veggies from Shelly's indoor garden was packed in a cardboard box next to the sink, awaiting their morning bath. I scarfed down my dinner and ventured up to my room, a museum of my former self.

The tiny hairs on the tail of my neck tingled as I hung my suits, still bound in the post-dry-cleaning plastic. The clash of time transcended between my Armani suits next to high school t-shirts, like plunging into a parallel universe. A red phantom raced past my open door. My pulse popped as I twisted my head and watched another red revenant pass by. Under my tongue a metallic tang grew, a dissolvable sheet of tinfoil.

*Was that me? The little adopted boy said.*

No, it couldn't be.

*That was me!*

No.

*That was me soaked in blood running to the shower!*

Could it be?

I peeped down the hall to a rotating night light.

Black coffee and butter-fried eggs carried me downstairs where Shelly and I soaked up memories of morning rituals past, then onward transition to giving the rest of the day to the sun.

Swaying off on the back porch on a rocking bench, finishing the pot of coffee while pecking a bowl of fruit. Shelly asked me again what I do for work, and her understanding led deeper after every explanation. The story became simpler after becoming a wealth advisor. "I advise on wealth to wealthy people." After our gradual morning awakening, we both found ourselves on our hands and knees, fingers deep in cool loam to prepare for summer. Her garden took off from when she originally launched this hobby, establishing its own prestige around town for producing juicy bites and aromatic whiffs when sliced. Youthful robins were playing between the branches and flowers, white as cotton. I couldn't remember the last time my mom and I spent a day like this. It was nice, letting yourself go to flora and fauna.

After lunch, I drove to Dana's house, a five-minute drive to the side of town that was once up and coming. Acres of earth turned up and loosened to prepare for residential construction surrounded by blocks of wheat farms, forecasted to produce bushels of goods. Forecasts and growth lost blood supply in the wake of 2008: a bluish tint of chapter seven. The leaven rose into an opportunity for the banks who ran the U.S. housing market into the ground, buying the foreclosed farmland to use as a strategic path for the Silverstone Pipeline, a project owned by Blue Horizon to transport crude oil from Alberta, Canada, to the Texas Gulf Coast, passing through the heart of Litchfield, and financed by Kauffman Schwartz. The ripples traveled to my dad's business, forcing him to close up shop, liquidate his assets of livestock, equipment, and patches of land. Leaving him no choice but to work on the Silverstone Pipeline, the town's main employer post-crisis.

It ate at my dad. I know it did.

It broke his heart to sell the business his father built, so much so, I believe, that it contributed to his premature heart attack two years later.

Dana was out front with yellow gardening gloves trimming her hedges, wearing a purple vizor and a paint-splashed Nirvana tee. I pulled alongside and lowered my window.

"You work that hedge!"

"Ted! You little *devil*, why didn't you text me when you got into town?" Dana tossed the clippers and ran toward me. I jumped out as she picked me up with her hug.

"God, I've missed you. Your hair is so long."

"Jim liked it short. You look so handsome, I can't. Is this your truck? Look at you."

"It's a rental."

"Nice ass rental. How long are you in town for?"

"The weekend." I winced as Dana rolled her eyes. "I know, I know. It should be longer." I scratched the back of my head then adjusted my glasses.

"Well, shit. What do you want to do? I'm yours all weekend. Let's go do something."

"My mom wants to do dinner tonight with everyone. So, I was thinking of treating the family to dinner at Crossroads, in town. But I want it to be a secret. Reserve the entire back room."

"Love Crossroads. How can I help? I'm good friends with the manager."

"Hop in. Let's go network."

THE SECRET CROSSROADS DINNER WAS A SPLASH HIT. THE mission of seeing everyone together over delicious food and wine-saturated laughs was a success. Dana and I worked quickly to assemble the surprise and reserve the space while brainstorming ways to make the experience memorable. Fun. We arrived at creating name tents, adults on one side and kids with their crayons and Legos on the other, which led to purchasing long stem candles and flowers facing near death to sprinkle around the table. From there, we shopped at the general store to find hideous tuxedo-pressed tees everyone sported like matching Christmas pajamas. A picturesque ensemble.

The family reconvened at our house, where I taught everyone the luxury of enjoying a cup of decaf coffee after dinner while playing cards. Throughout the evening, I would spot my mom, glowing with laughter and eyes warm with peace. The risky gamble of loving family time was having members who don't feel as passionate. The members who are comfortable with spaced gatherings. So, seeing my mom in the environment she adores was priceless.

Naturally, town gossip found its way into conversations as our mothers brewed another pot and uncles cracked another beer crease as foam coated the rim, giving Dana and me our cue to pack some beer and snacks into a backpack and retreat for cousin time. We both changed into sweaters and sweatpants and drove around back to Dana's parents' storage shed and packed up their white rowboat with blue horizontal stripes, headed to Litchfield Lake, surrounded by a forest of oak and hickory trees. Dana and I used to explore all over the lake in the rowboat and found hidden beaches barricaded by cattails and ducks. It was out on the lake where I came out to Dana, all those years ago. Gray nimbus clouds had grown above as I stuttered with the words, but Dana's embrace of acceptance drove the darkness away.

The moon's reflection glistened off the glass lake and the first batch of ripples as the rowboat was launched, spinning like a kaleidoscope of memories. The inhales of algae and fish oil sped up the time warp of childhood remembrances.

"Row! Row! Row!" Dana yelled as we pretended to be on a university-level crew team for the great state of Oklahoma. We rowed about fifty yards into the lake, then floated aimlessly as I pulled out two rechargeable lanterns.

"I haven't been out on the lake in so long," Dana said, sorting the snacks and opening a Pabst. The snap of the crease cracked across the lake.

"It feels the same."

"I'm opening all the bags. All the snacks."

We cheersed yet again and admired the silent darkness and constellation.

"Dude, I am so proud of you. Honestly. You've come so far. Got away from all the bullshit of growing up here, and you made it. You are out in the world."

*You will sit upon your throne.*

"Thanks. It hasn't been easy. Fucking soul-sucking, but I guess that's what I signed up for. It will be worth it in the end."

*But, a part of you will be dead.*

"Since you got promoted, will things slow down? Give you time to rest?"

"I don't want things to slow down, there is a larger plan in place. One of which depends on the work I did yesterday."

"What do you mean?"

"I'm building a company."

Dana's excited thoughts stretched across her face as she slapped me on the arm.

"Ted! You're starting your own company. I knew you were special. I knew you'd do something great."

An idea struck and tattooed itself to the walls of my skull. It's brilliant.

"I'm going to get you out," I said. "I'm going to help you get out of here."

Dana melted in appreciation. "Thank you, Ted." She sucked in air, following a sip. "All I wanted in high school was to get out. Dreams of moving to the city or out of state. College and a career." Dana set a single Chex Mix on the lake's surface, where she sailed it forward until a fish gobbled it up. "Then I met Jim, fell for his charm, and settled."

"Are you getting divorced?"

"We are. We are. I filed a few days ago. We'll both be better off if we got a divorce. He just doesn't see it yet. He still wants his wife and home and his bitches on the side with a bottle. But I'm done. I'm so done. I need to focus on me now. The past few years, it's all been about him."

"Good for you. It takes strength to go through with something as emotional as a divorce. Jim has never been my favorite."

"He's an asshole. I gave up so much of myself for him. I want to go to college, get my degree. Pursue my dreams, whatever they are."

"Yes!" We cheersed again.

"Do you still have crazy dreams?" Dana asked.

"I was good for a while, but they started back up again. A lot about work."

"I remember getting jealous, because you remembered so much of your dreams. I don't think I dream. I never remember mine."

"Lucky. Aside from being about work, the old slaughterhouse has been making appearances."

"Still? You were afraid of it when we were little. I don't blame you, it's creepy as fuck."

"All the death that happened in there didn't bother me. It was what else went on." I took a sip, then another. "My beer is empty. Are you ready for your second?"

"Please, kind sir." I handed Dana a fresh can. "But what do you mean? What also went on in there?"

I paused.

*Tell Dana the truth, the little adopted boy said. It's safe.*

"Mason would do some fucked up things to me in there."

"Really?" Dana took a sip. "What would he do?"

"Behind the scenes, he was never nice to me." The rowboat rocked as I found comfortable seating. "I'm not saying in like an, oh, you aren't being nice for not sharing your toys, kind of mean. I mean, locking me in the slaughterhouse."

*It's my fault he's dead, the little adopted boy said.*

Dana went silent. The sound of a still night filled the hollow space.

"If I refused or fought back, he threatened me with butcher knives. Tie me up with twine and remove my clothes. Cackle at my naked body, then leave me tied up."

*I'm glad he's dead.*

Dana grabbed my hand.

"Ted, I don't know what to say other than I am so sorry."

"He said if I told my parents or anyone, I would get hurt. No one would believe me, and they would take me back to foster care." My eyes darted up at the stars. "He used those lines a lot. *Going back to foster care, and I am not a true Sullivan. I was bought and used, like the dead carcasses in the room.*"

One drop, then two drops, fell from Dana's eyes. She looked away so I couldn't see. When she turned back around, her eyes were bloodshot and soaked.

"Ted, I'm so sorry. I'm so, so sorry."

"It's okay. I have moved on, and well, Mason got what he..."

"What he did to you is not okay. I love you more than anything and completely consider you a part of this family. You are my family."

Dana and I hugged as I felt this weight off my shoulders. I finally said the tragedy out loud—it had haunted my subconscious for years, eating at my self-worth.

"I believe in Karma. Whether it be with Jim and his cheating or what Mason did to you. Why was he so evil? His accident was so sudden and shocking. Why are all men in this town such disgusting assholes?"

I felt the size and weight of the pebble pressed against my hand—the soft run of the tractor engine. On my knees, hiding behind a bush with the force of the band as I pulled it back, twitched my biceps. Then the release and all those feelings vanished.

"We can't be sad during cousin time. Tell me about this company you're starting?"

The moon dance across the nights sky as we finally decided to throw in the towel and head back to land. I arrived home to a dark quiet house. I tiptoed up the stairs, a surreal experience as I'd never climbed them drunk. I plopped down on my small creaky bed as exhaustion struck. A fast siphon of energy and angst swirled and swirled and swirled away. My breathing relaxed and my body went numb with comfort.

*Suddenly, the streets of New York were empty and wet. They lacked traffic, people, and life—a black holograph-like somber sepal rife with rain. The soggy feeling of disdain covered me as I walked out of the St. Eleanors Hotel. The rain sounded like the quick closing of a clasp knife as it hit the concrete—hundreds of Chilean rain sticks rotating side to side. I grabbed an umbrella leaning against the wall and strolled the streets. The dreary street lights changed colors in quick succession, catching the eye. A dancing light show of flashing phosphorescence.*

*Green, Yellow, Red.*

*Emerald, Butter, Ruby.*

*Grass, Honey, Blood.*

*The streetlights remained, in an instant, all the same hue of crimson. The intersection next to me; the corner behind. The intersection far beyond, and the conjunction close and near.*

*All red.*

*I turned the corner and noticed a woman in a black hat and dress walk up a short flight of steps and into a building. The first sign of life. I got closer and closer until I stood at the foot of the steps and faced a church. Another sign of life walked behind me and up into the church.*

*Another, and another.*

*I walked into the church to see dozens of people sitting in grief. Salty tears rolled down blushed cheeks and into damp tissues. I walked past a collection of ladies in midnight hats; confused, sad toddler; and grown men in sunglasses. A bereavement-filled schoolhouse with an open casket sitting patiently at the end. A white stained wooden sarcophagus patted with dove pillows covered with personal possessions once owned and cherished by–Chaz Perez.*

*His face looked like it was etched from porcelain with an inch-thick purple and raven line across his neck—the result of a durable bed sheet and the sturdiness of a ceiling fan. I felt back into his living room where it happened. Watched his body twitch and convulse as it tried to maintain life, like a dangling earthworm pierced through a fishing hook. His purple tongue protruded under bulging eyes as blood engorged his face: a water balloon on the verge of bursting open. Chaz's abs curled one last time as if being tickled by a ghost until, finally, they relaxed. His muscles went limp, his body dangled soundlessly as an orange tabby with fish line whiskers scratched and nuzzled their head against the tip of his red velvet loafers.*

*I looked down at the lifeless body in the casket with disbelief that turned dismal and aghast. I got sidetracked by gloom. I forgot what once angered me about Chaz. Lost sight of his evil ways, his venomous pheromone.*

*"Was it okay?" I whispered to myself.*

*The priest standing above the casket heard and answered, "Was what okay, my child?"*

*I looked up, pondered, looked back down, and back up, "This man was a predator. He preyed on the naïve and intoxicated." I turned to face the crowd. "Do you all know what he has done? The pain he caused?" I turned around, and hundreds of maggots were oozing from Chaz's eyes and mouth. Rotting musk barreled out as giant horse flies swarmed and crawled up and down the corpse. I slammed the casket closed. "I forbid this demon from hurting another. His evil will not spread, and his cancer will die with him." The crowd gasped in shock, following the loud THUD. People yelled and stood up as I dashed out the side door and into a damp alley. A black cat quickly scampered away behind steam rising from the ground.*

*I looked around and yelled, "Hello?" but got no response. I walked farther down the alley and screamed again, "Hello?" Trash bags and dumpsters smashed on both sides—a sea parting. On the ground sat a little old man, bound down in his own campground, holding up an all too familiar sign. Unnerved by the sight of those words, the calligraphy of those words, I ran.*

*The old man hollered with foam oozing from his mouth, "Always on the go. Always on the go," echoing until I was finally out of the alley and back on the empty New York streets.*

*I headed back in the direction I thought was the hotel. Around a corner, straight, left, forward, right, until I finally saw the signature collection of flags of The St. Eleanor's Grand Luxurious Hotel and Suites. Gold trim around every window and entryway. Every room was lit from top to bottom. I counted the windows until I got to the 22nd floor, where I noticed the lights were a blueish purple, happiness and ambition, with the silhouette of a man overlooking the city.*

*Alec?*

*I rushed inside the hotel and to the elevators, anxiously pressing button 22 twenty-two times until the doors finally closed. The elevator's ding as it passed every floor made me pace around the small box, wishing for it to travel faster.*

*The elevator stopped, and when the doors opened, I was no longer in the hotel. There was no hallway lined with plush carpet and luxury-sized paintings. Rather, the bitter sound of water dripping echoed through the space. The doors remained open as I tried to press the down button, the close door button, then the emergency button.*

*Nothing.*

*Rattled, I edged out of the elevator and into the slaughterhouse.*

*Metal hooks dangled and swayed from the ceiling next to chains used for hoisting. On a pallet in the corner were salt bags used to prevent decomposing. The cement floor was wet with blood and water as I stepped over a green garden hose still running. A fresh spray, a crisp clean up of the equipment. Mixing together like congealing mud. The doors behind me slammed shut, locking me in as a sickening laugh reverberated.*

*A voice drawled, "If you want out, pour the pig's blood over your head." On the ground was a bucket brimming with steaming blood, "but first, take off your clothes and show me that wiener."*

*Warm blood was poured over my head, splattering on my glasses and filling the crease in my lips as it trailed down my chest, branching out in all directions like fast growing tendrils. My arms and hands engulfed. The blood oxidized like mud within an instant, glued to my skin as it cracked around the wrinkles and creases of my fingers, wrists, and elbows.*

*I ran through the slaughterhouse and pushed the side door open, falling into grass warmed by the summer sun. My heart pounded as I clenched my fist, grinding my teeth while I took in my surroundings.*

*Distraught, I heard a humming that didn't seem too far, a slight unbecoming rumble of an engine. I crawled to the closest bush, tossing aside sticks and shrubs. Through the leaves, like a sly little tiger, I saw Mason on his tractor.*

*In my back pocket, safely tucked, was my slingshot, a defensive rocket. I picked up a pebble and cocked the band back. I closed my right eye and stuck out my tongue.*

*Three.*

*Two.*

*One.*

*The pebble took flight, hurtling toward the shred tractor under the sundry air, and struck Mason on the side of his head. Within an instant, no time for a scream, Mason lost consciousness, and fell into the blades of the grain extractor.*

# 13

## Alec Young

A caffeinated twitch under Alec's right eye rattled his overexcited nervous system. Yet, Alec remained focused and confident. Every time the client spoke, whether deal-related or shooting the shit, Alec planted both elbows on the conference table, open palms with occasional head nodding and mirrored eyebrow reactions. Subtle but effective. Alec also noticed how Andre spoke with his hands, no matter the subject or the pacing. His hands became a device in the way he told any story. The way he secured a deal, won new business, or congratulated on a close. Deal-making was showbusiness, theatrics, and the clients were the attentive audience, as well as Curt the Critic. Alec had been an intellectual little sponge floating in Andre's rich presence: soaking up every professional trait he observed, while adding his own style.

A grin surfaced as he glared out the window with damp palms, leaving sweat beads on the surface of his phone. The black leather hide of the Escalade perfumed with notes from the conference room he and Andre conquered: smokey juniper and lavish fabric softener. Andre called a Kauffman partner to report the news that after weeks of shopping around and hitting up all the top investment banks, the client tapped Kauffman, Andre's team, to lead their vertical merger. An automotive company set to join with a parts supplier, all in the name of synergies. Alec's favorite sound. A three-syllable word that got his blood pumping. Syn-er-gies. Alec shouted the word over and over in his skull.

Traffic back to the hotel rode clean as the SUV approached five green lights in a row. Alec glanced at the serious driver in the rearview mirror. He was a big man in a suit wearing tight Oakley sunglasses resembling a federal or secret service agent. Alec's phone beamed with a text from Dawn.

> Your dad gets the final say. Things are not good. I'll work to get you those docs.

The fate of Young Industrials stood a recurring theme between the two. Factory closures, layoffs, and debt repayments delinquent were all on the table, the threat clear, though zero plans to adapt. Words easy to tell, but Alec lacked proof. Data.

Andre ended his call, faced Alec, and said, "You did a great job in there."

"Thanks. I wasn't sure if we would win. How long does it take you to come down?"

"Oh, you'll be feeling it all day." Andre played with his tie, running his hands through the silk layers. He too couldn't help smiling a prideful smile while bobbing his head to imaginary music.

"I noticed the CEO did all the chatting. You two seem to have a good relationship," Alec said.

"Well, that's the thing. Be a good listener. It's important the client feels heard. When it comes time to speak, ask open-ended questions. Not questions ending in a yes or no answer, but ones that require explaining. And they don't have to relate to the deal. You know, instead of asking the client how is the weather? You can say, how do you like the weather outside? Make them explain. The more they talk, the better they feel."

"Got it." Alec pulled out a pocketbook and scribed elegant notes with near-perfect handwriting.

"Are you writing in cursive? I didn't think anyone under thirty knew how to write in cursive." Andre smiled, revealing more and more of his laid-back leadership style.

"It's a lost art."

"It sure is. Okay, the next piece of advice I would give, a common mistake I've noticed in client coverage not everyone becomes a strategic advisor. They don't take the opportunity to engage on matters outside of the subject they are hired to do."

"Can you elaborate?"

"So, you know we were hired by Tay and Co. who want to buy Candor Royalty."

"Yep."

"Did you notice how I pointed out that a sizable chunk of their revenues come from Argentina? And that the government of Argentina said that they are going to devalue their currency. So that revenue coming into Tay and Co. as peso is more than likely going to decrease in value. Being a strategic advisor, I suggested hedging their exposure against the peso."

"And that's why you said, 'if it drops by five percent, you will lose three hundred million dollars in revenue.'" A lightbulb in Alec's head.

"Exactly. Another way to engage the client is to point out what their competitors are doing. Interest rates are low, money is cheap, have they thought about debt financing instead of equity financing? It's important to wear multiple hats and become an everything banker and not only a merger banker. Be creative in ways you can help the client."

"This is all great stuff."

"It's great to have a healthy work-life balance, but it's important to work hard and always be available. If the client can't get a hold of you at two a.m. regarding important matters, the next time they decide to buy another company, they will go to someone who is available. So, think of work-life balance in terms of months and years, not so much days and weeks."

"Important life events only happen once a month for me," Alec said facetiously. "These were all great tips. Thanks again, Andre."

"You're going to do great Alec. Are we on the same flight?"

"No. I'm staying an extra night. Don't worry, it's not on the company's dime."

Andre laughed, exposing his pearl white teeth, which believe it or not, are not veneers and the perfectness isn't the result of braces, but genetics. His mom, and her mother before her, all had perfect chompers.

"What will you be doing while you're here?"

"My girlfriend's parents live in Boston."

"Ah, got it."

"They want us over for dinner. Do the rounds."

"Are you and your girlfriend getting serious?"

"We're at a comfortable level. I don't want to think about *marriage*. The whole life after death thing. Sorry, not to be rude."

"It's all good," Andre interjected. "Marriage is hard work. Hard, hard work. But I think I've been lucky. Chantel is amazing, and she recognizes how important work is to me. She is my partner in every sense of the word. If you aren't ready, don't jump into it. You're young." Andre got excited and tapped Alec's chest with the back of his hand. "Ah, see what I did there? Mr. Young."

"So clever Andre, so clever."

THE KITCHEN IN THE GREEK REVIVAL-STYLE PETERSON Townhouse off Cambridge Street was by far Alec's favorite room. Built with raw light top-of-mind, the cathedral ceiling holds a peaked skylight that extends the entire space, like a conservatory or biodome. Sharing its effervescence with all who stroll in and infusing each with their daily vitamin D intake. The surfaces in each of the six bedrooms were first plastered with an ivory silk cloth, then hand-painted sunny yellow, neutral grey, afternoon blue and in Emma's room, a lively green backdrop with chinoiserie cherry blossoms growing from the floorboard up with shy bluebirds resting on the branches.

During the summer months Grace Peterson filled the wood-burning fireplaces with thick pillar white candles in descending order: the tallest in the back and shortest up front like class photos of toddlers smiling toward the camera. The wicks melted the edges as the tops deformed. Wax trailed down. The dining room candles were unscented so as to not mix with the fatty air of roast beef, salted blanched asparagus and warm fullness of baked garlic bread.

"Alec, sweetie. We've made up the guest bedroom upstairs for you," Grace said as she fiddled with her necklace, a large seashell in the center.

"Mom. Alec doesn't need to sleep in the guest bedroom," Emma said, passing a bowl of rolls to Alec.

Roger froze mid drink and said, "Emma, you know the rules. Just because you're an adult doesn't mean you can throw them out the window."

"I don't mind. Thank you, Grace. And thank you again for making this lovely meal."

Emma went silent and draped her napkin across her lap. She didn't argue with or challenge her father, out of all people. Her mother, sure. But she wanted to be Roger's little girl, and keep an innocent image of herself frozen in his mind. Being his good little girl, still calling him daddy when she really wanted something, the effect had its advantages. She knew how to work him when it suited.

"How's life at Kauffman?" Roger asked.

"Things have been great. Since getting promoted to senior associate, I've been doing a lot of traveling."

"Where to?" Gracc asked.

"All over. New York, Chicago, Dallas, Seattle, San Francisco. It's with my MD Andre about once or twice a month."

"Oh, how wonderful," Grace said.

"I've only traveled solo once, and that was to answer client questions in person. The deal was sensitive. Offer the white glove service, ya know?"

Roger nodded at every word Alec uttered, taking whiskey sips here and there, then patting him on the back. "Proud of you, son."

Alec clenched down on a bite of roast beef.

Son.

*I'm proud of you, son.*

A phrase Alec hadn't heard in months, years, *decades*. They ping-ponged around with every bite and swallow.

"Your parents must be so proud," Grace said. "I would love to meet them someday."

"Alec's sister made it to the championships," Emma said.

"It must be a treat to watch."

Emma caressed her toe up Alec's leg under the table and said, "God, I would have loved to learn to ride like that when I was younger. It must be so fun to ride without a saddle." She sipped wine with sultry eyes toward Alec for the entire pull.

"We took you a few times to the Burches stables, dear."

"That doesn't count," Emma said, snapping eye contact with Alec. He hated when Emma would try to get sexual with him in front of her parents. When Alec thought about it, he hated pretty much everything about Emma. Regretted over extending his relationship with her. His over-leveraged position kept bleeding more and more into the red, with no straightforward path to hedge his way out. If one good thing came from being with Emma, it was feeling a parental connection to Roger and Grace.

"How's Young Industrials doing?" Roger asked. "Damn, with these oil prices. That has to be hurting the farmers."

"From what I've gathered, they are doing okay. Not great, but okay. I can only imagine the spike has hurt orders and repair requests."

"Have you considered taking over one day? I'm sure they could use a brain like yours."

"Nah, I have no desire to run an old school manufacturing company. Plus, that would require my dad to step down. Which he never plans to do. "'til the day I die', he always says."

When entertaining guests, even a guest of one, it was customary to digest dinner on the terrace under string lights with brandy and cigars. Alec wasn't a fan of cigars. The way they dried his mouth and stung his tongue with the smoke burning his eyes, but he would give them another chance with Roger. Have Roger show him father-son how-to advice: this was how you fix a flat, this was how you can tell quality in your brandy, salt your steaks a day before grilling, honor your word especially in business, leave things better than you found it, always shine your shoes, and this was how you smoke a cigar. Roger struck a match and brought the flame to the tip. His lips looked like a goldfish as he pulled four large buffs while rotating the cigar, creating an even orange glow. Effortless. The two went back and forth discussing unique books they'd cherished like Homer's The Odyssey and found parallel opinions in Ayn Rand's Atlas Shrugged having way too many characters. Roger pulled out his glasses and phone and showed Alec first edition titles he purchased at auction.

Emma sat bored on the thick padded outdoor Raylan, scrolling social media. Her cheeks were wrinkled by her hand, holding up her head, feeling no desire to connect on the topics Alec and Roger were discussing. A child waiting for their parents to finish chatting up a friend they bumped into at the grocery store.

"Daddy?" Emma said.

"Yes, M?" Roger tilted his head up. His glasses rested on the tip of his nose while he held his phone, the light from the screen brightening his and Alec's faces like two kids telling each other ghost stories using a flashlight for effect.

"There is something you should know."

Alec got tunnel vision on the heels of sticky vertigo as he glared at Emma. She wasn't making eye contact with him, only Roger. Behind her, velvety moss covered most of the surrounding bricks, looking almost edible, thick and moist, like you could pick a bite off to taste sour apples. She wrapped her hair behind both ears at a snail's pace, as if to actively keep Alec breathless. It was games like those that prevented Alec from up and leaving her. Sweet dreams of him packing his bags in the dead of night would have destructive repercussions.

"Yes, dear?"

"Alec.... And I have been brainstorming about starting a company."

Roger removed his glasses and looked at Alec. The back door popped open, and Grace held a wedge of warm cherry pie topped with a tall Cool-whip tower that jiggled with every step.

"I'll be back with one for you Alec," Grace said, handing Emma the plate and shuffling back inside.

"It's something we have discussed," Alec said. "The American dream, am I right? To create something."

Roger brought his finger to his lips, like a pondering, pensive statue.

"I'm not saying it's a bad idea. It's great you both want to start a company. But I have to ask, why?"

Alec and Emma had their eyes on Roger. The pie sitting warm on Emma's lap and Alec holding a fist. The question didn't come off condescending or a stab at their intellect but a sound, non-biased question. One he often asked his clients, associates, and entrepreneurs when they told him of their own ambitions to create.

ALEC PLUGGED HIS PHONE IN FOR JUICE, TOOK A SIP OF water, and slid under the blossoming duvet cover. The vintage room, bed frame, nightstand, and window trim brought Alec comfort, although he did not understand how such objects and styles could resonate calm. Perhaps it was because Grace decorated them and intended to establish each room with its own sense of identity. A purple vase with sharp-cut full bloom hydrangeas stood under the bedside lamp. Alec wasn't sure if this guest room always had fresh flowers or if Grace added the touch last minute for his stay.

He preferred to ponder the latter.

Alec's emotions were in free fall, flung from a plane at ten thousand feet. His pounding heart rate made breathing laborious and the skin under his feet and hands fever sweat. This visit was not supposed to be about the plan. He had no intentions of making the hasty step of getting Roger involved.

The door opened to a darkened hallway, and in came Emma. Her hair was bundled in a sloppy bun, her body encased in a black spaghetti strap top and short, short, shorts. Shiny and satiny. She tiptoed across the beige hardwood and inched into bed with Alec.

"Emma, your parents' room is down the hall."

"So?"

"So, I don't want to upset your parents. We have to respect their rules. If your dad finds out...."

"What? He will take back his offer?"

"Maybe?"

"I was thinking. We should spend a few more days here to celebrate. Take a road trip down to Cape Cod or something."

"As much as I would love that, I have to get back. Theodore and I have dinner plans."

Emma twisted her eyes and said, "my dad offered to be our angel investor. This is huge and we should celebrate."

"I can't explain how excited I am," Alec said when noise from down the hall seeped through the door. Alec shot his head toward the sound and waited a few moments, internally begging not to have Grace or Roger come knock to say goodnight. "Your dad's offer is generous. It will go a long way in getting us off the ground. But I can't stay. Plus, we have work Monday, and like I mentioned, I have...."

"Dinner plans with Theo. Yeah, I got it," Emma said, leaping off the bed with a thud. She walked toward the door, scrunching her hair. Red strands falling loose. She stopped at the door, "sometimes I think you forget I am your girlfriend." And reeled around. "You need to stop putting other people before me."

"I'm sorry, babe. It's a work dinner we had scheduled for a while. I can't bail."

"Yep, got it." Emma twisted the antique doorknob and let it jerk back into place. "Tell your boyfriend I said hi." And closed the door.

# 14

Ted Sullivan

Due to client follow-ups and internal meetings in the afternoon, I ate lunch early. Reid had been open about his thoughts on my work, extolling my abilities to attract new clients and broaden our client base. The pantry stood lifeless as I heated leftovers and took a few seconds of silence.

"Early lunch?" John asked as he walked in. "Thank you for the piano book, by the way."

"Not a problem. I hope it helps," I replied as John vanished around the corner. A few days ago, I left the book I used when extending my knowledge of piano on John's desk with a brief note.

*I hope this proves itself useful.*

I arrived at the LGBT Network meetings a few minutes late. Alan posted a slide show on the TV with pictures from our recent volunteer event with the Big Brothers Big Sisters Organization. My prideful idea became a reality. Along with the foundation, colleagues' willingness to mentor and befriend a kid on the weekend surprised us. A few families brought their own kids to join in on the fun. We set up small booths with various games and minor prizes—a miniature carnival.

"I have some exciting news I wanted to share with you all," Alan said as the slideshow went on autopilot. "I got word Kauffman Schwartz LGBT Network will have a spot in this year's Phoenix Pride Festival." Everyone smiled, and a few let out an excited reaction.

I raised my hand. "Alan, when is the festival?"

"It will be this November. I know it's a few months away, but I wanted to fill you all in and maybe brainstorm some float ideas."

"Alright, great," I said. "Gabbie, do you want to lead the think tank for the float? It doesn't have to be now, but let's get the ball moving soon."

After the meeting, Alan held up one finger from across the room, hinting at me to stay for a chat. His dress shirt looked one size too big as he fixed his collar.

"What's up? Exciting news about the parade."

"We are putting the budget to good use. So, I am not sure if you are aware, but KS has been a big contributor to the Human Rights Campaign. Since we have an established LGBT Network, we have secured two seats for their end-of-year gala. There is a dinner, a silent auction, guest speakers, etc., etc."

"Well, that sounds like fun, and I'm assuming you are going?"

"I wish. I already booked my vacation back to Taiwan, so it will be you and John attending."

"John Barrett?"

"Yes, that John. Since he is the head of the network and I won't be able to attend, he asked you to be next for consideration."

"Thank you so much. Sounds exciting. I can't wait."

"All of Pheonix's gay society will be there, so look your best." Alan winked as he stood up.

A lightbulb lit up inside, an opportunity twinkling in my eye. The local elite gays will mingle under the same roof, and they handed me a free ticket to attend.

Since making the Forbes list the last few months have been a tornado. In April, I onboarded my first client post Forbes list, Shelby Turner. A sweet socialite who visits Dr. Plastic in Oldtown. She accumulated her fortune over time, but it wasn't until last summer that she hit the home run with her third divorce from MLB owner, Bill Turner. His net worth was a few hundred million because of commercial real estate and the railroad industry. Bill was undoubtedly someone's client at KS, but not Shelby; following their divorce, she was ripe. I snagged Shelby with my initial strategy, which involved studying recent and substantial divorce settlements in the valley.

My next step was to check LinkedIn to see if we had any mutual connections. However, most of these divorcees lack professional accounts, let alone job experience. Shelby, on the other hand, was friends with Emma on social media, so I got lucky. Shelby's discovery meeting was at a posh oyster bar after a five-minute call to Emma.

A discovery meeting was the first meeting with a new client, and I prefer to host mine over dinner rather than in the office, creating a relaxed atmosphere akin to a date. The initial meeting was critical to gaining a new client. I learn about who they are and what they love doing, and they learn about me. After four wonderful years together, I learned the judge had awarded Shelby $20 million and the keys to the G-wagon. The late thirty-year-old had everything she ever desired: money and no relationship. I voiced my main goal, to preserve and grow her wealth so she would never have to worry about money or change her lifestyle. I had her right there.

A few weeks later, the forecast swelled, as I added two new clients to the firm's roster. The second was Felix Hernandez. His family opened El Cabro, a daytime eatery that transforms into a tequila-filled nightclub. Felix, the current owner, had opened El Cabro within walking distance of all major Universities on the West Coast. Taking advantage of the burgeoning market of over-extended college students' thirst for a fabulous time. During our discovery meeting at an El Cabro restaurant, they overindulged me with goat meat tacos and avocado dip. His net worth hovered close to $12 million ($10 million was the bare minimum to be a KS client), so he made the cut. I found Felix after researching award-winning family businesses in Arizona.

Ed Harmon, the last member, completes the trio. I approached this differently, because he was already a KS client and had a fortune north of one billion. After a comprehensive search on Zillow for million-dollar homes, I came across Ed's property in the Foothills. The agent was reluctant to tell me the seller's name, but after some convincing, she spilled. From there, I searched LinkedIn and poured over his account. He was older, around seventy, and must have had an aide keeping his profile up to date as he was very active, *liking* several posts by The Arizona LGBT Foundation highlighting all the help they have done throughout the state. Ed was the foundation's top donor for three years, according to the foundation's records, so I purchased a ticket for their forthcoming event, a silent auction, and a mixer where all proceeds went to help LGBT youth in the state.

I threw on my favorite blue and gold paisley tie and Lyfted to The Phoenician, a grand hotel at the base of Camelback Mountain. I scoured the crowd and made my way in Ed's direction. He conversed with a few elderly gents while looking at some artwork for auction. I stood next to him until we established eye contact, which was a quick, casual glance, followed by a smile on his face.

"Ed Harmon?" I asked. "Sorry, I don't mean to be a creep. I recognized your photo on the foundation's website. I'm Ted, Ted Sullivan."

"Oh no, no. I didn't think that at all. I'm flattered someone recognized me. It is nice to meet you, Ted. Are you enjoying the event?"

"I am. These art pieces are amazing, it's hard to decide which to bid on. But I placed a bid on the far-right one." I pointed in the direction. "It's blue with the swans."

"A nice one, and I know the artist. He's a super talented young man who spent his entire life in foster care." I took a sip of my wine.

"Would you mind showing me around, Ed?"

"Not at all. Come, I'll introduce you to a few people."

Ed talked a little about each painting for auction and introduced me to the foundation's president. A tall salt and pepper shaker with suspenders. I felt at ease networking with people older than me. Listening to their stories and tales of life. I complimented Ed on his philanthropic work to help the community, envious of its impact.

"If only a foundation like this was around me growing up, and someone like you supporting it, then coming out would have been a lot easier," I said. "I value and honor all the work you are doing. Please never change. These kids need you."

Ed refilled my wine glass as we admired the sunset over the mountain and the large garden fountain. I learned Ed was selling his house because he came out to his wife and family. Ed hoped it would go over smoothly, but it didn't. The first hurdle was a divorce.

"This last quarter of my life, I want it to be lived authentically. No more hiding or denying. Martha is still processing the news, but I know at the end of it all, she will support me," Ed said. "I admire you, Ted, for coming out as young as you did. Your level of courage and pride. Things were different when I was a young boy. My father would have cut me from the family will." Ed chuckled and probed more and more about me. Where was I from? Where did I go to school? What do I do for a living?

"I'm proud to say I am the first gay wealth advisor for KS in Scottsdale who made Forbes list of top wealth advisors. It has been a rollercoaster this past year. Meeting so many interesting and clever people, traveling to New York, and meeting our clients. I wouldn't change any of it."

Ed reacted to the news I was a wealth advisor at KS. His left brow rose with a slight purse of his lips. By the end of the evening, Ed pulled me aside and confided in how he wanted me to be his wealth advisor. I ran him through the steps on how to make it work. He must first contact his current advisor to tell him the news; it was Ed's decision. And we would all jump on a call and begin the transfer of assets onto our books. The process took a week.

Now this Forbes Top Wealth Advisor tornado, known as moi, was on the precipice of becoming an F-5 on The Fujita Scale with winds speeds of 300 mph.

Since my return from New York, my mental and physical well-being had improved because of my efforts to maintain a healthy equilibrium. On days when I don't work out at the gym, I sprint around the park in sports shorts and a tank top dangling from my hip. While using a light bit of sunscreen, I jogged bare-chested and got a wonderful golden glow as the temperature climbed past a hundred degrees. I noticed a few people staring at me as I hobbled by or stretched my leg over a fire hydrant.

Today felt a little cooler as I finished my third lap and walked in circles to cool down. People and kids were in every direction, and to my left, under a tree in warrior pose, were Emma, Sloane, and Chrissy. Each wearing a different shade of red leggings, messy perfect buns, and arms stretched out. Emma and I made eye contact, followed by a wave.

"Ted, you look like you had a great workout," Emma said, bending over to grab her water bottle.

"Yeah, I don't know how you don't burn up," Sloane said.

"Thanks, I finished my third lap." I pulled my shirt out to put it back on. "Looks like y'all found the perfect spot under this tree."

"It's my favorite," Chrissy said as she sat on her mat.

"Congrats on passing level two of the CFA exam. Alec told me the great news," Emma said.

"Thanks, only one left. It was more difficult than the previous one. When I say more difficult, I mean it was less multiple choice and more writing your answers out."

"That sounds awful. I've been debating about taking it."

"How has work been going? I feel like I haven't seen you in so long," I asked.

"Demanding, but you know how it is. I got promoted to a more managerial type role. I oversee ten people, which is so demanding."

"I think Alec mentioned something about your promotion! Exciting news."

"Have you heard from Alec today?" Emma asked with a slight tilt of her head.

"Yeah, we're getting dinner tonight to celebrate our firmiversary."

Emma turned and glanced at Sloane and Chrissy.

"You two hang out a lot," Sloane said. "Like, a lot."

"What's a firmiversary?" Chrissy asked.

"Umm... It's similar to an anniversary, but with the firm. We've been with KS for three years."

"Are you dating anyone new, Ted? Anyone worthwhile?" Emma asked as she took another sip from her Hydro Flask. I scratched the back of my head and squinted my eyes. She glared at me while drinking.

"I wish, but the days go by so fast, you know, and by the time you know it, it's dark," I said. "If I'm going to use what remaining time I have, I want to make sure it's with someone special."

"Keep me posted," Emma said as she laid back on her mat and reached for her toes.

I TOLD ALEC I WASN'T IN THE MOOD FOR A PRICEY MEAL IN A dimly lit converted warehouse encircled by desert titans. Greasy wings, cheap beer in jeans, and a soft t-shirt were what I wanted. Not only for the sake of my sanity but also because recently they've made me feel like I'm part of a posh social set, complete with way too many bottles of champagne. Resilience and grounding are important reminders to keep in mind. It was easy to lose sight of the larger picture, the ultimate aim, the objective that appears alive but isn't when surrounded by luxury.

Alec stood in dark shorts and leather sandals as I entered Papa Wings. He stood with both his hands in his pockets, watching a tennis match on one of the plasma screens while balancing on his tiptoes when the game got intense. We tried Papa Wings a few times when we were new to the city and fell in love. A zesty collection of sauces with a cold beer in a fun atmosphere.

We scored a table facing three screens so Alec could indulge his obsession with Rafael Nadal.

"I can't believe I forgot my Armani suit back in Oklahoma," I said to a preoccupied Alec.

"Come on!" Alec let out while chewing on ice.

"And the nervous chewing begins," I taunted as a commercial break gave me his attention. "Not to direct the attention away from your game, but when are you going to cash out on your Emma investment?"

"Can we take in this moment for a little first?" Alec took a sip of his beer, and ran his hands through his hair again.

"You've been with her for a little over a year."

"I know, I know."

"Then what is the hold-up?" I let Alec do his thing with no check-ins, but it had been going on long enough—time for the audit.

"I am this close to securing a deal with her father. I didn't want to tell you and get your hopes up if it falls through. We were at their house in Boston, Emma was pretty drunk, and they began talking about her career path, what she plans to do, or what she wants to do. She joked about starting her own business, and her dad said if she did, and we did it right, he would invest. It perked my ear. And."

"Did you tell Emma about our plan?"

"Not exactly. I made her a fresh martini and probed her thoughts about starting a company. I said, we could build something great, and maybe we should take her dad up on his offer."

"So you told her. Emma is now involved."

"We could use her father's money to get things started. I mean, it's not ideal, and it's not how I wanted things to go or predicted how things would go, but the investment would go so far. We could hit the ground running."

I took a drink and smiled up at the server, who brought us our collection of sauced wings. The lemon and garlic aroma coated my nose, followed by the Cajun kick, my mouth salivated.

"What would be the size of this investment?" I said, while taking a careful bite.

"Five million."

My eyes widened as I choked, coughing on the sauce and five million dollars.

"Shit. That is an enormous investment." I glanced up at the screen and washed the chicken down. His money could go a long way. I know I didn't want to, but I'm pragmatic, and so involving Emma in a limited capacity would be worth it. "Okay, keep working her dad. And if Emma is involved, it will not change what we have or our purpose. This is a twosome, not a threesome."

"Of course. It will not change what we have. But, it will complicate things. I could suggest to Emma after we've received her father's investment; it would be best if we could work together professionally and not romantically."

"As it should be."

"What were you saying about your Armani suit?" Alec asked as his phone buzzed against the table. He tapped the screen. "It's my sister." He froze, re-reading the text. "My dad is back in the hospital."

"He's going back? If that's the case, things don't sound like they're going good, Alec. Have you thought about going home to see him and family?" I asked. Alec shrugged with ambivalence as stood up to answer a call.

Our family approach was inverse; Alec stood a distance, whereas I tried to maintain a connection. My parents are not my biological ones; however, I don't feel it impacted their ability or mine to care for each other. Could it be having biological parents allows for the ability to love but not care? Qualifying for an entitled, 'we are blood, so I can keep you at a distance' approach.

"How are those wings, Ted?" Sloane said, as she walked up to the table.

"Hi Sloane, they are great. I didn't think anyone knew of this place."

"I've been coming here for years. Grabbing dinner with a few colleagues. Where is Alec?"

"He's here somewhere. He took a call but should be back soon if you wanted to chat with him."

"Not really." Sloane squinted her eyes and rubbed her hands together. "Look, Emma is my best friend, and I don't know what is going on between you and Alec, but I hear things. Don't hurt her. I'm watching."

Sloane's forwardness surprised me.

"Sloane, I'm sorry you feel the need to watch out for your best friend, but Alec and I are friends. I'm not sure what you've heard or by whom, but I can assure you they are rumors—a classic case of paranoia."

"Let's hope so." Sloane gave a half-ass smile. "You have a lovely evening."

# 15

Alec Young

Alec's leather sandals slapped the concrete as he stepped outside, his phone vibrating with rapid pulses tickling the bones in his hand. A group of hungry strangers flowed around Alec like a river boulder as he pressed the green accept button on his phone, hearing snuffles and a man's voice echoing above.

"Alec. Dad... is back in the hos-*pital*," Alice said with an adolescent stutter following silence as her vocal cords twisted in knots. Alec heard more background announcements overpowering the breaths Alice made into the phone.

"Dad is a fighter." Alec sat on a wooden bench next to an cigarette ash pillar with a few butts dug deep into the black sand.

"It's serious this time."

"Serious how?"

"Mom said they think he had a stroke, and he's in the ICU." The more Alice talked the more her anxiety swelled and swelled, reaching max capacity then collapsing back, like inflated 55-liter horse lungs hooked up to air pumps. Despite Bradley and Alec not having a healthy father-son relationship, he didn't want his father to die. A genetic reaction rooted deep in his subconscious and colorful double-helix DNA, an inkling to make his father proud one day. A challenge he couldn't achieve if Bradley withered away.

"Where are you?" Alec asked.

"I'm at the airport. I board in thirty." Alice cried. Worst-case scenarios playing a continuous loop, ten-second videos projected in her mind like a drive-in theatre of her father flatlining, code blue echoing across the hospital floor following a stampede of doctors and nurses, and her sitting first class, alone at the Blue Grass Airport. "Will you please come? I need you here."

Alec bit his lower lip and his foot teetered faster and faster against the gum-spotted concrete. If his father was in as bad of condition Alice was panicking about, a family crisis will unfold and with every crisis lies opportunity.

"Yes, I'll come. Let me call my boss, I'll be on the next flight out."

"Okay."

"Everything will be alright.. Remember when you were learning to ride, and we got that shipment of alfalfa for your horses and those idiots unloading stacked one on a weird angle and a small bale came down and hit Dad? Everyone started freaking out, thinking he got hurt. Nope."

"Oh god," Alice relief chuckled. "Poor Dad. I remember, then he got that man fired."

"You're missing the point," Alec said in an upbeat tension-diminishing tone. "He's strong, and he will get through this."

A fresh wave of sauce and beer coated Alec's nostrils as he walked back into the restaurant searching for flights to Des Moines, so distracted he didn't realize he walked past Sloane who had her eyes fixated on him like a hungry lioness, crouched under dried terrain grass ready to pounce. Ted could sense the call was not good and Alec affirmed his suspicion, taking a sip of his beer and continuing to research. So, Ted ripped open the post-wing moist hand wipes, cleansed his fingers of tangy sauce and oily meats, and helped Alec find flights.

~

Alec juggled the idea of bringing Emma along. He outlined in his head why he should and why he shouldn't. The latter drafted simple. If he cut ties with Emma soon, hauling the extra baggage would send the wrong message. He was still learning all he could from Andre and Ted was networking, building his client list. They were at cruising speeds regarding *the plan* and would someday strike an angel investor who was not the parent of the interloper.

They have plenty of time, or so he thought.

Alec was fast approaching a fork in the road because the former drafted urgency to bring Emma along. If his father's health was dire, they must meet opportunity. Taking advantage of the chaos starts with being on Ruth's good side. Spun in a web of illusion: Ruth will get the only thing she desired from Alec, a wife and grandson, so showcasing Emma to her like a boy at the state fair with his prize-winning swine, waddling toward the center of the arena, would help.

Alec took a bet, a risky gamble his father's health would worsen, so he booked him and Emma two flights: first to Iowa, then to Massachusetts a few hours later.

The two arrived in Des Moines early the next day, strolling small carry-ons to save time. They bolted to MercyOne, located a hair north of downtown off I-235. The ICU waiting room hummed a soft buzz, stuffed like a Thanksgiving turkey with tension and love. A wound-up woman demanding answers, huffing at passing staff, her kids sleeping across chairs using their hands for pillows. In the corner sat an older gentleman in overalls reading a book while sucking on a hard butterscotch candy. Another guy buried his head in his hands, his foot bouncing against the cold linoleum while whispering on the phone. And sitting on the opposite end, upright and expressionless, was Ruth.

Ruth Young is a woman of class. Even as a young girl she was what they call an old soul, and now, her age and soul coincide, making her whole, but not genuine. Her stature and sense of self-worth have morphed into subtle condescension: tip-to-toe eye looks at everyone deemed less worthy, written, verbal grammar correction, gaudy plump pearls as if the oysters were fed steroids in condition tanks, and Chanel every day. Whether it be orphan shoes, suits, jewelry, sunglasses, or perfume. A coincidence, she says, number five *also* being her lucky number.

Since Alec was young, third grade young, Ruth was adamant he only wrote in cursive. "Santa Claus only knows how to read cursive, so make it *perfect*." Maybe it was the firstborn curse, but the cursive-only rule diminished and loosened; the strict policy was overturned when Alice reached the same age. Perhaps it was her high expectations parenting style, the life she envisioned through her son, the test case on what worked and didn't work for the second born. Since Ruth was a timeless woman of class, still to this day, she wrote every letter with a dip foundation pen on thick creamy stationery with custom letterheads. An inside joke between Alec and Alice of another example of their mother being *extra*.

Ruth stood above average height in sheer black hosiery, running up to a dark blue tweed skirt with fringe trimmings and matching over-stitched, woven blazer. Thick, ageless, and indestructible.

"Sweetie, you made the trip," Ruth said as she tilted her head and kissed Alec on both cheeks. One peck, two pecks. Then looked over at Emma. "And who might this be?"

"Mom, this is my girlfriend, Emma Peterson."

"It's very nice to meet you, Mrs. Young," Emma said, reaching her hand out.

"Please, call me Ruth." She leaned over and kissed Emma on both cheeks. "It's nice to meet one of Alec's girlfriends. Despite the circumstances." Ruth hovered her finger toward Emma's ear. "These are darling. They go well with your complexion."

Emma smiled and said, "Thank you. My mother got me these."

"Alec! You made it," Alice said, turning a corner. She ran and threw both arms around Alec, holding his embrace with closed eyes. "Emma, so happy to see you." And gave Emma a gentle hug, following a hand stroke up her back.

"So, do we know anything more? What have the doctors said?" Alec asked.

Ruth placed two fingers to her forehead as if she was experiencing a mind-shattering migraine and shook her head. The ivory pearls tugging at her earlobes swayed.

"It was a severe stroke." Ruth rummaged through her tiny leather purse, pulled out a silk handkerchief and dabbed the outside of her eyes. The dark ocean of uncertainty soaked her in fear; death swam around her like a circling shark, revealing its fleshy scarred fin. "They put him in an induced coma to decrease brain swelling."

Emma gave Ruth a consoling arm rub and slumped her head to the side with tender eyes.

"For how long?"

"They don't know. They said maybe a few weeks. But they don't know."

"Dad is a fighter. We will get through this," Alice said, nourishing the optimistic high Alec hammered.

"That's right," Alec said.

"Is there anything I can get you, Ruth?" Emma asked. "Coffee? Water? Wine?"

Ruth chuckled when Emma offered wine and said, "Coffee would be great, thank you."

"You got it."

"Decaf."

Ruth sat on the bland ICU waiting room chairs folding her handkerchief as Alice, Alec and Emma left to find the cafeteria in the MercyOne labyrinth. They rode elevators, walked long hallways, and tried deciphering the dangling hospital road maps.

"An induced coma for a few weeks?" Alec said in an astonished tone.

"That's what they said. I still can't believe any of this."

"I want to dress like your mother when I'm her age," Emma said. "She's like royalty."

"Who is stepping in to run the company?"

"Scott is acting CEO."

"Scott? Last time I heard him and dad weren't talking."

"They are always going back and forth, but they listed Scott in the business continuity plan if something were to happen to dad."

"Scott isn't fit to run a company."

"Do you want to tell your uncle that?"

Alec's brain warmed his skull, sifting through tubs of ideas, pulling out scenarios and actions like tools in a toolbox. Organizing them into two piles: certain and plausible.

"How long are you guys staying? I see you brought luggage."

Alec glanced over at Emma.

"It's a quick trip," Alec said. "We have a business meeting with Emma's father tomorrow."

Alice's face soured in an unimpressed reaction.

"What kind of business meeting? Don't you think it can wait? Our dad is in the hospital."

"In a coma. Look, I wanted to see you and Mom, get a pulse check on how things are. And it looks like all we can do is wait. There is nothing I can do here to help him, besides continue on."

Alice rolled her eyes while snapping the lid on two decafs and said, "Mom will not be happy."

"I know, I know. But if things take a turn for the worse, I'm only a plane ride away."

"I would say things have taken a pretty serious turn."

"Alice, I'm sorry. I know you're scared, but you have to remain positive. Dad will get through this and life around us keeps on spinning."

Ruth cherished her decaf cradling it with both hands, absorbing the warmth. The news did not surprise her that Alec and Emma would not stay long; instead, she seemed more glee-ridden at the prospect of having a grandson, a hopeful prophecy to distract her mind. A man in a white coat walked toward Ruth.

"Mrs. Young? We have your husband's private suite ready."

"Do you know more?" Ruth asked.

"We do not, other than Bradley needs rest. The private suite has comfortable accommodations for you and your family."

"Thank you, doctor," Alec said. "Well, Emma and I should head to the airport."

"You should at least go in and see your father before you leave," Ruth said.

Alec stood silent.

"Go ahead," Emma said. "Security check-in shouldn't take too long."

Alec nodded with a long, quiet inhale.

"Come, you can sit next to me, dear," Ruth said. "Tell me about yourself."

A nauseous sensation bellowed up in Alec as he inched into the room. The image of his father lying on the bed became clearer.

Half-dead, half-alive.

His face looked like aged leather, but weak, with a tube running across, pumping cool oxygen up his nose. His forearms had blobs of dried yellow iodine underneath clear tape holding in place more tubes pumping solution cocktails into his body. The room was somber, sterile, and silent except for the ominous rhythmic beeps of the heart monitor displaying real-time data in green squiggles. His feet wrapped in grey socks poked out at the foot of the bed. His belly still full and round like a balloon, despite his towering height, he was a little overweight. A physical appearance Alec had known since he was a boy: dad and his bulldozing belly.

Alec stood over Bradley, keeping his hands at his side as if frozen. The scar on the back of his skull throbbed and itched: unsettled and anxious that at any moment, Bradley's eyes would open, look up at Alec and ask, "*why* are you here? I *don't* want you here." Alec thought about strapping on a blue surgical mask, flexing his fingers through skintight latex down to the base of his suit jacket, and using surgical tools to crack open Bradley's mind, unspooling his memories to pinpoint how Bradley feels about him, the real him. Squeezing Bradley's memories between his hands like clear Jell-O, slimy but warm, and shoveling the *happy* memories into his mouth.

For the agricultural market to be transformed, Sullivan Young is the tantalizing dessert, like the first scoop from prize-winning dairy cows presented in the Baccarat crystal tulip cup launched the countdown to phase one. *Alec and Ted's long-term strategy to acquire Young Industrials with the clients Ted had secured is on track.* Renovate it like you would an old house with a solid foundation and a bright future. *In Alec's mind, his subconscious hope, this would force Bradley to open his eyes and finally look at his son.*

~

A SILVER SUV TURNED INTO A CURLED COBBLESTONE driveway. The ride from the hospital was quick. Alec and Emma hopped out of the Lyft in front of Dawn's house, a country French-style home with an attributable hip-roof design. The tan-colored stone popped against the window with black coats above rectangular bushes jetting out along the confine.

Alec opened the metal and glass door to an aroma wave of dahlias and ivy. The room was generous with sprawling windows that offered views of their courtyard, where Dawn and her husband Phil were savoring lemonade. Phil was a seasoned, lanky high school superintendent. Dawn and Phil were among the trope of being high school darlings. They waited years before having kids, as Dawn's career at Young Industrials appeared endless. A competent candidate to one day succeed as CEO. But when the trophy of running the show fell apart, column by column, her legacy shifted to creating a family. Dawn and Phil were watching their kids play in the grass, dashing all over their wooden swing set, loaded with a yellow cork screw slide and tips like a castle, roofed turrets with spires. They treated every inch of the yard in dense grass. A fresh-cut essence lingered.

"So this is where the party is," Alec said as they walked outside.

"Alec! It's so good to see you," Dawn said, setting her glass down, and gave Alec a hug. Phil followed suit.

"Dawn, Phil, this is my girlfriend, Emma."

Another round of hugs and chitchat as they sat down. Phil poured some lemonade into a blue highball glass.

"Your yard is beautiful," Emma said, following a sip. "Wow, this lemonade is wonderful."

"Thanks. The kids pick the lemons from the tree and Dawn helps them make it," Phil said.

"How's your mom doing?" Dawn asked.

"Stressed. She corrected the doctor's grammar like three times. Emma was a pleasant distraction for her."

"Oh, good," Dawn said as she threw Phil a look. We-need-family-alone-time, look.

"Emma, let me show you our newest addition to the family," Phil said.

"The kids wanted a goat," Dawn said. "Most kids learn responsibility through a dog or cat, but they wanted a goat." Phil took Emma to the small stable they built, with the kids leading the way.

"How are you doing?" Dawn asked.

"I'm doing good. Scatter brained. I know my dad will make it out, but I'm just worried about Young Industrials."

"Things have only gotten worse since we last spoke."

"I can imagine. And Scott is acting CEO? How did that happen?"

"He's still listed in the continuity plan. After their previous fight, Bradley vowed to update it. He never did. He always says those things. I lost count of how many times he threatened Spencer with a demotion."

Dawn and Spencer still oversee operations, and Scott Young was the President of Young Industrials and second in command. Well, until Bradley's stroke.

"Were you able to get those documents?" Alec asked.

"Let's go inside. They're in my office."

Alec followed Dawn as they returned to bond over mutual understanding the family business was in trouble. Chapter 7 bankruptcy trouble: liquidation of assets to pay creditors.

Dawn drew out a binder sandwiching stacks of financials and said, "We've already had to shut down several dealerships and manufacturing plants across three states, but that hasn't stopped the bleeding."

"What's causing the hemorrhage?" Alec asked as he thumbed through the documents.

"No one's buying our tractors. We can't compete anymore."

Alec's left eye jerked as he studied the full extent of the company's losses. Year after year, the red pool of blood widened. "Jesus. And I see the C-suite is still getting nice bonuses."

"I told your dad we needed to cut managements salaries, but he disagreed. And I doubt Scott will approve of having his income reduced. He's still busy keeping up with the Joneses."

"Despite all the red. This is good. We have an idea. It's pretty radical, but I think it's just what Young Industrials need to get us out of this fucking hole. To be competitive again."

"Please don't tell anyone I gave you these," Dawn said.

"I won't. And thank you again. We're meeting with Emma's father about funding for Sullivan Young, so these documents will strengthen our pitch. Once we get Sullivan Young off the ground, then the big meeting happens."

"I'm already dreading it."

# 16

Ted Sullivan

Good things never transpire when double asterisks surround the word, URGENT. Our operations team discovered some suspicious activity in one of Felix's accounts. My blue checked tie constricted my neck, growing tighter and tighter the more I read the email. Fuck. I picked up my phone.

"Gabbie! Hey, it's Ted. I got your email. What is going on? Sorry I haven't been responding. There must be something wrong with my rules in outlook as this email has not been going to the right folder. I'm so sorry."

"We found unusual transaction activity in Felix's personal account. The alarms went off, so we checked, and it seemed odd, but it happened again. So, we escalated to compliance."

"Fuck, I can see they're added to the email."

"If you scroll down, they are asking you for more information from Felix."

"Fuck, they looped in the anti-money laundering team."

"Yeah, it looks like they are asking for an updated copy of Felix's business financials."

"What transaction activity prompted this search? I can see he recently purchased a large stack of Anheuser-Busch and sold a few of Snap."

"We see deposits into his account that are not ordinary. As well as transfers to third party accounts, submitted by your new hire, Zoey Fields."

"Did you initiate the transfers?"

"We kicked the transfer request to our review team, and they denied the request. We get requests like this all the time, but those weren't what placed a cherry on top of this entire situation."

"What else did you receive?"

"An ACATS transfer to move funds to another broker, an overseas broker, one in which no one on my team has ever wired funds to. Zoey also submitted the request."

"Goddammit!" I pinched the bridge of my nose while shaking my head with disgust. Why and the fuck is she not catching these? It's alarming how none of these requests by the client seemed suspicious to her. "Please tell me you did not complete the ACATS request? And we still have the funds in-house."

"We still have the funds."

"Thank heavens. Okay, thank you so much, Gabbie. I'm going to escalate this on my end and get all the right people together. I'll come back to the email in a sec. Thank you again," I spun around in my chair. "Reid, we have an escalation. Can we pop into your office?" Reid was quick to stand while grabbing his tea and phone.

"What's going on, Ted?"

"Felix Hernandez has recently submitted some suspicious transfer request followed by an out-of-the-ordinary deposit. Our Operations team denied the transfers and has escalated to compliance."

"AML?"

"Yes. The anti-money laundering team is asking for updated financials from Felix. I haven't yet reached out to him. I wanted to fill you in first."

"I appreciate it. So, we can get ahead of any windfall this may bring.

Let's fill in John, so he is aware, and come back on the email looping John and myself in, and if she is not already, maybe Catherine."

"Will do." The sun's rays were warm as they pierced through the glass. Rays hitting the round table and warming my hands. "Thank you, Reid. Internally I was exploding as I've never had to deal with something like this before."

"Not a problem. These things sometimes happen. More often than not, it works itself out. You've followed the Know Your Client policy, you are close with him, and you know his business. Is this the first time you're hearing of this?"

"Yes. Our Operations team reached out after receiving this ad hoc transfer. Our new hire, Zoey, submitted them all. We need to have a chat with her. Attention to detail, she cannot be asleep at the wheel."

"I agree. I'll have a chat with her now if you want to send her my way and stop by John's office to post him."

I marched down the hall, nostrils flaring. Reid's wisdom soothed my anxiety, but not my frustration.

"Zoey? Reid wants to see you. He's in the team room at the end of the hall."

"Okay, thanks, Ted." Zoey got up, and Mel cocked her head at me. I rolled my eyes and continued marching.

I gave two gentle knocks on John's open door. He sat at his computer reading the news while man-spreading in his leather ergonomics. Papers were neatly stacked on his desk's outer edges and tenure awards from the firm were on various shelves. Next to them were brown wooden frames housing pictures of his wife, kids, and golden retriever.

"Ted, come on in. Shut the door behind you, please."

"John, there is an escalation I wanted to post you on," I said, pulling the chair out. "I am about to loop you in on an issue with compliance regarding suspicious activity with one of my new clients."

"Who?"

"Felix Hernandez."

John scratched the back of his head. "What phase are we at?"

"Compliance is asking for more information from Felix. I'm scheduling a meeting with him to retrieve those documents."

"Sounds great. Thank you for updating me."

Why did it feel easier than I was anticipating? "Thanks for your time, John."

"You're doing great work, Ted. Some advisors get involved in a situation like this and freak out. You were calm and knew exactly what needed to be done. It's an extraordinary talent. Maintaining control and doing what we ask."

I sat down and crossed my legs. Soaking up these compliments.

"I appreciate hearing that, John. I do my best at delivering and doing what you ask of me." These compliments powdered rouge on my cheeks and corrected my posture. "You're a big inspiration to me. The way you command a room, actively listen, and charm an audience." Okay, maybe the last bit was a stretch, but he opened the door to kiss his ass.

"I am sure whatever the compliance issue you are dealing with, I have confidence you will know how to handle it. You know how to use the surrounding resources. So, I was curious what your plans were tomorrow?"

"Tomorrow? I have nothing set in stone."

"There is a small barbeque hosted by some influential people if you wanted to stop by with me," John said. "It will be up in Fountain Hills."

"Thank you for the invite. I'll most definitely attend it with you." A managing director had never invited me to attend an exclusive party. "Could I bring a friend along?"

"I've invited many exceptional colleagues to my place throughout the years and to parties. Show my appreciation for their hard work and devoted service to our clients. Many colleagues have been, but none of them talk about it." John smirked. "Almost like being a member of a secret society. Invite only type of party. Simply because there will be a few high-profile people attending."

"I get what you're saying. Thank you for the offer. I look forward to it." I sent a confident acceptance smile. John's invitation was feeding my ego. Gorging on every syllable, the little monster inside feeding on the words, *Invite only*.

"Sounds good. Welcome to the club," John said as I opened his door.

"Open or closed?"

"You can leave it open."

I ran to my desk, threw my headset back on, and dialed Felix's number as Mel turned and hovered over my shoulders.

"What is going on?" she asked.

"I'll fill you in soon. I gotta make a few phone calls."

The line kept ringing and ringing. The same vibrating tone every two seconds for twenty seconds. Nothing. I hung up and dialed again. My blood pressure rose with each passing ring. Please answer, please answer. Voicemail again, fuck.

I GOT IN MY CAR AND PULLED FELIX'S PROFILE INFORMATION on my phone. His profile detailed his net worth, attached legal documents, and his onboarding questionnaire regarding his risk appetite and investment strategy. I copied and pasted his home address into my maps and headed to Cave Creek. A particular ranching community off the border of northern Scottsdale. During my drive, as the city lights turned away, I saw the stars and the terrifying emptiness of space.

Once I arrived in Cave Creek, my maps took me down a quiet, thin street. Light post surrounded by expensively manicured cacti and desert shrubs. Suddenly, my phone notified me I had arrived, but I didn't see any houses when I peered through my window—instead stood a stone wall with brass metal gates. I drove on the driveway as far as I could before hitting the closed gate. I rolled down my window to a gawking ten-digit pin box. I scanned for a call button when the path lights tracing the driveway filled in the empty spaces of trees and brick from the other side of the gate. I reversed my car, fearing the gate might hit it, if someone was arriving home. I continued to drive down the road as I couldn't pull off to the side. Instead, I'd flip a bitch at the next stop.

Okay, let's try this again; maybe I should try to call Felix one more time? As I drove back to the house, a sea of black Escalades poured out from behind the gate. Each perfectly distanced from the next, like a unified flock of birds. Four, to be exact. An unusually high number to be all matching. My left eye twitched as the words FBI flooded my mind. Felix sitting in one of those SUVs, handcuffed next to men in black windbreakers.

I have to get as far away from this scene as possible. Fuck. My paranoia mutated as I raced back toward the city lights. I searched for cameras tucked on the poles at every stoplight I passed. There was footage of me being in the area during the arrest. Literally outside his house. If Felix tells them I took part in his money-laundering scheme, me, deciding to fucking drive up here tonight, would strengthen his argument.

I instinctually pulled out my phone to call Alec, but I stopped as soon as I looked at my phone. Seeing his concerned face during our meeting. How could you let this happen? Anger mixed with disappointment. If I were to tell him what I saw, I would see that face again.

Once I got home, I took a Benedryl and crawled into bed. Fearing Monday when I'd arrive back at the office. Or, if things escalate, what phone calls would await me tomorrow?

~

I STOPPED AT TERRIBLE'S NEAR MY PLACE FOR GAS AND picked up a case of Stella, so I didn't look like a cheap ass showing up empty-handed with John at this elite barbeque. John didn't say how formal to dress, so I wore a white button-up beach shirt and pastel blue shorts. I checked my email every hour since I got up, and with each refresh of the page, my lungs stopped. There hadn't been a single email or phone call from Felix, an unusually long period of silence. The alarm grew louder and louder with each passing minute. I refreshed my email once more as I leaned against my car, the hot metal pressing against my back and a sliver of sunlight burning my legs.

John's residence was in a gated community east of the office. As I went on, these cookie-cutter Spanish-style homes with adobe walls and thick wooden accents appeared ideal for families. A couple was cleaning their cars, an old lady reading in her rocking chair, and four pre-teens preparing a lemonade stand.

I rang the doorbell and checked my email one last time. Nothing.

John answered the door in an almost identical outfit to mine, but with his sunglasses strapped around his neck and ankle socks.

"I wasn't sure If I needed to bring anything, so I stopped and got a six-pack," I said as a wave of cold air pulled me inside.

"How kind of you. But Giovanni usually has his barbeque's catered," John said as I followed him to the kitchen.

"Giovanni?"

"Yes, you might meet him. He's an old friend who hosts these annual get-togethers," John said as he unplugged his phone. "Let me grab my shoes."

"Sounds good. You have a charming home."

"Thanks, my wife does all the decorating," John said from down the hall.

"She's done an outstanding job." Everything seemed open. The kitchen and eating areas were together in one space, with a fireplace, living room and second living space across the hall. Out the window, I saw the gravel and a grassy backyard. There isn't enough space for a pool, but a decent-sized jacuzzi was snuggled up against the wall.

"John, I'm a little nervous. I haven't heard from Felix. No email or phone call. I don't know what to do at this point. I've exhausted all of my options. Besides, driving to his house."

"Don't *do* that," John said as he strapped a silver watch to his wrist. "It's okay to feel a little anxious. You have questions about an interesting situation. But I wouldn't dread it. Come Monday, Compliance will take over if those questions still go unanswered and will more than likely contact the Feds, who will get those answers."

"Wait, so the firm hasn't reached out to anyone outside? Like the IRS, or, I don't know, the FBI?"

John chuckled and opened one of my Stellas. "No, they haven't contacted the FBI. Here, for the nerves."

I took a sip as the four black Escalades replayed over and over, "Thanks. As bad as I want answers, Monday is looking gloomier."

"Focus on what is right in front of you, and when Monday comes, we will act," John said. "Finish your beer. I'm going to give Roxie her food, and we can head out."

As we drove up the driveway, it was getting harder and harder for me to keep my hand away from the jagged edges of my beer caps. The sophisticated mansion was like a hunter in the woods, seamlessly blending into the mountainside. The glass walls mirrored the sky and intermittent clouds were carefully supported by dark maroon, brown, and brass metal.

"Did you bring any business cards?" John asked.

"I did. I wasn't sure about networking that would happen. So, I came prepared."

"Good. Glad you thought ahead."

"Is that a helicopter on top of the house?" I asked, leaning forward, only to be restrained by my seatbelt.

"It sure is. Giovanni isn't the type of man to sit in traffic," John said. "He flies into Sky Harbor and charters his copter to his palace."

"It's so big. I like the dark green color."

"Like I mentioned, this will not be any ordinary gathering. Think of the best networking event you have ever been to.... Now times that by one hundred."

"No pressure," I said, as we reached the top amid purple Lamborghinis, engine-red Ferraris, and pearl white Bentleys. My palms, grasping the beers, became damp and aching. I took a deep breath as I ran my hands down the hem of my shorts.

An iPad-wielding staff member greeted us as soon as we reached the seven-foot French doors. In keeping with the rest of the staff, she presented herself as polished and well-versed in her job duties.

"Hello! And welcome. May I have a name?"

"Yes, it's John Barrett and guest."

The lady flipped the screen with her finger and made a few taps.

"It is so great to have you again, John," she said. "Your guest will need to sign this form." She handed me the iPad with blocks of legal text. The words look like a texture of hieroglyphics.

"What is this?" I asked.

"It's a standard non-disclosure agreement."

"It's okay, Ted. My signed document is already on file," John said, and with the tip of my finger, I squiggled my rights away.

"Thanks. Alright, you are all checked in. We will pass around the lunch menu shortly. In the meantime, please grab a drink at any of the bar tops and enjoy some appetizers floating around."

"We can take those for you." The lady said as she pointed. I smiled and handed her my gift. "If you need one, it will be at the bar top inside."

"Thank you so much."

Outside and inside were ambiguous because no walls separated the two areas with a landscape of concrete and grass surrounding an infinity pool, which was the focal point of the gathering. Pockets of three or four people formed around standing tables with drinks in one hand and food pinches in the other. I followed John up to the bar's highest ledge. I felt like I was being watched as we passed concrete sculptures adjacent to blank walls and random abstract portraits—the epitome of minimalism.

"Can I get a Macallan? Neat," John said. "Do you want anything?"

"I'm good for now. I'll wait until I eat before having some drinks."

"Well, when you do, try the Macallan 1926. It will change your life."

While waiting for John's drink to be prepared, I saw that apart from a few Filipino-looking employees, I was the only one under 30 in the room. They were all dressed casually, with salt and pepper hair and thin-rimmed sunglasses, an equal number of male executives to female moguls. I followed John as we sailed from table to table. To begin, they always extended a handshake, gave an update on how things were going in the KS empire, and made a particular acknowledgment of how well their grandkids were doing. They also complimented the appetizers and Giovanni's exceptional hospitality. John would always put me in the limelight.

A warm smile spread across the faces of the three men at table one as we exchanged cards, and John introduced me as the "rising star" of the night.

To the second table, John added, "This is our superstar advisor, Ted Sullivan."

"You always find the top talent," an elderly lady said, adjusting her floppy straw hat as the server topped off her champagne.

"You'll all wish you had an advisor like Ted," John told table three.

"This is our MVP, Ted Sullivan. He made this year's Forbes list," John told table four.

"Have you all met our rising star, Ted Sullivan?" He asked table five.

My cheeks were hurting from smiling. Behind us, a courteous server appeared.

"Hello, sorry to have interrupted, but we wanted to let you know lunch is now ready. Here is the menu." She handed everyone at the table thick postcard-shaped menus. "We have three options. First, is our wagyu beef burger topped with gourmet fries and truffle oil. Second, we have jumbo shrimp tacos topped with cotija cheese, avocado, and cabbage. And last, we have a vegetarian chopped salad with a vintage Giuseppe Giusti balsamic vinaigrette." My mouth salivated with each description. I wanted all three.

"I'll take a salad," the three ladies said one at a time.

"Wagyu burger," John and another gentleman said.

"Make that three." I chimed in.

"Absolutely. I will bring those two over in just a second."

After lunch, I asked the server to crack open a Stella's I brought and continued to shadow John, back to the same routine-like conversations. Hours later, my Stellas were gone. I now realized why John went for the drinks first. The finest of liquid for the bravest of courage. It seemed like the sun was waving farewell to the mountains as the titans cashed in their valet tickets and called for their town cars.

"Did you get lots of business cards?" John asked, since the first time we've been here, holding a glass of water.

"I did! I replaced all of mine."

"Good job. I'm going to say goodbye to Giovanni, and we can head out."

"Can I come with you? He's the one person I haven't met yet."

"Maybe next time, this is more of a business conversation."

"Not a problem. I'm going to the restroom. This water went right through me."

Various talks echoed throughout the mansion's halls as classical music accompanied me inside. When I opened the door, two young Vietnamese boys were using the powder room, drawing fine ivory lines on the black marble-like ground-up bones and elongating the borders with a credit card.

"You want?" The shorter one asked.

"Sorry, I didn't mean to barge in. No, thanks, I'm good." I closed the door and continued down the hallway to a glass staircase. As I ran up to the second floor, the ceiling towered three stories above, and each entry remained locked. Dammit. Gravity applied more and more pressure to my bladder. Finally, an unoccupied toilet.

I stood in silence for the first time all day as the music from downstairs failed to reach me. When I closed my eyes, groans could be heard coming from another room. Possibly the door to a different part of the house? It got louder and louder as the clapping got faster and faster.

The music of fucking.

Hard thrusting, hate fucking as the grunting grew more obnoxious, the sultry sounds morphed into death metal following more aggressive vocals. The video of John fucking Chaz played in sync.

"Who's my little whore?" A man's voice said over and over. "Who's my little whore?"

A slight dialect made me more and more uncomfortable. The submissive bottoms *cry for more* hinted to be foreign, an international performer.

I flushed and felt my phone vibrate as I ran downstairs. A text from Alec:

> Emma and I are heading to Boston for a few days to pitch to her father so we can get that 5-mil investment. Ready to pull the trigger on phase one of our plan. Are you free to chat?

# 17

Alec Young

Alec hovered his phone to his ear while blindly watching travelers with colorful neck pillows strapped to rolling suitcases drink overpriced beer with eyes glued to the surrounding flat screens or touch screen devices killing time. The simple pleasures of unfocused leisure. Off to the side waiting for a delayed flight was a tall father helping to take his boy's animated Buzz Lightyear backpack off, around six or seven with sleepy eyes and blue light-up shoes. His socks were uneven, scrunched down on one leg and normal length on the other. The boy stood sleep-deprived, not your typical cranky crying, but more innocent like a puppy after a long walk. The father set his backpack on the open chair next to him, picked up his son and gently laid him to sleep on his chest. His dirty blonde hair nestled under his stubbled chin.

"Alec," Ted said on the other end.

"Hey, Ted."

"So I am not going to be a part of the presentation? What is going on?" Ted asked.

"What? Sorry this group of people walked by."

"I'm not going to be a part of the presentation?"

"We need to move quickly. I'm sorry. I want you to present with us, but we need to act now."

"Why? We had a detailed timeline as to when we would begin constructing the company. And now, we have to get it done tomorrow? Why are we shedding an entire year off our timeline? Does this have something to do with..."

"Yes," Alec said. "Bradley is in a medically induced coma." Ted remained silent. "The doctors are optimistic, but now is our time to act. I know your client numbers are not where we wanted them to be when this time came, but...."

Ted interrupted, "We can do a roadshow. I've connected with a few institutional investors and hedge funds executives at this barbeque. God if you can call this shit a barbeque, but anyway, we can go on a tour across the west coast, east coast, middle fucking America if he have to. We will make it work."

"Young Industrials has potential," Alec said. "We both know that. This is what we've been gearing up to do."

"Phase one of many. Now, when you say moving fast, exactly how fast?"

"Well, if the meeting with Emma's dad goes well, I'll be using the rest of my vacation, which is about two weeks' worth, then turning in my resignation."

"Shit. Okay. Yeah, that is fast. Okay. So, what is next? Are you at the airport?"

"Yeah. Emma is in the lounge. Our fucking flight got delayed due to thunderstorms in Boston. But we're going to put together the pitchbook and I need to connect with my aunt to try and get a few financials for Young Industrials. I know they've been in the red. Bleeding money from various departments, zero cost-cutting and losing revenue to competitors due to inferior technology and equipment. I just need the numbers."

"How can I help?"

"Actually. Let me conference Emma in. We want to include a limited partnership slide and to appease Roger, we can include the client you do have. One sec'."

"Alec?" Emma answered.

"Hey, I got Ted on the line."

"Emma," Ted said.

"Hi Theo," Emma said. "Alec where are you?"

"I'm wandering the airport. But do you have the presentation open?"

"I can pull it up."

"Okay. We're going to include Ted's clients on the limited partner slide."

"Good. I had a feeling my dad might ask. We have to be prepared. Five million is a lot of money, and I know my dad. If he feels like we aren't one hundred percent about this, he won't invest."

"What was your goal again, Ted? Eight clients?" Alec asked.

"I wanted to have about eight solid clients I could approach about investment opportunities."

"And how many are we at?" Emma chimed in.

"I have three, currently."

"Almost halfway there," Emma said. "And what are the names of the clients you would be going after? So, we can add it to the potential investor slide," Emma said.

"Well, there is Ed Harmon, ultra-high net worth. And Shelby Turner, high net worth. In case Roger asks, ultra-high is anything over a billion."

"Got it, but I thought you said you had three clients?" Emma said.

"I do have three, but we had an escalation. I wanted to fill you in on, Alec. One of our fucking analysts submitted multiple requests for my client Felix Hernandez, and those requests, along with abnormal deposit levels, triggered a compliance review."

"A compliance review?" Alec asked.

"Yes, with our AML team."

"Theodore, what the fuck? The anti-money laundering team? What is going on?"

"It's all theory-based at this point. AML wants updated financials from Felix, and once I get those, we will be all good."

"Okay, and what if the firm cannot deem the money as clean, then what? They contact the SEC, and you will forever be a stained client advisor who had a client try and launder money? Shit follows you. You know, the majority of advisors whose clients laundered money were a part of the scheme. I'm letting you know for optics." Alec's tone cut deeper and deeper. "Why are we now finding out about this?"

"Because I barely fucking found out about it, Alec. This will work itself out, people escalating and being paranoid. Nothing has been proven."

"So, for the record, we only have two clients?" Emma said.

"Yes, we only have two clients," Alec said.

"While we have you on the line, Ted. Can we pivot to management positions?" Emma said.

"Yes. We want to approach her father with names already drawn up for management positions. Obviously, us three, and after I talk with Raj, I know he will get on board as our chief information officer. Build out the company website and investor portfolio portals."

"I like Raj," Ted said. "We can also put down possibly a few guys on my side. If the money is right, they should jump on board."

"Is there anyone at KS you both could think of?" Emma asked.

"Well, my team is a bunch of fucking idiots. But possibly a few names. Again, the money has to be right as this would be a huge risk they are taking."

"Let's plan to meet back up when we return from Boston. Hopefully, things would have resolved themselves regarding your client, Ted," Alec said.

"Let us hope," Emma said.

"You can hop off the call Emma," Alec said.

"Bye, Theo."

Alec and Ted stood in silence.

"Theodore, I'm sorry I got heated. Everything is delicate right now. I shouldn't have used that tone with you. I'm sorry. I think what I'm most embarrassed about is talking that way toward you in front of Emma."

"It's okay, Alec. Really, it's okay. I know it came from a good place with the right intentions. You're right, I don't know what to do next if things escalate."

"Then we will tackle them as they come. Together."

~

Droplets wormed down the window while sudden flashes lit up the black clouds proceeding rolling booms and cracks across the sky. Alec's mind mirrored the angry weather, his anxiety in sync with his throbbing jugular, thoughts coursing up then splitting behind his ears and scattering about his skull like bolts of lightning. Fast and loud.

"Do you think your mom liked me?" Emma asked.

"I think so."

"Me too. We've already evolved to a texting relationship. She wants to know when my birthday is. So *cute*."

"Sir, the house is going to be up on your right," Alec said to the driver. His mind was too preoccupied. "Right here is good. Thanks."

Rain pounded the Peterson townhouse and all of the surrounding areas. The gutters spewed gallons into gardens and shrubs. Alec and Emma looked like cats scurrying up the concrete steps, leaping over the middle only to be greeted by another rumbling crack from the sky while closing the door behind them.

"You made it," Grace said, her voice mixing with the aroma of sugar and peaches as she poked her head from the kitchen, still wearing a white apron with over-stitched pockets and flowers.

"Ugh, barely," Emma said, upset at whoever, the meteorologist for a wrong prediction, the airlines for delaying the flight, nature, God, you name it.

"It smells lovely, Grace. What are you making?" Alec asked as he used his dry hand to comb back his wet hair then dried his now wet hands with a Delta napkin he had in his pocket from several flights ago.

"Peach cobbler."

"Yum! I can't remember the last time I had some peach cobbler," Alec said, bug-eyed.

Emma sat at one of the high-top chairs in the kitchen, fixing her hair. "Where is dad?"

"Your father is on a work call in his office."

Since Grace pointed out the fact, the unidentifiable chatter running down the hall made sense.

They finished dessert and relaxed in the sitting room, the largest room in the house with built-in wall to wall bookshelves, a central fireplace flooded with candles, a reading nook window that gave flashes from the mayhem outside and a black grand piano whose string lid and keys were covered. Towered lamps with tassels dangled from their mustard-colored shades produced a yellowish tint. The carpet under the couches and centerpiece table could easily cover four king-size beds. The shiny majestic piano reminded Alec of Ted and the first time he played for him. Alec had flown down to Stillwater a few months after their KS internship. Spent the weekend with Ted in his studio apartment. His piano nestled close to his bed where Alec lay, his face lit from the full moon piercing through the window, listening to Ted run his fingers across the board.

"Do you play the piano, Grace?" Alec asked.

"I know a few melodies and tunes."

"She never plays on it," Emma said, standing at the mini bar, also built into the wall, her hands flowing around the various bottles, unsure of which potion to whip up.

"Yes I do," Grace said.

"I dunno, the dust would say otherwise."

"Can you play, Alec?" Grace asked.

"I can't. Always wanted to learn though. It's one of those things where you say and want to learn when it's brought up in conversation but afterward, escapes."

"You know, *Roger is the real piano player in this house*," Grace said. "He tried teaching Emma when she was a girl, but could never get her to sit still long enough."

"She's *always on the go*."

"I can hear you both."

"Maybe Roger can teach you sometime," Grace said.

"Alec?" Emma said.

"I would like that." His eyes and attention were still on Grace.

"Alec," Emma said, turning her head to the side in an attempt to make it sound more clear. "Do you want a drink? Whiskey? Brandy?"

"I'm good."

Conversations from Roger's office shifted to an assertive almost reprimanding tone, which caused the sitting room to go quiet, even catching Grace off guard. Alec feared whatever business call Roger was deep into would alter his mind, take him to a pessimistic valley where he'd reject the plan. Reject Sullivan Young. Poisoned by negative thoughts of economic loss and hard conversations of inadequacy like the pungent aroma of bitters, sharp spices, and dried flowers from Emma's coupe glass, overpowering the uplifting peaches.

"Do you think we should turn in? Call it a night, it has been a long day, and have the meeting tomorrow?" Alec asked.

"That might be for the best. I don't know how long he will be in his office," Grace said.

"We can wait," Emma said, nibbling on a pierced cherry and then swirling it around in her drink. "Power through. I'm sure he won't be too much longer."

Before Alec could protest further, the inkling to wait and let the dust of angst settle in Roger's office, the sliding French doors opened.

"Dad," Emma said while getting up from her chair. "Sounds like you were having a fun time."

"Come in, come in."

Alec had never stepped foot in Roger's spacious, paper-ridden office. Files were stacked on his desk under fossil and jewel paperweights. Others were scattered upside down, right side up on the floor, and around the table next to a window. His office had the townhouse's signature built-in bookshelves with a small collections of books, tasteful antique objects, and pictures of the family.

Roger sat behind his desk with his face half-visible, covered by his enormous monitor, and let Alec and Emma lead the meeting. Alec took charge, having had months of practice with Andre, clearing his throat and handing Roger an iPad with the presentation cover page begging to be read. Alec started off strong, beginning with a question he figured Roger would eventually ask. SLIDE TWO: WHY PRIVATE EQUITY

AND HOW WOULD THEIRS BE DIFFERENT FROM THE REST? He said enough without the purging of word vomit. He said the right words knowing Roger would be more focused and interested in profits over environmental impact, considering that most of the clients at Peterson Consulting are oil-rich and mineral-dense.

SLIDE FOUR: TARGET COMPANIES OF SY ONE FUND. And before Alec could utter a word, Roger spoke and said, "I thought you weren't interested in running your family's company?"

"We want the flexibility to have our hands in multiple buckets, and so running Young Industrials from the inside would be limiting. Operating Young Industrials from the outside gives us that flexibility, as well as outside observations."

"Given the size of Young Industrials, it seems quite futile. Wouldn't you say? I was expecting to see smaller fish in this brochure."

"Slide five, Daddy," Emma said, folding her hair behind her ears. "We already have a lineup of potential limited partners who would invest in the SY One Fund. Some names you might recognize, and for those you don't, we put their net worth and possible investment size into the fund."

Roger remained quiet, raising his finger against pursed lips. His reading glasses were on the verge of falling off his nose as he remained still and pensive.

"Who is Sullivan?" Roger asked.

"Ted Sullivan," Alec said. "He is the other partner and fellow KS colleague who works on the private wealth side."

"Why isn't he here?"

"He's out getting us those clients on the list."

Roger sat silent again, flipping forward with his finger against the iPad screen like an anxious reader who flips to the back of a novel to read how it ends. He took off his glasses, putting the iPad to sleep and took a sip of the potion Emma made. The red cherry bobbing around.

"M, can you give Alec and myself a moment, please."

"Sure."

Emma shut the sliding doors; her footsteps hovered down the hall along with her shadow under the lip of the door. Alec put his hands in his pockets and tried to control his breathing. What did Roger want to talk to him about? Alone. Alec began mentally listing random objects he saw to control the anxiety: desk, chair, clock, monitor, cords, books, paper, pens, iPad, glass, cherry, ice, Roger. He remained quiet, as if to force Alec to speak first, a possible power play. It worked.

"Is there something about the pitch?" Alec asked.

"Nothing about the pitch. It looks great and thorough. So, I'm prepared to invest so you can get off the ground. Five million like previously mentioned."

"That's great! You won't be disappointed. I promise."

"There's just one thing I need first," Roger said, leaning back in his chair. "I want her name on the wall."

"I'm sorry?" Alec said, taking an anxious step toward Roger like it would somehow improve his hearing or at best, clarify what Roger said. To Alec's hope, it wouldn't be what he heard.

"Emma. I want her name on the wall."

# 18

Ted Sullivan

When the market opened Monday morning on October 19, 1987, it showed a severe and sudden selloff. The Dow Jones Industrial Average sank twenty-two percent. Malaysia, Mexico, and New Zealand lost thirty to thirty-nine percent, with Hong Kong being struck the heaviest with a forty-five percent plunge. Twenty-three global markets experienced sharp losses when the dust cleared—complete hysteria, fear, and worry about what would transpire next.

Today was my Black Monday.

"Ted, do you have an update from the client?"

"I don't. I've dropped numerous emails, phone calls and voicemails, but they went unanswered."

"Well, shit," the AML associate said. "Per the policy, when we are investigating suspicious anti-money laundering activity, and we have not heard from the client, we will place a freeze on all of his accounts and pass all our data to the authorities."

"Ted, can you send us over a detailed list of all the client's accounts and transaction activity spanning back to his onboarding with the firm?"

"You bet. I'll get started right away. Question though, what kind of scenario would play out if your team cannot contact Felix? As a hypothetical."

"We will give all the assets we currently have to the authorities."

"Would the authorities question me?"

"Depending on what they find in their investigation, it is a possibility."

"But don't worry about it, Ted," Legal said. "You will have the full backing of the firm's resources."

"Okay, great. Thank you."

I drew Reid into a team room to update him on Felix. Our recent interactions have been me looping him in on escalations—the corporate love story of being a leader. The situation was out of our control, and now we wait. But Reid showed ambivalence to the news, his mind elsewhere.

"Mel left the firm," Reid said, pursing his lips.

"Really? When? Where did she go?"

"She landed an advisor role at J.P. Morgan. So, it will stretch us pretty thin with her absence. I haven't told the team yet. I was on a call about it this morning. There's going to be a feeding frenzy for her clients."

"When it rains, it pours," I said. "Let me know where I can help." Like I have fucking capacity. Throwback to the bottom after climbing the corporate mountain. "I'm going to post John on Felix."

"Good idea," Reid said, opening the door as I trailed behind.

John came barreling out of his office.

"Hey, John, can I update you on Felix?"

"Tell me on the way to *Keira Bean*. Let's go."

One of my favorite waves of experience was strolling into a bistro. The raw ground beans glazing the nostrils, flakey buttery pastries eyeballing from inside a glass bowl. We didn't have a coffee shop back home, let alone a Keira Bean convenient in the town center. The coffee we appreciated was brewed in our home or at Sue's Cafe, which trains in Folger's black or black with walnut creamer.

"Since neither Compliance nor I have heard from Felix, they are freezing his accounts. Passing the baton to the authorities," I said, walking behind John in line.

"When are they handing everything over?"

"Today. I'm compiling all the evidence and account information for AML, and they will forward it on."

"Okay, good. I told you not to worry. Compliance knows what to do next if something looks fishy," John said. "Do you want anything?" The barista stood ready, looking at me.

"Sure, I'll take a tall cold brew. Black."

We rested in a booth. These shops have predictable storm hours of lavished coffee fiends. We arrived at the right time as two ladies studied the newspaper while the sluggish baristas were stocking shelves.

"Did you have fun on Saturday?"

"A great time. Thank you again for inviting me. I met a lot of fascinating people. Sad, I didn't have time to meet Giovanni."

"More to come. I saw you pounding those beers. Were you a *naughty* boy?"

"I... um," How do I respond?

"If you keep down this path. Outstanding at work with a discretionary demeanor, I will see to it you have the largest bonus this year, and fast-tracked to VP," John said, planting his palm above my knee. "You're a great guy to have around. And to look at."

"Thanks, John." How do I respond? I took a slow sip of my brew. I could feel myself freezing, doing nothing as his fingers trailed up my thigh. *He shouldn't be touching you, the little adopted boy said.* His whimper oozed from the ceiling speakers.

"So, you won't tell me what trouble you got into? After I left to talk with Giovanni."

"I networked a bit. Nothing too crazy."

"Tina updated me about another gathering at Giovanni's penthouse in Miami. It could be fun."

"Who is Tina?"

"She's a business associate of Giovanni. She usually sets up his parties and manages the guest list. I believe she said it would happen in about two months? So, clear your calendar." The more and more I am brought into John's personal lifestyle, 'colleagues' and friends, the more I'm getting an Eye's Wide Shut vibe. Could this submissive obedience be a factor that promoted Chaz Perez? I can envision him feeding off this type of attention mixed with his predatory promiscuous past.

My phone vibrated inside my suit causing my skin to tingle. Alec freed me.

"John, excuse me, I have to take this call. I'll meet you back in the office. We can go over Felix's account activity before sending it to Compliance, if you'd like."

"Sure, let's do that." John slid his hand off my thigh.

Rushing out the door, my blood bubbled with resentment and sharp pressure of suspense.

"Please tell me you have good news?"

"We fucking got the investment!" Alec said. "A transfer of five million into our business account once we set it up later today and file the incorporation paperwork! We fucking got it!"

All I feared and dreaded about today was gone. Poof. Like witnessing the emergency helicopter swoosh in after being stranded on a mountaintop, inundated by spiteful snakes and cold-blooded reptiles.

"We *got* it?" I said in disbelief. "We got it! Fuck yes. Alec, this is amazing news! We can finally begin building our company."

"After all the planning and spending countless hours building our reputation. All for this moment."

"I'm so proud of you, Alec. So, so proud of you."

"I'm proud of us. We did this together."

"How was the presentation? Did he give any feedback or stipulations about the investment?"

"Roger left impressed with how much we have planned and outlined. From investment sectors to employee quality. Our growth projections and strategy. The investment came with a few requests regarding management and oversight."

"Such as?"

"Emma, holding an executive position. Head of consulting and advisory."

"Did you tell him we were leaning more toward only private equity?"

"I started off detailing, but he said it can be done. It has been done," Alec said. "More room for growth, he said. It will round the firm in its ability to perform services."

"We need to go over our game plan."

"I have my resignation email already typed out and ready to go. My manager approved my two-week vacation, so Emma and I are spending a few days here. Let's have a dinner celebration when we get back. Then we can outline and plan the next steps."

"I'm in shock. I should do the same. Use up the rest of my allocated vacation. Suck every penny out of KS before quitting."

"Do it. Let me know if they approve it."

"I'll draft letters to my clients for when we are ready to approach them about investing in the fund and, of course, my reason for leaving KS."

"I cannot wait to say the words, our firm. Our empire. *Sullivan Young and Company.*"

Excitement, gratitude, pride, and joy are potent emotions I haven't known since I accepted my KS internship offer two and a half years ago. I recalled the day like it was yesterday. Circled by piles of notecards, textbooks and highlighters tucked deep in the library, flying on four hours of sleep, bracing for our first finance exam of the semester.

My phone shivered under mountains of papers with a New York area code. My pulse stopped. The air in my lungs exhausted and filled as I stumbled to answer. I assured myself it was another dream. Another glorified subconscious mind story, so unreal it could only be real. Ending the call with, I accept.

Before *I found Alec*. Before, *we conjured up and sewed our dreams together to strive for something beyond our imagination*. When I was a naïve business student, my shaky knees were influenced by my aspirations. I was wielding any pain I'd experienced into ammunition to tackle what was necessary to, one day, receive the offer call. Or to fast forward to the call from Alec about our investment.

I walked into Pacific 16 late and followed the host to our table. Alec and Emma were at the white cloth-covered table and a fresh candle stood tall and plumb in the center.

"You look dashing," Alec said, standing up and giving me a hug.

"I've finally developed style. God, I feel like it's been so long since the last time I saw you," I said. "Or you, good evening Emma."

"Theo, so good to see you."

Our hug felt light and forced.

Alec held his finger up to a server. "Can we get a bottle of champagne, please?"

"Absolutely. Our champagne selection is toward the back."

"Let's do a bottle of Dom," Alec said without flipping open the menu.

"You bet. I'll get that right out."

"This is a celebration," I said. "So tell me how everything went?"

"My dad was so impressed with our presentation. Poor Alec was all shaky before the meeting."

"Okay, I wasn't too nervous."

"You could hear his tongue get stuck to the roof of his mouth."

"My mouth gets naturally dry. But yes, we impressed Roger."

"I wish I could have been there."

"I've already talked to Raj, and he is on board; we can go over his salary and signing bonus this weekend."

The server brought us a silver icebox with the gold Dom Pérignon shield peeking out, pouring tasteful amounts in our flutes, disappearing after.

"How delicious," Emma said, salivating.

"Cheers, team. We've worked so hard for this moment. We're close to something big. Cheers to our company, our legacy, our empire," Alec said, as we let our rims kiss and tasted the brut bubbles.

"This is better than I remembered," Alec said, taking another sip.

His toast took me back to our room at the St. Eleanors during the innovator award ceremony. Everything mimicked the same feeling, except for one unwanted addition. Déjà vu struck.

"Sorry, I'll take the eight-ounce filet mignon, rare."

"Excellent choice. Those will be right out," The server said, picking up our menus.

"So, I think I'm going to submit my vacation request and ride it out," I said.

"You haven't already?" Alec asked.

"No. They're short-staffed I didn't want to put more pressure on Reid or the team."

"Fuck 'em," Alec said. "We got our investment. Let's do this."

"I agree with Alec."

"What is the update on your client?" Alec asked.

I pinched the bridge of my nose. "It's out of our hands now."

"Meaning?"

"Since I nor compliance could get in contact with Felix, they froze his accounts and handed all the documents to the authorities."

"Yeah, you definitely need to get out," Emma said.

"I agree with Emma."

"Okay, Okay. I'll submit my vacation request tomorrow, and if it's denied, I'll hand in my resignation," I said, taking in more bubbles.

"There is no point in delaying the inevitable," Alec said.

"No, you're right. I've been nervous, so I've been putting it off."

"Did Alec tell you the great news?"

"No, I didn't," Alec said as he chewed on the ice from his water glass.

"Didn't what?" I asked.

"One stipulation for the investment my dad said is for my name going on the wall."

My stomach curled, following a nauseous sensation.

"Have your name on the wall? So, what now it's Sullivan Young Peterson? People are going to think we're a fucking law firm. What did you put on the incorporation paperwork, Alec?"

"Also, I was talking with Sloane, and when we're ready to launch, she was going to write an article about us. Well, the company, not Alec and I." Emma laughed. "The article will sound something like, two Kauffman Schwartz associates leave to start a private equity firm with Emma Peterson, daughter of Roger Peterson, founder of Peterson Consulting."

"Will the article say Peterson enough?" I snarled but caught myself. "But no, that is really great. We need all the publicity we can get. Cut through the noise."

"Hopefully, it catches the attention of some big news outlets, and they do their own story," Emma said, looking at Alec, who was still munching on ice. "Alec, do you think Raj could help push the article?"

"Oh yeah, sure. We can allocate a marketing budget for him to advertise across the internet."

"Well, congrats on the article," I said.

"Ted, that's not the good news I'm referring to," Emma said, raising her left hand from under the table, revealing a diamond. "This is! We're engaged! So, yes, my name will be on the wall."

A wave of goosebumps covered my arms, back, and legs. The baby hairs on my head stood at shocking attention. Smacking my face into a brick wall.

"Umm...wow, congratulations!" Those words felt automatic, a default response.

"Let's make another toast," Emma said, raising her glass. "To Alec and I."

"To you and Alec," I said, piercing my eyes at Alec, following a sip. He avoided eye contact with me. I looked at him for five seconds, and his eye never met mine. He knew I would react to the news. Angry. Betrayed. They are fucking engaged. The server slid our plates onto the table while asking if we needed anything in the meantime. A to-go box?

Pain, anger, betrayal, duplicity, and sorrow are also potent emotions I haven't felt since I received news about Emma a year ago. Alec munching on ice chips as he fumbled with the words to tell me in the hotel cafe. His reassurance she was temporary, borrowed, and used.

I sat at my piano with my eyes closed and only a faint light tucked in the corner. The dark hues echoed off the strings as I could no longer feel. Tear droplets covered the keys as I inhaled the music, tasting the salt.

Why did this have to happen?

Why is this the only way?

A lost part of me saw this coming, saw the true love I deserve, fueled by troubling thoughts and submissive actions. My lost soul predicted my outcome and waited for the unfolding.

*Why doesn't anyone ever love us? The little adopted boy cried.* His words seeped through the vault walls.

*Why does everyone leave?* His voice grew grim, wedged between shallow breathing and innocent hiccups.

I pressed the keys harder, nearly snapping a bone to drown out his voice.

~

Seldom do I get migraines, ones where you want to wrap your head around a pillow and bury the buffer inside a cold, quiet cave. Today was one of those few days.

"You look bloody awful," Reid said, shutting the door to the team room.

"I have a terrible migraine," I said, closing my eyes to the sounds of Emma's shrilling laugh.

"Shite. I didn't know you got migraines?"

"I don't. These last few days have been stressful. I slept very little last night," I said, taking a sip of water while pushing reheated scalloped potatoes around in my Tupperware. "Which is why I scheduled this meeting. Sorry for it being last minute."

"I'm going to take my two-week mandatory vacation starting tomorrow."

"Tomorrow?" Reid said, his voice picking up. "I can't have you do that, Ted. But, sorry, it's too short of notice. Mel already stretched the team thin. In a few months, sure. After we onboard new hires."

I took one last bite, closing the lid to my Tupperware.

"John spoke highly of you in the management meeting the other day. Some spiel about him receiving client calls regarding your excellence," Reid said, raising his left eyebrow. "You don't want to fuck that up, do you? Let's keep up this winning streak, hit a few more home runs, and celebrate afterward. You got this, mate." Reid's appearance signals the end of this meeting. A quick brush of his tie with a half-ass grin.

"I have put in countless hours for this team and brought hundreds of millions worth of assets to this firm. I pick up the slack when our teammates are too hungover or lazy to show up, and so I am telling you. Starting tomorrow, I am taking my two-week mandatory vacation. My body and mind need a rest. I can't recall the last time I got a migraine, and now I'm getting them on the regular. This is not okay. I am arguing mental health, and again, I'm taking that vacation."

The thickening air made it more and more difficult to breathe. I never stood up to Reid and always did what was told of me. He was silent, and I couldn't determine the root cause. Shock or anger? Will he continue to push back? Again, this haggle for my vacation surfaced around sucking every penny out of Kauffman before leaving, following in Alec's footsteps.

"You can have one week," Reid said, pursing his lips.

"Two weeks."

"One week and you can have first dibs on Mel's client list."

"Two weeks."

Reid got up and as he left the room, he agreed. Steam barreling from his ears. Light from the open door punctured the back of my skull and rattled the razor blades inside my head. I was gone from KS, mentally and ready to pour everything I had into our company.

I sat at my desk debating whether to text Alec that I had gotten my vacation approved. I felt a slight release when I pulled up his company profile within our instant messaging system. The pain and pressure were subsiding. I saw his corporate photo and steel eyes smiling toward me above the words, offline, next to his status.

*Offline.*

Our relationship these last few months had felt offline, and the rhythm between us shifted, hurdling us into free fall.

*They were fucking engaged.*

Q3

# 19

## Ted Sullivan

I took a long sip of my iced hazelnut while getting comfortable on my living room floor next to my faux wood coffee table, on top of a Target Collection rug. Emma flitted over my living room, expressing her disapproval of the size of my television, furniture selection, and random Better Homes and Gardens decor.

"I drafted up these categories for our budget. These are essential for sure costs we need to incorporate," Alec said, moving papers around the table. "They vary from the legal fees to start a fund, paying back the cost of getting our articles of organization. And the fun part, office space."

"I did some research on the median price for office space in New York's Financial District. With that, I have narrowed it down to three options," Emma said. "We're going to tour these spaces with Alec still on vacation. When is our flight again, dear?"

"Wednesday at ten," Alec said. "Sorry, Theodore, I want you to come, but with work—"

"I got my vacation approved."

"You did? That's great! Should we try to get you on our flight?"

Alec's eye-widening. His voice turned genuine like he wants me to come.

"No, it's okay. You guys tour the spaces. I need to meet with my clients to tell them in person why I am leaving. This step needs to be handled with care if we're to have them follow me."

"I agree," Emma said.

"And did you—"

Interrupting Alec, I said, "Yes, I did. I've already sent my resignation email to Reid and John, scheduled to be delivered at six a.m. the day I am set to return."

"Happy Halloween," Emma said.

"I also sent separate emails to all of my clients, reminding them of my departure, set to be delivered at the same time. And, I won't lie, I'm nervous."

"Nervous about when they get the email?"

"Yeah. My clients will already be aware when reading it, but I'm unsure how Reid or John will react. I want the thirty-first to arrive already."

"Great work," Alec said, grinning with pride.

"My apartment is month to month, and I was considering moving out at the end of the week so that I'm not paying for the entire month if we plan on moving soon."

"You can stay with us in the meantime," Alec said.

My head shifted from Alec to Emma.

"Yeah, I don't see why not," Emma said. "While we're in New York shopping for office space, we'll also be out there browsing for a condo. I suggest you look now, Ted. I know many places won't consider you unless you're moving within the next few weeks of touring."

"And you're good financial-wise? For the first and last month? We could dip into the investment if you need it," Alec said.

"No, I'm good. I've been saving. The rent here is cheap. But thanks for the offer."

"Not a problem. Okay, so, back to office space. No matter which we choose, rent will be around fifty-four thousand a month, which equates to six hundred-fifty thousand a year," Alec said. "Once we find the one, we're hoping to sign the lease and complete the order to receive office supplies and furniture."

"My dad put me in contact with the company they use, and with the size of our office and quality of the furniture, we're looking at around one hundred to one hundred twenty thousand."

"And that will encompass?" I asked.

"Everything. Oakwood desks, leather chairs, forty-inch computer screens, pens, paper, printers, HP computers, everything."

"Once our system is up and running, Raj is ready to connect the company servers. He's already begun a few website and client portal mockups. They look great," Alec said. "Also, I expected we would each wait for our payday, and use the investment to pay Raj, the lawyers, and whoever else we onboard."

"I agree with that. Since we're on the topic of employees and money aside for salaries. I have someone in mind for the receptionist role. My cousin Dana is so personable, and I know the clients will love her."

"I don't know. What's her background in?" Emma asked, fidgeting with her need to control everything.

"Her background is she is very personable. Years of excellent customer service experience," I said. "I wouldn't recommend her if I didn't think she would do a good job."

"Let's add her to the list. Set aside funds," Alec said.

I was not sure if every suggestion would be met with opposition. Emma had some set schedule for every little detail, as though she'd built a company dream diary and now gets to execute on the aesthetics of the office.

~

My Monday morning alarm went off like a typical working day, but this day was far different from what I had done before. Yet, despite its abnormality, I met the alarm with eagerness and a dash of peace.

This morning I'm heading to my favorite park one last time. Appreciating all the little moments I got to experience while strolling or jogging. Take one last glance at the school of drifting swans below families of nesting sparrows. Confirm if the city replaced the broken basketball hoop or patched up the cracking concrete one last time.

The drive took a little longer than usual from Oldtown, even at five-thirty in the morning with the eager ants racing to their work hills. But, as painful as sitting in rush hour was, I took this opportunity to appreciate it. This would be my last time sitting in Scottsdale rush hour and my last time driving my car. Things you wouldn't expect to miss until you're met with the day before they're gone. I was substituting the familiar for the unfamiliar. Ricocheting myself out of my comfort bubble and into the abyss.

I took a seat at my familiar bench after strolling one lap. Some Halloween fanatics decorated the park with jack-o'-lanterns, fake spider webs, and Styrofoam tombstones. With everything going on, I'd lost track of time. I filled the last few days with client meetings, more client meetings, packing my clothes, selling my furniture, and researching a new apartment.

I forgot about Halloween. These holidays can reassure you what month you're in.

For me, what overshadowed everything and blocked me from the outside world? *Today, in five minutes, I will no longer be a wealth advisor at Kauffman Schwartz.* The thought left me dizzy and my mouth dry: I have sacrificed so much of myself to this company. I met many brilliant people from all over the world and grown a considerable amount, day after day, month after month, year after year.

*Three minutes remained.*

I was risking everything by morphing my success into an entity, into our company that will forever live—withstanding the test of time, challenging the status quo. If working at KS had taught me anything, it's that I never want to conform. Coasting at my desk, as so many did around me. Heads down, stomachs empty, bladders full.

*One minute remained.*

My phone let out a quick vibration following a ping sound. Without looking, I knew which email had hit my inbox. The next phase of my life was now in motion, the small gears rotating, transferring motion to other small gears, and building torque to move the larger pieces. Looking around, the swans from the nearby pond became more and more communicative with each other, and the flow of traffic remained the same. The day-to-day mechanics of life continue. Unfazed by my life-altering decision.

My phone vibrated. I could sense anger with every shake and tremble.

"Hello, Reid."

"Really, Ted? Really?" His accent sounds a tad more British. An angry brit. "Why are you trying to fuck me? What have I done to make you do this?"

"Reid, I'm not trying to fuck you over."

"Well, it sure in the hell looks like it. Where are you going? Are you following Mel to JP?"

"No, I am not following Mel." I pause, sifting through my thoughts. Do I tell him? Or make something up?

"So, what are you doing? Who all did you send this email to?"

"Just you and John."

"Total bollocks."

"I'm sorry?"

"So, where are you going? Have you contacted any of our clients?"

"You mean my clients?"

"Ted, have you thought this through? Or did you forget about the non-solicitation agreement you signed when becoming an advisor?"

"Reid, I have thought this through. Over the past three years, I've been thinking about this," I said, walking through the grass and making my way to the nearest tree shadow. "I have not forgotten about the non-solicitation agreement. I studied it so much I don't think it will hold up. It specifically prohibits me from poaching former clients regarding wealth management purposes for a certain time frame. But says nothing about private equity."

"So that's what you're doing? I cannot believe we are even having this conversation." Reid's exhale blasted through the speaker. "The firm's legal department is better suited to handle this conversation, and I'm telling you, Ted, this is not something you want to fuck around with. The way you quit will have you black-listed from ever working at the firm again. Then challenging your non-solicit will only piss them off. You don't have to do this. Come in, we can leave early and talk this out over a beer, and we will forget you even sent this email."

"Reid, it was a pleasure to work with you. I have learned so much, and with that, I want to say thank you."

I could hear a few telephones ringing in the background. His frustration was something I can understand. The team was already lean, and my departure will emaciate it. But our plan doesn't have time to factor in the well-being of my stepping stone team.

"I wish you the best of luck, Ted," Reid said before disconnecting the call.

A smile stretched across my face, my heart beating a constant, accelerating thump.

THE CONDO WAS A MAZE OF MOVING BOXES AND BUBBLE-wrapped twenty-pound picture frames. An assortment of *donate, trash,* and *keep* piles corralling us from the kitchen to the bedrooms. It's funny how substantial moves, the move across states, fuel us to purge our closets. Like snakes shedding their skin, moving on from the items that once defined a significant portion of your life. I reflected while cleaning out my apartment, now, when I say cleaning, I'm referring to throwing ninety percent of everything away or donating, dropping memories off at the thrift store. Goodwill should use that in their marketing campaign.

*Goodwill: the marketplace of abandoned memories.*

I felt little attachment to most of my things, so shedding off those parts of myself came easy, simple, ambivalent. Of all my belongings, my piano, a small collection of photos, and the cufflinks Alec got me were the most *significant.* Those are the memories I never want to let go of. When tackling my junk drawers, I found the DNA kit Emma had gotten everyone. My insides made a grumpy; *I didn't want to,* noise. But my mind went silent. My past and my story lived on the horizon of this test. The true ethnicity question with the words Double Helix gawked at me. Enticing me to open, spit and submit. Fucking Emma. I am still not sure if giving me this test was a calculated dig.

Emma might have a hoarding problem. Most of the boxes in the keep pile were hers, along with six suitcases full of clothes, shoes, and who the hell knows what else. She had lots of *baggage*.

As I made a sandwich with what little food remained in the fridge, I sent off a chain of texts—a quick life update tour.

My thigh vibrated.

"Well, well, well, if it isn't Miss Oklahoma."

"Please, no interviews. You'll have to talk with my publicist," Dana said.

"Deal. How are you? How are things?"

"Things are looking up. Jim and my divorce got finalized today. I'm a free woman!"

"Yes! Congratulations. This is a huge deal. You are done with him, and you can move on. Fucking Jim."

"It feels amazing. Jim is going to keep the house, but I'm like, I don't care, take it."

"Where are you going to be staying?"

"With my parents for a little, until I can save enough to get a place of my own. I might go back to school or work as a flight attendant, so I can see the world. It feels so good to have all these options."

"Actually. Dana, I've been meaning to call you. I have a job for you!"

"Wait, what? Are you serious?"

"Well, nothings set in stone, but it could get you out of Oklahoma. Start a whole new life. I'll know more in a few weeks, but it's a thought."

"Oh my goodness, Ted. I would give anything to get out," Dana said.

My phone vibrated.

"Hey, my mom is calling."

"Let's chat tonight?"

"Yes, please. And thank you for calling to tell me the good news! I'll keep you posted on the job offer."

"You are the best; love you."

I needed to hear her voice. Dana's aura could transcend space and time, lifting my soul out from inside any hole. A direct hit of serotonin into my bloodstream.

"Hey Mom, did you read my text?"

"I did, Ted. It sounds very exciting. I read your aunt the text, and she asked what kind of company you're starting?"

"A private equity firm."

"They are starting a private equity business, whatever that is," My mom said off to the side. "Your aunt wants to know what that is? And when do your doors open?"

"It's a little complicated, but in a nutshell, we collect money for a fund from investors to buy companies. Once we buy them, we restructure, cut costs, find the profit centers, dust those off, then re-sell the company a few years down the line."

"Oh boy, that sounds complicated," my mom said. "When does it open?"

"Sometime next week! I'm moving to New York this Sunday. I have a flight booked, and we hired movers to transport all our belongings."

My phone vibrated once more. It was Alec. I rarely talked to my mom, so I let him go to voicemail.

"Wow, what a move. I would be too scared to drive in a city that large."

"I sold my car—no need to drive. Oh, and, since our company is looking for a receptionist, I offered the job to Dana. We got off the phone not long ago."

"You offered your cousin a job? Ted, that is so great of you. She has been through a lot, and you know, I was telling Carol she needs to get out of here, go find what she likes to do, like what you did."

My phone buzzed again as I pulled it away from my face to check.

"Mom, can I call you back? My partner has called multiple times. I should take it."

"Oh yes, okay. No problem. Bye-bye, Ted. We love you."

"Love you too," I said. "Hey, Alec."

"Where are you?" His voice was fast.

"I'm at the condo. Where are you?"

"Did you not see the news alert?" Alec said in a firm, rapid-fire tone.

"No, what news alert? I've been on the phone."

"Turn on the TV, go to MSNBC."

"Okay, one second, I have to find the damn remote."

"It should be on the island."

"Ahh, yes."

A lady in a light blue blazer appeared on the screen, the audio connecting to the home theatre system as she mouthed empty words.

"Did something happen in the market?"

My pupils dilated as my eyes enlarged, and my hold on my phone slackened, lifeless. My heart was thumping on the roof of my mouth.

"We are still awaiting more information at this time," the anchor said. "But we can confirm that authorities arrested Felix Hernandez, owner of the popular Mexican restaurant, El Cabro, this morning."

"Alec, this is not happening...."

"On money laundering charges. Investment bank Kauffman Schwartz alerted the authorities when suspicious activity by Felix prompted a compliance review."

"Ted, stay there. I'm coming back to the condo now."

"Investigators then found sound evidence of criminal activity. Let me bring on financial crime attorney Ben Wentz— Hello Ben."

"Hello Sharon, thank you for having me."

"So, Ben, what's involved with money laundering charges?"

Alec did not hang up as we stood in silence. His breathing through the phone had a calming effect—a live conscious connection to the person I deem as my other half.

# 20

ALEC YOUNG

ALEC DASHED THROUGH THE CONDO, ONLY TO DISCOVER Ted standing in the living room, white as a sheet, holding the remote in one hand and his phone in the other.

"Ben, how common is it that the wealth advisor was in on the scheme from the beginning?"

"Sharon, it's not as uncommon as you would think. I've seen multiple cases where the advisors were the chief architect and getting paid for it in cash on the side. Now I don't want to assume that is what's going on in this situation, but it is telling that KS has yet to offer a statement saying the advisor was not aware."

"That mother fucker actually tried to do it," Ted said. "He tried to launder money through me."

"But he didn't. Focus on that."

"What is with these outlandish questions? Give me a fucking break. Why else?"

"Ben, what are some of the top reasons criminals try to launder money?" Sharon asked, placing her hand below her chin.

"Another great question, Sharon. So, there is a list of reasons, but majority involve the individual laundering their own money for tax-evading purposes, and another involving laundering on behalf of someone, such as drug money from a cartel or mob organization."

"Drug money," Ted said as if playing jeopardy. "The second we accomplish our KS mission, this bullshit brings us right back."

"Your name cannot be said. Ever." Alec ran his hands through his hair.

"I know. The media's asking questions if Felix's wealth advisor was involved."

"Do they know you were his advisor?"

"Not yet." Ted placed the remote on top of a box. "KS has not made a statement, and the longer it takes, the more questions people will start asking."

"KS needs to issue a statement saying you, but no names involved, Felix's wealth advisor was not involved. Something along those lines. Can you leverage your connections at KS?"

"I can view the ashes from the burned bridges. Maybe? With the way I quit, I don't know."

"Reid?"

"It has to be higher up. John's level. I could reach out to him."

"Do you think he'll take your call?"

"We should still have a relationship. After all, he invited me to his house and the networking barbeque," Ted said as he pulled out his phone with darting focus for John's contact details and flipped the call to speaker. Alec's ears pop at the first ring, then again at the second.

"Hello, you have reached John Barrett. Sorry, I missed your call. Please leave a message, and I'll get back to you as soon as possible," John's voice said, following a long beep.

"Hi John, this is Ted. I'm calling about a serious situation I know you are aware of. Please call me back as soon as you can. Thanks." Ted looked up at Alec.

"Let's draft that email," Alec said.

"What if I overestimated our relationship?" Ted said as his thumbs pecked his screen like hungry birds gorging on cracked corn. "I mean, he tried to...."

"What?"

"Sorry, I mean. What if we don't hear from him?"

"Do you know of any places he likes to visit? We could stage a run in?" Alec asked, walking toward the kitchen.

"I don't know. Even if we saw him out in public and approached him, he could argue about harassment or stalking. I don't know."

Alec plucked a green apple from the island and bit into it. Juice sprung in all directions as the sour sting puckered his lips and tingled his jaw. He tossed the apple across the room to Ted, who caught it with one hand and hovered the bitten chunk to his lips as he scanned his phone, searching for a name, a lead, a connection. He stopped scrolling and took a neighboring bite.

"HRC Gala," Ted said, shifting apple chunks to one side of his mouth and tossing the half-green half-white apple back to Alec.

"What about the HRC Gala?"

Ted walked toward Alec as rings echoed from his phone.

"Hello, Ted!" a hoarse but aged chipper voice said.

"Ed, how are you? Your voice sounds rough."

"I'm getting over a cold. Golly, they hit you out of nowhere. Too many meetings, no time to rest."

"Ed, you best be taking care of yourself."

"And I learn my favorite advisor is leaving to start his own company." Ed's tone hummed proudful amongst phlegm and wedged in between tissues. "That news alone should have cured me right up."

"It's an exciting time and I'm looking forward to diving into the specifics of the fund with you, but the reason I am calling is to ask a question."

"Alright, what's your question?"

"Do you or your foundation know the president of the Human Rights Campaign?"

"Leonard, of course."

"Wonderful. I want to attend this year's HRC Gala, but the website says they are all sold out of tickets. If an anonymous organization were to donate... I don't know, five grand? Could we possibly score two tickets?"

"A generous donation and I don't see why not. Let me call him."

"Thank you so much, Ed. Before I let you go, how much did the gala raise last year?"

"Umm... I believe they raised around two-hundred K."

"Sounds like big players attend the gala."

"Oh, yes. Some go for the social aspect, others to be known as the top contributor within the valley."

"You're a rock star, Ed, for reaching out. And I'm going to set up some time to discuss more about the fund."

"I look forward to it. Bye-bye, Ted."

Alec stood against the marble island entranced, watching Ted flourish in chaos. He was like a kid in a candy store, manipulating items in a whirl of art, watching each piece roll down the tube and into his hands. Alec bit his lower lip, collecting the last remaining sour juices as he set the apple stem on the ledge, where it stuck a tilted axel landing.

"John will be at this gala?"

"Yep. Before quitting, I got invited to attend the gala with John. Surprise."

Alec thrust his hip forward and took a step, running his hand through his hair as he walked toward Ted.

"And now you're going with me." Alec ran his thumb against Ted's lips. "Should we rehearse what you're going to say?"

"I have an idea in mind. Best to keep the suspense," Ted said, tilting up and kissing Alec as his hand grazed around Alec's hip, trailing his fingers against the surface of his lower back. Ted squeezed his ass as the two smiled at each other. "Thanks for the bite of that apple."

"You need to keep up your strength."

"And you still need to get us coffee, because I see you forgot it when you went to the store."

"Dammit," Alec said, jerking his head around to scan the kitchen.

"We're going to have a busy few days. We won't survive without coffee. We need to keep up our strength." Ted winked as Alec grabbed his car keys and headed out the door.

# 21

Ted Sullivan

"Hold still," I said, shoving the S cufflink through the tight slit on Alec's left wrist. "And, done."

Alec and I stood in front of his bathroom mirror, gazing at one another than ourselves. He looked perfect as always, with his tux tailored around his broad shoulders. Cutting off a few inches below his belt, revealing just a glimpse of the goods. I couldn't recall the last time Alec and I lived under the same roof for a few days, got ready for some event, preparing for battle. We prepped to perch in dark corners or tiny nooks, observing and analyzing the crowd. Telling the opulent anything they want to hear, what they need to fuel their thirst for more.

It's also been calming having Emma not within spitting distance as she visits her folks in Boston these past few days. Especially with everything going on with Felix and John, the last thing I want to hear was the little interloper dishing unwanted remarks or eye-rolling suggestions. I still need to have a word with Alec about this sudden engagement. Get a pulse check. Kneeling down on one knee to profess his fake love, following a life-altering question. I hate being in the dark. What does Alec have planned?

The bathroom counter was spotless and wiped down, with all the unused products placed below the sink, like leaving a vacation summer house when the first leaf fell. The rest of the condo looks the same. All the tubs and boxes are in transit to Lower Manhattan, with one stop in Tribeca for me and somewhere in the Financial District for Alec and Emma.

The shipping company estimates a Monday noon arrival time with a two-hour unpacking window. I don't understand how moving my six boxes up a freight elevator could take two hours, but as long as I am not doing it, take however long you need. We kept a small suitcase with a few outfit choices, enough to last us the weekend.

Five days have passed without a single call or email from John. Not a single text, voicemail, or out-of-office autoreply. On all accounts, he was ignoring my two calls a day and follow-up email chasers. I'm attributing his silence as retribution for quitting KS. The only punishment he can inflict on me, his cold shoulder approach. The unanswered question by the media about my potential involvement bestowed John with another punishment device. A more painful crack, leaving welts and swelling red splotches. Skin to skin. The power to leave a permanent mark slashed across my face. I must remove his ability to inflict such pain, to forever tarnish my appearance and reputation. This motherfucker will not derail all the hard work we have put in. The meticulous planning, conniving, and sacrifices will not be for nothing.

"I wonder who went in my place?" I said, tugging on my dark purple button-up sleeve, then readjusting my tux, followed by a tightening of my charcoal silk tie and a brush down both arms.

"What are you going to say to him?"

"Do you think I should call him one last time?" I grinned at Alec through the mirror as he swung between the doorways. "Eleventh times the charm?"

"Eleventh-hour appeal?"

"I'm not sure what I'm going to say. All I know is that I'm going to play him like a fiddle."

"Once we get a lay of the land, just tell me where to go and when and I can be close by," Alec said. "We need to make sure we leave by nine. Nine-thirty at the latest to make our flight. Please tell me you already checked in?"

"I'll keep track of the time. Please tell me your family is aware of our arrival and the importance of the meeting?"

"They are aware," Alec said as a lingering vibration echoed. "Speak of the devil, Dawn is calling." Alec placed the incoming call on speaker. "Please tell me you have good news?"

"From what I can tell, the entire family is coming to the meeting tomorrow."

"Do they know what it's about?"

"I don't think so. Scott thinks you're going to pitch to take some management position. Probably worried you're after his seat."

"Well, he's half right."

"Are you already in Iowa?" Dawn asked.

"No, we're still in Arizona. Gotta lay one final nail in this KS coffin, then we'll be on our way. Our flight is tonight."

"Safe travels and I'll see you tomorrow." Alec ended the call and looked over at me.

"I hate this small side shit," I said.

"Me too, Theodore. Me too."

"Do you mind if I use your cologne?" I asked, admiring his small collection peeking from his toiletry bag.

"Use the Aventus by Creed!" Alec said from down the hall. "Also, I ordered us a Lyft."

THE LINE TO THE DROP-OFF AREA INCHED CLOSER AND closer, and with each gas, brake, gas, my palms grew more and more clammy. I did not plan for a contingency if John shuts me out, because there was no room for a backup plan, only plan A. Putting all my teal, robin eggs into one basket and watching that basket. Shoveling my energy into resolving this tonight. Unearth the truth with no loose ends or gaps in the fabric. A jolt of reality, a snapping back to the present thanks to Alec's hand squeezing mine as our car made its last stop.

"Are you ready?" Alec said.

"Let's fucking do this."

A young blonde wearing a cheap cotton tee with the word "VOLUNTEER" steam pressed across the front strapped our passes across our wrists, and pointed to the the place to stand for a photo-op in front of a massive backdrop of repeating gold equal signs inside blue squares. The infamous logo for the Human Rights Campaign and the popular equality bumper stickers. They ushered Alec and me onto a blue velvet rug, hovering over an X, marking the spot following a big bang. The blinding fireworks are humpback cameramen, raising one hand to get our attention, following a flash. Then another, and one more.

The Phoenician had a copious flamboyant discharge, like rainbow PlayDough oozing through star and heart shape doorways with glitter replacing dust, collecting in dark crevices or a top life-size lion statues. We entered the primary ballroom swimming among dozens and dozens of high-profile politicians, socialites, activists, fortune five hundred executives, C and B list celebrities, and mid-level influencers. All here with an agenda, highlighting nuanced legislation, impressing the community through monetary generosity, or posting thirty-second snippets with #HRCGala. Whatever the reason, people were here to talk and make things known. The second noticeable thing, how could they make chandeliers so extensive? The unimaginable cuts and logistics of assembling such a vast decorative light fixture seem almost limited? The ceiling could come crashing down by the sheer weight of the six dangling cubic zirconia galaxies, and no one seemed to talk about them.

Alec and I made our way from art to art piece, entertaining us with their abstract color pallet and radical political statements. I stood enthralled at the artists' ability to engage the audience and make them stop, ponder, contemplate, and question. To tantalize emotions of sorrow or satisfaction. Delight or displeasure.

"I want to bid on this," I said, walking up to the auction clipboard.

"What is it?"

"I'm not sure. But I like the way it makes me feel." I scanned the bid sheet and added fifty dollars. "I'm now the highest bidder at four hundred." I took a step back, reanalyzing how the artist made color variations out of black and gray. All the diverse ways to describe power and what it represents.

"I'm going to find our table and get a drink," Alec said. "And remember, nine-thirty at the latest." I gave Alec a nod while continuing to appreciate my surroundings when a tap on my shoulder caught me by surprise.

"Ted?" the familiar softening tone said. I turned to see Gabbie McClintock in black kitten heels, complimenting a carmine off-the-shoulder with a lumpy bow on her hip. A bouffant she hadn't worn since her high school prom days; that's assuming she even went.

"Gabbie! What a wonderful surprise! How are you?"

Gabbie giggles before replying, "I'm doing great, and this is a fun surprise seeing you. I didn't think I would see you again after Alan told us in our LGBT meeting that you left the firm."

"Oh, you know, off to bigger and better things. How are things going with you?"

"Great. I'm on track to get promoted to VP at the end of the year."

"Well, it's about time. Are you still in operations?"

"Yep, and with this new promotion, I'll be the team lead. Which sounds a little scary, to be honest."

"You will crush this new role. I guarantee it." I've always thought Gabbie was too good to be working within the firm's operations division. Processing documents and resolving breaks because asshole advisors like me sold shares without going through proper steps beforehand. She was smart but not pretentious, and her homely demeanor makes her a suitable candidate for a client-facing role. Calm, cool, and collected. If someone gave me bad news, I'd want Gabbie to do so. "Are you here with anyone?"

"Yes, I came with John Barrett. I guess the firm had two seats, and Alan asked me a few days ago to attend. It's John Barrett. I couldn't say no." Gabbie giggles and displays her domestic smile.

"You can never say no to John. Where is he, by the way? I'd love to chat with him."

"Ummm." Gabbie scanned the room. "I'm not sure, but when I see him, I'll let him know you're looking for him."

"That would be wonderful!"

I floated around and drifted away from the gala. Searching, searching, searching for the spot. Far enough away for privacy, but not too far that sparked concern.

"I found the perfect spot. Past the silent auction room and down a marble hallway, there is a small conference room," I said, sliding into my chair next to Alec. He turned and looked, imagining in his head the path I drew up.

"Did you see the name that is on the table? Was that your doing?" Alec asked, following his signature half-grin.

"Where?" I scan through the togetherness of the table. A film set touch of perfection with each plate, silverware, water glass orbiting a blue cylinder centerpiece, and between two sets of china, on a small white card read, *SULLIVAN YOUNG*. I smiled at the realness of those words.

"I need to find Ed Harmon and thank him for squeezing us a table last minute. I'll send you a text if things move quickly." My eyes shift from left to right and back as I scanned the room for Ed. And there, shuffling into the silent auction room with two other gentlemen.

"Found him. I'll be right back." I got up and bolted in his direction.

"Ed Harmon, you look so dashing in your tux."

"Ted, so glad you could make it. And, thank you, it's an old one that still fits."

"Glad to see you're feeling better."

"I'm a new man. Are you enjoying yourself? Have you admired the art up for auction?"

"Yep, I placed a bid on one; fingers crossed, I don't get outbid. I should check to see if anyone else threw down some extra cash to outbid me. But, first, I wanted to say thank you for finding us a table last minute."

"You don't need to thank me. I was more than happy to make a quick phone call."

"We appreciate it."

"What I appreciate is you informing me about this environmental investment opportunity. I understand you're off to forge your own path and do what makes you feel complete, but I will sure miss having you as my wealth advisor."

"My partner and I are very excited to begin this next chapter. We've been working very hard at it, and I can guarantee this investment will be worth it. This side of finance is a little out of my wheelhouse, but my partner is very knowledgeable about finding the right companies that need fixing. My expertise is more finding the right people to get on board, like yourself," I said when I saw John at a booth chatting with a few people. "I know you will be taken care of at KS, even with my departure. Reid is an excellent advisor, and who knows, maybe if we offer wealth management services, I can be your advisor again."

"I would love that."

"Let me introduce you to someone. John Barrett is the managing director of the Private Wealth Division at KS. He's the guy who will make whatever you want come true." The stars align at the right moment. Now John can't dismiss me or make some off-color comment about quitting in front of a KS client. One of his clients. He must remain cordial and professional.

"John Barrett, what a pleasure," I said as he turned around, his face running sour at the sight of me; a once joyous bright eye reaction was now met with indignation. "I want to introduce you to Ed Harmon. Ed was my client when I worked on your floor at KS." I made it seem like decades ago. The type of tale your grandparents tell you. Back when I was your age, type story. "Since Ed is still with the firm, I thought it would be good to put a face to a name." Ed and John shook and gave each other a sturdy, nice to meet you, look.

"It's very nice to meet you, Ed."

"Oh, likewise, likewise." I could sense Ed was gearing up for one of his long-winded stories. "You know, I've been a KS client for several years, but only until back in, I don't know, March? Ted became my advisor. He really did a fantastic job. Way better than my previous advisor." John's appearance remained forced. Clear strings used to stretch a smile and widen his eyes to fully engage with Ed. The room emptied; one by one, black tuxes and formal gowns found their seats following a few taps on the microphone. Ed turned his head.

"Well, looks like we better find our seats. The show is about to begin." He turned back and re-thanked the pleasure of meeting John and my generosity. I pulled out my phone and sent Alec a ready text.

John turned away, walking toward the French doors leading to the ballroom, when I tapped him on the shoulder.

"John...please?" I could tell he enjoyed having this power over me, this hierarchy pyramid where he was at the top, like at KS, where he looked down at me as I begged for his attention. "It will only take five minutes. Please."

"Fine, five minutes. Then I need to return to my seat."

"Thank you." I walked down the cold stone hallway, signaling John to follow. A quick tilt of my head, "So we have some privacy." John exhaled with a fit of pique and followed behind me. I got to the entrance of the empty conference room and spun around.

"What is it, Ted? What do you want? Is this about Felix?"

"John? Stop it. Why are you acting like this?"

"Like what?"

"You know what you're doing. Why? We had such a great time at Giovanni's, and you showed me around your house."

"I prefer people who are loyal," John said. "You weren't loyal. So don't be surprised by the outcome."

"So, this has something to do with me quitting KS."

"Like I said, you weren't loyal, so why should I be?"

"But I still want to be loyal to you. Me quitting has nothing to do with what we have. I'm more flexible now... I left to distance you from what I'm craving."

"And what are you craving, Ted?"

"What I've been trying to ask is if Miami is still on the table? Giovanni's next party. If so, I would love to join you."

"Well, that depends."

"On?"

Suddenly, two young hotel caters came bustling by, laughing with each other while carrying silver drink trays with white aprons tied around cheap cottony black button-ups. John and I froze our conversation as we waited for them to fade into the distance.

"Depends on what?"

"If you're going to be a naughty boy in Miami."

"Well...only with your permission." I scan my surroundings and take one step closer to him. "You know. I was a naughty boy at

Giovanni's that night." John tilted his head upward as though a flow of blood rushed from his head down to his groin. Leaving him dizzy and throbbing.

"You were?"

"He was so rough, but I liked it." I smirk. "I didn't think I would like it. He was powerful. Forceful, and around your age." John bit his lower lip, leaving it glossy and slippery. "I want to be a naughty boy in Miami, but only with your permission."

"Good answer. I'll send you more information when the date gets closer," John said, tapping my right shoulder, following a wink. He halfway spun around when I realigned his attention.

"Now... about Felix."

"What about him?"

"Why haven't you offered a statement saying I had nothing to do with his scheme? Why is that one question still being dragged out?"

"Because Ted, the firm doesn't know for sure...I know you weren't involved, but the firm doesn't. That is until Miami happens. If you can show me what true loyalty looks like then I will issue a statement."

"You promise?"

"I've always kept my promises," John said, turning around to head back to the ballroom when Alec walked out of the empty conference room. He held his phone up toward the ceiling, capturing the upscale bulbs and gaudy finishes. Custom Victorian-style molding on every crack, corner, and baseboard.

"Oh, I'm so sorry, John. I should watch where I'm going," Alec said.

"It's fine."

"John, meet Alec Young."

A soft rumble of applause made its way to us. "I should get back; I can hear they are starting the guest speeches."

"I love how The Phoenician granted all video recording access to social media influencers for this gala. Being on private property and all, they have a say," I said.

"Goodbye, Ted."

"Because I was taking a video of this beautiful gala to show my followers when I caught some background noise. Let's replay it to make sure," Alec said, turning his speaker on full blast.

*"I know you weren't involved, but the firm doesn't. That is until Miami happens."*

"Interesting. That is your voice, right?" Alec scratches his chin stubble.

"John, you're going to pull out your phone right now and send a concise, straightforward email to Catherine McKay, absolving me from having any knowledge of this money laundering scheme. And, before you can say, or what? Which I think you already know. But, just to make it crystal clear. You have ten seconds to send Catherine that email or the *Arizona Tribute* will receive the video clip Alec took instead. I can see the breaking news headline now. Managing Director at Kauffman Schwartz knowingly withheld—"

John cut me off. "Nice try, Ted. I'm not sending Catherine any emails. We need to let the authorities continue their investigation. Have a goodnight."

I nodded at Alec, following a half grin. "You're right. The authorities do need to finish their investigation." Alec handed me his phone, and playing was the video clip of John fucking Chaz. The sound was on full blast—the climax scene. "I wonder which they and the public will find more intriguing? Again, I'll count to ten."

Grunting and heavy breathing seeped out of the phone speakers tangled with squeals from Chaz begging for more. "This ass is yours, daddy!"

The blood from John's face vanished. His lower lip throbbed in fear, and his left eye twitched regretfully.

"How did you? You're bluffing," John said.

"*Nein*," I replied.

"Plus, I don't respond to blackmail. This is a felony."

"*Eight*."

"Like you bartering Miami with absolving Ted in an open federal investigation," Alec said.

"*Seven*."

"Your wife's name is Melissa Barrett, correct? Email Melissa dot Barett at—"

"Stop," John ordered.

"I can CC her on the email to the AZ tribute," Alec said.

"*Six.*"

"Your eldest daughter, Shannon Barrett, email—" Alec said when John cut him off.

"Okay, okay. Fucking enough. I'll send Catherine the email."

"Your phone still isn't out," Alec said.

"*Five.*"

"Wait! Fuck. There, there. See. Catherine, I am absolving Ted in knowing any part of the money-laundering scheme with our former client, Felix Hernandez... Happy?"

"Press send," Alec said.

"*Four.*"

"I pressed send!"

"Show us your outbox," Alec said.

"Are you serious?"

"*Three.*"

"Okay, Okay. Here, see, it's there."

"Good, now fuck off," Alec said, then slowly looking at me as John stormed off, shaking his head with clenched fists.

"Now we wait; once the headline is posted, this will all be behind us," I said, looking at Alec. I could tell he was flustered. Hearing those details about me fucking some fictional older man did not sit right with him, as it shouldn't. He let out a gentle exhale of relief. "I'm going to call Emma; she called twice."

"Okay, I'll meet you back at our table? We can have dinner, then head to the airport."

"Sounds good to me."

# 22

Alec Young

Alec sat motionless on the drive to the airport. He walked the entire distance with his lungs squeezed, as if bands were tightening around his chest. Alec felt he was to blame for letting the stillness envelop them, with each passing minute making it more impossible to talk or check in on how the other was feeling. Because their flight was delayed yet another time, they were even more irritated by the TSA pre-check process. Alec and Ted were relaxing in The Centurion Lounge, people-watching and enjoying the free food, when Ted broke the silence.

"Alec?"

"A part of me knows you were making up that story for John, but the other part. An encounter. A misstep John took towards you."

"Yes, the stories I told John were lies, but I knew they would work. He came on to me and offered the trip to Miami."

"What kind of encounter?"

"We had a catch-up on the Felix's situation at a coffee shop, and afterward, he placed his hand on my thigh under the table."

"Why didn't you tell me?"

"You and Emma were in Boston. I didn't want to worry you or get you distracted and have it fuck up the meeting somehow."

"You should have told me."

"Like you telling me about the engagement? Communication goes both ways, Alec. Why did you get engaged?"

"I did it for the five mil investment. I did it for us. To get our company off the ground."

"We could have thought of other ways."

"Since we're laying all the cards on the table, I need to tell you something. It's about Emma. She's known about the plan for a while."

"You told me she brought it up to her dad when you both went to Boston. The five million looked great, so you picked her brain on the topic."

"She found out the night after we were at the UNICEF gala."

"She has known since then?"

"I wanted to tell you that night. I was going to tell you. But after seeing you stressed with work and studying, I didn't want to add any more pressure. I told myself I would figure it out."

"Sounds like you dug a deeper grave. What does Emma know and think she knows?"

"She thinks it's our idea. Our company. Mine and hers. A private equity firm. Bring you onboard to attract clients and investors with your private wealth background. Since she told me she could get an investment from Roger, I did everything to ensure the investment. Keep everything under wraps and commit. I always kept her thinking it was our idea."

"I need a moment." Ted shoved upright. He took off his glasses and squeezed the bridge of his nose. Applying more and more pressure as his eyelids pinched tight. "We could have found another investment. One that didn't involve you adopting a puppy."

"When you think about it, Emma's connections and the five million are getting us off the ground. It's a worthy investment."

"Is the engagement also a worthy investment?"

"I'm sorry."

"Don't apologize, just tell me what you were thinking. What is the plan? When you don't involve me, we can't coordinate. Our entire system is in freefall."

"I wasn't expecting engagement. I mean, I posted the scenario in my head, like I do all scenarios, but I never thought it would be." Alec scratched his stubble. "I think Emma may have talked to her dad behind closed doors. Roger kept saying how excited he was to see his daughter follow in his footsteps of creating their own company. And I quote, '*the entrepreneurial blood is strong*.' If we want his support and investment, her name has to be on the wall. And so, to get the investment, I proposed. They cornered me into making the proposal. Roger took her fucking grandma's ring out of the vault and put it in his desk."

"If you didn't like the deal, you didn't have to take it. We would have found a different way to start our company. We didn't need Roger's quid pro quo. Fuck that."

"But it was right there, at my fingertips. And time is ticking, with my dad still being in the coma. We needed to act now and come up with a solution afterward."

"Call the engagement off?"

"That is the plan, but not right away. Roger is our sole investor, so we would first need to pay back his investment with interest. Only then would he not have control over us. Control over our company."

"Does Emma not care how weird that is? The proposal is based on an ultimatum her father gave you. '*Marry my daughter, or you won't get the investment?*' Does she not care that it wasn't something you did on your own?"

"Emma's complicated and very ambitious. And, like I said, she put the bug in her dad's ear. It was a turn-on for her. A way for her to maintain control."

Both of their phones lit up with an update from the airline. The flight was delayed an additional hour. Alec stood up. "Better get comfortable. A fucking additional hour delay, Jesus. I'm going to get a beer."

Alec shifted in his seat, reaching up to regulate airflow against his face. A soothing flow cooled his feverish cheeks and relaxed the frazzled nerves. He leaned over to see Ted, reclining against the window, neck wrapped in a pillow. Alec closed his eyes, but they didn't stay closed for long as the anticipation of being close to the Young estate fluttered his lids. Memories crept into this skull like a drop of water on a paper towel, dragging fresh memory molecules, spreading remembrances of the past in a wet puddle.

"Alec, I want to start by noting how smart you are, and you to understand I know how much pain you've been in. You're not a bad person. Your parents love you. Your sister loves you. You're not a bad person. No one is born *bad*, no one is born gay," the man said as he sandwiched a bible between his hands. "Tell me you understand you're not bad. Repeat after me. I am not *bad*."

"I'm..."

"You can do it. I know you're not *bad*. Your mom knows you're not *bad*. Your dad knows you're not *bad*. Your sister knows you're not *bad*. I need you to know you're not *bad*."

"I'm..." Alec's gaze flitted around the man's office like a forlorn bird, passing a stack of religious nonfiction paperbacks alphabetically arranged beneath scenic portraits of Iowa in autumn. The yellows and reds glistened because of the glossy laminate surface and reflections from the anesthetized fluorescent bulbs above. The man held up the Bible so the title would be at the center of Alec's binocular vision.

"Jesus wants to help you. Jesus knows you're not *bad*. But he knows the hurt you caused your parents, and the hurt you caused him." The man handed Alec the Bible. "Flip to Romans one twenty-seven. Read it out loud for me."

Alec flipped through the Bible. His tongue swelled and words queued up in his throat.

"You can do it. It's even bookmarked for ya. Romans one twenty-seven."

"Can I go home? I want to go home."

"You can't go home just yet, Alec. We have to finish our meeting. Don't you want to make your parents, myself, and Jesus proud? You can do it. Come on."

Alec's mind rumbles like an intellectual shield of armor. A wit-pointed dagger welded to a clever rod. He blew a laugh from his nose as he fought his muscles to not hoist a smile.

"What are you thinking, Alec?"

"Ransom." The Bible lies unopened on his lap.

"I'm sorry?"

"Ransom is an anagram of Romans. Thought it was funny since I can't go home."

A fresh piece of pink skin. Alec's scab hums red with laughter. The surrounding skin was puckered and hidden by shaggy combed hair. It itched with every pulse. Forever covering its story of shame and heartbreak. Alec didn't want people asking how he got the wound in social gatherings, whether on the playground, by the lockers, lecture halls, or team meetings. Instead of serial lying, he would keep it covered. Forever keeping a business-oriented shag appearance, enough to never remind Alec. Remind him of the day when it happened, the moments before and the pain after. Watching the eyes of the one person whose sole responsibility was to love and cherish turned filicide black.

# 23

Ted Sullivan

I woke up to daylight shining through three large windows with stained glass rectangles bordering the outer edges, comprising blue and green hues. The sheets and pillows surrounding the bed emitted a refreshing scent of cotton. I tapped the top of my phone to check the time when I saw the news notification plastered across my screen: *Kauffman Confirms Wealth Advisor Not Involved in Money Laundering.*

I inhaled, savoring satisfaction and exhaling peace. I sat up and scanned the article, then admired Alec's bedroom. Though he had twice my bedroom space, only a few traces of him remained, as though they wiped it clean when he left for college. Two traces of his existence remained: a lacrosse stick leaned against the corner and a chess game set up on his oak wood dresser. They inscribed his first name in white pieces; his last name in black. I looked into one drawer, hoping it might contain some insight into Alec's past, but there was only polo socks and underwear in their transparent packaging, sealed shut.

We arrived at a silent sleeping mansion at 3 a.m. Alec took one of the guest rooms down the hall and had me get cozy in his room—or what they left of it. I tiptoed down the hall in my gray sweats and gave the door two gentle knocks, but no response. I opened the door to find the room empty, the bed perfectly made with Alec's travel bag napping on the edge.

I walked to the window and admired the view of their private lake from the second story. The lawn was cut; the trimmed hedges trailing a paved walkway to the dock, where I saw Alec drinking coffee while watching the sunrise. It was one of the most scenic views I'd seen in a while.

I threw on my shoes and tiptoed down the stairs, passing three living rooms, a study, and a washroom with two commercial-size washers and dryers. I opened the back door and became overwhelmed by the surrounding color. Seasons have their own color, a unique pallet of painted leaves and subtle hazy fog. Transitions from plush greens to rustic reds, then building piles and piles on the ground of dead yellows and withering browns. The air tasted sharp, a noticeable difference from Arizona. As I got closer and closer to the dock, I noticed Alec was still wearing his tux, still in his black leather dress shoes, and his bowtie still knotted and centered.

"The color is beautiful here," I said.

"Autumn is about the only beautiful thing here, and it only lasts a few weeks. Beauty, beauty, beauty. I miss it."

"Have you slept at all?"

"I dozed off a little on the plane, but no." Alec took a sip from his mug. "There is coffee inside; I made some not too long ago." Alec handed me his cup. The aroma woke my nose, eyes, and ears. I took a sip, waking my throat, stomach, and body.

"Is everything okay? You seem I don't know... distracted?"

"I'm okay, but I am a little distracted," Alec said. "I haven't been home in a while, and we have a lot at stake."

"I thought you and Emma came to visit when your dad went back to the hospital?"

"We traveled from the airport to the hospital, then to Dawn's, then back to the airport."

"The meeting with your family is at noon?"

"Yeah. I haven't seen or talked to a lot of my relatives, and now I'm going to ask them to sell us the family company."

"You said they have been hurting for years. I can only imagine the stress. You would think the thought of not having to deal with it anymore, plus a great payout would thrill them."

"You would think, but for some, it's a pride thing. They deeply wove their egos to Young Industrials fabric, so it's going to be interesting hearing what they have to say."

"And who are they?"

"Seven of us have voting power. My father and mother. Myself and my sister, and both of my dad's brothers."

"The twins?"

"And my aunt."

"Spencer lives in Wyoming and Scott will never leave Iowa. My aunt still lives within driving distance. But aside from her, I haven't talked to them in a very long time."

"How does the voting work? Do we just need a majority for the sell to pass?"

"Yeah, we need a four to three-vote count. Each person has one vote, but with my dad in his coma, my mother then has double voting power to vote on his behalf."

A dozen men in white polos began marching onto the back lawn, each holding steel poles, bricks, yards of rope, and folded white tent fabric that looked more durable than most houses in Okie.

"That must be Mother's doing," Alec said.

"What are they building?"

"More than likely the tent for lunch."

Two white catering vans pulled around back, and a few men unloaded boxes of food while a few others took each inside one by one. With one arm pointing inside the house, holding a coffee cup in the other, stood Alec's mother. Short hair curled and forked out with hair spray, molding it into shape. A blonde mound nested in her head. Her high-waisted violet dress spoke volumes with visibly textured material. A true country queen. She spun toward the lake and gave Alec and me a wave, following one last point toward the house directing traffic, then she began walking toward us. Collaborating with each worker, she passed, dishing orders and expectations. Keeping a tight organized setting while smiling big, following each command. How was she not freezing? Little blurry details came into focus as she inched closer and closer. The weight of her pearl earrings tugging at her earlobes matched the double-wrapped pearl necklace. Popping against the contrast of the violet. Her height grew taller and taller until she stood just shy of eye level with me.

"Oh dear, it's so great to see you. When did you get in? I didn't hear a thing," she said, kissing Alec on the cheek.

"We got in super early this morning," Alec said.

"Do you need anything pressed? Everyone is here. We can arrange it. Did you eat breakfast? I can have them whip up something quick."

"No thanks, Mom." Alec looked at me. "Theodore, are you hungry?" Then looked at his mother. "Mom, this is my business partner, Ted Sullivan." I smiled while extending my hand, and she grabbed it tighter than I expected.

"A pleasure to meet you, Ted. I'm Ruth." Her eyes dart at mine, following two quick blinks and a whiff of number five.

"You have a lovely home."

"We've lived here for twenty-two years." Ruth turns to face her massive estate, then back toward us. "Moved in when Alec was around... How old were you?"

"We moved in when I turned seven, remember? The first event you hosted was my seventh birthday party."

"Oh, that is right, and your sister was learning to walk," Ruth said. "Oh, Theodore, you should have seen her falling left and right all over the place, and Alec would get so concerned."

"Being a great older brother," I said.

"When does Alice fly in? Is she coming?"

"Where is your fiancé?" Ruth asked. "Ted, do you know I wasn't even aware Alec got engaged? It wasn't until sweet Emma called to tell us the great news."

"Emma is with her parents in Boston and getting our New York apartment set up." Alec's mind stuttered. Emma's a bitter person, and she's shown it to Alec over and over again. How cunning she can be when she's bored and he can't watch her.

"Send her my love. We miss those red cheeks of hers."

"Do you know if anyone else is coming down for the meeting?" Alec asked.

"Yes, people are coming down for this mysterious meeting you called," Ruth said, then took a sip of her coffee. "Honestly, Alec. People talk, and I know what you're going to ask the family. Just know, I can't support it. I'm sorry, but I can't. I can't make this decision while your father is in a coma at the University of Iowa Hospital." She pinched the bridge of her nose.

"When did he leave MercyOne?"

"If you ever called, you would know we moved him last week to Iowa City. We want the best people on this, and the University hospital is a research facility. We want all the best research done."

"I'm sure MercyOne has adequate doctors," Alec said as a lady tried to insert herself into the conversation. She appeared to work with the catering staff. Hair in a bun with a clipboard pressed against her spotless white apron.

"Mrs. Young?" The lady said, clearing her throat then swallowing. "I'm sorry to interrupt, but we have a slight issue with today's menu order."

"I'm sorry, I have to attend." Ruth began until Alec interrupted.

"Yes, figure out what's going on. We'll see you soon."

"Theodore, it was great meeting you." Ruth sent a wave, then began walking toward the house while the lady pointed to items on the clipboard.

"They sent us the wrong type of cheese for the grilled sandwiches," The lady whispered as Ruth shook her head.

"She seems... very forward," I said as Alec and I turned to face the lake.

"Everyone already knows and colluded to reject the offer," Alec said. "*Fuck*. I don't like this. This is not good. Who told her?"

"We don't know what the others think. Let's not reserve our grave lots just yet."

Alec and I walked inside, trailing a caterer, who took a sharp left turn toward the grand kitchen. I took a quick peek at the commercial-sized stainless-steel oven with each burner housing deep and shallow copper pots with dozens of other colorful pots dangling above his and her marble-topped islands. The kitchen looks double the size of my entire apartment back in Scottsdale. They sprawled and categorized veggies, dairy, meats, and fruit.

"If it isn't my first nephew here to take the keys to the castle," a man said, wheeling a leather suitcase while sporting a brimmed outdoor hat and phone holstered to his belt. "Are you still trying to kiss boys on the playground?" The man laughed while removing his hat and sunglasses. "I'm joshing. Come, give me a hug. You've gotten tall. Why are you wearing a tux?"

"Out of all my dad's siblings, you're the most I'm excited to see, Spencer," Alec said.

"We both know that's a bunch of horseshit. How long are you in town? Are you going hunting with us tomorrow?"

"I was only planning on staying for the meeting," Alec said. "By the way, this is my business partner, Ted Sullivan."

We shook hands. For a hunting man, his hands felt moisturized and uncalloused.

"Ted, what a pleasure. Can I call you, T?"

"Umm, sure. It's great to meet you. Alec tells me you live in Wyoming?"

"'Till the day I die. I snagged this ranch out with picture perfect shots of the Grand Tetons. I about cried myself to sleep when I got word about this mystery meeting back at the historic Young Estate," Spencer laughed. "I'll tell ya, this going back and forth between time zones will kill you faster than any chemtrail or asbestos outbreak ever could."

"It's an hour time difference," Alec said as a caterer holding an empty tray squeezed by. Spencer's ears perk up.

"Miss? Hi, hello! Can I get a Hot Toddy? I gotta warm up."

"Spence, I don't think that's what they are here for," Alec said.

"I gotta tell ya, your mom is pulling no punches on this lunch. It's almost like the last supper if you think about it," Spencer laughed.

"Uncle Spencer!" Two young kids ran up and threw their arms around his legs. Both are blonde, wearing blue and red puffy jackets. Spencer picked up the young girl, around four or five.

"Do you miss Florida?" Spencer said. "Do you remember uncle Alec?"

Both kids froze, staring at Alec and me.

"Katie, you don't remember me?" Alec said in a lofty tone. She put her fingers in her mouth and made no eye contact.

"And that's because uncle Alec is never around," Spencer sang while bouncing Katie in his arms.

"What is with all of those vans parked out front?" A voice said from down the hall. "I see the kids found you. I still don't know why you're their favorite."

"Dawn, this is my business partner, Ted Sullivan," Alec said.

"Good to meet you, Ted."

"Likewise."

"Dawn is the youngest sibling of my dads."

"Yeah, she's the baby," Spencer said, still bouncing Katie in his arms.

"And they always like to remind me." Dawn rolls her eyes. "Jake, come here so I can finish putting sunscreen on your forehead and ears."

"Sunscreen? It's freezing outside."

"Tell that to Phil's dad, who was diagnosed with melanoma."

"Speaking of Phil, where is your charming husband?" Spencer said.

"Out front chatting with Scott," Dawn said while shaking the lotion bottle.

"Ted and I are going to get ready."

"It was great meeting you both," I said.

"Get ready? You're already in a tux. How formal is this mysterious meeting?" Spencer asked.

"Too formal for Wyoming," Alec joked as we walked up the stairs.

"Scott is the twin to Spencer, right?" I whispered.

"Yeah. He's the hardass conservative who is still working at the company. Right now, he's the interim CEO until they get a good idea of where my dad's health is heading. Goddammit, everyone already knows and has talked about it."

"We won't know their position until the actual meeting. Let's stay focused."

# 24

Alec Young

One by one the family walked into the massive study, each taking a seat in the hide leather chairs tucked in corners and behind window shutters. Round seat pillows on the ledge of the fireplace. Bradley Young was a second amendment collector, hoarding all the arms to bear. Tacked to the wall, organized by size, inside glass cases, and even enough to use as legs for a custom end table. The room, as tasteful as it was, seemed dead and unlived in.

Two catering staff floated around, each balancing a round tray with a mixture of neat and on-the-rocks whiskey. They filled the room with hints of spices and cinnamon. Alec and Ted grabbed on-the-rocks.

Alec's stomach vibrated and rumbled, unsure if it should digest lunch or his anxiety first.

"Whoever thought of combining whiskey with cinnamon should receive an award," Spencer said, raising his glass to the bottom of his nose.

"They did," Dawn said.

"No, I'm talking like every year. Here you go. You automatically win for creating such a wonderful potion."

"Okay, let's FaceTime Alice," Alec said, scrolling through his phone.

"Great idea," Ruth said.

"Hello, everyone," Alice said as Alec propped his phone up behind some books.

"Hi, Sweetie," Dawn said.

"R, why aren't you here?" Spencer shouted from across the room.

"She's in school," Ruth said.

"I have homework and class tomorrow morning."

"Aren't you in college? You don't have to go to class," Spencer said.

"Not the day before an exam."

"Oh, you're going to do just fine. You're a Young, remember," Spencer said.

"You missed a delicious lunch," Dawn said. "Your mom did a great job."

Scott cleared his throat. "I'm sorry, but can we get this over with?"

The room went silent.

"Yes, let's get started. We have a lot to discuss," Alec said as Ted picked through his briefcase and passed around a ten-page presentation.

"Graphs! I love graphs," Spencer said. "This is adorable."

"*Sullivan Young and Company*," Scott said.

Alec took a wide stance, looking at heads bobbing up and down.

"We want to start by saying thank you to everyone for taking the time to meet."

"And why are we meeting?" Spencer winked.

"We first want to highlight Young Industrials' performance over the past few years and compare that with the growth projections for the industry," Alec said. "Now, if you look at exhibit 1-1 and the obvious downward trend while also acknowledging exhibit 1-2."

"Alec. Alec, I'm sorry," Ruth said as she sipped her neat pour then placed it down. "I've already mentioned it, and I don't want you to have to go through this entire thing. Like I told you, I can't support this. Your father will get better. He's a strong man." Ruth waved her hand as if to clear smoke from her face, fighting back the tears. She looked through the window. "I think the bouncy house we ordered for the kids has arrived."

"Mom, please hear us out. Just wait."

"Alec, I'm sorry," Alice said, everyone's heads darted toward the phone. Her live video feed was not in sync with the audio. "I agree with Mom. I don't support the decision to sell. Dad has built this company, and he can turn it around."

Alec and Ted exchanged glances and he gave Ted a nod of approval.

"On page four, you will see our plan to restructure," Ted said.

"We have a plan," Scott interrupted.

"Do you?" Alec asked. "And what is the plan for who will run the company if my dad doesn't make it?"

"Alec, don't say such things," Ruth said.

"What is the plan? People who invested in Young Industrials will want to know. The banks who loaned my dad money will want to know. Or is chapter seven the plan?"

"I will transition from interim CEO to full-time CEO," Scott said, taking a sip.

"So, then yes to chapter eleven," Alec said.

"Oh fuck off," Scott said.

"On page six," Ted said, trying to recenter attention. "You will see our strategy to make Young Industrials competitive again by aligning."

"You have no plan; admit it," Alec said. He was losing composure. His family pinched a nerve by not taking him or Ted seriously. Treating him like a little boy. "You are so against change, and the fact that you actively fight it is very concerning for your stakeholders. You have no innovation and no imagination. It's almost like you want to keep Young Industrials this old dinosaur that continues to tear apart our environment just to keep a pulse."

"Nephew, you know the lib invented global warming too—"

"Fuck off, Spencer," Alec said. "You know it's no hidden secret that out in the field, our combines are the least technologically advanced. At one point, yes, they were dominating the market for their size and extraction levels, but that was it. We did not modify them to meet farmer's demands or needs. You never upgraded your combines or equipped them with smart technology to compete. It takes three men to operate; why?"

Dawn raised a finger. "I agree with Alec. Something has to change. I'm not saying Bradley made some poor business decisions or Scott, you wouldn't do a great job, but we need something to change. I support the sell."

"You've been drinking that left-wing cool-aid little sis," Spencer said. "Listen, we have a story. Young Industrials has die-hard customers who prefer to do things the old fashioned way. You know what they say. If it ain't broke, don't fix it."

"It is broke, and you don't know what you're talking about," Alec said. "This would not be a quick fix overnight solution. I'm talking about long-term changes for issues we will face in the future."

"Sorry, nephew, but I can't support this," Spencer said.

"You already know my stance," Scott said, finishing the rest of his whiskey in one gulp.

"Well, I guess that is that. Ahh, I can see them setting up the bouncy house. The kids are going to love it. Goodbye Alice, we love you, love you, love you."

"Bye, everyone," Alice said. "Sorry, Alec."

"Dawn, can the kids go hunting with us tomorrow?" Spencer asked, pretending his hands were guns.

"Absolutely not," Dawn said, getting up from her chair. The room emptied, and the murmur faded behind the closed French doors. Alec and Ted stood in silence. Alec looked down at his shoes, the edge of the rug, and a dust mote tumbling under an end table. Did they lose? All their planning shot out the window? Countless hours of research and discipline, only to not qualify.

"This is fucked!" Alec said. "The fuck was that? I told you they all had met and discussed."

"They were not taking this seriously. Do they think everything is okay? The data is right here. I noticed Scott didn't even open the presentation. What now?"

"I need a second to think. As of right now, we are still short in funds. So even if they approved the sale, we wouldn't have enough to buy."

"Correct. We only have a few million. What do you think the price tag will go for? Do you know the value of their most recent 409A valuation?"

"My guess is anywhere between one hundred to one hundred fifty million to buy the entire company. Okay, let me think." Alec paced back and forth. "We should divide and conquer. With enough alone time, I can convince Alice and Spencer to sell. My mother is set in her ways, and Scott is suffering from little man's syndrome and will do anything to prove he's valuable."

"Okay, I can continue on as if we got the votes and begin planning the roadshow."

"Our only way is forward. I'll stay here a few days, go hunting with Spencer tomorrow, begin chipping away, then maybe fly back to Wyoming with him. If he's removed from the influence of Scott and my dad, he will cave."

"Start with the weakest link."

"After he agrees, I'll fly to Kentucky to visit Alice. She is a smart girl, but her fault is the constant need for the approval of our parents. Once I talk logic with her and close with, 'even Spencer agrees to sell,' she will cave."

"V.O.U.," Ted said as he kissed Alec on the lips and took an inhale following another kiss. "Let us get to work. We're going to have a busy few weeks ahead of us."

Spencer's Wyoming ranch was small, with no horses or livestock roaming the acres and no four-thousand-square foot mansion like his siblings. The real gems were the extensive network of hiking and jeep paths. Spencer stacked the days by showing Alec his best picturesque courses, accompanied by cheese and wine, to be appreciated once they arrived. A pleasant wide landscape with a powerful river hammering round stones and scraping dirt away from the shoreline.

Spencer led Alec to a few places in Jackson Hole, including their renowned Million Dollar Cowboy bar, where he continued to show Alec his hidden favorite spots like a single child with an overcrowded toy chest, glee-ridden at showing their treasures to a fresh face. Alec got up and flung his leg around the horse's saddle bordering the bar top, thinking about Alice and what he'd say to her next. The world was letting Alec know he was on the correct track. The saddles for seats in the pub he's in with Spencer, whom he's attempting to flip, was a sign. A sign he's on the right path. Alec laughed at his creativity as Spencer ordered them another round. The youngest found his nest in the world and did his own thing with occasional Young Industrial meetings. Alec felt a faint resemblance to Spencer, a similarity of not being inside the Young bubble, but being inside their own bubble that caught an upward draft, drifting it away from the other bubbles.

The attention to detail crawling up the mountains and down to the base, where a small shipping village looked hard at work, loading and unloading cylinder logs on the bed of several freight trains. Alec squatted down and hovered his face toward the tiny buildings, insides lit with a single LED bulb, the size you see wrapped around Christmas trees or those strands of accent lighting used to outline the ceiling in a bedroom, stuffed into a glass bottle for presentation, or brighten up a fish tank.

Since he was a boy, Spencer's guilty pleasure was trains: the history, their purpose commercially and economically, and how the transcontinental line transformed America and became the backbone of industrialization. The passenger and freight, diesel and coal, all tickled his insides like the rattling of rail tracks from a barreling metal snake. Spencer spent years building his train diorama. Painting, connecting, snipping, cutting, and gluing every piece. He even went as far as cutting a small hole in the wall, no bigger than a standard doggie door to connect two rooms, two cities, to the world he built in his mind.

"Spencer, I have to say, I'm impressed," Alec said, spotting deer and camping travelers hidden in the mountains. "Are those wolves eating a rabbit?"

"You betcha. And if you come over here, you can see a black bear and buck fighting."

"You thought of everything. Why is this the first time I'm seeing this?"

"Eh, I don't publicize. Your dad and Scott would think it's childish, plus you haven't come to visit nephew."

"Did you come up with the company names on the trains?" Alec said.

"No, Meek and Co. are one of the oldest freight companies. Boomed during the industrial revolution and both world wars, then nearly collapsed thereafter."

"Nearly?"

"They came back," Spencer said. "Not to the same success pre-war, but they came back. It should stand as a testament to resiliency if you just hang on and ride out the storm."

Alec stood up and said, "I take it you're referring to Young Industrials?"

"I don't know, nephew. The company has had turbulence before."

"Not like this."

"And we've always bounced back. Your dad knows what he is doing. Can I say some real shit?"

"Sure."

"I've not always agreed with what your dad does. And to be frank. I think it was fucked up to have you go through conversion therapy with that pastor when you were how old? Eleven? Twelve?"

"Ten."

"Ah, yes, Ten. I think their handling of it was shit and became dramatic, most of that I think was your mom's doing, but that's for another time. But I think your dad knows what he is doing regarding the business."

"Maybe, but that is another story. Our current trajectory is Scott taking over. Fucking Scott. You and I both know he doesn't have what it takes to turn the ship, which is heading straight for an iceberg."

Spencer picked up a half-painted diesel train to distract his anxious mind. "And you have what it takes?"

"Yes, Spencer I do. I believe my team has what it takes to repair the tracks before the train comes. Once Scott defaults on the first debt payment, the banks are going to raise eyebrows. I'm assuming they aren't aware of my dad's health. And the debt payment will continue to go unpaid, the banks will get spooked, forcing us into chapter seven and you will lose everything. The banks will sell all of Young Industrials' assets so they can pay themselves back. It's all about money. All the banks care about is making a bit more money on the dollar they loaned my dad, and someone has to pay."

"I need a cigarette," Spencer said, scratching his eyebrow.

"We want to pay. Sullivan Young wants to pay so everyone can continue life, unchanged. We have the capital. We have the resources."

Spencer opened his desk drawer, then another, as he balanced the menthol between his lips, "I'm looking for a lighter."

Alec peered down at the edge of the table to a box of half-melted crayons Spencer must have used for some decorative effect, picked up a Bic, and walked toward Spencer, igniting the flame and hovering it in front of Spencer, who sucked in air.

"Let Sullivan Young pay," Alec said. "So you can continue enjoying life."

Spencer turned and blew smoke out a cracked window, took another puff, and said, "okay, nephew. I'll agree to sell."

Alec smiled and said, "Now can you show me these trains in action? Turn this baby on!"

# 25

Ted Sullivan

When I opened the door, fireflies blinked in my stomach as I viewed our New York headquarters for the first time, a faint tingling bliss. Our office was nestled away on the sixth story, facing adjacent buildings and air conditioning machinery bulging from windows. Our gorgeous beige castle hummed off a rather quiet street, tucked between a three-star Italian restaurant and a three-story CVS.

"Well, good morning, good morning!" Dana said, popping up from behind a pile of discarded computer and printer boxes. "It's so good to see you in person again."

"You do not know how great it is to see you." We wrapped our arms and stood in each other's embrace. The calming energy of seeing a familiar face.

"Did you get in last night?"

"I did. Using my remaining intellectual stamina, I got myself to my apartment."

"Please tell me everything was there?"

"It was, it was. But my mattress and couch I ordered have yet to arrive, so I slept on the floor." I wrinkled my nose and rubbed my left shoulder. "I'm a little sore, but I was so tired I collapsed."

"Jesus, Ted," Dana said. "Can we get this man a blowup mattress at least?" Dana looked around the room as if to be speaking to an audience by raising her hands.

The space is bigger than I'd imagined," I said, admiring the industrial vibe of the room. Visible ceiling beams and metal air vents.

"Right? We got all the computer stuff and a few chairs yesterday that I began assembling, and today we should receive the remaining chairs, all the desks, and other small electronics."

"Wonderful, thank you so much. And what about you? How are you enjoying this new city life?"

"I. Am. In love. No, honestly." Dana put her hair in a ponytail to hold back her excitement. "I found this super cute townhouse in Brooklyn. It's only like a twenty to twenty-five-minute commute to the office. Every morning, I try to leave a little early and try a new breakfast spot or coffee house." Dana laughed at herself. "Gosh, listen to me, coffee house, new breakfast spot."

"That makes me so happy."

"My two roommates are sweet, and we jive so well. I can't wait for you to meet them. One is attending med school; I think she graduates next year? And the oldest roommate, she's lived in the townhouse for a few years; she does digital marketing for Peloton. So cool, right?"

"I knew I wouldn't have to worry about you. You are already making friends and making this city yours. I'm so proud of you."

"I feel rejuvenated. Alive again." Dana showed me the conference room and two private offices. "Also, you will be so proud, but I enrolled in online school!" Dana made a surprised reaction, waiting for me to do the same. My eye widened, and my eyebrows arched.

"This day keeps getting better and better."

"My first round of classes starts in January. I'm so ready for this. I think I'm going to stick with general business then eventually pick a more concentrated path. Yesterday I went and bought a few school supplies with leftover registration money, and I have been reading those books you got me."

"Basic accounting and understanding private equity, I was about to ask." I took a second to admire the realness of this space. Sullivan Young finally had an address. A place to grow roots and build a future. "I would start with the basic accounting. Business has its own language, and accounting is understanding that language." We walked into one of the private offices, one that will be mine or Alec's, or, yes, possibly Emma's. I haven't thought about her in the past 48 hours.

"Has Emma come around?"

"She came once when it was empty. I was measuring the spaces and trying to figure out where things would go. She said little."

"She's back from Boston, so she might come in today."

"Are you planning on staying here all day?" Dana looked excited at the idea.

"How good are you at multitasking?"

"The best."

"Okay, great. When you're not setting stuff up, I'm going to have you book flights for me as the dates come in."

"You got it." Dana scoured the ground, picking up a notebook and pen. I sat in the chair and pulled my laptop from my bag. "Where are you flying to? Also, I was chatting with my parents last night; they say 'hi', by the way. And they asked what type of company you started, and I tried to describe it to them, but the more I described, the more confused I got." Dana scratched the back of her head.

"Totally understandable. When you get to your PE book, it will be a refresher and a deep dive into the nitty-gritty. But, in a nutshell, we are creating a fund. Think of it as an empty swimming pool. We plan what to do with the funds when the swimming pool fills up, so we go on a world tour with the plan. A roadshow of fundraising, sending feeler emails to potential investors. Doing everything we can to fill up that swimming pool to buy our targeted company or companies. After we buy, we restructure, change things. Always with the question in mind of how can we make this company profitable in the coming years?"

"So, right now, you are in the fundraising stage?"

"Correct."

"And when you get the swimming pool filled up, the company you're going to buy is Young Industrials LLC?"

"Correct again. Alec and I were going to do the roadshow together but, we ran into some obstacles."

"What obstacles?"

"Well, word leaked to the family that we want to buy the company, and they got spooked. Alec is spending time with them, trying to persuade. So, in the meantime, I will run around the country looking for investors. And when the time comes for us to buy, we will have the swimming pool filled."

"What if they don't want to sell?"

"They will because there is no alternative. But factoring risk in the real world is that if they don't agree to sell, it's back to the drawing board. Lose months of planning, maybe even a year set back that will be filled with conducting more research, finding the next company to target."

"Plan A can't fail," Dana said. "Or as Greta Thunberg once said, Plan B stands for blah, blah, blah."

"Exactly!"

"How can I help?"

"I'll be scheduling a bunch of meetings all over. As they get confirmed, I'll need you to book flights as well as hotels. Now when I say they could be anywhere, I mean anywhere."

"How did you know that event planning is like my guilty pleasure? I'm going to crush this!"

"That's the spirit!" I remembered my curiosity. "Also." I peek into the front pocket of my bag and pull out a small, insulated bubble wrap pouch, and the words Double Helix splashed across the top. "Can you mail this for me? My courage and curiosity finally reached high enough levels for me to complete the test, but I can't find the *will* to mail it."

"Ted, this is an enormous step!" Dana reached for the wrapped specimen.

"I know. I lost count of how many times I kept going back and forth about what to do. Take the test or don't take the test? What will happen if you do? What will happen if you don't? How would you feel if you did? How will you feel if you don't? Will the results change anything?"

"They'll change nothing. You'll always be my family," Dana said.

"I'll only mail this if it's one hundred percent what you want. And no matter what decision you decide, I'll support you."

"Thank you, Dana. I've sat with the opportunity to peek into my past long enough to weigh all the options. And no matter what those results say, I know who my family is and where they come from."

Dana reached over and squeezed my hand.

"I sometimes get excited. Anticipation with a dash of anxiety."

"I'm going to put money on the results say... Let me think. Somewhere in Europe." Dana laughed. "Were Greeks tan? I'm betting on your ethnicity being in Europe, but I'm curious about the cause of your year-round golden tan. Lucky. Will you call me the second your results come in?"

"You will be the first person I call," I said. "What I'm nervous about is the test will scan for pre-existing conditions."

"Like?"

"Cancer, diabetes, et cetera."

"The fun ones."

"Whatever is flagged, I can get the opinion of a professional."

"You have thought a lot about this. I'd be terrified to know what I'm exposed to."

"Enter the nervous part."

"Just don't let your insurance company get your results." Dana laughed.

One would think, one could assume, if presenting the same presentation, the same spiel monologue on facts and proposals, it would get easier and feel less exposing. I sat with my hands clutching each other while resting on a sleek conference table, trying to be an active listener to this potential investor and not rehearse the pitch in my head. I tried saving the high-profile meetings for down the road. Investors that would make a significant impact on the fund. The real money makers and game-changers. Mr. Abrams and I exchanged business cards at Giovanni's, an event I was trying as quickly as possible to exploit as well as forget.

"A major decision you took," Mr. Abrams said. "Leaving your career behind to start your own venture. One that I promise you will not regret. It says a lot about a person. Having an appetite for risk in such a way."

"A few investors asked why we didn't leverage our positions at KS to fight climate change, why start a private equity firm, the world has enough of those. The answer was simple. We found our philosophy on sustainability differed from that of Kauffman Schwartz. Being pressured by management to push investments in heavy carbon emitting companies, doing anything to keep their oil money turning. We knew something had to be done. This level of polluted financing terrified us. We dragged the decision out for months. Countless hours of research and planning, my partner and I wanted to make sure we gathered all the data when exploring this opportunity. One that, I'm happy to say, looks amazing."

"Where is your business partner?"

"He's down the street securing funds from your competitors."

Mr. Abrams scoffed. "I'm very interested in hearing about this opportunity. Your proposal summary was vague enough."

"With change comes growth, and from growth comes returns on your investment. At Sullivan Young, we are creating our first fund called *SY One*. The main objective of SY One is to *disrupt*. Force change in the agriculture market to achieve sustainability. The driving force fueling this entire mission, sustainability."

"And the strategy behind SY One? How do you plan to achieve *change*?"

"*SY One will invest in three companies*. Each plays a major role in achieving change. The first one, the big tuna, is Young Industrials LLC. A private family-owned manufacturer of large agricultural machinery. Think combines and other RV-sized tractors. As they currently stand, they are more taxing on the earth than they are beneficial. The resources required to assemble, operate, and maintain have gone beyond the economic and environmental boundaries farmers need and want. The lack of innovation has crippled their growth and thus profits."

"I'm listening...."

"The second company we have eyes on is a startup that specializes in autonomous technology. Vision AI: using a combination of cameras, radar, and satellite communication, they have shown this startup to transform any vehicle into a driverless machine," I said, as Mr. Abrams pursed his lips over squinted eyes. The gears turned inside his head. "This technology will allow the farmer to cut operating costs and shift focus to areas still requiring human involvement."

"So, driverless tractors," Mr. Abrams said.

"There is more," I said. "The third and final company SY One will buy in is also a startup specializing in solar technology. *SolarX.*" Mr. Abram's eyebrows jumped. "Yes, I said solar. The company manufacturers Lego sized panels to cover any surface area with solar charging capabilities. The warehouse roof? Or tiny tiles built on the tractors to ensure they have enough juice to complete the job and make it back home. SY One will combine all three companies to form synergies resulting in sustainability for both the farmer and our planet. The merger of all three companies will yield *Young Robotics*, a solar-powered autonomous agricultural machinery manufacturer. Competing with John Deere, CNH, CLAAS, and everyone else. Young Robotics will be The Tesla of tractors."

Mr. Abrams stood up and poked his head out of the conference room. "Marcia? Reschedule my next meeting. The one I have now will go over." He sat back down and seemed comfortable in his chair. "you have my attention, Ted. A very bold and creative strategy. Do you have a background in agriculture? Or did you hire a consultant?"

"My undergrad is in agricultural economics, with an MBA and CFA, and I've grown up around it. My family back home in Oklahoma used to have a small ranch. That was before my dad sold the family business of selling livestock meat in the wake of the financial crisis, forcing him and most of the community to work on an oil pipeline that has ripped through our town. You know, Litchfield never got earthquakes, but once those fracking sites got erected, they are becoming a regular occurrence. So I guess I've seen firsthand the struggles and concerns farmers have and continue to face. It takes a while to see the positive effects of smart farming, which is why many don't value the benefit or believe in its ripple effect. It's not until you realize you don't have to change something that it sticks. You don't have to turn up the soil or buy gallons and gallons of diesel to fuel your tractors. You no longer need to scramble to find a driver who didn't show up because your combines are driverless. The costs decline, and the bottom line gets fatter... Now, Mr. Abrams, I don't know your stance on climate change, or your insights. But, I believe this fund, SY One, will create a positive impact on the environment. We will become the status quo for the next generation to come. The next time you're in an airplane, really get a good look out the window, seeing mother earth miles above ground, exposed, shy and alone. Only then will you understand the urgency to make sure she remains protected."

TWO PLANES TOOK OFF AS THREE MORE TOUCHED DOWN AND crept up to the gate as I continued reading Sloane's article on our company, on Sullivan Young. The title: *GROWING ROOTS IN PRIVATE EQUITY.* My eyelids flapped in rapid succession as the fluttering in my stomach dissolved. This piece was all about Emma. Her background of privilege sewed around her promotions through nepotism at the great consulting firm and the lessons she somehow learned along the way. Total fluff, a shit puff piece, wrapped around more shit and shoveling that shit into the reader's mouths. What was Emma doing?

I flipped my phone over and stood up to shake blood to my legs. It started a few days ago with my arches and yesterday my knees joined in on the sluggishness. Non-stop walking, traveling, waiting, moving, and thinking were the engines for my body and mind to rumble and boycott. Two out of the four meetings in Denver yielded positive responses and modest investment appetites. Before that, one out of four meetings in Dallas were green, but it's expected with Texas' love for oil.

Now I'm on my way to Seattle, eager for the five meetings scheduled, salivating green dollar signs. The folks in Washington are a little more environmentally conscious, tickled by the pleasures of sustainability. Afterward, I'm off to Palo Alto for two meetings with potential investors and check-ins with the founders of the two small startups we're buying, Vision AI and SolarX.

Next, I have a special meeting with Ed back in Scottsdale, which should take an hour or two, then I'm off to Chicago to meet with Investment Firm PPM America, who in 2014, managed $106 billion in assets. But the investment vehicle they created in the '90s had my intrigue, a niche investment group, a vulture fund specializing in bankrupt or bankruptcy-risk firms; the right eyes we need to tackle Young Industrials. Their support will go a long way, their advice and investment in any capacity. After Chicago, I believe I'm heading to the east coast, New Haven, or Boston.

Boston.

Emma.

I sat down and pulled up the article as my foot tapped the linoleum. I first skimmed sections I figured was about Emma growing up in Boston and the struggles she faced, but they were worse. An exploited rush crawled down my spine. This hidden section buried in the article was about her claiming to have already met with high-profile companies. This was not okay. I called Alec.

# 26

Alec Young

Alec paced the sidewalks of Lexington, a minimalist city of ancient stone surrounded by leafless trees, skeletons covered in premature holiday lights and soft drooping wreaths.

"Did you read the article?" Ted said.

"I did."

"It's all about Emma. Her background, her father, and what it means to him to see his daughter, and I quote, little girl, go off and start a company."

"I know, I know. What they published is not how she explained how the article would read."

"I wasn't expecting an article on Sullivan Young, so when she told us one was going to be published, I got on board. I waited for the interview email from Sloane, but it looks like Emma told her enough about us, well me, to fill two sentences. Maybe three. Have you heard from Emma?"

"Things have been moving so fast I haven't checked in with her."

"I don't care that they barely mentioned us. I mean, I hate it, but what concerns me more is the article saying she's met with several high-profile companies already. What companies? Who?"

"I'm going to call her."

"I don't like this, Alec. There is a weird feeling. God, it's like she is trying to get our attention. Play some game."

"Dammit. I'll call her and get this all sorted out."

"How are things looking at your end with Alice?"

"Good. We had a nice long chat last night, and she said she wanted to sleep on it, so tonight at dinner I should get an answer. She is leaning more on our line of thinking. The company's future is in trouble and something drastic must be done."

"Great, keep me posted."

Alec ended the call and glanced through the window of a boutique shop where Alice was still browsing, killing time before their reservation. Emma's mysterious behavior curbed his appetite. The more he thought about it, the more he played fake scenarios in his head about what she was up to, the deviant little fox.

"Hello, my charming *fiancé*," Emma said.

"I think you know why I'm calling."

"To tell me how much you love and miss me?"

"I saw the article Sloane published. What companies have you met with?"

"I've been getting so much press. I love it. I got invited to be on this podcast—"

Alec interrupted. "Emma, please answer my question. What companies have you met with? What did you discuss?"

"Relax. It was a couple of phone meetings. Establishing a relationship. We signed nothing."

"With?"

"It was with, let me think. Pebble Arrow, Epic Drilling, Blue Horizon, Rex Mining. The podcast I got invited to is a conversation with the CEO of GEO Sanderson. I'm so excited and a little nervous. I know my dad will listen in."

"Jesus, Emma."

"What?"

"Those are all fracking companies. They go against everything we're trying to build."

"You mean what you and Theo are trying to build? I have autonomy. I will not ask for your blessing every time I want to onboard a client."

"Under the Sullivan Young umbrella, which your involvement would be to work with the formed companies we've merged. Young Robotics."

"The umbrella my dad bought. I don't mean to throw that in your face, but I'm sorry. I'm not a green peace hippie. I would expect you to know this about your fiancé. But again, you never really asked about my stance, you assumed." Alec remained quiet as a sea of beanie-bopping teens bounced around the sidewalk. "Also, the end-of-year party invites for here in the city have rolled in. Should I RSVP?"

"I don't know, Emma."

"Well, I'm going to RSVP and you can go or not go. You must be so tired after all the traveling you've been doing, so I understand if you don't want to make an appearance. But, it will look *sus* if you aren't with me. I know people will ask. I will think of a lie. Maybe you're under the weather from all your traveling."

Alice walked out with two small bags with teal tissue paper oozing from the top.

"The restaurant called. Our table is ready," Alice said. "Also, I got mom and dad early Christmas presents."

"Emma, I'm heading into the restaurant."

"With your sister? Tell Alice I said 'hi'."

"I want to continue this chat. And so, we're clear, I'm not happy."

"I know, Alec. I know. But you'll be okay."

THE DINNER WAS GREASY AMERICAN GRASS-FED BEEF, DUCK-fat fried potato spears with a side of fry sauce (a basic combination of mayo and ketchup), a cold salad tossed in Ranch dressing, bacon bits, and fresh-baked croutons and yet, despite the mouth-watering smorgasbord, Alec took slow small bites. His stomach flooded with acid, Emma inducing acid. Her rogue behavior ate away at his stomach lining, spewing up into his esophagus like a volcano.

"Are you not hungry?" Alice asked as a glob of acidic reddish-yellow sauce dripped off her fry and onto the table.

"I'm sorry, what?" Alec said, his mind snapped back to reality.

"Alec? Are you okay?"

"Sorry, sorry. I'm a tad distracted. Everything with Dad and the future of the company."

"A tad? You haven't touched your food and said four words. Please eat."

"Yes, Mom," Alec said with a half-grin when Alice's phone vibrated.

"Speaking of Mom," Alice said. "Hi, Mom!" She nodded and nodded, following a smile with brightened eyes. "Really?" She pulled her phone away from her face, mouthed to Alec, "Dad's awake!" and continued the mother-daughter banter. Alec gulped ice-cold water to dilute the bile his gallbladder continued to pump like the heart of a racehorse.

"Dad is awake!" Alice said, placing her phone on the table, missing the sauce blob. "This is such a relief."

"See, I told you he would be okay. What else did Mom say?" Alec tapped the top of his phone, and, to no surprise, he didn't have a missed call from Ruth.

"Well, he's groggy and confused. Can't hold a conversation. Doesn't know the date or his name." Alice sucked in air. "But the fact that he is awake is a significant sign."

"That is."

"Will you please eat now? Everything is going to be okay. No need to worry."

"There is still reason to worry, Alice. Dad is fragile, we both know that. The company is fragile and the stress of trying to run and fix it... Who knows what it will do to his health? Dawn is aware of the risk. Spencer is aware of the risk. I need you to be aware. If you agree to sell, you won't be hurting the family. You will help it. You will help Dad."

Alice sank in her chair, somber slouching while flipping pieces of lettuce to find garlicky croutons.

"What is your concern about selling?" Alec asked. "Because if your concern is the wellbeing of dad's health, then I think you know the vote to sell is in his best interest. The stress of trying to save the company will put him back in the hospital. Or worse." Alice froze and took a soft bite of her salad. "You can help dad by removing this stress. Come on, Alice. I know you, and if you don't sell and the stress of the company causes dad to have another heart attack, you will blame yourself. I don't want you to live with that burden. You have to think logically. Dad spent years working and earned retirement. So, what do you say?"

Alice's eyes darted away, made their way along the tables edge, across the collection of food, then back up toward Alec. "Okay. I'll agree to the sell."

"Yeah? Alice you are literally saving his life! I'm proud of you."

"But I think we should fly back home to see dad."

"I agree. When are you done with finals?"

"Next week."

"Do you want me to stay with you until then?"

"Are you sure?"

"I can extend my stay and work from the hotel."

Alice smiled and sipped her cola.

# 27

Ted Sullivan

I stepped onto the streets after leaving my final meeting in midtown. A grey, lethal fog lingered over the Manhattan skyline like 1950s London. It sang from tower and taxi lights. A flickering essence of police sirens and sloshing black river water from Hudson to East mixed with ferry horns trapped under the fog bubble. I arrived back in the city for a few deal closure meetings and last-minute investment touchups, and I felt, based on my non-stop tour, would collapse my limbs and intellect.

The SY One Fund reached its target goal of $300 million, the aftermath of seventeen meetings across five states in two weeks had set in, but my drive, my will to endure to nourish my child, mine and Alec's entity, roared like a bonfire engulfing stacks of hay pallets on a dry Oklahoma summer. Unstoppable. We filled our equity pool from individual investors, boutique hedge funds, and pensions thirsty for more sustainable opportunities, with the remaining chunk from debt financing across three green-hungry banks.

The capitalization table Raj built would make any Excel junky hard or wet. The investor-facing platform was sleek, sophisticated, and green.

The lingering fumes of wood fired pizza hypnotized me like a Looney Tune floating through the crowd. My cravings are fixated on roasted veggies, bombarded by cured swine pepperoni, sausage balls, and subtle notes of burnt, crunchy bread. As I finished the first slice, my phone dinged with an email notification previewed atop my screen, another email deal-related, until the sender left me frozen mid-chew. I tidied my fingers of powdered crust and grease, sucked in a gulp of oxygen and plunged into my past headfirst. Double Helix confirmed they completed my results. Tap the link to open the account and explore. Simple enough, but tough to swallow for folk like me.

*Don't click the link, the little adopted boy said. I know my tribe. Clint and Shelly.*

This won't change anything.

*Don't force me to the light. I'm happy where I am. Don't click the link.*

The page loaded and came to life in pieces across my phone screen as I resisted the urge to cancel, reload, cancel and reload again in this reception dead zone. Displayed was a rainbow pie chart and below a list of regions they reported the molecules inside my saliva originated from.

*Please don't.*

Sorry.

A little more than half of my origin, 56%, was Northern Europe. Ireland, Scotland, and the United Kingdom. An understandable insight. I pushed my glasses further up the bridge of my nose as if to correct my vision of what the remaining half-read. A confusing, almost surreal insight, like I was seeing for the first time what the adopted little boy inside my mind looked like. I had plucked him from pandora's box. Foreign and unknown. The second-largest chunk is 30% *Iberian Peninsula* and 12% *Italy*. My eyelids fluttered. This had to be an error. The method used to pinpoint DNA origins probably glitched. They somehow analyzed my results as one thing but labeled it another. I have a light tan, yes, but I attributed that to being outside most of my youth. A full-bodied farmer tan who still to this day sunburns too easy. Iberian Peninsula? Italian? I opened another tab and searched those results, storytelling me a generic answer: you had ancestors who lived in that corner of the world at one point. My ancestors, my story, me.

Alec's face appeared on my screen as my phone seized in my hand.

"Did you make it to Iowa?" I asked.

"Yeah. I'm in the study printing the legal docs Becher and Caldwell drafted up."

"Since we're expecting Scott and your mom to fuss about the price tag, what number are you going to propose?"

"Considering their massive pile of debt we're going to suggest one-fifty. I know they are going to lose their shit since the Young Industrials team estimated their value to hover around one-ninety to two hundred."

"We can't spill over two hundred since we've already signed the buying docs with SolarX and Vision AI for fifty each."

"Hey," Alec said.

"What?"

"I'm proud of you for getting us over the fundraising finish line. I know it wasn't easy."

"It would all be for nothing if you hadn't convinced your family to sell. So tomorrow, what time is the family meeting to sign everything?"

"Eleven. But I'll prob call you around ten-thirty along with our attorneys to discuss any potential ad-doc obstacles before showtime."

"Sounds good to me."

"How about Emma's privation? Did you find out who she has met with? Or was she just fishing?"

Alec exhaled through the phone. "No, she wasn't fishing. She's been conducting her own meetings, and the clients she is chasing, well, let's say it will fuck Sullivan Young's reputation if she goes through with consulting any of them."

"Fuck. Like who? How bad are we talking?"

"She's met with every tentacle of the oil squid machine."

"All of them?"

"All of them. She's attending a live podcast interview with the co-CEO's of Rex Energy Corp."

"Please tell me you're joking. Fuck!"

"I wish. I've been calling and texting her, but she isn't responding."

"What can I do? Is she in the city?"

"Yeah. She is probably at the condo. Can you stop by and tell her to call me? And also tell her how bad the interview would shred our brand. Plead with her not to do it."

"I will."

"Once my family signs everything, I will fly back as soon as possible. Help try to contain the shit show if she goes through with it," Alec said. "We might need to hire a publicist sooner than expected."

"We should get the ball rolling on that. I'll send a few emails tonight after I talk with Emma and see when's the soonest we can get a meeting."

"Paying Roger back can't come fast enough."

"It will, I promise. We'll pay him back. We'll get through this. Emma does whatever damage, we'll say we let her go because her values didn't align with the culture of Sullivan Young, and let our publicist handle the rest."

"Damn it!" Alec said.

"What is it?"

"Ah, sorry. The paper in the printer got jammed."

"Smack it a few times. That always works."

"This thing is so fucking old," Alec said as I heard flesh smacking plastic in the background.

"So, I got my ethnicity results from Double Helix."

"You did? I didn't know you sent in a sample."

"I asked Dana to mail it and I kinda forgot. With all the traveling and meetings."

"What does it say? How do you feel?"

"I feel okay. A part of me didn't want to know, maybe just the fact I could know if I wanted, that it was possible to know. But I looked, and it surprised me to be honest."

"Did it say you're a genius?"

"I have some Spanish and Italian blood in me."

"You're shitting me. Really?"

"That was my exact reaction. I expected the other half. Irish, Scottish, and British."

"I love knowing everything about you. Mine was all Western and

North Western European," Alec laughed. "Poland, Sweden, Norway. And a small fraction of Ashkenazi Jew."

"Should we say L'chaim?"

"I think so. Should we display a menorah at the office?"

"Maybe we start with the condo first."

"I love knowing your results."

"None of it feels real. A part of me thinks it was an error."

"Nah, I doubt it. Otherwise, that would be a massive breach that someone would have identified already."

"Unless it began with me?"

"Nah," Alec said. "Hey my sister's calling my name."

"Go do your thing. I'll stop by and talk with Emma."

"Fucking Emma. Okay, thank you!"

"V.O.U.," I said.

"V.O.U.," Alec said.

My Double Helix rainbow results flashed back onto my screen after our call, along with Alec's echoing words about his love of my results.

See, it's okay. Nothing changed.

I lost track of time, staring mindlessly at my results like a winning lottery ticket. At the top banner of the homepage, I saw a little bell that was full purple with the number one, white and hollow in the center of the purple bell. A welcome to Double Helix message? A thank you for choosing Double Helix letter? An alert? Your results were tainted and thus voided. Please ignore and accept our apologies?

I tapped the purple bell, not once but twice, until the screen loaded. Load. Load. I stepped onto the city sidewalk, hoping to escape the dead reception zone. A simple fix, I told myself. The street was quiet, so only a few cars and taxis cruised down the one-way path. The walkway was light of pedestrians but heavy with black trash bags and flat cardboard. My fingers hummed red when I strapped my fleece-lined leather gloves on. My visible breath vanished as my lungs collapsed, and the blood in my hands, arms and head rushed to my heart as the beats pumped louder and louder, faster and faster, leaving me lightheaded and dizzy.

*No! The little adopted boy said. I don't want that to be true.*

A rush of adrenaline coursed through my veins, and the words on my screen beat in sync with my jugular. I stopped walking and stood in the middle of the sidewalk, appearing like a social media addicted asshole too preoccupied with my phone to appreciate or even acknowledge life around me, like the crowd that had to split around me, making a snarling pass to wake the fuck up. The purple bell rang to let me know there was a DNA match.

Her?

*No! He yelled again. Look what you've done.*

It's okay. It's okay. I... This is an error. This is an error.

*No, it's not. No, it's not. I know who I am. I'm not a part of her! She did this to mess with you. She did this to mess with you.*

But did she?

The words screamed and the bold font bled down my screen like syrup. This can't be. This can't be. I don't understand. How? How?

Emma and I shared 22.9% of our DNA.

Q4

# 28

Ted Sullivan

I gave the door two gentle knocks while peering down at my phone, my eyes still burning into the white page and black font. Bare feet smacked against hardwood flooring following silence. Her eyes were burning at me through the door's peephole, accompanying exhales of annoyance so potent I could smell the alcohol seep through.

"Theo," Emma said in an unimpressed expression, balancing a full clear martini with the tips of her fingers. The glass was so cold that the outside sweat beads of condensation with the shadow shape of a green olive bouncing about the bottom. Her cheeks are moulin rouge, and her eyes are red October with a white satin robe draped across her shoulders and loosely tied around her waist.

"Emma, there is something important I need to talk to you about," I said, slipping my phone into my pocket.

"God. I already know." Emma turned around and walked back toward the living room.

"You do?" I said, taking my first step inside their 77 Pine two-bedroom condo with stargazing views of Wall Street and Freedom Tower as they played peek-a-boo behind the dense fog. I felt exposed without saying a word and stopped behind their island counter, a safe barricade between us. On one end of the island sat two half-drunk bottles of The Botanist gin and Mancino vermouth, an open jar of green olives surrounded by juice droplets, a tiny fishing fork, and a stainless-steel shaker. They scattered the other end with mail and a robin's egg blue Tiffany's bag, small but eye-catching.

"Yes! Alec has been up my ass about it. And I'm still doing the interview." Emma sat down on an uncomfortable-looking black leather couch, boxy and modern.

"Emma, you can't. You will destroy Sullivan Young's credibility. Our brand. Those people you're interviewing with, what they are striving for, their goals, go against everything we stand for. The market will forever label us hypocrites. And that is something you can never recover from. Losing the trust of our investors."

"Your investors."

"Our investors, Emma. What will those people you're meeting with think when we publicize SY One Fund? The change we're striving for impacts them. We want to sustain the planet."

"They won't care," Emma said, taking a sip of her martini and licking her wet lips. "Plus, some are already aware. I told them. It's a sham. This whole fight against climate change, piss green bullshit. It's a political tool. Climategate confirmed it."

"Alec and I believe the opposite. Sullivan Young believes in fighting climate change. And you are a part of it."

"Oh Theo. You keep saying Sullivan Young this Sullivan Young that, but you do not know. No fucking clue."

"No clue to what?"

"Everything," Emma said. "We brought you in for a reason. Not because of your stance on climate fiction, but because of your client list. You were our quick ticket to attracting investors." I placed my hands on the cold marble and bit my tongue. "Listen, I know you and Alec are gay for each other. We all have little secrets. What I'm more shocked about is that he didn't tell you. We were using you. This isn't fun to hear, I'm sure. Knowing I've been a part of this since finding Alec's little hidden stack of business cards a few months ago. Or finding out it was my idea to expose Chaz. Do you think Alec is smart enough to think of something like that? Attention Sloane Marshall. All me. I got you on the Forbes list because we needed it. I finally have a company. And on behalf of the company I'm a part of, I'll meet with whoever the fuck I feel like meeting with. Tell your little fake boyfriend that. Go on." Emma shooed me with her hand like I was a dog.

"Leaking the story about Chaz, was you?"

"Don't look so surprised. It got you Forbes. And that is all you wanted, right? Now if you should be mad at anyone, it should be at Alec for keeping this from you."

"Does Sloane know it was you?"

"God no," Emma chuckled. "I've made her career over the years. She was writing shit pieces no one read until I learned how to use her voice for her. And don't think about trying to expose me to her because I'll deny, she'll believe me, obviously. And who knows, maybe a new article will surface about how an adopted boy from Oklahoma benefited from Chaz's suicide."

My throat went bone dry and my hands thumped to the beat of my heart. I pulled my phone out of my pocket and said, "Emma, I underestimated you."

"What are you talking about?"

"I wanted to talk to you about your interview tomorrow and plead with you to not take it."

"Well, I am."

"Can you let me finish? But there is something important I need to talk to you about. Something I discovered."

"Let me guess, you're here to tell me to not marry your boyfriend? Also, plead with me not to go through with it? I want you to do something for me. Look inside that bag." Emma pointed with her martini. "The Tiffany's bag." I took a few steps, reached across, and slid the bag toward me. I glanced up and Emma had an evil grin. A plotted half-smile. I reached my hand inside and felt a small box and knew. A ring-sized box. An engagement-sized box. "I got it for Alec. Do you think he will like it?" I pulled the box out. "The ring is Tiffany's, of course, but I liked this box better," Emma said as I held the box Alec got us, the matching box to go with our matching S and Y cufflinks. I took out a platinum wedding band from the package. My mind glitched as it was accustomed to seeing our cufflinks. Inside, the two of us cozie together. Y and S. "What do you think? Beautiful ring, right?"

Word vomit brewed hot until it bellowed up and out of my mouth. I pulled out my phone.

"Emma! I used that fucking DNA kit, and I got an alert saying my DNA had a 22.9% match. With you."

Emma sat on the couch, raising her glass to her lips until it was empty. She stood up and moved toward the island, spinning the empty glass with the tips of her fingers. Her steps are a little louder and a little dizzier than before. She didn't look at me as she laid her empty glass down and lifted the lid off the gin.

"You said earlier that you underestimated me," she said as she let The Botanist pour continue and continue into the shaker, following Mancino that splashed onto the marble. "But I think it's the other way around. Can you pour me some ice?" Emma picked up the tiny fork and fished for the plumpest green olive, piercing down, then sliding it off the fork and into her glass. I spun and filled her shaker with ice, trying to not let the potion splash while scrambling to understand what game she was playing. She doesn't believe me. I slid the shaker across the island and she popped the lid and began a slow shake. "I underestimated you, Theo."

"Emma, what are you talking about?"

"All I am saying is that I underestimated you." She filled her glass to the rim and the olive, so dense and plump, remained at the bottom unfazed. She took a sip. "I thought you might try, worse case, to threaten me to not do the interview. Or to not marry Alec. Threaten to leak something about me to the press or whatever. But now I see what you're doing."

"What am I doing, Emma? You don't believe me, do you?"

"Oh, I believe you're a slimy snake who has resorted to say we're related to get me to back down," Emma said as she walked back into the living room. She steps once loud, now appearing loose.

"It's true!" I walked toward her and showed her my phone. The results back up my argument. The facts. Her head swayed as she blinked several times to correct her blurry vision.

"And now you're going to use this to get to my dad, try to be part of the family, get your name added to the family trust."

"What? No. Do you not care what this is saying?" I sat my phone on the marble island.

"Theo, this company is new. This feature is in a beta stage and something went wrong. Because what you're saying is my father cheated on my mother. Is that what you're saying? Going to use this to extort my family for money?"

Emma leaned into the couch and ran her fingers through her hair. I took a step back. She was too drunk to have this conversation with. Unable to process, brain flooded with gin and vermouth.

"Let's talk when you're sober," I said, walking toward the kitchen.

"How pathetic must you be to have this be your strategy? Or I could be wrong, and you're just scrambling from person to person until you find someone who loves you."

I stopped and faced the door as if something had rooted me in place. My feet melted into the hardwood.

"Ah, is that it?" Emma said, noticing me stop mid-walk to her last remark. "Your adopted parents didn't love you, so now you cling to this DNA results error, hoping to find someone to love you? Is that it?"

I closed my eyes as a moist draft crept across my back with the sound of a wooden door creaking open and Mason's vile laugh. *You know she is right. No one will love you. No one, no one, no one, Mason said.* The sting of iron and blood coated my tongue.

"Alec doesn't love you. Your adopted parents probably wished they had returned you...." Emma's voice drowned out, a slow fade in the distance as Mason confirmed her every word while throwing in his blood-soaked comments: *you're going to let her talk to you like that? faggot. My body was ground up like it was in a meat grinder because of you and you're going to let her get away with saying shit like that, homeless boy.*

"Shut up!" I covered my ears, but still, the faint voice of Emma's last words cut in.

"So, cheers to you for giving me Sullivan Young." Followed by the gulping of her martini like spiraling water down a drain, then sudden glass shattering into thousands of pieces and silence.

Mason's words have never been this loud, this long duration of words and phrases slicing through my marrow. It wasn't my fault he fell off the tractor. It wasn't my fault. I only wanted to make him feel the sting of the pain he had caused me. A thud to the side of his head. Maybe crack his skin open, draw blood, and get blood in his mouth. It wouldn't be hogs' blood like what seeped into my mouth when he would force me to get naked, tie me up, and have me pour the bucket over my head. It wouldn't be that, but it would be something. I didn't mean to kill him. I wanted to show him I was strong, I could fight back, but *vengeance* steered my hand to the perfect pebble, and *vendetta* directed my hand on the slingshot, pulling as far back as it would go as *revenge* guided the rock through the air to crack the precise spot on his soft temple, to an unconscious collapse into the tractor's blades.

Emma's words weren't slashing my skin like a thousand cuts and weren't flooding the room with poisonous vapor. I lowered my hands and turned around to see Emma squeezing her throat with both hands, hunched down and facing the ground as her hair dangled down, ripping through the air.

She was choking.

Emma took several trepid steps toward me, pointing at her throat: over and over. Her frightened eyes were wide and her eyebrows stitched together with flourishing purple lips.

She took another step toward me.

I diverged.

Her shattered martini glass was strewn across the floor as she knelt, still supporting her neck as her stomach convulsed, and fear-induced urine poured down her inner thigh as she went flat. Her mouth opened and closed like a fish, desperate for more oxygen.

My eyesight was merging as it crawled into the center like fog that rippled with the fast beating of my heart. As a terrified sweat slid down my neck, my hands became swelled with blood, wet and heated. I stood there for what felt like hours, days, and the whirling blackness didn't go away. I took a wobbly step closer, then another, until Emma's face, her open eyes, looked at me. Her blue hands were frozen around her throat, with strawberry strands of hair glued to her lips, like a doll thrown across the room.

My stomach twisted and swirled as I ran into the sink and drive heaved. I removed my glasses, slapped cold water on my face, and stood with my wet hands covering my eyes, inhaling the perfume of martinis and olives. The condo's silence was deafening.

I grabbed the nearest cloth to dry my hands and face, threw on my jacket, and dashed out the door. When I heard the click of the door closing, I was halfway down the hallway. I hit the elevator button nonstop until it opened, only to be greeted by a couple dressed in business casually behind bulky parkas and scarves. As we switched positions in the elevator, my shoulder bumped the gentleman's, following an automatic apology from him.

I was mute.

# 29

## Alec Young

Alec paced in the study, dialing Ted for the third time and arranging the many stacks of paperwork on the table. The phone rang but went unanswered. Alec's face wrinkled as his family entered the room one by one. Scott gloomed with a dejected face as he was going to sign away ownership, allowing the kid they all shared to go live with someone else. Dawn and Spencer were the only ones who made small talk with Alec, admiring his suit while standing next to the fireplace. Alec set the attorneys on standby and tried for the fourth time to reach Ted.

Nothing.

Alice tugged on a loose string to her sweater looking distorted with an uncomfortable demeanor, all she wanted was for Bradley to get better. Healthy and clear. Ruth was the last to arrive, with the family lawyer clutching a stack of documents when an unidentified woman with a stethoscope dangling around her neck popped her head in, and Ruth responded with a sharp directive.

"Thank you, everyone, for coming," Alec said. "Before we begin, I first want to say how proud I am of all of you in your decision and understanding that Young Industrials, in order to survive and flourish, needs to adapt. I know this isn't easy, which makes it even more impactful. Pride would have sunk this company, and you've all put pride aside to deliver change instead."

"Great intro, nephew," Spencer said with a wink.

"We have our attorneys on the line if anyone has questions," Alec said, pressing the speaker button on his phone just as the screen notified him Roger was calling in. His attention glitched, but re-centered. "I believe your attorney already reviewed the signing docs?"

"We did," the suited old man said from the corner of the room. "Pretty standard boilerplate. Our only concern after having the discussion with the family is the price tag."

"Are you saying you don't agree with the Deloitte auditor's valuation of one-fifty?" Alec said.

"We agree with the set valuation by Deloitte. But for my clients to sign today, that price tag will need to be adjusted to encompass more of their emotional duress and financial security."

"We are open. How does one sixty-five sound?"

"You're just asking for us all to leave this room, aren't you?" Scott grumbled.

"The price tag will also have to be adjusted to account for the emotional duress of having to sign today, otherwise my clients will have to re-schedule until we can come to an understanding."

The negotiation was going according to plan. Alec and his attorneys planned for this pushback as he froze in pensive thought. It was time for Becher and Caldwell to speak.

"We are prepared to go to one seventy-five," they said from the phone.

Dawn, Spencer, and Alice looked around. An enticing number that left Scott and Ruth unfazed but heading in the right direction. Alec knew Scott would want this transaction to be painful for him, so making the appearance he was going against the advertisement of his council would satisfy that itch. The study remained quiet and Alec's phone screen alerted him again to Roger on the other end, but he remained focused.

"One eighty," Alec said.

"Our final number," the attorney echoed from the phone.

The Young family lawyer looked around the room to gauge interest, with Ruth tugging at her pearls with a half-smile of agreement, but Scott was not.

"I think we are heading in the right direction," the family lawyer said.

"One eighty is our final number," Becher and Caldwell's attorneys said.

Alec was ready for his trump card, the number he planned.

"Two hundred. But everything has to be signed today."

"Alec, we don't advise that."

"Noted."

And finally, a grimace came from Scott as Alec and his attorneys went back and forth. Scott spun around to Ruth and the family lawyer with a satisfied expression.

"My clients are prepared to sign with the price tag of two hundred."

"Great. My attorneys will update the signing docs now and fax them over."

"Who wants mimosas?" Spencer said, shooting up from his chair.

"Congratulations, Alec," Spencer said. "You've finally bought out your family. Let's just hope you weren't blowing smoke up our asses and you actually have what it takes to turn the company around."

"And you finally admit the company needed turning around," Alec said. "I should congratulate you."

The family signed one by one as the docs came in and each left the study thereafter. Ruth was the last to sign as she held the pen.

"Your father is on his way home," she said.

"I thought I saw a nurse."

"Just taking extra precautions in case he needs anything. Are you going to stick around for when he arrives?"

"I want to, Mom. But I have to be getting back to New York. We have a lot to do."

Ruth nodded as she signed the document and left the room. Alec tucked all the docs in his briefcase and checked his phone to see three missed calls from Roger. He got secured in his Lyft, recalling the awkward goodbyes from his family in the kitchen. Half already tipsy and the other half drunk on what the future of Young Industrials holds. As Alec rode off down the long driveway, the estate shrank in the distance. His phone pressed to his ear while nibbling on airline pretzels.

"Roger, hey, sorry for not picking up. I was in a meeting. Did you make it safely to the city?"

"Have you heard from Emma?"

"I haven't. Is everything okay?"

"We haven't been able to get a hold of her all morning. We were supposed to have breakfast before her podcast interview."

"Hmmm. That's weird," Alec said. "Where are you now?"

"We were in the lobby at Seventy-Seven Pine, but since she is not answering, we headed to Whisk, thinking maybe she is already at the restaurant waiting for us."

"I'm headed to the airport now. I should be in the city in a few hours, but let me call her," Alec said as he glanced up through the windshield of his Lyft and a black van cruised on by heading toward the estate. He knew who was in that van and how word of what transpired over the past few weeks didn't make its way into Bradley's ear. Not yet. Cocoons rattled inside Alec's belly, ready to be hatched from Bradley's response to the news. *Proud, proud, he will be proud,* Alec thought. Movie clips play inside his head, snippets of Ruth showing Bradley the SY pitch deck with all the data they gathered fitted to a sound strategy. Alec blinked several times, missing replies from Roger.

"Sorry. I think you cut out, Roger. What was that?"

"Let us know if you hear from Emma and call us when you land. We're going back to the hotel."

"I will. She is probably stuck in a subway somewhere and lost service. I wouldn't be worried."

The call ended and the excitement of finally owning Young Industrials dissolved in the unanswered phone calls to both Ted and Emma.

# 30

## Ted Sullivan

My memory shot like slow flickers of a strobe light in a black room. An abrupt onset dark fugue state. *Black*. Emma's hollow eyes peered up at me. *Black*. I'm wandering down the hall. *Black*. I'm outside my apartment building. *Black*. I'm standing in my bathroom. *Black*. I undressed and tiptoed into the shower. The water was icy. Freezing cold to silence my mind. I scrambled to unlock the vault. Trying to control my rattling hand as it twirled the combination. Frantic. A dry heave of fear bellowed up. I got the vault door open and slammed those memories inside. The only lingering trace was the sound of the adopted boy crying. Endless sobbing. His cries were still bleeding through the cracks of my shivering body.

*Look what you've done, the little adopted boy cried.*

I sat on the shower floor and closed my eyes. The knob twisted to the base of the blue. The adopted boy hiccupped in between deep inhales, doused in tears. He wouldn't stop.

*Look what you've done!*

I didn't dry off as I rested on my bathmat, catching my blurry wet figure in the bathroom mirror. I planted on my bed, glaring at the soundless ceiling fan. My mind was rapid fire: static noise, child cries, and Emma's laughter. The shattering of glass and thump of knees dropping onto hardwood. I rummaged through a small plastic box of bathroom supplies and popped two Benadryl's into my mouth, swallowing them dry. My bed sheets felt cold as my heart bludgeoned my rib cage, sending throbs up my neck and a shockwave through the outer edge of my eyelids. I focused on my breathing. Relax. A deep inhale through my nose then a slow release. Again and again. And soon my body was calming with a swirling sensation of weightlessness.

*I stood in the kitchen of the condo enchanted by the stars twinkling out the windows. Sprinkling around hydrangea tinge gas bubbles, aftermath of collapsing suns, winkled from Hubble. A time lapse all scintillating and still. Indicating an ever-expanding darkness—cold and soundless.*

*I wandered to the window and maundered over shreds of Mason. Fatty intestines wrapped around his corpse like a ribbon. Taboo Beef patty. I continued through and stepped over a beige extension cord: twisted and knotted around Chaz's neck. His face maroon-spotted—his eyes coup de grace.*

*I veered outward, guarding empowerment—eternal life bearer, while disregarding Emma, who remained hunched. A gun-punch position, clutching her neck with terror, for the stars outside mesmerized my eyes and the mission was nearly complete.*

*"So much dark matter. Yet invisible," I said.*

*Emma collapsed to her knees with her mouth fully widened, lips pulled back, wet eyed. And her tongue was suctioned to the back of her throat, desperate for more oxygen as I let out a gloat.*

*"Dark fact of the matter is I've known about you, Emma, since before we met. Back when you were this ambitious consultant caught up keeping up with the Joneses. Throwing the most exclusive game nights." I adjusted his glasses and turned to pity Emma. "What? You don't believe me?" I inched closer and closer to Emma, gritty and witty as she slid her arm across the hardwood, reaching out her hand as she went cross-eyed. Her index finger extended. Her nails dug deep into the wood, animal-like scratches carved out.*

*I retreated, far enough to greet her nail as it grazed the top of my dress shoe.*

*I rose and with my fuck-you-finger-knuckle, nudged my glasses back up the bridge of my nose and said, "you know I find it quite ironic your nickname for me is Theo. I kind of like it. It's very fitting. Do you know what the Greek word for Theo is?"*

*Saliva dribbled through the crease on her lips. Her blue eyes were a tint bluer and face a juicy plum. Achieving eternal peace.*

*"Do you?"*

*I twisted his head toward the window and spotted a shooting star zip across, and while peering out, I said, "it means God."*

*I buttoned my suit, and as I strolled toward the door, shattered martini glass cracked under my shoes like pop rocks. The crunching soon morphed into screams. Constant whales over crying hiccups.*

*Look what you've done. Look what you've done, the little adopted boy said.*

*I covered my ears as I bolted out the door.*

*A click confirmed, and I shoved the vault door open, stumbling inside my room as a kid. The little adopted boy's room, where he sat crying on his bed of dinosaur prints scattered around a blue blanket, frozen in time, yet somehow running backwards. The little adopted boy continued to cry and peeked with one eye over his shoulder up at the night sky. I stood above him, and the hovering brought a wave of cold cruelty and bold malice. He looked away, and his cries echoed louder, slicing deeper. Succumb to the dominance and evil intentions.*

*Look what you've done! Look what you've done! Look what you've done! Look what you've done! Look what you've done! Look what you've done! Look what you've done! Look what you've done! Look what you've done! Look what you've done! Look what you've done! Look what you've done! Look what you've done! Look what you've done! Look what you've done! Look what you've done! Look what you've done! Look what you've done! Look what you've done! Look what you've done! Look what you've done! Look what you've done! Look what you've done! Look what you've done! Look what you've done! Look what you've done! Look what you've done! Look what you've done! Look what you've done! Look what you've done! Look what you've done! Look what you've done! Look what you've done! Look what you’ve done! Look what you’ve done! Look what you’ve done! Look what you’ve done! Look what you’ve done! Look what you’ve done! Look what you’ve done! Look what you’ve done! Look what you’ve done! Look what you’ve done! Look what you’ve done! Look what you’ve done! Look what you’ve done! Look what you’ve done! Look what you’ve done! Look what you’ve done! Look what you’ve done! Look what you’ve done! Look what you’ve done! Look what you’ve done! Look what you’ve done! Look what you’ve done! Look what you’ve done! Look what you’ve done! Look what you’ve done! Look what you’ve done! Look what you’ve done! Look done! Look what you’ve done! Look what you’ve done! Look what you’ve done! Look what you’ve done! Look what you’ve done! Look what you’ve done! Look what you’ve done! Look what you’ve done! Look what you’ve done! Look what you’ve done! Look what you’ve done! Look what you’ve done! Look what you’ve done! Look what you’ve done! Look what you’ve done! Look what you’ve done! Look what you’ve done! Look what you’ve done! Look what you’ve done! Look what you’ve done! Look what you’ve done! Look done! Look what you’ve done! Look what you’ve done! Look what you’ve done! Look what you’ve done! Look what you’ve done! Look what you’ve done! Look what you’ve done! Look what you’ve done! Look what you’ve done! Look what you’ve done! Look what you’ve done! Look what you’ve done! Look what you’ve done! Look what you’ve done! Look what you’ve done! Look what you’ve done! Look what you’ve done! Look what you’ve done! Look what you’ve done! Look what you’ve done! Look what you’ve done! Look done! Look what you’ve done! Look what you’ve done! Look what you’ve done! Look what you’ve done! Look what you’ve done! Look what you’ve done! Look what you’ve done! Look what you’ve done! Look what you’ve done! Look what you’ve done! Look what you’ve done! Look what you’ve done! Look what you’ve done! Look what you’ve done! Look what you’ve done! Look what you’ve done! Look what you’ve done! Look what you’ve done! Look what you’ve done! Look done! Look what you’ve done! Look what you’ve done! Look what you’ve done! Look what you’ve done! Look what you’ve done! Look what you’ve done! Look what you’ve done! Look what you’ve done! Look what you’ve done! Look what you’ve done! Look what you’ve done! Look what you’ve done! Look what you’ve done! Look what you’ve done! Look what you’ve done! Look what you’ve done! Look what you’ve done! Look what you’ve done! Look what you’ve done! Look what you’ve done! Look what you’ve done! Look done! Look what you’ve done! Look what you’ve done! Look what you’ve done! Look what you’ve done! Look what you’ve done! Look what you’ve done! Look what you’ve done! Look what you’ve done! Look what you’ve done! Look what you’ve done! Look what you’ve done! Look what you’ve done! Look what you’ve done! Look what you’ve done! Look what you’ve done! Look what you’ve done! Look what you’ve done! Look what you’ve done! Look what you’ve done! Look what you’ve done! Look done! Look what you’ve done! Look what you’ve done! Look what you’ve done! Look what you’ve done! Look what you’ve done! Look what you’ve done! Look what you’ve done! Look what you’ve done! Look what you’ve done! Look what you’ve done! Look what you’ve done! Look what you’ve done! Look what you’ve done! Look what you’ve done! Look what you’ve done! Look what you’ve done! Look what you’ve done! Look what you’ve done! Look done! Look what you’ve done! Look what you’ve done! Look what you’ve done! Look what you’ve done! Look what you’ve done! Look what you’ve done! Look what you’ve done! Look what you’ve done! Look what you’ve done! Look what you’ve done! Look what you’ve done! Look what you’ve done! Look what you’ve done! Look what you’ve done! Look what you’ve done! Look what you’ve done! Look what you’ve done! Look what you’ve done! Look what you’ve done! Look done! Look what you’ve done! Look what you’ve done! Look what you’ve done! Look what you’ve done! Look what you’ve done! Look what you’ve done! Look what you’ve done! Look what you’ve done! Look what you’ve done! Look what you’ve done! Look what you’ve done! Look what you’ve done! Look what you’ve done! Look what you’ve done! Look what you’ve done! Look what you’ve done! Look what you’ve done! Look what you’ve done! Look done! Look what you’ve done! Look what you’ve done! Look what you’ve done! Look what you’ve done! Look what you’ve done! Look what you’ve done! Look what you’ve done! Look what you’ve done! Look what you’ve done! Look what you’ve done! Look what you’ve done! Look what you’ve done! Look what you’ve done! Look what you’ve done! Look what you’ve done! Look what you’ve done! Look what you’ve done! Look what you’ve done! Look what you’ve done! Look done! Look what you’ve done! Look what you’ve done! Look what you’ve done! Look what you’ve done! Look what you’ve done! Look what you’ve done! Look what you’ve done! Look what you’ve done! Look what you’ve done! Look what you’ve done! Look what you’ve done! Look what you’ve done! Look what you’ve done! Look what you’ve done! Look what you’ve done! Look what you’ve done! Look what you’ve done! Look what you’ve done! Look done! Look what you’ve done! Look what you’ve done! Look what you’ve done! Look what you’ve done! Look what you’ve done! Look what you’ve done! Look what you’ve done! Look what you’ve done! Look what you’ve done! Look what you’ve done! Look what you’ve done! Look what you’ve done! Look what you’ve done! Look what you’ve done! Look what you’ve done! Look what you’ve done! Look what you’ve done! Look what you’ve done! Look done! Look what you’ve done! Look what you’ve done! Look what you’ve done! Look what you’ve done! Look what you’ve done! Look what you’ve done! Look what you’ve done! Look what you’ve done! Look what you’ve done! Look what you’ve done! Look what you’ve done! Look what you’ve done! Look what you’ve done! Look what you’ve done! Look what you’ve done! Look what you’ve done! Look what you’ve done! Look what you’ve done! Look done! Look what you’ve done! Look what you’ve done! Look what you’ve done! Look what you’ve done! Look what you’ve done! Look what you’ve done! Look what you’ve done! Look what you’ve done! Look what you’ve done! Look what you’ve done! Look what you’ve done! Look what you’ve done! Look what you’ve done! Look what you’ve done! Look what you’ve done! Look what you’ve done! Look what you’ve done! Look what you’ve done! Look done! Look what you’ve done! Look what you’ve done! Look what you’ve done! Look what you’ve done! Look what you’ve done! Look what you’ve done! Look what you’ve done! Look what you’ve done! Look what you’ve done! Look what you’ve done! Look what you’ve done! Look what you’ve done! Look what you’ve done! Look what you’ve done! Look what you’ve done! Look what you’ve done!*

*“Shut up!” I lunged toward the little adopted boy’s face, knocking off his round glasses and wrapped my hands around his throat. The little*

*adopted boy gagged and thrashed about, jerking his legs, kicking his feet and trying with his tiny hands to shove me off as his face swelled a violet coloring. I held my entire weight on the boy's throat until his brown eyes rolled back into his skull. One final hard constriction caused a crunch sensation in my hands. The little adopted boy stopped jerking his leg, kicking his feet and his hands coasted down my arms—*

*Silence.*

I DON'T RECALL WHEN I FELL ASLEEP, BUT I AWOKE WITH A slow movement of my eyelids. A fuzzy awakening, like a dream hangover. Worse, a nightmare hangover. I snuggled myself under my comforter, with only my eyes peeking out. The shape of beige towers circled me. With all my nonstop traveling, I had not yet unpacked. What time was it? I ran my hands across my bed, searching for my phone.

Nothing.

I got up and found my glasses on my bathroom counter. My pile clothes were in the center of the floor. I dipped my hand into each pocket.

Nothing.

I shuffled into the living room and collected my peacoat off the floor as a heavy all encompassing panic erupted.

Nothing.

I pressed my mind to expose my steps, more snapshots, and the only explanation howled. I left my phone at Emma's. In the room, somewhere, feet away from her.

No! No! No!

I darted at the clock on my stove. It's one.

I grabbed my parka off a wooden rack in my closet, bought some coffee at Kiera Bean a block from my apartment, and headed for the office. The cold snipped at my nose while the hot roasted beans warmed my throat. My sips turned into drags the further I hailed, the longer I continued in this bone-crushing frigid air. Mainly for the caffeine. My eyes felt sluggish, glossy, even. After the fog dissipated, I could see. I would give Alec a time and place to hear it. Blurry somewhat, but visible. Aware. Lucid. I knew what I must do, what I must say, how I must react. Observe. *Lie.*

I left the condo after our conversation. We said our goodbyes. I pleaded with her not to do the interview one last time, and I left. End of story. I think I'll find a better time to tell Alec about our DNA match. I prefer to say it that way. DNA match. It tastes less bitter than saying, sister. God, I still can't believe it. A part of me still doesn't believe it, and that's the side I'm clinging to. I will give Alec a time and place to hear it. It was like how it took me fifteen years to explain to Dana who Mason was.

I recognized what to do. The vault of secrets was completed the day Mason dropped into those tractor blades, and I discovered my *superpower*. My drags soon turn into chugs. I was chugging time for when my brain would sharpen the soft edges—chugging to warm my throat, chugging because my life turned upside down and the little adopted boy. *Gone.*

I walked into our office. Dana had surrounded herself with open books and scattered paper in the conference room. She used this space on weekends to study. I took a seat and dialed Alec. His phone rang and rang. The time in between rings kept getting shorter and shorter. I hung up and sent him a blank email with the subject:

`I misplaced my phone. I'm at the office.`

# 31

Alec Young

Alec landed and made another round of calls: Ted rang and rang until voicemail, and Emma did the same. Unease settled at the bottom of Alec's belly. *Neither one had gone this long without responding: maybe a few hours after a fight, but nothing like this. And it was the both of them. Something was wrong*, Alec thought as he stormed the city.

The lobby of 77 Pine was where Alec met Roger and Grace. The Lyft was braking as Alec leaped out, tugging his suitcase, following a thank you as the door shut. His exhaling was visible in large bellows like he was out of breath. Anxiety and adrenaline pulsated through his body. *Where was Ted? Why isn't he answering?* Emma was probably pissed about something and her chosen form of punishment being silence, she disengaged from Alec, Roger, and Grace. A soundless tantrum.

"She is upset about something and is taking it out on us," Roger said as Alec pondered if Roger could read his thoughts.

"Or she's stuck in a subway somewhere. If something major breaks down, you could be stuck down there for sometime," Alec said. Alec sensed Grace was applauding the attention to detail within the lobby, the spaciousness of the elevator, to divert her mind as a finger fidgets with the string dangling from her tea, warm in her hand. Overload her senses with color to silence the sole question. *Where was Emma?* But the longer the elevator lifted them, the higher a sense of vertigo dizzied their emotions.

"Should we try her again?" Grace asked, and without speaking, Alec replied by pulling out his phone, and in a split decision, tried Ted one more time. The phone rang as they approached the condo, and it continued to ring as Alec fumbled for the keys in his pocket and unlocked the door. The room was sunny with natural light from the towering windows, engulfed in notes of olives and gin. A buzzing vibration echoed off the marble island. Alec stepped inside with Ted still ringing, saw the phone buzzing, and knew.

It's Ted's phone.

"Oh, there's her phone," Grace said as she and Roger entered the condo. "I love the view, my goodness." Following a shrieking gasp, the sound of being confronted with your worst nightmare. Roger ran across the room and picked up Emma's head. "Emma, baby?" Shards of glass cut into his palms like tiny droplets of tragic love seeping through his jeans, right at the knee.

"No! No! No!" Grace cried, falling to the floor, inching closer and closer, trying to evade glass. Her voice robbed the world of its beauty. Alec froze at Emma's body, lying face down. Paralyzed, he stood, a trauma response. Her hair was gleaming, and her body stiff like a doll.

Roger held Emma in his arms and wailed, "Someone call 911! Someone call 911... Someone call..." His vocals popped. His words melted into silence. A gradual disappearance for reality was setting in. Emma was gone. Their daughter was gone. It's too late.

Alec sucked in air, snapping back, and realized he was still calling Ted. He ended and dialed 911. He placed one hand on top of his head while he paced around the bedroom, stumbling with his words, unable to fathom the verbiage. Powerless to grasp. The utterances sliced his throat from the inside on their way up.

"We... We found my fiancé unconscious."

"Is she breathing?"

"No... No, she's not."

"Okay. I'm going to walk you through how to perform CPR."

"Her face..."

"First, I need you to turn her over on her back. Let me know once that is done."

Alec interrupted. "Her face. Her face is so discolored." His dry voice cracked.

The dispatcher assured Alec help was on the way, while the sound of grief in the living room traumatized the other ear. Tears saturated with love and anger: unconditional love for their daughter and anger at life, God, for stolen years, time with their daughter cut short. Each tear evaporated into guilt and suffering: guilt for why they didn't come into the city earlier and pain for their purpose.

Their little smart-talking, red-headed monkey was gone.

THEY PRONOUNCED EMMA DEAD AT THE SCENE. No timestamp or exact cause, but theories of asphyxiation sometime last night. Grace rested on the bed with Roger standing over her, his hand wrapped in medical tape resting on her shoulder as the coroner strolled Emma's body away in a gray body bag. The wheels of the gurney made a rolling rumble against the hardwood. Grace closed her eyes as they hurried past the doorway, and Roger squeezed her shoulder, looking away, then back to the deputies.

"Again, I'm so sorry for your loss," the bearded deputy said, following a pause as his partner, a fresh out of the academy youthfulness, mimicked the same condolence.

"We see no sign of foul play involved. No forced entry or visible wounds. Just a random tragedy. When was the last time you spoke to your daughter?"

Grace's eyes swelled.

"Umm. It was last night," Roger said. "We chatted on the phone, around six. She was a little nervous about this podcast roundtable she should've had today. So, we were talking through it. We got into town this morning to all grab breakfast before the interview."

"And that's when you noticed she stopped responding?"

"Correct. We texted her before we left and called when we landed. And never stopped calling."

"Did she respond to your text this morning?"

"No."

The bearded deputy sets his views on Alec.

"You're the fiancé?"

"Yes, sir. My name is Alec."

"When was the last time you spoke to your fiancé?"

"It was also last night, also about the interview. I was in Iowa, closing on a deal for our firm. And landed this morning around noon."

Ted's phone shivered against the marble. Capturing Alec's and Grace's attention.

"Oh, is that Emma's phone?" Grace asked, twiddling with her necklace. The bearded deputy strolled over and grabbed the phone. Alec's eyes followed like a curious cat, and his body tensed.

"We thought the phone on the island might have been hers, but there was a phone on the couch," the youthful deputy said. "Do you know who the other phone belongs to? Is it a work phone?"

The bearded deputy handed Grace and Roger the phone, exposed on the screen, read Ed Harmon.

"I don't know who Ed Harmon is," Grace said. "Do you?" Looking up at Roger.

"Ed Harmon?" Alec walked over. "That's Ted's phone."

"Who is Ted?" Grace asked.

"He's a partner at our firm."

"Was he here last night?" Grace handed the phone to Alec. "He may have been the last person to see Emma. Do you think something stressed her about the interview? Could Ted tell us what her mood was?"

"They were discussing the deal, and I'm sure the interview," Alec said. "He must have forgotten it." Roger sent a side-eye to Alec.

The bearded deputy whispered into his partner's ear; he nodded then left the room.

"We're going to review the security footage to get a better sense of the timeline."

"Timeline?" Alec said.

"Eliminate uncertainty. That's all."

"I want to know how her mood was," Grace said. "Ted could tell us what was on her mind. Something which may have caused her to drink so much. Something. Anything!"

"I would be interested to know what they discussed," Roger said. "Because from what Emma told me, you and Ted weren't on board with her doing the podcast. So, was Ted here to talk her out of it?"

"I'm not sure what they discussed. We can confirm with Ted." Alec's body tensed tighter. He wasn't aware Roger knew they opposed the interview. The scar on his head itched like a parasite crawling under his skin.

"Why weren't you on-board?" Grace asked.

"There were multiple factors involved. Now isn't the time to grudge it up. We can discuss business later."

"Alec, where is Ted?" The bearded deputy asked.

"You pressured her not to do it!" Roger said. His grief progressed to anger. "Didn't you?" Roger pointed his finger at Alec like a father scolding his son. Bradley's voice gushed out of Roger, the disappointed tone. The 'father knows best, so you should do what you're told' expression. The hostile manner of the pointed finger. "You thought it would go against what you stand for."

"Roger, I only said I didn't think it was for the best."

Roger cut him off. "Let me be very clear. This company wouldn't exist without my investment, and my daughter, your co-partner, will meet with whoever she feels is best for your sole investor. Me."

"Please. Please, I don't want to fight," Grace pleaded. Her eyes floated around their bedroom like a delicate bubble, cherishing the small traces of Emma. A museum of her: a gallery of her life from the half-drunk glass of water on her nightstand, her rolled-up yoga mat nestled in the corner, and against the bathroom wall on a table sat the box—the custom box to her one-of-a-kind Monopoly game. Roger didn't realize the museum, not like Grace. Anger prevented him from cherishing the fresh traces of his daughter. Alec remained gentle. He knew grief rooted and fed his comments.

"Alec, we'd like to have a chat with Ted. Where can we find him?"

Alec inhaled. "Let me call the office. He is probably there." Alec dug out his phone and saw the email from Ted. "Yes, he's at the office. He sent me an email saying so, and that he misplaced his phone."

"Grace and I are heading back to Boston," Roger said.

"Have a safe flight. We'll be in touch," the bearded deputy said.

"Alec, sweetie. We'll make-up Emma's room for you," Grace said as another stream of tears caressed her face and filled the crease in her lips.

"Thank you. I'll book the earliest flight out."

Alec looked at the deputy.

"Do you want to lead the way?" The bearded deputy said. Alec acknowledged and as they were both stepping out the door, the youthful deputy returned, carrying a scribbled notepad of times stamps and negative adjectives.

# 32

Ted Sullivan

I tried working on updating our strategy for Young Robotics, scanning excel data, and transcribing it into a demonstration as though nothing had changed. Favoring the gears of Sullivan Young to stay spinning: resolving urgent emails with Ed Harmon while arranging follow-up meetings with our investors. All the time in between, I took a crack at Sudoku from a puzzle book in Alec's office since I still never tried, and Alec raved. I pressed the tip of the pen against my lips. Alec would always beg me to get into Sudoku, find little circumstances to slip me a newspaper cut out, or text me a link. He even went as far as surprising me with a book, Sudoku For Dummies. He thinks he's so funny. I miss him. I want to feel connected to him and because it looks *normal,* like nothing changed.

The door opened, and Alec walked in with two police officers in puffy black jackets tucked into their duty belts of radios, guns, and handcuffs. I sucked in air while scribbling the number three in the last box and walked out of my office.

"Alec. Is everything okay?"

"Um... no, things are not okay," Alec said, his tongue suctioned from the roof of his dry mouth, expressing at the floor, then up at me. "Emma is dead." His eye melted along with his voice. "We... Um, Roger, Grace, and I walked into the condo and found her on the living room floor. They think she may have choked on something."

I bundled Alec in my arms, dissolving everything around us. Even the two officers vanished.

"I'm so sorry. I'm so, so sorry," I said into Alec's ear, my skull settling on the base of his shoulders, pillowed against his cotton white button-up. "Please tell me if there is anything you need. If there is anything I can do." Alec's phone vibrated against my chest.

"None of this feels real. A dream I'm going to wake up from. Wake up back in Iowa, prepping for my family to sign, with you on the other line."

Shattering glass against the hardwood popped my ear drums. Again and again. Smash. Smash. Shrill.

"I'm so sorry this is all happening," I said as we glitched back to reality, noticing our office lighting, the warm air, and the two police officers waiting. "You were Emma's entire world, and what you two had was special. Never forget that."

"Ted?" Dana said, her head tilted out of the conference room. "Is everything okay?"

"I'll fill you in," I said, then twisting my head to the officers. "Do you guys want anything? Coffee? Water?"

"I'll take a coffee, thank you," the bearded officer said.

"I could use a coffee," the pubescent officer said.

"Alec?" I said.

"Water. Please." Alec pulled out his phone and silenced another call. Dana smiled and walked to our tiny kitchen tucked in the back.

"Hi, I'm Ted." I shook hands with both as they sent teethless smiles.

"Ted, these officers have some questions for you," Alec said.

"Okay. About what?"

"You were the last person to see Emma," the bearded officer said. "And because of that, the family is curious about what you discussed and how her mood was."

"Um, she seemed distracted. Her mind, in a hundred different places. The perk of starting a company." I regretted trying to lighten the room.

"Because of what you two were talking about?"

I don't understand their desire to know what we talked about, to know word for word. Asking what we spoke about seemed pretty specific if I wasn't someone they had an eye on. But there was nothing there, nothing for that eye to find. Unless they are probing to determine if I caused her emotional distress, which impaired her ability to fucking swallow.

"I wouldn't argue with the fact that what we discussed got emotional. To be honest, our conversation went by so fast I'm having trouble pulling together quotes. But the cliff note topics were deal-related, her podcast roundtable, and personal."

"You said it went by fast, but the security footage shows you were in there for forty-three minutes." The bearded officer said, then glancing to his partner, who said.

"And you looked upset when you left."

Are we really having this conversation?

"Also, why did you leave your phone on the kitchen island? It stood out against the white marble. You seem like an important and responsible guy. So I feel what kind of responsible guy forgets his phone, especially the day before closing a deal."

Dana arrived back, juggling three mugs and a bottle of water, and she passed them around and escaped back to the conference room. I blew at the meniscal curve of my cup of black coffee.

"Do you have my phone?"

"Yes, but can you please answer our question? For the family, you were the last person to see her. Can you gauge at all how she was feeling? Was she upset about anything that may have increased her drinking so much she choked on an olive?"

"If you would please hand me my phone, I will show you what we were discussing, and I will show you what may have induced such stress. If you must know."

The bearded deputy handed my phone over, and within seconds, I handed it back over. Displayed on the screen was the notification from Double Helix about my 22.9% DNA match with Emma. The officers went quiet while staring at the screen, then shifted their eyes to me. Alec nudged over.

"Yep. This would cause anyone to go into shock."

"What does it say?" Alec asked. The officer's eyes shifted from me to Alec, then back to me. He handed Alec the phone, and I swallowed the fast-growing lump in the back of my throat.

"What the fuck?" Alec said under his breath, glancing up at me with those puppy eyes, delicate and concerning. He walked over and gave me a hug. "Are you okay? This is insane. When did you get this notification?"

"Last night. They included it with all the other results, but I was so curious by all the ethnicity graphs I took me a minute to realize I had an alert."

"When we talked last night?"

"It was after we hung up that I found it and went straight to the condo."

"Does Mr. Peterson know about this finding?"

"He doesn't. And if you could tell him for me, that would take an immense weight off my shoulders. For me, there will never be a good time. He's our angel investor and the father to our co-partner."

"We will update the Peterson's on what the two of you discussed. We appreciate your time." The two officers re-centered their black beanies on their heads and walked out. Alec gave me another hug, and I responded by hugging back harder.

"I am so sorry, Theodore."

"You're right. None of this feels real."

Alec's phone vibrated again as we morphed back into two units, standing inches apart. He pulled out his phone to a random number with a New York area code.

"Who is that?"

"I don't know. Everyone's been calling. My sister, this random number, and Sloane twice."

"Shit," I said, skimming my phone. "There's a news alert about Emma's death. It's trending."

"Jesus. A resident or maintenance worker at seventy-seven Pine must have leaked it." Alec ran his fingers through his hair. "Fuck. What does the article say?"

"It's saying it's a developing story, cause of death under investigation."

"I should head to the airport. Roger and Grace are flying back to Boston to make service arrangements. I'm on the next flight out."

"Okay. Let me know if that is anything I can do. I think it would be best if I attended the service. For optics. She was our business partner."

"I think so as well, but are you sure? I don't want to put you in a situation you're not ready for. You uncovered some heavy stuff, and I don't want you to feel overwhelmed. A lot of her family will be there, and well."

"I'll be okay. I can handle small talk if I went. If I didn't go, I wouldn't be able to control the narrative. I can already see the news headline."

# 33

## Alec Young

"I first want to thank everyone for being here today. Knowing Emma's emphasis on hospitality, she would correct me if I didn't," Alec said, following a few chuckles. The tightness of his suit was oddly comforting, somehow keeping anxiety and grief at bay. *It's all my fault*, Alec thought. "Emma was a firecracker, in every good sense of the word. Since the first day we met in grad school. They grouped us into the same team, and she was delegating tasks and following up on assignments we hadn't even gotten yet. I fell in love with her instantly."

Alec held a deck of flashcards, remaining confident amongst a sea of black, forlorn faces. Digesting their grief, the crowd wrestled a war inside their minds, their brains swimming in stress-releasing hormones. Pumping out the chemical more than their bodies had ever experienced, releasing the buildup of pressure with a gush of tears from each eyeball. Some more than others and a few less than some. Alec's eyes, his gentle gaze, belonged to the crowd of mourners. A beat of an eyelid and a bob of his Adam's apple as his words hugged all two-hundred and twenty-six while echoing up to the vaulting peaks of the cathedral. Breathtaking edifice, all gothic revival and stained, painted glass. Every wooden beam carved and stone block chiseled to form marvelous shapes and neat details so tiny the eyes glimmer over. Alec sucked in air and peered in front of him at Roger and Grace holding hands and the lineup of family.

"Roger, you were her idol, and Grace her role model. Together, you were her very best friends. And that is what I love about Emma. I would be standing up here all day if I were to list everything I love about Emma," Alec said. "But what comes to mind first? Emma was always helping others. She made sure her family and friends were taken care of and was always willing to step in and help when things got rocky. Her positive spirit was striking. She truly believed everything has a solution. You just have to look hard enough, she would say. There is always a solution. She had a glow about her that would light up every room and warm people from the inside out. Instill motivation and love. Acceptance and trust."

*Trust. Trust. Expectation and assumption. Dark intentions. I never loved your daughter. I had no intention of ever loving your daughter. I used Emma to dangle the prospect of a grandson in front of my mother to nudge her to sell my family company. So, it's my fault. I'm the reason your daughter is dead. It's my fault. And for that, I'm sorry. I regret involving her in Sullivan Young. I regret staying with her for as long as I did. I regret being with your daughter. I regret my intentions*, Alec thought in between pauses.

"And that is why I love Emma. I not only lost my fiancé, my support system. I lost my best friend and the love of my life."

Alec's view continued to scan, easing to the next row. Ruth rested, wearing sunglasses next to Alice, crying with her head down. Both holding balls of tissue they would dab under their noses and cheeks. Behind sat Ted in a full black suit and tie, doughy-eyed and dipped chin. Dana rested her hand on Ted's as his shoulders slumped. She looked at him through side eyes squinted in pain. They filled the back of the cathedral with business executives, politicians, Whartonites, sorority sisters, and off to the side, up close: Sloane and Chrissy, eyes hollowed out.

"Please watch over me, sweetheart. I love you."

Silence swirled around Alec as he drifted off stage and back into his seat next to Grace.

~

Alec turned the vent flap to redirect the balmy air along his face in the back of a somber Suburban. A dazed silence that swelled and swelled, popping as Ruth lauded the beauty of the service, tugging at her Tahitian pearls cultured and plucked from the tissue of a black lip oyster. Triggering Alice to mirror with runny eyes. Alec remained stalled in place, staring out the window, blinking sandpaper. Why hadn't he cried like everyone else? His mind refused to flood his tear glands to allow him to grieve: the day of her accident, the minutes or hours after, telling Ted, trying to sleep in Emma's bed, at the cathedral, during his eulogy, and now. Instead, a perpetual sensation of free-falling, reaching terminal velocity with breathless mouthfuls of shallow breathing. Alec could splat against the ground at any second. Ruth did not surprise him when she mentioned Bradley's absence, his swift under the weather, unable to fly state Alec felt resulted from the sale, but could it be the dawn of a period in which Bradley never talks to his son? Not even when news about Emma flew to Iowa and slithered inside Bradley's ear or on the day of her funeral service?

The reticent state further submerged Roger, who rested in the passenger seat, facing forward in sunglasses next to a silent, unrecognizable driver. Roger was in the aftermath of grief's tidal wave, post ship sinking, circled by family. Every day, every second, another reminder of the wreckage, like a grotesque scar scrawled on his chest, above his heart. At dinner time the past few days, he wouldn't eat, yet would still rested at the table with family, savoring endless bourbon, chiming in here or there, but mostly talking to the wall with his eyes. Beyond exhausted, as his grip would tremor, gently rocking his tumbler above his lips.

Alec's hand rested on the wing of a black Steinway and Sons. He skimmed across to the bare slit on his wrist where his S cufflink would occupy. *Ted*, he thought, *I need you here*. Dozens of mourners striding up the path through the window grabbed Alec's attention. They would step from the present and into the *repast* one by one. Alice brought Alec a sharp pour as the occupancy into the Peterson townhouse neared capacity. Appetizer and drink trays floated around the entire first floor by quiet tuxes who wouldn't ask if you'd like a quiche bite but drew their time showcasing.

"Can this day be over?" Alec said under his breath.

"We're in the home stretch," Alice said as she rubbed his shoulder. "Have you seen Mom?"

"No."

"I'll be right back. I'm going to track her down. I still have her phone." Alice gave Alec one last tap and vanished into the crowd as Ted, Dana, and Raj drifted in. A state of discomfort from being surrounded by strangers and a certain thickness in the air. A stickiness to it, the humidity of grief. Alec bolted over; his eyes dilated.

"Your eulogy was beautiful," Dana said.

"Thank you."

"Yeah man. It was very lovely," Raj echoed while squeezing Alec's shoulder.

"Thank you."

"How are you doing?" Ted asked.

"Overwhelmed, to be honest. These past few days have blended together." Alec pinched the bridge of his nose. "I should ask how you are doing?"

"I'm okay. Haven't been sleeping much."

Sloane emerged from another room, holding a glass of pinot. Her tattoos covered by a black suit and belted trousers. The memory of Emma weighed at her lips as she gravitated toward Alec in tight-jawed silence.

"Hi Sloane," Alec said.

She took a sip. Tension rippled between them. Taking note, Dana and Raj looked at each other in agreement, exiting to seek a drink and finger food. A hand that tapped Ted on his shoulder replaced their space.

"Hi Ted," Roger said. The knot on his black tie was lumpy and off-center, and his eyes were the color of popcorn kernels. "Can we talk?"

Ted looked over his shoulder at Alec, then back at Roger.

"Sure."

The two faded into the crowd.

"Sullivan Young has been getting a lot of media attention," Sloane said. A stab, jab, cut hidden in her words, tied to ruthless truths, for Sullivan Young was in the spotlight. Emma's sudden death rattled all inside their bubble, the daughter of Roger Peterson, the five degrees of separation, feeling the shock waves. Articles on her life and work cleaved spin-offs and more questions. What is this private equity firm she co-founded? Who is Sullivan Young?

"Yes. We have received a little attention."

"A little?"

"I get nervous thinking about how many emails are sitting in our inbox."

"The day of your fiancés funeral and you're worried about emails?"

"Sloane, you know what I meant. We were on media attention and endless articles on Sullivan Young."

"Endless articles that I feel are asking the wrong questions." Sloane took a sip of her wine, winding up for another slice of the jugular. Alec braced. Sloane and Emma were two peas in a pod, and he knew she was up to something.

"And what question is that?"

"Was Ted in the room when Emma choked to death? How involved was he? Because I think something more happened."

"Sloane."

"I'm looking at it through a journalistic lens. An investigative journalist. Why did he leave his phone if he wasn't in a hurry? Or distracted." Sloane folded a loose strand of hair behind her ears. "Listen, I know there was something between you and Ted, and Emma knew as well. To me, it sounds like she was viewed as an inconvenience. I think there is more to the story. I do. So much so I think I should write my own article asking those questions."

"Emma's death happened after Ted left. End of story." Alec's skin became gooseflesh, and his tiny hairs shot to attention as heat traveled to his chest in a slow wave. "We are both hurting. Ted, maybe even more. I lost my fiancé and Ted lost his sister."

"What?"

"Don't turn this into some tabloid click bait bullshit. You're better than that, Sloane. We gave you a platform. A platform of legitimacy and fame so you could start telling the stories you've always wanted to tell, to everyone."

"What are you talking about? You gave me a platform?"

"I hate to be the one to change your perspective of her. Especially on the day of her funeral, but Sloane, Emma has been feeding you stories. Anonymously." Sloane's eyebrows stitched a strict line as her pupils doubled in size, stationed on Alec. "Long before we met. Long before, Emma and I started dating. She lived her life on the inside. She was having fun, especially when she set to benefit. Like your article on Sullivan Young."

"They were a favor for a friend. A dear friend of mine who achieved this huge milestone."

"Scottsdales most exclusive game nights. In that article, you mentioned Emma and her one-of-a-kind monopoly game. Or, how Scottsdales young professionals celebrate Friendsgiving."

"It was a favor for a friend, one I knew she was behind. We talked about it."

"What about, oh god what is the headline? The co-head cheating CEOs? Or your older stories exposing the number of DUIs of the kids to business executives? You think Jane Smith submitted those leaks tailored to you? The all-seeing eye."

Sloane pulled a sizable gulp and hovered the glass over her nose, sucking in the tannins.

"What about Chaz Perez?"

"That one I don't know. I don't want to go through your catalog of stories to tell you which Emma fed you. All I wanted to do was open your eyes. Emma was a complicated and private person, but that doesn't change the fact that we are all hurting. We are all grieving. Please, don't add to that grief with outlandish stories. I know you're hurting, Sloane.

You were her best friend. Your grief is justified. Just please heal in a healthy way."

Sloane tumbled into her thoughts. Sending a quick smile to a familiar face across the room, she scratched her eyebrow and said, "what did you mean when you said Ted lost his sister?"

# 34

Ted Sullivan

If I'm feeling a wave of anxiety, Alec taught me a nifty trick to tame my breathing and distract my mind from wandering into the abyss. The grounding technique: subvocalization. Say in your head objects, the first objects you identify to help your brain recognize where you are, to pull you back to earth and away from the black hole of panic.

Flügel Steinway and Sons, keys, leather bench, hardwood, rug, tassel, blue, doorway, chair, human, dress, wine, whiskey, black, black, black.

Roger.

My thighs and calves flex and release as I follow him up a circling wooden staircase saturated with a plush carpet. Carpet, white, fuzzy and staticky. Railing, sturdy and black. The ceiling was ever-expanding, with frames lining the wall. The skylight was bright and tender.

As much as I don't want to, how badly I would give to be in the sanctuary of our office, building our future, I know we have to have this discussion. *I must address the bull in the room.* The appearance game was where we are at, and it's vital we conquer it, for appearance was nothing more or less than what we reveal, and what we reveal was in the details. Attending the funeral service, allowed me to experience the grief happening around from a glistening eye to a hand on a shoulder. Listening over talking. Attending this reception at the residence of a man I found out was my biological father. As we entered the spacious townhouse, passing decorative arrangements along the path, Emma's oval stainless steel urn greeted everybody. Nesting on a high-top table hemmed by white scentless candles and a gold gaudy framed picture of Emma. A professional headshot. I ran my mind blank and distracted when I squinted down, and it was when I noticed it. In the center of the urn was engraved cursive, *we're waiting for you.* My head turned over my shoulders as if to spot eyes on me, as though someone was watching me, lingering to see my reaction. My eyelids fluttered, and the center engraved *Emma Peterson* when I read back at the urn.

The chatter and whisper from downstairs dissolved as we met the second floor. A pulse inside my suit tickled my rib cage. I plucked out my phone to my mom calling, her face beamed at me like she was nudging me not to continue upstairs, pleading with me through every vibration and tremor. The task of the little adopted boy, bare bedroom, gone.

We turned a corner and went into a guest room. The wood slab produced a crackling creek as we stepped through the doorway. Still silent. They draped a daisy scattered floral duvet over the bed with purple hydrangeas breathing on the nightstand. *A desire to understand.* Its presence was unavoidable. Roger sat on the bed and tugged at his earlobe. I slid my hands inside my pockets. My posture, a little wider. The essence of regret filled the room, smelling of burnt bacon when left in the pan for too long, or fast evaporating gasoline spewing from your tank to your freshly washed car, salty sweat rushed down the skin of an elderly man as he was met with the consequences of a past transgression. The aroma was so thick in the air you could slice it.

"I... I like your tie," Roger said.

"Thanks."

"It's nice to put a face to a voice. You're a handsome young man."

"You're taller than I thought."

"You gotta eat your veggies," Roger said with a thin smile. "Emma hated greens. She never finished her broccoli or Brussels sprouts. I hope you finished yours."

"I did. Roger, I'm so sorry for your loss and the revelation that still has me shocked."

"It was a double whammy. But who would have ever thought, you know?" Roger scratched his eyebrows, then held his tumbler with his hands as if he were warming his skin with ice. "You go on, continue life, or at the very least, try to make sense of it. I don't think I can or ever will. I feel as though a part of me was chopped off. A massive limb. Gone."

My analytical vision was processing his body language, physical features, and overall disposition, as though the selfish genes inside me hummed at the proximity of their origin. Is this what I'm to look and sound like? Perfect my leadership and influence while developing an unquenchable thirst for alcohol and adultery. My mind kept rationalizing my accomplishments being unearthed by Roger. I am a part of him, after all. I got this far on my own. Making my way into the bubble, not knowing a piece of me was already inside. An out-of-body experience rushed over me where the little adopted boy was me and I was Roger. Overcome by the truth of who he was. At any moment, Roger would leap up from the bed, wrestle the little adopted boy to the ground, and in a monotone voice, count to three hundred with his hands wrapped around my neck. Roger sighed as a fragile tear dripped from his right eye and into his whiskey, feeling the phantom pain of his missing limb.

"Who is *she*?" I asked.

Roger picked his head up and his eyes danced about the room until he landed on me, and I gently sat on the bed.

"Ted, I want you to understand something first. I was a different man nearly three decades ago. I was doing a lot of traveling when Peterson Consulting was taking off."

"I understand."

"I love Grace more than words can describe. Since things have come to light, I have beyond apologized, and I think we will make it through this. We have to, for Emma."

"Are you saying you don't remember who she is? What she looks like? What her name is or how you both met?" I craved the fine print, the little details to paint a complete and full picture, story, memory. From there, I would lock them in the vault, a mansion filled with compartments and the stories written on the walls.

"I'm sorry, Ted. I'm very ashamed of myself. How I've behaved."

I couldn't determine if I preferred the truth over the unknown.

"It's okay." My palms were dry and my pulse, calm. Creaks, like an aged rocking chair, caught our attention as a little girl, around four or five, with strawberry blonde hair in a black dress and matching flats, stood in the doorway.

"Hi, sweetie," Roger said as the little girl placed two fingers in her mouth with shy eyes. I pictured Emma as a little girl with big blue eyes and long white lashes. The innocuous early years.

"Uncle Roger, my mom said to grab her phone charger," The little girl said.

Roger combed the nightstand and passed me his drink as he reached down. The little girl skipped off after Roger handed her the cord and shuffled back to the bed.

"Cute kid."

"She's a splitting image of Emma. A little shyer than Emma was, but still." Roger took a sip and bowled the whiskey with his tongue before swallowing, rewarming his insides and spirits. "Ted, I want to see the positive side. Try to make sense of everything, try to heal. A blessing has sprouted in this tragedy, and I want to focus on that. It's entirely your decision, but I will welcome the opportunity to be in your life. If you'll have me."

"I don't think it's a good idea. Best to move on." Roger gave a few nods while still zoned out. "The best way to heal is to create distance." Roger rewarmed his insides and peered down at the floor. I stood up in slow motion as if trying to sneak out of the room.

"It's okay. It's okay. I know what you mean. You're right," Roger said in a tone not matching the spirits of those words.

"I want to help create distance and remove your obligation from us."

Roger twisted his head at me. "What do you mean?"

"Your angel investment. We will never forget how helpful you were, how impactful your investment was, but I think for you to fully heal, we must remove your involvement in Sullivan Young." The ice ball in Roger's whiskey dinged the glass walls as his hand twitched. His face turned into an ombre of white and red as blood left his face. A double whammy. "A wire transfer of five million, plus interest, is being transferred to your account. Again, we will never forget about your insanely generous investment." Since getting word about Alec and Emma's engagement, I plotted how I could prevent it, stop it. The cleanest strategy would be to remove Roger as our angel investor by replacing his investment with another, thus removing his control. The only man I trust to handle the job was Ed Harmon. Given our track record and his awareness of Sullivan Young, he jumped at the opportunity to be our sole angel investor. I already updated our company filings and Raj had updated our Key Investors page on our website. All that remained was this conversation. *The bull in the room.*

"What if I waive the interest payments and push back the maturity date?"

"Things are already in motion," I said. "We're not doing this to hurt you, but to help you heal and move on. I hope you see that."

Roger sat silent. Took one last sip before standing up, sending a flutter of eyelid bats from lightheadedness. He was too exhausted to put up a fight. Roger gave me a gentle 'take care' tap of his palm on my shoulder and shuffled out of the room. The creaks in the wood confirmed it.

Down the hall, I saw a door to a bathroom. After flipping the light, the reflection from the bleached white tiles and porcelain toilet stabbed my eyes. The tub had little copper legs, pranced and ready to scamper away at my presence. I sent a chain of texts to Alec and Dana, asking for their location. I didn't want to wander from room to room like a *lost boy*. My foot seemed to tap and fidget uncontrollably despite the calming lavender scents. As impatience swelled, I distracted my attention by counting unread emails, checking the status of the wire transfer to Roger, and then remembering the four voicemails from Alec. I pressed play on the oldest.

"Hey, Theodore. Just checking in, we're about to start the meeting. Talk soon, bye."

I played the next voicemail.

"You probably overslept. I'm heading to the airport now. Call me when you get this. I'll call you when I land. Love you, bye."

The pulse up my neck popped at the shaky tone in Alec's voice. At his inner workings, he optimistically rationalized my absence to a gentle morning cat nap. I played the next voicemail.

"Theodore, you're scaring me. If you don't feel like talking, please just send me a text that you're okay. That you're safe. Okay, I'll talk to you soon. I love you, Theodore. Bye-bye."

My heart sank. I never heard those worrisome vocals. A rose with thorns, his trembling voice gave glimpse into how much Alec loved me, a concrete sound that moved through the air and flicked at my heart. I readied for the last voicemail, a tone from Alec I'd never experienced. I sucked in air and pressed play.

Disturbing sobs mixed with slicing screams. Raw and animal-like.

"Someone call 911! Someone call 911!" Roger cried. "God, no! Please, no!" He whimpered with Grace, who wept as her voice sunk to the floor.

I breathed notes of olives and gin aerosol.

# 35

Alec Young

Alec drew Sloane aside, reciting with urgency the need for discretion. He chewed his tongue as he speculated the remark would slip under her radar, a risky but necessary card to play.

"Sloane, I trust you. You can't tell anyone. The family wants to keep it a secret. We will be the first to know if they want us to."

"I told you I wouldn't tell anyone. Jesus, can you let me process? This is huge, let me process." Sloane glared at an odd shaped vase stretching out on an artifact shelf built into the wall. She drew several low sips.

Number fourteen opus twenty-seven, like they delivered it from heaven. Melodic immortality swam through the room, hypnotizing the mourners as it furnished the space around Sloane and caressed Alec's cheek. His ears perked and his senses tingled. It was his favorite score. Everyone was facing the same direction, like a pack of bunnies snared in a spotlight of dark euphoria. Alec followed the music, maneuvering between bodies as the hammers struck three bass and treble strings. He followed until he reached the main living room. The vibrations rumbled off the wing, and his suspicion was right. Ted rested at the black piano with his head dipped and eyes sealed, his fingers danced from key to key like a grieving ballerina. A black swan. Ted cast a shadow from the evening light beaming through the arched windows. His silhouette looked as if he was holding up a crown of swan lake or stigmata thorns while producing rays of *Moonlight Sonata*.

~

ALEC AND TED, HAD RETURNED TO THE CITY, SAT IN ALEC'S unboxed office, nursing coffee and silence. Grace begged Alec to stay one more night after the service, but life needed attending, so he sat aside with her for the last talk. The 'we'll be in touch this isn't goodbye' talk. One he couldn't have with Roger as he scurried off to bed halfway through the reception: too much whiskey and phantom pain. The cremation dust of Emma was settling, leaving a gray film on the surface of everything. Alec and Ted's hair, shoulders, and shoes looked post-apocalyptic, the eruption aftermath of Mount Saint Helens. Ash film covered the office keyboards and papers, floating like duckweed in their coffee.

Alec cleared his throat.

"I dreamt of Emma last night," Alec said. "I never remember them, but this time. I don't know. We were back in Philly walking around a cemetery. I woke up and couldn't fall back asleep."

Ted grabbed his hand.

"She isn't letting me sleep either," Ted said. "More like I don't want to sleep because I keep having the same nightmare. Every night since."

"I've never heard you describe your dreams as a nightmare."

"It's warranted. They're all there. Mason, Chaz, and Emma."

"Roger and Grace proposed something to me," Alec said. "They said they understand we weren't legally married yet. The act of signing the document doesn't mean we already weren't, Grace told me."

"Okay."

"They want me to have her trust. Emma's Trust."

"What did you say?" Steam from Ted's mug fogged his glasses.

"I told them I couldn't. Said to donate it."

"Good answer."

"They didn't like that answer. But they are still grieving, so I understand. I think they are trying to hold on to something from Emma's past."

"I can see that. Roger gave some push back when I told him we bought out his angel investment. He agreed to waive the accruing interest along with extending the maturity date."

"Only time can heal these types of wounds. On top, to find out he has a son, it's heavy."

"The witch was right," Ted said as he fidgeted with papers, then picking up a silver envelope opener, resting the tip against legal docs. "A part of me died. Like she predicted."

"Don't. It's not healthy to dwell. She also said I would be alone, craving some unknown."

"But she was spot on about one thing. We are sitting upon our throne."

"Yes we are."

Alec's smiled soon dissolved as his phone came to life: BRADLEY, plastered across the top. It sucked more and more oxygen out of the room with every vibration. A cyclone siphoning air. Alec's eye flung to Ted, then back. He answered.

"Hi Dad."

"Hi, son." Bradley's voice was deep yet pleasant, all spit tobacco and milk.

"Glad to hear you're feeling better."

"How was the service?"

"Beautiful. It was inside an eighteenth century cathedral."

"That's what your mother said. She also told me some other things. Some not so beautiful things."

"Dad, hear me out. We both know Young Industrials was hurting, bleeding cash. I did this so we can pump fresh blood in and turn the company around."

"That's what your mother said."

"You can remain as CEO for as long as you want. When you're ready to retire, we can transition you out."

"Remain as CEO," Bradley scoffed. "I can remain CEO for as long as I want. Words my son is saying to me. Words my first born is saying to me."

"We will handle strategy and oversee the business mergers with SolarX and Vision AI. You will still run the same day-to-day CEO responsibilities as well as execute the strategies we've proposed."

"Young Robotics," Bradley said in a tone bordering the edge of impressed and proud or embittered mockery. "The day we brought you home from the hospital, you slept and slept and slept and never cried. You just looked around with those big blue eyes. Your mom and I had a joke that you were already independent."

Alec sent a laughless smile and said, "I grew up fast."

"When you were a little boy, you would sneak into our room every night. You would sometimes crawl into bed and other times we found you sleeping on your mother's vanity sofa. You hated sleeping alone."

"I don't remember that—"

"You were little. Very demanding and defiant. Every sentence ended in, why? Why? You would ask questions you already knew the answers to invoke superiority. Over me, over your mother. Your schoolteachers. I don't think you've changed one bit."

"What do you mean?"

"While your fiancé was choking to death on your living room floor, you were busy stealing my company. Taking advantage of your mother, who was beyond stressed with my health and brainwashing your little sister and my siblings into agreeing to sell my company. Your priorities, son, they're fucked. You're selfish. You disappoint me. You only ever serve yourself and you don't care about other people. Maybe it's something medically wrong with you. Who the fuck knows? But it's who you are, since you were a young boy. It's in your bones. It's who you are. And I think it's who you are is the reason why..."

Bradley paused, delaying.

"*The reason why I never loved you*. You thrive in chaos. Always have. I never knew you, and I still don't. I never want to. Let me be clear, you are no longer welcome in this house. You are being removed from the will as we speak. You got what you wanted, you're removed from this family. You stole my company. This means war. Now fuck off!"

Alec's lashes beat with the words *never loved you,* coasting over his eyes as a tear slide down his cheek, dashing past his nose where it dripped off his jaw. He bit his lower lip, recoiling in pain. The three floating sounds crushed the dam Alec built to hold the dreadful feelings at bay, releasing manageable floods and rivers of emotion. Alec sobbed as he lay his head on Ted's lap. His face hummed red. Ted's deadpan reaction harbored ominous energy as he gripped the back of Alec's neck. The scar on Alec's scalp gawked up at Ted like a cyclops through strands of hair as he stroked his head consolingly. One stroke, two strokes, three.

"We have our investors' interest to think about now, and they want skulls," Ted said. "So, that's what we're going to do." With his palm still relaxing on Alec, Ted leaned forward, plucked the phone, dialing a memorized number.

"Hi, it's Ted."

Alec's bloodshot eye under clumpy eyelashes peeked up at Ted. His skin from his chin to the top of his suit was baby smooth, with a sharp jawline. Ted's Adam's apple bobbed once like a cork in water.

"Process the termination docs for Bradley Young." Ted looked down at Alec and dried his eye with his thumb, then graced his eyebrow and ran his fingers down Alec's cheek. "Time to find a new CEO."

# 36

Ted Sullivan

Ed and I stepped onto the cottage-style terrace with ivory wooden beams serving sporadic shading, looking over the Pacific on a cloudless day, a light salty breeze, and seagulls swooping overhead, patrolling the beaches for leftover snacks.

"You found a gem, Ed," I said. "This place is amazing, and the location is perfect."

"I have a good friend over at Berkshire," Ed poured us sweet tea from a teal pitcher as we both applauded the view. "How's Sullivan Young?"

"Full steam ahead. We've onboarded one new hire, with two in the third interview stage. We're making significant progress."

"You guys have been busy."

"We're still shopping around for a new CEO to run Young Robotics, but we've received a good chunk of interest. We will narrow down our decision by end of the week."

"How about the wrongful termination lawsuit by Bradley?"

"A judge tossed it. We were well within our powers to remove him."

"Bradley didn't think so. Well, enough to sue."

"Theatrics. But I have a feeling this isn't going to be the last time we hear from Bradley. The last time we spoke he told Alec and I we're at war."

Ed laughed.

"Bradley is a very prideful man, and stubborn. The type you have to force into retirement."

"I couldn't jump on the retirement train fast enough."

"Because you're smart enough to know when it's time to step aside and enjoy life."

"Nothing screams enjoy life like living ocean front in San Diego."

"Exactly."

"And how have you been?"

"I'm happy to report things are going great. The firm is becoming self-sufficient, which has been a stress relief. It's surreal seeing the office buzzing with productivity."

"What about Alec? How's he doing? It devastated me when I learned what happened to his fiancé and your co-partner."

"He's doing well. I mean, there are days when you're reminded, but Alec is in a healthy place, finally."

"Oh my, how could I have forgotten the big news!" Ed said as he shot up and shuffled inside.

"I was wondering how long it would take you."

"Ted, you don't know how proud I am. This is an enormous deal," Ed said while carrying Forbes magazine. "Something I can say has never happened to me. You and Alec making the cover to *Forbes thirty-under-thirty*."

"I pinch myself every time I see it."

"Did you hang it up in your office?"

"Framed and everything. If it wasn't for you."

"Please. I may have nominated you and Alec, but it was the both of you who caught the attention of the judges."

That's right, Alec and I made the cover of Forbes thirty-under-thirty. Fucking *Forbes*, the face of this year's issue, with the fun headline:

*Green PE Firm Is Here to Clean House.*

In the shot, we both stand side by side with our arms crossed. The photographer wanted a relaxed business casual vibe, so we wore a navy suit jacket and no tie with our cufflinks poking out. Every time I see the cover, my view admires Alec, staying fearless with his handsome stubble while emanating his three hundred-million-dollar fund smile. SY One. I declared this our first official article, as it paints the details of the Sullivan Young story. Every decision we made was etched into our history, growing up in a farming town, only to watch it dissolve in oil and drain from fissures in the earth's crust, highlighting Alec's struggles of losing his family to challenge our nation's dependence on oil, snippets on our time at Kauffman, why we left, and why we felt compelled to act, describing where we found that courage. You see, it's not only the product you're selling or the unique investment opportunity that hooks big-money investors.

It's having a great story.

I DON'T THINK I'LL EVER GET OVER THE SURREAL JOLT OF pride I feel every time I walk into our office to Dana's warm smile, neighbored by our of hard-working associate crunching numbers, playing arts and crafts in PowerPoint, perfecting the presentations, or playing real arts and crafts using a stylist on their phones during quick relaxation times. The surreal jolt of seeing our work culture developing, placing our people front and center of that culture, rewarding bold and creative ideas, built on a foundation of transparency and trust. Free and fair with zero room for cutthroat tactics against the team, directing that competitiveness to the market, to our competitors. We set ourselves apart with this culture of valuing our employees, bringing them into the Sullivan Young family, us, together, expanding the team motto. *Valuing only us*.

A bouquet of purple hydrangeas sat on my desk, soaking in a tulip-shaped vase wrapped in Tiffany's blue ribbon.

"Those are gorgeous," Dana said, poking her head in and adjusting the collar on her charcoal blouse. "The card doesn't say who they are from."

But I know.

"All it says is V.O.U.," Dana said, walking up to give the florals another whiff. "Is V.O.U. another business acronym I should know?" She smiled.

"No, it's not a business acronym, but it should be." I picked up the thick stationery. The acronym was cursive in red ink and had perfect curves and edges. "It stands for *valuing only us.*"

"The team motto."

"Yep."

"Who came up with valuing only us?"

"Alec. It was toward the end of our internship with Kauffman years ago. We were at his apartment drinking coffee and watching a documentary. Inside Job, narrated by Matt Damon. Anyways, he just said it. Confusion turned into admiration after he explained it. I don't know how he came up with it, but he said it was like two sides of the same coin."

"I'm listening."

"One side being the face value, what those words mean in its normal context. Valuing us and only us. Valuing the team. The other side acting as a reminder of our dreams of starting a company. So it was almost like a code. Only we knew the encryption."

"What's the code?" Dana said, her eyebrows harbored fuzzy confusion with smooth intrigue.

"The code is that valuing only us is an anagram. Somehow Alec's analytical, sudoku loving mind stumbled upon it."

"So, do I have to rearrange the words until I find the new word? Or is my awesome boss and favorite cousin going to slide me the answer key?"

"Only if I can get those compliments in writing." I smiled, admiring the card. "*Valuing only us is an anagram for Sullivan Young*. Again, it was Alec's doing. I wish I could take credit."

"What a little genius."

The handsome genius knocked on my office doorframe and said, "glad they finally arrived."

"They are beautiful," Dana said. "But next time, it's customary to get one for the front desk." She winked and trailed back to her desk to a ringing phone.

"How was California?"

"Sunny and sandy. Ed found himself a magnificent spot, and from what I could see, he's leaning more and more into his true gay self. He's flourishing. Told me about all the evenings at the theatre, art galleries, and queer owned restaurants."

"Good for him."

"Thank you for the flowers."

"You can thank me by showing up at this address," Alec said, handing me a folded piece of paper. It's an address. New York, NY, 10011.

"What is this?"

"Just be there, around five."

"Okay mystery man." I rolled my eyes as I felt my cheeks grow warm.

"Alright, I gotta head. Your gift is being delivered soon." Alec knocked twice on my wall, an over-and-out expression as I watched through my window him say goodbyes to Dana, the team of associates, pat Raj on the back, and waltz through the front door.

I opened my desk drawer and pulled out our cufflink box. New as the day Alec surprised me with it. I spun my chair to admire the framed Forbes article while buttoning on my cufflinks.

*We had our throne.*

Jasmine from the bouquet representing fresh with each inhale. Purple hydrangeas were the first flower Alec got me, the desire to deeply understand someone. Those were the words Alec said to me. The symbolism of purple hydrangeas, he said. Desire. Understand. Me.

I know Alec understands me. An unseen connection. A magnetic bond. And it was that bond that built this company. Bloody hands and broken backs. Strategy and trust. Complete trust that what the other does is for the best. That we would value only us. Being as one.

The life, or partnership you might say, between Alec and I is complex and dynamic and with those recipes, it gets messy and complicated, soiled with secrets — Secrets that protect him from the truth. The events that happened were necessary for our survival. They will remain locked in the vault, to protect both of us. It was necessary, for we now had our empire. Alec and I became one. A merger of two elements with unlimited potential.

Sullivan *and* Young.

The vault must never reopen, for Alec's sake. Maybe one day, but not now.

For now, I'll continue to ruthlessly charm and lie, gently.

# ACKNOWLEDGMENTS

This story, a shapeshifting 130k-page monster, underwent a four-year transformation. It slowly shrank, crystallized, and sparkled, thanks to the contributions of many who chiseled and fine-tuned every nook and cranny.

Thank you to my fantastic editor, Rachel Eve Moulton, for instantly connecting with and understanding this unconventional love story. The cherry on top is how you've become a friend and mentor. I can't think of Ted and Alec and not think of you. You're a rockstar!

To my husband, Taylor, for always supporting and pushing me in my creative endeavors. You've seen the roughest of the rough drafts (and still stuck around). I love you!

To the remarkable duo of Carlee and Julia. I will forever cherish the mark you both left within this story. Thank you for always helping to guide me out of dark caves and into the light with your support and cheerleading.

Thank you to my early readers, Christy Carter, Heather Enriquez, and Sam Battis, for your feedback and insights as this story morphed. We did it!

Thank you to Greg Dudley, the only man in finance who can successfully pull off the mustache, for helping flesh out all my private equity hypotheticals and questions. What a pearler!

Thank you to Alexandria Brown. Your feedback forever changed this story, and I'm very thankful for your time.

Thank you to Richard Ljoenes for designing a beautiful cover!

# ABOUT THE AUTHOR

Cory Desmond Wolfe earned his B.S. at the W.P. Carey School of Business at Arizona State University. He works in finance. Although his career has taken a business turn, he always loved telling and writing stories. He self-published his first cartoon-drawn picture book in third grade. Some of his favorite authors include Gillian Flynn, Bret Easton Ellis, and Andy Davidson. He lives in Idaho with his husband and cuddly felines.